SO-AUI-610

SACRAMENTO PUBLIC LIBRARY
828 "I" STREET
SACRAMENTO, CA 95814
NOV· 2005

DEADLY ERRORS

DEADLY ERRORS

ALLEN WYLER

A TOM DOHERTY ASSOCIATES BOOK

New York

This is a work of fiction. All the characters and events portrayed in
this novel are either fictitious or are used fictitiously.

DEADLY ERRORS

Copyright © 2005 by Allen Wyler

All rights reserved, including the right to reproduce this book or
portions thereof, in any form.

This book is printed on acid-free paper.

A Forge Book
Published by Tom Doherty Associates, LLC
175 Fifth Avenue
New York, NY 10010

www.tor.com

Forge® is a registered trademark of Tom Doherty Associates, LLC.

Library of Congress Cataloging-in-Publication Data

Wyler, Allen R.
    Deadly errors / Allen Wyler.—1st ed.
        p. cm.
    "A Tom Doherty Associates book."
    ISBN 0-765-31311-1
    EAN 978-0-765-31311-9
    1. Hospital patients—Crimes against—Fiction. 2. Medical
records—Management—Fiction. 3. Conspiracies—Fiction. 4.
Hospitals—Fiction. 5. Surgeons—Fiction. I. Title.

    PS3623.Y625D43 2005
    813'.6—dc22

                                            2004061961

First Edition: August 2005

Printed in the United States of America

0 9 8 7 6 5 4 3 2 1

To Susan Crawford and Natalia Aponte-Burns

— — — — — — —

ACKNOWLEDGMENTS

In no particular order, I thank Daryl Gardner, Jean-Pierre Wirz, Marci Brajcich, Marsha Martin, Don Donaldson, and Mary Osterbrock for suggestions, encouragement, and advice. To Mike Long for designing *www.allenwyler.com* and to Lily for being there.

DEADLY   ERRORS

PROLOG

Maynard Medical Center Reduces Medical Errors
By WILLIAM BARR
Seattle Times staff reporter

SEATTLE — In a statement issued today, Maynard Medical Center CEO Arthur Benson reported a twentyfold decrease in medical errors since becoming a beta test site for the highly touted Med-InDx electronic medical record (EMR). This makes it by far the safest West Coast hospital according to JCAHO, the accrediting organization for hospitals. "This is a remarkable improvement in patient safety," said Sergio Vericelli, chairman of the JCAHO committee charged with selecting a benchmark EMR within the next year.

Vericelli added, "In November 1999, the Institute of Medicine concluded a study entitled *To Err Is Human: Building a Safer Health System.* It focused attention on the issue of medical errors and patient safety by reporting that as many as 44,000 to 98,000 people die in hospitals each year from preventable medical errors. This makes preventable medical errors this country's eighth leading cause of death—higher than motor vehicle accidents, breast cancer, or AIDS. About 7,000 people per year are estimated to die from medication errors alone."

In support of its mission to improve the quality of health care provided to the public, JCAHO reviews a hospital's response to sentinel events in its accreditation process. A "sentinel event" is an unexpected occurrence involving death or serious physical or psychological injury. Such events are called "sentinel" because they signal the need for immediate investigation and response.

AUGUST

". . . the needle, sponge, and cottonoid counts were correct. The estimated blood loss was 350 ccs with no blood or blood product replacement. This has been dictated by Tyler Mathews."

Neurosurgeon Tyler Mathews finished dictating his operative report, returned the beige dictation telephone to its cradle, and leaned his weary body against the acoustical tile wall of the small dictation booth. The sweat-dampened scrub shirt chilled his back but he was too exhausted to move to a more comfortable position. For an uncharacteristic moment he savored the professional satisfaction and pride his work gave him. The benign brain tumor, a meningioma, had been a particularly nasty one involving a fifty-year-old woman's nerves for sight and eye movement. He'd spent the past six hours peering through a surgical microscope, picking bit by bit at the knobby, cream-colored, grape-sized hunk of tough fibrous tissue until every visible nubbin was removed. A total removal was one thing. But the real trick—and the thing that made this case so satisfying— was getting out of there with the surrounding nerves functioning perfectly.

It was meticulous, demanding work. He loved the challenge.

With a deep breath he palm-wiped his face.

Ignoring the familiar fatigue created by six hours of continuous mental exertion, he pushed off the bar-height stool and headed for the recovery room to once again check his patient's progress recovering from anesthesia.

"Dr. Mathews, there's a man wants to see you." Matilda, the ever-smiling unit clerk, nodded toward the automatic doors leading to the rest of the hospital. The man appeared to be close to Tyler's thirty-eight years and perhaps two inches shorter, maybe five feet nine inches. He wore a summer-weight dark gray suit, white shirt, and abstract black and white tie.

Tyler thought, *FBI,* without knowing exactly why.

"What does he want?" By now the man was approaching with a self-assured strut Tyler recognized as characteristic of law enforcement or military types.

"Dr. Mathews?"

"Yes?" The questioning stares of nurses and anesthesiologists tingled Tyler's back, their interest already sharpened by a stranger in street clothes in a restricted area.

The stranger glanced around. "Not here. Let's move this out into the hall." His tone carried an irritating edge of authority.

Tyler didn't move. "Not until you tell me what this is about. I'm wrapping up a case. Who are you?"

The man pointedly surveyed the room again. "I think it's better we continue this discussion in the hall."

Tyler told the clerk, "I'll be back in a minute," as his gut tightened into a square knot.

Out in the hall the automatic doors slid shut at their backs. The man studied Tyler a moment before his hand appeared holding a wallet. "Agent Dillon, DEA." The wallet dropped open exposing official-looking identification.

The square knot in Tyler's gut began to send sharp stabbing pains up through his diaphragm. "Yes?" He'd wondered about reprisals from his chairman and how they might come. Was this the beginning?

"Mind if I have a look-see in your locker?"

Tyler's heart started galloping. "Why would you want to look in my locker?"

Legs spread in military at ease, Agent Dillon hooked both thumbs over his belt, throwing open his suit coat just enough to flash a shoulder-holstered firearm. "And why would this be a problem, Doctor?"

Tyler spread his legs too, folded both arms across his chest. "The problem's your attitude. It sucks. I want to know what you're looking for and why."

Dillon laughed. "Hey, not my problem. And I *will* look in your locker . . . one way or another."

Tyler shook his head. "There's nothing in my locker that would interest the DEA. Period."

"Hey, have it your way. But, we can do this one of two ways. Either you open it for me, or I'll have security do it." As he spoke, his right hand replaced the ID wallet with a folded paper from his inside breast pocket. "This is a signed order to search your locker." A shrug. "Your call, Doc."

Seeing no other option, Tyler marched toward the dressing room, anger constricting his chest. "What's the deal, you guys don't have enough to do in the War on Drugs? You have to get your jollies now by bullying doctors?"

As they rounded the corner to the narrow passageway between rows of identical gray metal lockers he came face-to-face with two security guards, one leaning against his locker, the other one blocking the aisle, telling a joke. Their conversation stopped abruptly when Tyler appeared.

Tyler turned to Agent Dillon. "What are they here for?"

Dillon flashed irritation. "Just open the fucking locker."

Tyler glanced at the guard leaning against his door. "Mind?" The guard moved away with an embarrassed grin.

Tyler's mind started racing as he reached for the combination lock. What if someone placed something in there? How long ago had he opened the locker to change into scrub clothes? He checked his watch. Six hours. A long time. Long enough for anything to have happened.

"Well? You going to open it?"

Tyler spun the dial and missed the third number. He started over and missed again. By the third time his fingers, trembling from anger, hit the combination and the lock dropped open. He stood aside. "Go ahead, knock yourself out," and drilled the closest security guard a questioning look. The guard glanced away.

Agent Dillon snapped on a latex glove, stepped up, opened the door, and stood there a moment before reaching up to the single shelf above Tyler's hanging clothes. "My, oh, my, what have we here?"

"What the hell—" Tyler reached out but the DEA agent slapped his hand away.

"Don't touch a thing." Dillon pulled down a vial from the shelf. The label read Morphine Sulfate. He turned to one of the security guards. "Open one of those plastic bags for me, will you. And neither one of you is to touch anything before I drop it in a bag. Understood?"

OCTOBER

Attorney Mary McGuire's richly appointed office occupied the southwest corner of the fifteenth floor, and commanded a magnificent view of San Francisco's industrial district. The morning sky was so dark with late October fog and drizzle that cars snaking along the streets below had headlights on at nine o'clock in the morning. It would rain soon. Tyler was sure of this.

"You have a choice. You can accept their offer, which by the way, I think is extremely generous under the circumstances, or you can take your chances in court. I shouldn't have to reiterate the consequences should you lose the case, but just for the record, I will. In this state, as is the case in most states, a felony conviction would mean loss of your professional license. Bottom line, you lose the case and you will never practice medicine again. Ever."

"Goddamnit," Tyler said, his frustration and fury building. He continued to stare out the window, fists shoved deeply into his pockets, shoulders hunched as if protecting his body from the chilly, foggy, autumn gusts outside. "Say we go to trial, what do you estimate my chances of winning?'

His lawyer sighed. They'd been over this how many times this morning? "If you hadn't come up with a positive urine test, well,

I would've said pretty good. But, considering that particular bit of ammunition . . ."

"Goddamnit, just give me the odds."

"They haven't changed from the last time we went over this," she said testily. "My guess, you have about a ninety percent chance of losing."

Typical. He'd asked for his chances of winning. She'd given his risk of losing. He grunted sarcastically and continued staring at the street below.

"Just so I understand this completely . . . so I have an informed consent . . ." His jaw muscles were aching again, producing tight throbbing across his forehead. He paused to work out the tenseness. "Tell me again exactly what the *deal* is." He glanced over his shoulder at her.

Peering back at him over the tops of her half-height reading glasses, sending him her stern-faced lawyer expression, she said, "First, you must complete a drug rehab program here in San Francisco. One that is certified by the California Medical Society's impaired physician program. Only after being fully discharged from such a program can you practice again. Second, when you *do* practice again, it must be outside the state of California."

"This is the part that baffles me. Can they really do that? Dictate which state I practice in?"

"Under the circumstances of this particular deal they can, yes."

"Final question. How long do I have to consider this?" He turned to fully face her.

She reached up, took off her reading glasses, her face deadly serious now. "What's to consider? It's a no-brainer, far as I can see. But, to answer your question, no time at all. They expect an answer from you today."

He knew what he had to do. He thought of Nancy, how he still had her in spite of losing everything else that mattered in his life. He drew in a deep breath, and gave his answer.

Later That Day

The moment Tyler opened the front door to their one-bedroom apartment, a bolt of intuition warned of something wrong. He hesitated, hand still on the doorknob, then shrugged it off as residual paranoia from a very bad day.

He turned into the living room and saw Nancy push up from the couch, fists clenched, cheeks streaked black from mascara. Confused, Tyler stopped. Two pieces of luggage stood neatly aligned to each other a few feet from the couch. She moved to them.

His heart stumbled, a knot of fear encasing it. "Something happen to your mother?"

Fresh tears trickled down her cheeks. "No, Tyler, she's fine but I'm not. I'm moving out. I've contacted a lawyer. I'm filing for divorce."

He placed a hand on the wall for support as his legs weakened. "I—"

She shook her head. "It's not debatable, Tyler. I've made up my mind."

"Not debatable? Who said anything about a debate?" He found himself unable to think clearly.

"I know how you are, that's all. I just don't want to discuss this."

"Jesus, I come home from a very bad day and you tell me we can't even discuss this . . . that you're leaving me? Why?" He pointed at the suitcases. "Christ, we've always been able to talk things out . . . that's been one of the really special things about our relationship . . . being able to communicate."

"Well, not this time, Tyler. I just don't want to be pressured out of my decision."

He straightened his legs back up. "As I remember, the vows went something like 'for better or worse.' Were we both on the same page that day?"

Before she could react, he held up a hand. "Hold it. I take that back. Let me start over again." He inhaled deeply. "Isn't there something we can do to work this out? I mean, why are you doing this?"

"It's the drug thing, Tyler. I just can't handle it. I believed in you. I really did. I was willing to stand by you if it went to a trial because I believe that innocent people win."

"But I *am* innocent. I've been framed."

"Then what are these?" She held up an amber prescription bottle.

"I have no idea. Here, let me see."

She handed it to him. "I know what they are, Tyler. They're OxyContin."

"But—"

"I found them in the back of your nightstand. I . . . I just can't deal with the fact that you lied to me." New tears began flowing down her cheeks making glistening new trails. "I'm not going to live with a drug addict."

She grabbed the bags and walked to the door. "Don't try to contact me. My lawyer will contact you."

CHAPTER 1

"Is this how you found him?" Robin Beck, the doctor on call, asked the paramedic as she quickly ran the back of her fingers over Tyrell Washington's skin. Warm, dry. No fever, no clamminess. Black male. Age estimated in the mid-sixties. Half-open eyes going nowhere. Findings that immediately funneled the diagnosis into the neurologic bin.

"Exactly as is. Unresponsive, pupils mid position and roving, normal sinus rhythm. Vital signs within normal limits. They're charted on the intake sheet." Breathing hard, the paramedic pulled the white plastic fracture board from under the patient, unofficially consummating the transfer of medical responsibility from Medic One to Maynard Medical Center's Emergency Department.

"History?" Beck glanced at the heart monitor as the nurse pasted the last pad to the man's chest. Heart rate a bit too fast. Was his coma cardiac in origin?

A respiratory therapist poked his head through the door. "You call for respiratory therapy?"

She held up a "hold-on" palm to the paramedic, told the RT, "We're going to have to intubate this man. Hang in here with me 'til anesthesia gets here."

The tech nodded. "You called them yet?"

"Haven't had time. It's your job now." Without waiting for an answer she rose up on tiptoes and called over the paramedic's head to a second nurse plugging a fresh line into a plastic IV bag, "Glenda, get on the horn to imaging and tell them we need a STAT CT scan." *Better order it now.* The scan's status would be the first question out of the neurologist's mouth when asked to see the patient. Nervously fingering the bell of her stethoscope, she turned to the paramedic. "I need some history. What have you got?"

"Nada." He shook his head. "Zilch. Wife's hysterical, can't give us much more than she found him like this." He nodded at the patient. "And, yeah, he's been a patient here before."

A phlebotomist jogged into the room, gripping the handle of a square metal basket filled with glass tube Vacutainers with different colored rubber stopper, sheathed needles, and alcohol sponges. "You call for some labs?"

"Affirmative. I want a standard admission draw including a tox screen." A screen blood test for coma-producing drugs. Then to the paramedic, "Did the wife call 911 immediately?"

He shrugged, pushed their van stretcher over so his partner standing just outside the door could remove it from the cramped room. "Far as I know." He paused a beat. "You need me for anything else?"

"That's it? Can't you give me something else to work with?" She figured that under these circumstances a hysterical wife was of little help in giving her the information needed to start formulating a list of possible diagnoses.

His eyes flashed irritation. "This was a scoop and scoot. Alright? Now, if you don't need me for anything else . . ."

She waved him off. "Yeah, yeah, thanks." She wasn't going to get anything more from him now. At least knowing the patient had been treated here before was some help.

She turned to the monitor. Blood pressure and pulse stable. For the moment.

She called over to the lead nurse. "We got to get some history on him. I'm going to take a look at his medical records."

At the workstation, Beck typed Tyrell Washington's social security number into the computerized electronic medical record. A moment later the "front page" appeared on the screen. Quickly, she scanned it for any illness he might have that could cause his present coma. And found it. Tyrell must be diabetic. His medication list showed daily injections of a combination of regular and long-lasting insulin. Odds were he was now suffering a ketogenic crisis caused by lack of insulin.

Armed with this information, Robin Beck hurried to the admitting desk where Mrs. Washington was updating insurance information with a clerk.

"Mrs. Washington, I'm Dr. Beck . . . has your husband received any insulin today?"

Brow wrinkled, the wife's questioning eyes met hers. "No. Why?"

Suspicions confirmed, Beck said, "Thank you, Mrs. Washington. I'll be right back to talk to you further." Already calculating Tyrell's insulin dose, Beck hurried back to Trauma Room Three.

"I want fifteen units of NPH insulin and I want it now." She figured, *Let him start metabolizing glucose for an hour before titrating his blood sugar into an ideal level.* For now she'd hold off calling for a neurology consult until assessing Washington's response to treatment.

"Mama, what's happened to Papa?"

Erma Washington stopped wringing her hands and rocking back and forth on the threadbare waiting-room chair. Serena, her oldest daughter, crouched directly in front of her. She'd called Serena—the most responsible of her three children—immediately after hanging up the phone with 911.

"I don't know, baby . . . I just don't know." Her mind seemed blank, wiped out by the horror of what life would be like without Tyrell.

Her daughter reached out and took hold of both her hands. "Have the doctors told you anything yet?"

"No baby, nothing."

"Nothing?"

"No, wait . . ." Amazed that she'd completely forgotten. "A lady doctor came, asked had Papa been given insulin today."

"*Insulin?* Why'd she ask such a thing, Mama? Papa doesn't take insulin!"

"Dr. Beck, come quick. Room Three's convulsing."

Robin bolted across the hall to Washington's room. The man's limbs were locked in extension, pressing the stretcher side rails out, jaws clamped shut, saliva bubbling out between upper front teeth. From across the room she heard the raspy stridor of a compromised airway. Luckily, the nurses had left the center restraining strap pulled snugly across his belly. A pool of sickening acid settled in Beck's stomach. She'd missed something. Either that or she completely miscalculated the insulin dose.

She yelled to the closest nurse: "Ten milligrams Valium. Now," then muttered, "Shit, where's respiratory when you needed them?" To a nurse just entering the room, she yelled, "Get some nasal oxygen on him." She looked at the suction to assure herself it was hooked up and functional. All she needed now was for the patient to vomit and aspirate. The best thing, she knew, was to turn a seizing patient on his side so fluids would run from the mouth instead of down the trachea into the lungs. But with his arms rigidly straight this would be impossible.

The cardiac monitor alarm rang with a slicing shrill.

Beck saw a flat green line streak across the screen and yelled, "Get a crash cart in here." She slapped the red "Code 199" wall button, scrambling the medical center cardiac arrest team from whatever parts of the hospital they were presently working.

LATE NOVEMBER

Oh, Christ, not again, thought Gail Walker. Two migraines already this month and the spots in her vision that signaled her typical onset were dancing again. She believed they were triggered by the recessed fluorescent ceiling lighting throughout the Intensive Care Unit. She'd considered requesting a transfer to another nursing service but loved the action of this Surgical Intensive Care. There were other ICUs in Maynard Medical Center, of course. Neonatology and Cardiac, for example. But she hated seeing newborns and preemies in heated incubators, with four to five tubes sticking out of their wrinkled little bodies. The Cardiac Care Unit depressed her, reminding her of her own mortality and the incremental age each day checked off of her life. From the fanny pack around her waist she dry-swallowed a pill. Catch those suckers soon enough, chances were you could abort them.

The centrifuge beside her stopped. She removed the small capillary tube and placed it against a chart. The deathly pale thirty-two-year-old real estate broker—one of Dr. Golden's stomach bleeders—now had a hematocrit of eighteen. Too low. Not unexpected. Especially since a half hour ago he had discharged a large amount of foul-smelling black tar into a bedpan.

From the little ICU lab she stepped into the nurses station and found a free computer terminal. On the wall above her left shoulder hung the white board—in spreadsheet format—listing each room, each row stating the patient's name, admitting physician, and assigned nurse. She double-checked the patient's orders on the electronic medical record. Just as she thought: she was to give him two units of packed red blood cells if his hematocrit dropped below twenty.

With another few keystrokes she ordered the two units of red blood cells from the blood bank and marveled at how much more efficient this sort of task had become since MMC had installed the new Med-InDx Computerized Information System—or CIS, as the Information Technologies techies called it. The electronic medical record, or EMR, was just one component of the entire CIS system.

Ten minutes later two clear plastic bags of red blood cells arrived on the unit. With a scanner similar to those used by grocery clerks, she verified the bags as those typed and cross-matched for her patient. Before the advent of the Med-InDx CIS, this job would have required another nurse to cross-validate the blood. Now the task could be done in a fraction of the time with absolute accuracy. God bless technology.

She entered the room and asked, "How you feeling? Still short of breath?"

The pale man turned his head to her. "Man, oh, man, it seems like it's getting worse."

"That's because you're anemic." She held up the bags of red blood cells for him to see. "Once I get these into you you'll be feeling much better."

With both bags of packed cells dripping into the patient's IV, Walker checked on another patient—a post-op open heart who'd probably thrown a blood clot to his brain during a coronary artery bypass operation to unclog three Big Mac–encrusted arteries—where she ran through a NIH stroke assessment and recorded it into the chart.

An alarm from a cardiac monitor shrieked.

She glanced at the row of nursing-station slave monitors, did a double take. What the hell? Her patient. Golden's GI bleeder. *Shit, what happened?*

She raced around the corner of the desk to join the flock of nurses and doctors funneling into the room.

JANUARY, THE FOLLOWING YEAR

"It's been the shift from hell. I'm outta here."

William Thornton threw a mock salute to the nurse he was replacing. "Have a good one."

Walking past sliding-glass doors to a string of patient rooms in the MMC Cardiac Care Unit, Thornton began mentally organizing the next sixty minutes of his ten-hour shift. He stopped outside room 233. As an RN he had responsibility for three CCU patients instead of two—a thin staffing pattern brought about by the nursing shortage. A staffing pattern the administration deemed acceptable because of using nursing assistants as extenders. A practice Thornton knew the nurses union intended to make a hot issue during the next round of contract negotiations.

Might as well start by making rounds on the patients, he decided. Tablet computer in hand, he entered room 233.

"Hello, Mr. Barker, I'm Bill Thornton." He reached out to feel the fifty-five-year-old man's pulse, an unnecessary move since he could read it off the monitor, but one he knew personalized the contact. "How are you feeling?"

"Bored. Why the hell can't I have a TV in here?"

Thornton scanned the patient's vital signs. Heart in normal sinus rhythm, blood pressure 144/76, pulse 78. Color good, patient responsive.

"Don't want to get you excited. Not for a day or so." He already knew Barker's story but asked, "Tell me, what happened to you?" to test his memory.

"It was the damnedest thing, I'm down in my basement workshop—I do woodworking, you know . . . furniture, pretty good stuff too, if I do say so myself—when I get this chest pain." His right hand massaged his left breast. "Just like what they tell you? Ya know, like a fucking elephant stepping on my shoulder. Well, hell's bells, I knew exactly what it was. Scared the bejesus outta me too. I didn't want to move so I called my wife and she called 911. Doc says two of my arteries were almost completely shut down."

Thornton nodded approval at the story. "But that's all taken care of, right?"

"Yep."

"Except for the fact you're still having some irregular heartbeats." An understatement. Barker was still on high-dose IV medications for life-threatening arrhythmias.

With his notebook computer, Thornton logged into the EMR and checked Barker's medication schedule. To his shock he noticed the nurse he just relieved had neglected to give a critical anti-arrhythmic medication. Horrified, he moused the pharmacy tab, double-clicked on the medication, then clicked STAT.

"Matter of fact," he said, trying to mask any anxiety from his voice, "you're due for another dose of medication right now. I'm having it sent up right away."

Ten minutes later Thornton returned.

"You're in luck, Mr. Barker," he joked. "The pharmacy still carries this." He held up a syringe of clear colorless fluid, squeezed out a drop of air, and injected the drug into the IV port.

Finished, Thornton dropped the empty syringe in the wall-mounted "sharps" container just as the cardiac monitor began shrieking. He turned to see the tracing go flat-line.

JANUARY, ONE WEEK LATER

For the first time since starting their discussions, second thoughts began eroding Sergio Vericelli's confidence. It wasn't the proposal evoking the toenail nervousness that had started creeping in waves from his feet up to his chest, filling his gut with a tightness. It was the man sitting across the small bistro table from him.

He realized the man had asked a question. "Sorry, I became distracted. You will repeat it?"

A flicker of irritation in the man's penetrating dark eyes broke the emotionless mask he wore so effectively. "How would you like to receive the money? I suggest it be wired to an offshore account. I assume you have one?"

Sergio studied the man's face for a hint of what disturbed him so. Chiseled, rugged features that he supposed women found handsome. From his perspective the only mar was a shock of white from the widow's peak—a contrasting streak against black hair combed straight back. A flaw Sergio would have taken care of if it were his. Maybe there was nothing sinister there at all, he decided. Maybe his nervousness was nothing more than the muffled voice of his conscience shouting to be heard above the cacophony the hundred-thousand-dollar offer caused. An additional fifty thousand, if all went as planned.

"No, but I will open one tomorrow."

Sergio realized he'd just moved one step closer to consummating *the deal*. Did he really want to do this? He thought of childhood stories of men who made pacts with the devil. *But this is not the devil,* he reminded himself.

Are you very certain of this? Do you know this to be fact?

Sergio Vericelli felt a shiver snake down his vertebrae only to be chased away by the thought of what one hundred thousand dollars would buy.

"Excellent. Then we are agreed?"

Sergio swallowed only to find his mouth dry. "Agreed."

The man with the shock of white hair held out his hand.

A primitive gut-level fear caused Sergio to hesitate a beat before clasping the dry warm flesh. But the moment the other man's fingers wrapped around his, dreams of further riches smothered those fears.

CHAPTER 2

Larry Childs wiped sweat from his brow with the back of his forearm and tried to ignore the pounding in his temples. It was hotter than hell behind the grill, the smell of sizzling fry grease cloying, nauseating him more and more. Suddenly, bitter, bilious gastric acid shot up his esophagus. He swallowed what he could but a small residual burned the back of his throat. He remembered the dark olive, vile gunk spewing from his mouth ten minutes ago as he had bent over stained, urine-scented porcelain. He gagged again at the mere memory. This time a bolus of stomach juice shot upward, rushing toward his mouth so fast he knew he wouldn't make it to the john. Eyes wide with fear, right hand clamped against gritted teeth, he frantically scanned the greasy work area for a wastebasket.

The warm liquid hit his palate with the force of a home run. Both knees buckled. His vision dimmed. His right hand shot out, connecting with something solid. With his lips and hand forming a tight barrier, the path of least resistance became his nose. The sickly green fluid spewed from both nostrils onto the hot grill.

At that moment pain signals from his burning palm hit his brain. Through blurred double vision, he watched in horror as his fingers clawed the hot grill only inches from three sizzling hamburger patties.

He screamed in pain and jerked his hand away, the balance it managed to provide now lost. He crashed to the greasy concrete floor and immediately curled into a fetal ball of pain, nausea, and shame.

His consciousness seemed to waver on a precipice. Only the throbbing arm pain kept him from slipping into blissful unconsciousness. His left hand gripped his right wrist, trying to strangle the agony radiating from the burnt tissue.

He heard, "What the . . . ahhh, Jesus Christ, someone barfed."

On his side, knees against his chest, Larry Childs struggled to roll onto his stomach when something kicked his leg. A white-hot ember glowed in the back of his mouth above his tongue, stealing his breath.

"What the hell . . ." that voice said. "Oh, Blessed Virgin Mary, Larry, s'that you? What's wrong?"

Mr. Jorgenson was kneeling over him now trying to turn him onto his back. But he wouldn't let him. He didn't want his boss to see his hand and send him home or to the doctor. This job—the only real job he'd been able to land in his twenty-one years—was just too important to him. Reliability and dependability had been drummed into him during the vocational rehab sessions. No, he wouldn't let Jorgenson send him home.

"I . . . just need to get to the men's room . . . wash up."

The stench of frying vomit and the burning in his sinus sent another ripple of bile racing up his esophagus. But there was nothing much to come this time. The headache kept squeezing in from both temples as if a vise were being cranked slowly closed. Both eyes felt ready to pop from his skull.

Again he tried rolling onto his stomach, but Jorgenson kept trying to turn him onto his back. The really bad thing was the headache was much more intense lying down here on the floor— worse than during the past two days as it grew to the point he couldn't sleep flat without it becoming intolerable. So each night he had waited until his parents went to bed before sneaking downstairs to sleep upright in Pop's La-Z-Boy recliner.

Out of the mental haze he heard, "Frank, call Larry's mother. The number's on the Rolodex on my desk."

Larry struggled to push up, to tell him no. She'd only take him home and that would ruin everything. Dr. Fraser at Voc Rehab had warned him . . .

MAYNARD MEDICAL CENTER

"Dr. Mathews."

Tyler turned from the patient he was examining. "Yes, Teresa?"

"Phone call for you. I'll put it through to your office."

He cast the clinic nurse a questioning look. The only reason to interrupt him during a patient visit would be a call from another doctor. In such cases she always mentioned the physician's name.

She nodded toward the hall, suggesting she'd provide an explanation out there. He told the patient he would be right back and exited the room. Before he could ask, she said, "It's your ex-wife."

"Nancy?" His heart accelerated. How long since she walked out on him? *Ten months, ten days,* he knew. *Is this it? Has she unleashed her pit bull lawyer?* His stomach knotted.

"Is there another one I don't know about?" When he didn't respond immediately, she added softly, "Yes, Nancy. That's why I thought you might want to take it." Her eyes twinkled against her flawless brown Filipino skin.

A strange brew of hope and dread infused his chest, causing him to freeze.

She shot him a questioning look. "Is there a problem? I thought you'd be overjoyed, the way you still mope around here, pining away about her."

"I mope and pine?" He was trying to make it light.

She gave him a playful slap on the arm. "You're changing the subject. Is there a problem?"

He started walking. "Are you always this nosy?"

Teresa laughed.

Sitting in his small office, hand wavering over the phone, he thought, *This can only be bad news. It's finally over.* He palm-wiped his face, sucked in a deep breath, and picked up the phone. "Hello, Nancy?"

"Hi, Tyler." Her voice sounded upbeat and friendly. A good sign?

"What's up?" trying to sound casual, trying to mask the dread in his voice. He visualized the day he'd met her at UCLA—a molecular biology grad student hunched over a microscope. At the time he was a chronically fatigued first-year neurosurgical resident.

"I'm in Seattle now, working at the Fred Hutch." She laughed. "Mom's ecstatic, says that by leaving the academic womb, I'm finally acting like a grown-up and putting my degree to good use."

Tyler rubbed his temple. "This a consulting thing or what?"

She exhaled audibly. "No. It's permanent. I mean, like any grant it's for as long as the money holds out. Oh, heck, I'm not very good at this, at making myself vulnerable, but . . . I was wondering . . . if we, you know, you and me . . . if we might still have . . . damnit, Tyler, let me just say it. I miss you. I have since the day I left you. Do you think we might try . . . I mean, are you seeing someone?"

"Hold on a second." A sudden dizziness forced him to lean back in the chair next to his desk, the small office cramped with filing cabinet, bookcases, one wall choked with framed diplomas, and both his California and Washington state licenses.

He rubbed his lips and tried to calm his voice before uttering another word. "No. I'm not seeing anyone."

"Then can we meet for dinner, say next week?"

Tyler's heart leaped with joy. Then his beeper started ringing. "Hold on a second." He recognized the phone number for the Emergency Department. The digits 911 after the message signaled an emergency. "Yes, I'd love to but I just got beeped . . . an emergency. Got something to write with?"

"Yes."

He gave her his apartment phone number. "If I don't answer, leave your telephone number. I'll get back soon as I have a chance." On second thought, might as well write it down now. He glanced around his cluttered desk and found a ballpoint advertising a new antibiotic. "What's your number?"

She recited it. He scribbled it on a Post-it.

"I really want to see you again, Tyler."

His throat constricted, his eyes misted. "Me too, Nancy. Gotta run. Bye." Reluctantly he hit the disconnect button and dialed the ED.

"Dr. Mathews answering. What've you got?"

"Thanks for getting back to me right away. Remember a patient, Larry Childs?"

Tyler's heart sank. "What? He have a seizure?"

"No. Worse than that. Looks like he's herniating."

"*Herniating?* People with epilepsy don't herniate, they seize."

"That's all well and good, but that's sure as hell what it looks like from this end. Guy's left pupil's blown, both disks show four-plus papilledema and he's Cheyne-Stoking." Papilledema. A bad sign meaning the nerves at the back of the eyes were full of fluid from elevated pressure inside the skull.

"Cheyne-Stoking?" An abnormal breathing pattern. "Damn." Obviously, something other than his epilepsy was causing the problem. A subarachnoid hemorrhage? "Ordered an MRI yet?"

"Scanner's full with another emergency. He's on his way to CT as we speak."

"I'll be right down."

"Man! Now that's what I call U-G-L-Y," whispered the CT technician so the nurse from the Emergency Department on the other side of the lead-impregnated glass couldn't hear. The tech was an overweight, thirtyish woman with a duck's ass haircut and a white polo shirt cut sleeveless to showcase tattooed barbed wire encircling linebacker biceps. Tyler liked her because she could whip out three top-quality scans in the time most techs took for two.

Tyler stood in the scanner control room watching "slices" of

Larry Childs's brain appear as infinite shades of gray and black on a finger-smudged twenty-one-inch monitor. The air was stale from poor ventilation and smelled vaguely of electronics.

Tyler mentally ticked through several possible causes for Larry's problem. The entire left side of the kid's brain was swollen, flattening the surface against the inside of the skull and obliterating the normal convolutions that characterize human cortex. Even more alarming was that the swollen left brain was compressing the normal right side and in the process had twisted the brain stem, causing Larry's coma.

Tyler leaned out of the control-room doorway, said to the nurse, "I want twenty-five grams of Mannitol and ten milligrams of Decadron pushed STAT."

She cast a hesitant glance at her patient while untying the lead shield. "You'll watch him?"

"Of course, now go!"

Tyler stepped down one step into the room that housed the GE-built scanner and accepted the lead-impregnated shield from her. Since the scan was over, he draped it on the wall holder over two similar protectors, then moved next to the table as the sliding gantry withdrew Larry Childs's head from the huge cream-colored donut. Thin, gaunt, Larry's pale white skin blended with the sheet covering him.

Larry's breathing was becoming more labored. Before the CT tech could leave the control-room phone, Tyler yelled to her, "Page anesthesia and respiratory therapy, STAT. He needs to be intubated."

She flashed a thumbs-up.

Tyler pulled a penlight from his white coat to shine in Larry's pupils. The right one was normal size and reactive. As billed, the left was dilated and nonreactive. Not bothering to test the corneal reflexes, Tyler tapped his reflex hammer against Larry's biceps and patella tendons. The right-sided reflexes were distinctly more brisk than the left. All findings consistent with the CT picture of swollen brain pushing on the delicate brain stem regions controlling consciousness.

"Anesthesia's tied up in the cardiac ICU." The imaging tech stood beside him now.

"God, every time you need an anesthesiologist . . ." He shook his head and recalculated the need to intubate Larry. "Respiratory therapy?"

"On the way."

At that moment the nurse returned with a syringe, a vial, and an IV bag. "Here's the Decadron," she gasped between breaths. "Give that. I'll push the Mannitol."

"Wait a second." Tyler held up his hand. "We need to cath him first." Giving a powerful diuretic like Mannitol without a urinary catheter in place could burst the bladder.

"I'll do it," the tech offered.

The ED nurse's brow furrowed. "You certified to do that?"

"Fuckin' A." She thrust a thumb at her own chest. "Served as a navy corpsman before this gig."

Tyler cut off the ED nurse: "We don't have time for any territorial pissing matches." To the CT tech he said, "Grab a Foley set and get to work." To the nurse, "If there's a problem, I'll deal with it later."

She shot him a withering glare before jerking a blood pressure cuff from the wall holder.

"Stow it. We don't have the time," he shot back.

From the small glass vial, Tyler drew into a syringe ten milligrams of a steroid to combat brain inflammation. As he injected the drug into Larry's IV line a respiratory therapist—a Japanese woman, no taller than five feet—jogged into the room. "What's up?"

She looked no more than twenty-one to Tyler. "We need to tube this patient *now*. You have an intubation tray ready?"

"You bet, but anesthesia's tied up for ten minutes or so. Can it wait?"

Tyler glanced at Larry again. His right arm muscles were

tightening into rigid extension, signaling his brain function was deteriorating. "No we can't."

"Well then—"

"I'll do it," Tyler interrupted. "Just get the tray."

Soon as the words flew from his mouth a feeling of panic shouldered aside his confident reply. Unlike the well-lit operating room where a few anesthesiologists allowed him to practice this skill, this area had poor lighting and he was wedged awkwardly between the scanner and the wall.

"All done." The CT tech pulled the white sheet over Larry's exposed genitals. Pale yellow urine flowed down the plastic tube toward the collection bag.

The nurse gently pushed Tyler aside as she wheeled a stretcher next to the scanner. She asked the group, "Ready to transfer him onto the stretcher?"

Using a plastic transfer board to bridge the gap between the scanner gantry and stretcher, they used the draw sheet under Larry to pull him onto the stretcher.

A moment later the respiratory tech rushed in carrying a tray wrapped in a blue surgical sheet sealed with strips of autoclave-sensitive tape. She asked Tyler, "Where do you want this?"

Tyler sucked in a deep breath, glanced around, and nodded at a stainless-steel Mayo stand against the wall. "Over there."

She placed the package on the stand and expertly unwrapped it, keeping the contents sterile.

Just then Childs's respirations stopped.

"Shit," Tyler's gut knotted.

The respiratory therapist shot him a nervous look. "You sure you can do this? I could put some O-2 on him until anesthesia gets here." She didn't sound convinced this was such a good solution.

Tyler glanced at the opened tray and back to Larry Childs, "We can't wait."

CHAPTER 3

With deliberately unhurried movements Tyler snapped a medium curved blade onto the laryngoscope handle. *Start to rush, you make mistakes,* he reminded himself. After checking to see if the light at the end of the blade worked, he pulled the chrome Mayo stand to the head of the stretcher. He told the respiratory tech who was struggling to keep Larry's lungs full of oxygen by using a face mask and an Ambu bag, "Open me a seven point five." Then to the nurse, "Suction ready?"

"Yes."

He sucked in a deep breath, trying to quell the anxiety making his hand tremble. *One shot's all you get, pal . . . Aggravate the vocal cords into spasm and the resulting lack of oxygen will cause Larry's brain to crush the brain stem.*

He lifted Larry's chin, tilting the entire head back toward him, and opened the mouth. Laryngoscope in left hand, he slipped the silver blade into the mouth and over the tongue, inserting almost all the curved part before pulling straight up. The pale pink larynx popped into view, both vocal cords glistening in the light. Holding the scope steady, never losing sight of the cords, he held out his right hand. "Tube."

And felt the smooth plastic contact his fingers.

Gently he worked the endotracheal tube over the steel blade and through the opened vocal cords. "Got it." A paradoxical adrenaline rush hit, making him giddy.

Stethoscope to her ears, the short respiratory tech listened first to Larry's left lung and then to his right. "Airway sounds good," she said with palpable relief.

Tyler exhaled the deep breath trapped in his lungs since inserting the laryngoscope. He placed a bite block between Larry's jaws and taped the tube into place.

As he stripped off his gloves the nurse asked, "His mother's in his room. You want to talk with her now, or should I tell her you'll be out later?" Her way of dumping responsibility of breaking the bad news on him rather than the ED physician. Nurses tend to protect their own, he knew. In the ED he was the outsider.

He glanced at the respiratory tech. She nodded toward the door. "I have him under control until anesthesia arrives."

"Which room?"

"Trauma Six."

Tyler sucked in a deep breath, stepped out of the cramped scanner room, and stood in the hall wrestling with an explanation Larry's mother might understand.

Radiation necrosis. That has to be it.

He considered this diagnosis more carefully. Four months ago Larry Childs became subject number twelve in a multicenter clinical trial evaluating highly focused radiation as an alternative to traditional surgery to obliterate seizure-triggering brain tissue. The one-shot treatment came from the Z-Blade, a third-generation radiation device touted as state-of-the-art.

A bolt of gut-churning anxiety hit. *Did I make a mistake? Did I do this to Larry?*

No, he reminded himself, *the system doesn't allow only one person to determine treatment.* He mentally ticked off the steps required. He, Tyler, provided the tissue targeting volume. Then Nick Barber—the study's Principal Investigator at the University of Pittsburgh—calculated and then electronically transferred the radiation dosage back to Larry Childs's MMC chart. Only after Tyler confirmed this dose had the Z-Blade accepted it. Even then, the computer was programmed to never accept a dose outside a reasonable range without a cumbersome override entry. This technique was supposed to provide bulletproof protection from such errors.

No, he assured himself, *it's something other than radiation necrosis that's swelling Larry's brain.*

Despite reassuring himself, he couldn't shake the nausea twisting his stomach.

Face etched with deep stress lines, Larry's mother perched rigidly on the edge of a molded plastic chair, right hand clutching a magazine rolled into a tight baton. She glanced up as he approached, pessimistic fear immediately replacing the glint of recognition that flashed across her eyes. Tears followed in anticipation of Tyler's words.

"Is he going to be alright?" she whispered tentatively.

He hedged. "I don't know yet, Mrs. Childs, I need more information." He pulled a burnt orange plastic chair next to hers, reached out, and placed a reassuring hand on her arm. "All I know is the left side of Larry's brain is swollen and pressing on those deep areas that control his consciousness."

"It's the radiation, isn't it." Making it a statement, the fear in her eyes changing to self-incriminating anger. "Lord! I knew he shouldn't have that radiation."

Tyler shook his head. "Whoa, let's not get ahead of ourselves, Mrs. Childs. We don't know that." He caught himself from punctuating the sentence with "yet."

The corners of her mouth turned south in an expression that rippled a taste of guilt down Tyler's throat for not confirming her suspicion. He swallowed. But why speculate on a diagnosis now if not completely certain they weren't dealing with something totally off the wall? Something like a herpes infection, for instance.

"Ma'am, I need to take Larry to surgery to remove that temporal lobe, the one causing the seizures, to relieve the pressure off his brain stem. And I need to do this as soon as I can get an operating room geared up."

"He's going to die, isn't he?"

He swallowed again. "Not if I can help it."

Her pessimistic eyes said she didn't believe he could.

"I'll be right back with a consent form, Mrs. Childs. I'll need you to sign it."

"Teeing up a case this late in the day?"

Tyler pulled on his scrub shirt. He recognized Bill Leung's tenor voice without turning. Bill, a senior partner in their group, occupied the locker flanking his.

"Long as you're here, might as well give me your opinion on something." Tyler cinched the pulls on the scrub pants, then tied a bow, which he tucked inside the pants—a long-ingrained habit to prevent dangling ties from contaminating a sterile field. Finished dressing, Tyler reached into the narrow locker and came away with a white and brown MRI envelope.

"Here," handing it to his partner. At fifty-seven Bill still looked like a Marine drill sergeant. Lanky, not an ounce of extra fat. *From running every day,* Tyler thought. *Compulsive about it.*

Also clad in green scrubs, Bill held up a rectangular oak box the size of a small jewelry case. Loupes. Magnifying eyeglasses worn by most neurosurgeons. "Let me get rid of these first." His partner spun the combination lock to his locker. A triangle of sweat darkened the midline of Bill's scrub shirt by at least two shades.

"Tough case?"

Uttering a sigh weighted down with cynical fatigue, the veteran surgeon opened the gray metal door. "Aren't they all?" After setting the mitered wood box on the single shelf he turned, hand extended. "Let me see those pictures."

Tyler passed over the envelope and followed Bill into the adjoining tiled shower/toilet area. Without a backlit view box available the best place to examine the images would be against one of the frosted windows. Bill quickly sorted the films, zeroing in on the most telling. With his left hand pinning it flat against the window, he slipped on a pair of half-height reading glasses and leaned forward, chin up, to examine the images.

Bill gave a slow whistle with a headshake. Removing the film from the window, he turned expectant eyes on Tyler. "Herpes?"

"That your first choice?"

Bill peered over the top of the tortoiseshell glasses at him before stealing another glance at the film. "Could be anything, I guess . . . Glioblastoma, infection, you name it. All I see is a shitload of edema"—tapping the film with an index finger—"no well-defined mass . . . yeah, herpes is the first thing comes to mind. Why? You going to tell me it's CPC material?" Clinical Pathologic Correlation is a weekly conference at which difficult to diagnose cases are discussed.

Tyler recited Larry Childs's history.

Bill slipped the film back into the envelope. "Well, there you go. Seems to me like your patient has a bad case of radiation necrosis." He paused. "Not that any case of radiation necrosis isn't bad, mind you, it's just that this looks *really* bad." Envelope now intact, he handed it back to Tyler.

"I was afraid you were going to say that." They headed back to their lockers. Tyler needed to slip on his shoes and grab his own set of loupes before heading for the operating room.

Bill pulled the sweat-stained scrub shirt over his head, balled it up, and threw a double pump jumper toward a linen hamper. "Word of advice?"

Tyler watched the shirt miss and fall to a green clump on the floor. Tyler bent down, pulled a pair of air-cushioned Nikes from the locker floor, then dropped his butt onto a wood stool. "What?" Tyler suspected he was going to advise not operating and wondered how much of his partner's surgical conservatism came from wisdom and how much came from plain old grind-it-out fatigue of years in the OR.

"I wouldn't do anything more than needle biopsy that mother

of all edemas." Leung was sending him that dead-eye Chinese look Tyler found difficult to evaluate.

"I was planning on taking out his temporal lobe." He started tying the laces.

Bill slipped off his pants and this time tried a hook shot. Missed again. "That, my friend, is a huge mistake."

"Why so?" He jerked the knot tight and turned to the other shoe.

Bill's face turned even more serious. "Kid's temporal lobe isn't your biggest problem here. Hell, with that scan the kid's probably a goner anyway. The problem is you can bet your bippie that family will have some sleazeball lawyer licking his chops before the sun sets. You operate that kid and he'll have you in the knee-chest position so fast it'll make your head spin. And he won't provide you the courtesy of using K-Y jelly, either."

Tyler sighed. "Point noted, but that's the risk we all take when we schedule cases."

"Sure, but look at it this way. If it's herpes the biopsy will show it and you can treat him with acyclovir. If not? Like I said, with a scan like that, he's screwed blue and tattooed anyway. Best to keep as much distance from this tar baby as possible. Hell, even if it *is* herpes he looks like a goner. I just can't see any upside to operating the kid."

Loupes and MRI in hand, Tyler kicked the locker door. It slammed shut. He met his partner's questioning eyes. "Way I see it, if it's radiation necrosis, there's nothing I can do to increase or decrease my odds of getting sued. It's either going to happen or it's not. But if I don't take out that kid's temporal lobe, he's going to die. It's that simple."

"Tyler, let me put it to you this way: what're you really going to accomplish by opening up that kid's head?"

"Don't start with me again, Bill. We've had this debate before. It's philosophical, not medical. Boils down to one thing—you and I see risk differently. Isn't that it?"

"Humor me and walk through this little exercise just for drill. Okay?"

Tyler couldn't be certain if Bill was intending to be fatherly or condescending. He gave his senior partner the benefit of doubt. "Why? I know exactly where this is going and I really don't want to get into a heated debate minutes before opening this kid's head."

"Way I see it, that kid's brain's trashed as it is. What the hell difference is it going to make if you're a little hot under the collar when you crack his coconut?" Leung took a deep breath. "I took a huge gamble hiring you, Tyler—"

Tyler sliced a hand through the air. "Whoa. Hold it right there. Don't confuse issues, Bill. I have too much respect for you to tarnish that opinion now. Whether or not I operate on this kid's brain has nothing to do with what happened in the past."

"Maybe not directly," Leung interrupted, "but indirectly it sure as hell does."

Tyler double-checked Bill's face and realized the conversation was about to take a completely different tack. "Mind explaining that?"

Bill leaned against the row of lockers opposite his own, cheeks and eyes sagging with weariness. "Remember you telling me how come you missed that scholarship to UCLA?"

Tyler flashed on his high school basketball coach warning him to stop unloading impossible shots with only seconds on the shot clock, that it was ruining his average.

"Sounds rhetorical to me." Tyler checked the wall clock. "They should be wheeling my patient into the OR any minute now."

"Point being, you didn't listen to your coach, did you." He waved a dismissive hand. "Yeah, yeah, I know—another rhetorical question. But the end result was you didn't win that basketball scholarship you wanted so much. Which, in turn, changed your whole life. Who knows, you might've ended up a point guard in the NBA and never gone to medical school."

"Look, Bill—"

"Don't worry, you'll have plenty of time to get that case started. You want to hear me out on this one." Leung adjusted his lean body against the locker. "You're not listening to me, Tyler." He punched Tyler's shoulder softly. "Hey, think of me as your high school basketball coach giving you advice. Try not to make the same mistake twice."

Before he could answer, Leung continued. "What you don't know is that the Quality Assurance committee is looking at your M and M stats and they don't look all that terrific, Tyler." He shrugged.

"What the hell you saying? I'm a bad surgeon?"

"You know damn well *I* don't think that. I know the quality of work you do and the type of Hail Mary cases you elect to do. Hell, look at this one," with a nod at the MRI folder in Tyler's hand. "But the cubicle grunts on that committee don't know a craniotomy from a pepperoni. In their eyes all surgery is created equal. If your case morbidity and mortality pops up above the average for gallbladders and hemorrhoidectomies they start crooning the bottom-line anthem."

Tyler let out a sarcastic grunt. "Far as I'm concerned the Quality Assurance committee can have any of my cases reviewed by an independent panel. But until they can convince me my decisions are wrong, I'm going to practice the best I can. Now, if you'll excuse me, I have a case to do."

Leung called after him. "Take my advice, Tyler, just pop in a burr hole and needle that gobbler and get the hell out of there. You open that kid's head and you'll have a tiger by the tail. All that edematous brain comes oozing out into your lap like The Alien, you're going to wish you never went in there."

Michelle Lawrence, the anesthesiologist, asked, "Any land mines I should know about?" They were standing next to the heavy steel operating table in the warm glare of two sets of parabolic, high-intensity spotlights, a scrub and two circulating nurses scurrying around still opening and arranging instruments. Tyler, absent-mindedly focusing one of the lights more directly on Larry's shaved head, said, "ICP's elevated." Meaning intracranial pressure. "How much, I have no clue, but he's got four-plus papilledema so that tells us something. Plus, his scan looks like the monster that ate Chicago."

Tyler turned to a wall-mounted X-ray view box, slapped the edge of a film up underneath the clips, securing it. "Right here, for example." Tyler tapped one particularly ugly spot on the MRI to emphasize the point.

Michelle emitted a cynical snort. A little over six months ago Mike Lawrence's sex change operation created one of the most unattractive, overweight, middle-aged females Tyler ever laid eyes on. Although estrogen therapy suppressed such male physical attributes as facial hair, it certainly hadn't bestowed Michelle with the grace genetically created females learn from infancy. To make matters worse, rumor had it she underwent surgery to become a lesbian. *Go figure,* Tyler thought, while watching her return to the anesthesia cart with the broad-shouldered swagger of an NFL linebacker. "Lawrence of A Labia" the other anesthesiologists jokingly called her behind her back.

Tyler double-checked Childs's positioning on the operating table. Head held solidly in a three-pin clamp bolted securely to the table, chin pointing toward his right shoulder that was propped up with a towel roll to prevent undue neck strain. Childs's freshly shaven scalp glistened in the high-intensity light.

For one last moment Tyler surveyed the OR, mentally going through his preflight checklist before exiting to scrub. The chilly air raised goose bumps on his exposed skin. His brain already had submerged the white noise of the nurses' preparatory sponge counts and the rhythmic respirator wheezes into a subliminal zone, giving him full concentration on the task. Satisfied, he turned and pushed through the heavy swinging doors into the hall.

Minutes later he returned. The scrub nurse held open a sky-blue paper scrub gown like a matador for him. Next, he pushed his hands into a pair of gloves as the circulating nurse tied the back of the gown. He handed off the final tie to the scrub nurse to hold while he did a 360, wrapping it around his waist. This he knotted, finalizing the ritual.

With a sterile felt-tip pen he drew a large question mark incision starting mid-forehead and ending just in front of the ear. All of the head except for the proposed operative field was draped with four blue surgical towels and then covered with a sticky Saran Wrap–like plastic barrier. A larger blue paper drape shrouded Larry's entire body. Next, Tyler injected local anesthetic along the proposed incision.

"Ready?"

The scrub nurse and Michelle answered, "Yes," in unison.

Tyler held out his hand. "Number ten Bard Parker." She handed him the scalpel.

Even without an assistant Tyler worked swiftly, placing clamps along the skin edge to stop bleeding.

The circulating nurse asked, "Want me to see if I can find you an assistant?"

Considering the time of day and it being an emergency, he hadn't thought to request one. "That's okay. I'll be alright."

Michelle said, "If anyone can muddle through a craniotomy, it's Tyler. But you better get moving, his pulse is starting to drop." Meaning the pressure in the brain was increasing.

An anxious fluttering awoke in Tyler's chest. He remembered Bill Leung's warning to not open Childs's head. "Can you hyperventilate him any more?"

"He's maxed."

"More Mannitol?"

"He's so dry right now, he's pissing dust."

"Shit!"

He peeled back the scalp and the jaw muscle, exposing white skull.

He held out his hand. "Perforator."

The scrub nurse handed him an air-powered instrument. He drilled two nickel-size holes through the bone, exposing the tough brain-protecting membrane, the dura.

He handed it back to her. "Change it over to the craniotome." A side cutting saw.

This he used to connect the two holes with two arcing cuts, forming a circular piece of skull that he carefully removed from the dura.

He ran his fingertip over the rock-hard membrane, muttered, "Shit."

"What?" Michelle peered over the barrier—a blue paper sheet clipped to an IV pole and the patient—isolating surgeon from anesthesiologist.

"This is worse than I expected."

"They're always worse, Tyler. You suffer from the bane of any good surgeon—optimism."

To the scrub nurse Tyler said, "Fifteen blade." Then to no one he muttered, "When am I going to learn how to stay out of trouble."

Blade in hand, he sliced a two-inch incision through the dura, staying low, keeping away from arteries on the brain surface. Gelatinous white brain tissue oozed from the elliptical opening, slowly at first until Tyler began removing it with a sucker. Once the final membrane broke—encasing cortex—watery brain tissue began spitting out.

"Give me a specimen cup and some culture swabs. Aerobic and anaerobic. And while you're at it, some glutaraldehyde for electron microscopy." That covered infections from bacteria and a virus, he decided. "Oh, and call a pathologist. I want a frozen and viral cultures." He mentally ran the list he'd just ordered, checking for anything he might've forgotten.

Between collecting the various specimens he sucked at the exuding tissue, purposely not enlarging the incision yet, allowing the internal pressure to push out the damaged, necrotic-looking brain like a fetus. This way the pressure would decompress slowly and gently, to minimize any compensatory shift on the brain stem.

"What's our game plan, Ace?" Michelle again, eyes wide, the skin above the bridge of her nose conspicuously plucked of fine hairs.

"For now, just easing the pressure down. After that? Plan to snatch out his temporal tip . . . give him more room."

"Any wild-ass guess what diagnosis we might be dealing with?" she asked anxiously.

"Doubt it's AIDS or hepatitis related, if that's your worry."

The anesthesiologist let out a little gasp. "Heavens to betsy, no. I never would've thought of that."

"Could be just about anything. But my money's on radiation necrosis." Tyler filled Michelle in on Larry's history of epilepsy and the clinical trial to destroy seizure-triggering areas of the brain with focused radiation.

"Dr. Mathews."

Tyler looked over at the scrub nurse. She nodded, eyes directed over his shoulder. He turned. A bearded stranger dressed in a green jumpsuit, scrub cap, and mask stood watching him work.

"You the pathologist?" Tyler asked.

"Correct. I assume you have a frozen for me?" He spoke with the flattened vowels of an Australian.

While explaining Larry's story again, Tyler accepted a specimen cup and a biopsy forceps from the scrub nurse. While talking he slipped the forceps past the dura, blindly into the brain, then closed the tips. This he did several times, removing lima bean–size chunks of tissue that he tapped off the end of the forceps into the sterile plastic container. Finished, he capped the cup and handed it off to the pathologist.

Holding the container up to the operating lights, the pathologist squinted, turned it back and forth, inspecting the small gray chunks of tissue. A moment later he nodded. "Doubt I'll be able to tell you much more from the frozen than you already suspect, but we'll see, won't we."

Tyler held out his hand to the scrub nurse. "Scissors." He began enlarging the opening in the dura in preparation to remove the temporal lobe.

"But it *could* be herpes?" Michelle again.

"It *could*," Tyler agreed. He noticed the cut edges of the brain oozing more than before and another jolt of anxiety surged through him.

As he struggled through distorted dead brain, snippets of recent conversations with Bill Leung and Michelle replayed over and over again like a commercial jingle that becomes an annoying endless loop in the shadows of consciousness: *"Tough case?" "Aren't they all?"* and *"It's always worse face-to-face than what you expect from the MRI."*

"Yo, Tyler!"

Without moving his eyes from the surgical field. "What?"

"Just asked you what his chances are?"

Tyler straightened up, relieving the cramps in his neck muscles from holding his head in an awkward position for so long. "Depends on the diagnosis. But no matter what, if the rest of this hemisphere looks like the crap I'm pulling out of here, it's trashed."

"But assuming it's radiation necrosis like you suspect . . ."

Tyler started working again, sucking out gray mushy gunk from low in the lobe, trying to find tissue that wouldn't crumble away and bleed unnecessarily. He decided to keep going until he could define the dura at the base of the brain. At least this would give him a solid landmark from which to judge any further dissection. The tissue bleeding increased, the small vessels just as rotten as the brain, making them almost impossible to coagulate. This was now a major worry. How the hell to stop the bleeding?

"Radiation necrosis sometimes subsides if you get the initial portion—the site the radiation targeted—totally removed. That's the reason I'm going after this temporal lobe. If I can remove it, then sit on him with steroids for a couple of days, he might just have a chance."

"Always the optimist, aren't you, my friend. Anyway, that's good to know."

Tyler turned to the scrub nurse. "Surgicel." A thin meshlike material used to help control bleeding.

She handed him a folded towel with half-inch squares of the silver-colored mesh. He picked up several squares with forceps and laid them individually over areas of oozing brain surface. Blood seeped through each one without slowing.

Michelle asked, "Did I hear you correctly when you said this poor boy has never had any prior radiation?"

"More Surgicel." Then, to Michelle, "Look, Shellie, can we talk about that later, right now I have a problem. I can't get any hemostasis."

"Oh, dear."

A hushed conversation between the scrub and circulating nurses stopped abruptly, leaving the steady piping of the heart monitor and the plodding whoosh of the respirator the only room noises. Both nurses looked at him with alarm. He ignored them.

Tyler covered the oozing area with more squares of Surgicel, then layered this area with several white cotton strips, each about two inches by a half inch, over them. He held these in place with his fingers as a Roto-Rooter ground away at his stomach lining. *Maybe I should've asked for help. Christ, maybe I should've listened to Bill.*

"Shit," he muttered. Tightness enclosed his heart. His hands started tingling and he realized he was hyperventilating, his face mask now soggy against his lips.

After thirty seconds he let up the pressure on the cotton strips, hoping they would stick against the Surgicel as a sign of clotting. They didn't. They fell away as more blood started oozing again from the raw, crumbling brain.

"How much blood we have on hand?" he asked Michelle.

"Didn't type and cross him, I'm afraid."

"Oh, great!" Tyler said to the scrub nurse, "Irrigation."

She handed him a blue rubber bulb, like you would use to baste a turkey. Gently, he squirted sterile saline over the brain surface, washing away the useless Surgicel.

"Load me up again, but this time cut them postage-stamp size." He rolled his neck, working out the kinks. "Sponge."

Tyler held a sopping wet cotton sponge against the raw edge of the cavity as the scrub nurse cut more squares of the blood-clotting agent.

"Whatcha going to do?" Michelle asked.

He didn't know, but he sure as hell wasn't going to say that with both nurses listening. "We're going to get it controlled."

"But, how?"

He shot her a look. "Goddamnit, Shellie . . ."

The scrub nurse held out a folded blue surgical towel, the squares of Surgicel aligned in neat parallel rows. One by one he placed them over the oozing brain. Once the entire lemon-sized cavity was lined this way, he packed it snugly with cotton sponges, then backed away from the operating table, both nurses avoiding eye contact.

He said, "Five minutes by the clock. Starting now." He glanced up at the round face clock over the gleaming stainless-steel autoclave and decided to give it every second of the five minutes to clot. Not one second less.

Michelle sidled up next to him as close as possible without contaminating his sterile surgical gown and whispered, "Thought about just closing him up and getting the hell out of there?"

Tyler looked at her. "You mean before we get the bleeding stopped?"

"Seems to me like that might not happen. Besides, you plan on staying here all night?"

"Jesus Christ, Michelle, it'd kill him," he whispered while drilling her a look.

"Seems to me he's a dead man either way you cut it," Michelle snipped. "You wouldn't be the first to bail out on a hopeless case. I've seen a few of your esteemed partners fold the tent and load the camel on lesser problems than this one."

When Tyler didn't answer she added, "Like the Nike ads used to say . . . just do it."

CHAPTER 4

"Slick . . . very slick. Where did you learn that one?"

Tyler glanced up. Michelle was peering over the drape at him. "Surgery 101. Apply pressure, wait, and try to strike a bargain with God." He made no attempt to hide the huge relief from his voice. He used saline to irrigate the cavity where the tip of Larry Childs's temporal lobe had been. He stopped irrigating and waited for the bubbles to clear. The water remained free of blood this time. "Time to play hooky."

Michelle laughed. "Watch it, Tyler. You'll ruin your image."

Tyler held out his hand to the scrub nurse. "Load me up with dural silks and keep them coming as fast as you can." Then to the anesthesiologist, "What image is that?"

"Dr. Dour. Surgeon Serious. The man who doesn't joke around in the OR."

Suture accepted, Tyler began the first stitch. *I haven't always been like that,* he mused. *It wasn't like that when I was with Nancy.*

Twenty minutes later Tyler leaned over to inspect Larry Childs in the recovery room. The area was populated with only a few stragglers from end-of-the-schedule cases. "He's not waking up. You given him anything since the OR?" After helping to load Larry Childs onto a recovery-room stretcher, he'd ducked into the dressing room to dictate an op note. Now, standing over his patient, he tried again to evoke a response by pinching the skin over his chest. Nothing.

Michelle Lawrence, sitting at a stainless-steel counter between two patient bays, glanced up from the computer terminal she was typing on. "Give him anything? Heavens no. I ran him the last hour on just nitrous and oxygen." She began playing with the mask still hanging around her neck.

"Good." Tyler preferred his patients awake soon as possible after the end of the case so he could examine their brain function. Tyler continued to examine Larry in more detail.

The endotracheal tube was out and the kid was breathing on his own, so at least that much was okay. Tyler gently opened Larry's eyelids. The left pupil remained dilated, the eye deviated to the left. No worse than pre-op but still a sign of damage to the third cranial nerve—probably from the shift of the temporal lobe before he decompressed it. The right eye also appeared to be the same as pre-op. Tyler rocked Larry's head side to side. The left eye didn't move, but the right did. Next, he pulled the cotton tip of a Q-Tip into a wisp, which he used to gently brush each cornea. Both eyelids blinked a weak response. Larry's respirations, however, were Cheyne Stokes. Abnormal, signifying a poor connection between the brain stem and cortex.

"Doctor Mathews?"

The RN assigned to Larry drifted over from her other patient. She wore a blue scrub suit with a gray hospital-issue stethoscope draped around her neck.

"Yes?"

"The family's been increasingly inquiring about Larry's condition for the last hour. They seem quite anxious. When can I tell them you'll be down to talk to them?"

He'd become familiar with the various family members during discussions leading up to Larry's enrollment in the radiation trial. He didn't want to deal with Larry's antagonistic sister right now.

"I'll call down and talk to them. I don't want to go face-to-face with his sister until I have a better idea how soon it'll be before Larry wakes up."

She seemed to accept this but wasn't happy with his plan.

Tyler glanced at the anesthesiologist. "Hey, Shellie, you interested in grabbing a bite before the cafeteria closes?"

The anesthesiologist checked her Swiss Army watch. "Sure. I have enough time. There's a potential C-section cooking upstairs, but if we go now . . ." She slipped off the stool.

An idea hit. "Hold on a sec. Want to check something first." He took the stool Michelle just vacated and logged onto the medical record system. He called up Larry Childs's chart and moused the radiation therapy tab. A smaller window opened. Tyler blinked, moved in for a closer look. He realized a patina of sweat now coated his body in spite of the chill. An urge to vomit battled his self-control.

"Holy shit, Mathews, you okay?" Michelle reached out, grabbed his shoulder to steady him.

A tingling floated over his skin, his equilibrium faltered. He inhaled deeply and planted both palms squarely on the stainless-steel counter for support.

He found his mouth too dry to speak so he cleared his throat and swallowed. "Ah, can you tell me what the screen says?"

"Which one? The dialog box?"

He nodded, the dizziness starting to clear enough to release one hand from the counter.

A second later Michelle gave a slow whistle. "Oh, dear . . . Two hundred. That's—"

Tyler grabbed her arm, whispered, "Hold it 'til we get downstairs." With a shaking hand he withdrew a pocket computer from his coat, then fumbled with pulling the stylus free. Slowly, deliberately, he worked through the screen to where he kept notes on research patients. He scrolled through the record to the entry he'd made when Nick Barber determined Larry Childs's radiation dose. The number jumped out at him: 10 Gr.

He handed it to Michelle. "Check it out."

She accepted the computer but kept staring at him. "Hey, you want to lay down or something?"

"Look at it, damnit."

Michelle handed it back with a nod, her face drained of color. "You're right. Let's discuss this downstairs. You up to walking now?"

"If that isn't radiation necrosis then what the hell could it possibly be?" Michelle dragged the end of a French fry through red ketchup mounded at the end of the oval plate. Her short precisely manicured fingernails were coated with clear lacquer.

Michelle waved the fry. "What I'm saying, I don't buy this business about herpes or a wildly malignant glioblastoma. Holy shit, the brain's necrotic and he apparently received enough radiation to melt an aircraft carrier. What more is there to say?"

Tyler had also chosen the fish and chips. He took a bite of cod. It tasted like cardboard. He pushed his plate away and forced a swallow. "I know. It's logical, isn't it. Just hard to accept."

"Okay then. The kid's got a case of radiation necrosis. That's the easy part. The next question is how the hell could that kind of overdose happen? Way you describe the protocol, it's impossible. Besides, you showed me your Palm computer. I'm no radiation therapist, but that dose is more like what I'd expect."

The chill in Tyler's gut intensified. "It has to be radiation necrosis. Can't be anything else." He looked at her. "Jesus, I couldn't have made a mistake like that and typed it in wrong."

She frowned at him. "For Pete's sake, stop this mea culpa routine. You don't make those kinds of errors. We both know how tight-assed compulsive you are about things like this. I don't for one minute believe you allowed that crazy a dose to blow right past you. No way, no how. Besides, the computer would've caught it and asked you to verify."

"Then what else could've caused it?"

DEADLY ERRORS ⬛ 57

"What about dear old U Pitt? Don't tell me they don't have a license to screw up once in a while just like the rest of us mortals." She popped another fry into her mouth.

"Sure, but the dosage value is double-checked by the radiation therapists before being sent. *And,*" he remembered at the last minute, "the value has to be within safe-range parameters or the U Pitt computer chokes and won't allow the data transfer. And, like you just said, it's the same with our computer. If it isn't a reasonable value, we won't accept it. It's a one-shot deal, you know, the zap. And believe me, *that* protocol's bulletproof too. Had to be for NIH and the local IRB"—referring to the institutional review board that oversees human experimentation—"to sign off on it. No"—he shook his head thinking about it—"there's no way in hell that kind of dosage mistake could've happened."

Michelle coated another fry. "Get real, Dr. Pollyanna. I've seen the bumper sticker . . . Shinola happens. It's Murphy's basic rule, the one all the other Murphy's rules derive from: if something can go wrong, it will."

He mentally ran the protocol again, searching for a way to go wrong. "But the way this is set up, something *can't* go wrong."

The anesthesiologist sat back with a smirk. "And how, dear boy, can that be? Something can *always* go wrong. Believe me, I know."

Intuitively, he knew Michelle was probably right. He just couldn't see how. "Okay, let's walk through this again. The patient's MRI is sent to the Principal Investigator at the University of Pittsburgh with the targeted area overlaid on the images. The PI's radiation boys determine the dosage, it's double-checked, then sent back here electronically where it goes into the patient's chart automatically. It's only after I double-check the dose that Larry's given treatment. It's all done by computer. No chance for human error."

"Right. No chance of *human* error. But what about computer error?"

He considered this suggestion a moment. "I dunno . . . the protocol is supposed to be infallible."

Michelle threw up both hands. "Okay, okay, you made your point. The *protocol* is inviolate. But what about someone else? Couldn't someone else change it?"

"Impossible. Only the treating physician can do that. That's me. And I can guarantee you I didn't."

"I realize that. What I'm suggesting is a hacker."

Tyler thought about this a moment. "Jesus, Med-InDx's made a point of absolute security that that possibility didn't even cross my mind. Huh!" Made sense.

Michelle smirked again. "Absolute security? Just like Microsoft?"

"Good point."

"So what are you going to do about it?"

The question triggered a cascade of thoughts. "Shit, Shellie, I just realized . . . this would classify as a sentinel event. Which means whatever the cause of Larry's problem, I need to report it to NIH and our administration. First thing in the morning too."

"Oh, dear, that probably means JCAHO too." JCAHO—the body charged with accrediting hospitals.

Wrong treatment dosage, Tyler mused. Exactly the types of mistakes electronic medical records are supposed to eliminate. But how could this one happen?

"Holy shit!"

Tyler snapped back out of thought. "What?"

"I just thought of something. Did you ever know Robin Beck? The ED physician?"

"No. Why?"

"Now that I think about it, she had something similar to this happen. Hold on, let me see if I can get my facts straight." Michelle pressed her fingertips against both temples and closed both eyes. A moment later her eyes popped open. "Okay, I think I got it straight." She sat back in the booth, hands folded on the table. "She injected a patient with a whopping dose of insulin. The only problem was, the patient wasn't diabetic. She swears the chart unmistakably showed the patient on a combo of regular and long-lasting insulin."

"Jesus. What happened?"

"Patient died."

A finger of nausea stabbed Tyler's gut. He thought of Larry.

"Now that I think of it, there was another one too . . ." Michelle snapped her fingers. "Okay, yeah, yeah . . . a nurse—what was her name?—gave a GI bleeder a couple units of mismatched blood. Patient ended up having a mondo transfusion reaction and boxed."

Tyler smoothed out a napkin, removed a garish purple and blue drug company ballpoint pen from his white coat. "You remember the nurse's name now?"

Michelle paused to think a moment. "Gail Walker? Yeah, Gail Walker."

Tyler wrote that down. "And the other doctor's name is Beck? Robin Beck?"

"Right."

"How'd you know about this? You know them personally?"

"No. Just heard about them."

"Where?"

Michelle shrugged. "Doctors lounge I guess."

Typical, he thought. With no office to tend to or patients to see, when not sleeping a case, most gas passers hang around the lounge drinking coffee and taking the pulse of the medical center. They become the staff's CNN. Want to know which hospital administrator is having an affair? Ask your favorite anesthesiologist. Want to know what line items are being cut from the budget next year, ditto.

"How long ago did these complications happen?"

"Oh, man, you would have to ask that, wouldn't you. Let's see." Michelle's brow furrowed, accenting penciled eyebrows. "You know what, I can't honestly remember. Last fall, I think. It's been a while. I know that much."

"Both of those sound exactly like the kind of screwups EMRs are supposed to prevent."

"My point exactly. Which makes a pretty good argument for a hacker diddling the system, doesn't it?"

Tyler groaned. The thought of Larry's brain being irreparably damaged by some pimple-faced techno-geek made him almost vomit. "What happened? I mean, those cases must've been investigated, right?"

Michelle looked up surprised, as if not having considered this angle before. "You know, I don't really know. I do know that Beck was slapped with a huge malpractice suit. Ten million's the word on the street. Other than that . . ." She shrugged.

Tyler glanced at his watch. "I'm going to call the Med-InDx tech."

Just then Tyler's beeper began chirping. It displayed the recovery-room number followed by 911—meaning an emergency. "Jesus, here we go . . . the ICU."

Michelle waved him away. "Go ahead. Answer it. I'll call the technician for you. You want to meet tonight, right?"

Tyler nodded and pushed out of one side of the booth as Michelle did the same.

When he answered the page a moment later the nurse told him, "Dr. Mathews, you better come quickly. Your patient just blew both pupils and stopped breathing. He's getting Ambued now."

Tyler made it from the basement cafeteria to the second-floor recovery room in record time. Gasping for air, he pulled up alongside a respiratory tech squeezing the black Ambu bag connected to the tube into Larry's lungs. Larry's eyelids were wide open, both pupils so large and black only a thin rim of green iris showed.

"Shit," he murmured. Then, to one of the nurses hovering, "Call CT, tell 'em I want a STAT scan." *He bled into that resection,* was his first thought.

The nurse glanced up from the computer keyboard. "Figured that's what you'd ask for. Already called. A transporter's on the way."

Tyler grabbed the head of the bed, started pushing. "Don't have time for that. I'll take him myself."

CHAPTER 5

One by one Tyler watched black and white images fill the oversized GE monitor as he scrolled the CT series once again. Through the lead-impregnated glass window his peripheral vision caught the recovery-room nurse, the CT tech, and the respiratory tech transferring Larry's supine body from the scanner to the recovery-room bed. *Larry's body,* he mused, already preparing his emotions for the eventuality he saw in the scan.

"Where do you want him to go?"

Tyler glanced up at another recovery-room nurse who had entered the room undetected. He knew the guy, an ex-corpsman, if memory served correctly. "Take him up to ICU." It would be better to have the family see him there than in the recovery room. Besides, the recovery-room nurses had finished their shift by now and were closing down the unit until tomorrow morning's cases started rolling in. "But before you do, I want another look at his pupils. I'll be out in a minute."

"Thanks." The ex-corpsman moved off to help the others.

Tyler returned his gaze to the huge blood clot filling most of the area where Larry's brain should be. *Return to surgery and evacuate the clot?* Why? Larry was, by now, brain dead. Besides, getting in and out of Larry's head a second time without the clot reaccumulating was about as likely as winning the Lotto. No, he had nothing left to offer the poor kid.

Tyler wondered what sort of hopeful dreams the prospect of a life without seizures had spawned in Larry Childs's imagination.

Probably included a raft of trivial daily activities most of us take for granted, he supposed. Conveniences and privileges that allow independence. A driver's license. Employment. Being able to sit in a theater without fear of soiling himself or having moviegoers goggle in horrified interest at a convulsion. Gone now, all of them.

Suddenly Tyler's shoulders seemed twenty pounds heavier as the fatigue from operating and the depression of seeing his effort fail seeped through his bones. He thought of the family downstairs—waiting, unaware of this terrible complication, still holding out hope for Larry's survival.

His beeper started chirping. He called the unfamiliar number.

"Tyler, Michelle. Got hold of that technician for you. I told him what we're thinking—the hacker and all? He doesn't believe it. Thinks we're full of shit. Much as said I'm crazy. Claimed it's impossible for anyone to penetrate their security. Bottom line is there's no way he's coming back tonight to even discuss it. Said he'd meet me tomorrow at the latte stand."

"Which one?"

"The one in the cafeteria."

"Thanks." He almost hung up before realizing he needed more information. "Oh, what time?"

"Seven."

"You going to be there?"

"Probably not. Depends on whether I'm finishing up a case or not."

"Got it. What's his name?"

"Jim Day."

Wearily Tyler rolled back and pushed out of the task chair. For a moment he stood, hand on the chair back, and sucked in a deep breath before palm-wiping his face. He stepped into the scanner room and over to Larry. For a moment he studied his half-opened eyes. Believing only in the reality his own senses provided, Tyler had no idea what clerics conceptualized when speaking of a person's soul. He doubted it was some sort of metaphysical energy packet that, at the moment of death, levitated from the lifeless body into heaven or dropped into the abyss of hell. What he knew for certain was there came a time in the dying process when an immeasurable sign of life vanished from a person's pupils. He'd witnessed it too many times to not believe in it. He had never known a patient to survive once that light disappeared. It had vanished from Larry's eyes sometime within the past few hours.

He told the nurses, "You can take him up now. I'll go talk with the family."

Tyler found Larry's family occupying a waiting-room corner where the three of them had set up a small camp. A rumpled thermal blanket piled on one end of the couch, newspaper sections stacked on the other. Latte cups strewn over a commandeered coffee table, two club chairs liberated from nearby. A priest with basset-hound eyes stood silently to Mrs. Childs's left. Tyler assumed he was from their parish. This time of evening the large surgery waiting area was deserted except for a middle-aged couple across the room in adjoining chairs, apparently watching CNN Headline News. Tyler suspected they would eavesdrop on this interchange in hopes that any forthcoming bad news might lessen their odds of the same.

A second after eye contact, Leslie Childs, Larry's older sister and self-appointed family spokesperson and legal counsel, jumped up from the couch but stayed put. The parents' heads snapped toward him but they remained seated. All three pairs of eyes zeroed in on him. Tyler dropped down on the couch next to Leslie so as to speak directly to her parents, even though he expected her to dominate the conversation.

Knowing no other effective way to broach the subject Tyler began with, "I'm afraid it's not good news." He paused for the full impact to register. "Larry's not waking up. In fact, his condition is worse. He bled into the area I removed."

Mrs. Childs sobbed, burying her face in both hands. Her husband reached an arm around her shoulders while his other index finger pushed up his bifocals to pinch the bridge of his nose, his head bowed.

"It's that damned radiation, isn't it!" Leslie Childs stood pillar straight, fists planted solidly against her narrow hips, flared elbows forming an imaginary barrier beyond which no family member dared to cross. Larry's parents huddled behind this five-foot seven-inch alpha primate in worried silence.

Her outburst came as no surprise. Fully expecting her opening salvo he'd rehearsed a firm, but not too defensive reply. Meeting her eye to eye, he said, "Ms. Childs, I appreciate your concern for your brother, but we'd all be better served if we carry on this discussion on a less antagonistic basis."

The mother looked up at her daughter. "He's right, dear."

With acetylene-torch eyes on Tyler, she forced a smile and dropped into a club chair next to her mother. Mrs. Childs reached over and grasped her hand. The priest began fingering rosary beads.

Round two coming up, my friend, get ready, bell's about to clang.

"Here's what's happened," Tyler began. For the father's benefit he rehashed the CT findings and the explanation given to Mrs. Childs earlier. Then, to all three family members he explained the findings at surgery, how biopsies were submitted to the pathologist, the time needed for a pathologist to make any sense of the tissue, Larry's failure to awaken long after the anesthesia should have worn off, and, finally, the terminal hemorrhage.

When he finished Leslie asked, "All you've given us so far is a string of medical mumbo jumbo. What exactly does it mean?"

Fair enough question, Tyler told himself. It was her sanctimonious tone and attitude that grated. Then again, her brother lay dying in the ICU. He took a moment to mentally rephrase his explanation before attempting another pass at it. "I'm afraid your brother's brain is dead."

"He's dead?" Leslie asked without her prior defiance.

"Yes."

Larry Childs Sr. hugged his wife more closely but she seemed to accept Tyler's words as a grim anticlimax.

"But his heart is still beating, isn't it?" Leslie asked.

Tyler slipped into words explained many times before. "True." He paused. "But the heart isn't the essence of human life. The brain is. The heart is a symbol of love perhaps, but life can go on if it's replaced. You can't say the same for the brain. Once your brain stops working, your spiritual and personal essence stops too, leaving behind only a physical body carrying on a series of metabolic functions." He braced for a theological rebuttal from the priest but none came.

Leslie nodded, accepting this explanation.

"I have to ask something," Tyler continued, "that I know will be very difficult for any of you to answer, so if you wish, no answer will be sufficient for me to proceed."

Leslie offered, "You want to turn off the respirator."

Again, Leslie's cooperative tone surprised him. "Yes."

She thought about this a moment. Then, without conferring with her parents, "That's what Larry would've wanted."

"There is one more unpleasant issue I need to bring up." Another pause. "I would think you'd want to know for certain that it was the radiation that caused his problems. I want you to allow me to order an autopsy."

"He's the priest who baptized and confirmed Larry," Mrs. Childs whispered to Tyler as she walked into Larry's ICU room. "I think it's only right that he gives my son last rites." Mr. Childs, Leslie, and the priest followed.

Tyler pulled the sliding-glass door closed but didn't approach the bedside so as to not intrude on the family's private grief. For a long moment he heard only the heart monitor, the respirator, and sniffling. At the head of the bed, the three family members to either side, the priest pulled a long, embroidered sash from around his neck, kissed it, and began uttering words Tyler recognized as Latin.

Silence again encased the room. Tyler softly cleared his throat, softly said, "I'll show you where the waiting room is."

A few minutes later when he returned to Larry a nurse was already turning down the IV drip. She glanced at him. "Time?"

Tyler nodded, wrapped his fingers around the corrugated plastic hose from the respirator, his other hand gripping the endotracheal tube. He paused to reflect once again on what he was about to do. Once disconnected, air could no longer be pumped into Larry's lungs, causing his heart to stumble and die. *Is there a God? Is He watching? What would He do in my position?*

He pulled apart the tubes and thumbed off the respirator power switch. Over the past hour he'd allowed Larry's CO_2 blood level to rise to a normal value, just on the off chance some brain stem functions were still there and he'd been wrong and Larry would resume breathing.

For three minutes Larry made no attempt to breathe. Shortly after that Larry's heartbeat began to slow until it finally stuttered, fought for a minute, then became silent.

– – – – – – – – – – –

The man picked up the telephone on the third ring. "What!" His voice carried an alcohol slur and a hint of irritation that said he didn't appreciate being disturbed at night.

The caller said, "We may have a problem."

"At nine o'clock at night we may have a problem? Can't it wait until morning? I'm busy."

The caller wanted to tell the pompous egotistical sonofabitch to shut the fuck up and listen for once. "There's been a complication. A patient received a radiation overdose."

"So? That's life, shit happens."

"For christsake, listen up a second. This is different. We got us a doctor running around claiming hackers cracked our system."

"Well, in that case, there's no problem. No way no how can we have a security breach. You should know that."

The caller's irritation rose. For a smart sonofabitch, the man wasn't very smart. "That's not the point. She's got a wild hair up her ass about it, to the point she wants us to start an investigation. She says she'll have to report this to JCAHO."

He heard no flip reply this time, just a pause. Finally, "Who's the doctor? We know anything about him?"

"It's a her. I looked her up. She's an anesthesiologist by the name of Michelle Lawrence."

"Well? So what's the problem? Just have to make sure nothing comes of it."

– – – – – – – – – – –

Tyler fluffed his pillow and settled back onto his left side, the cool cotton pillowcase refreshing against his facial stubble. He listened to rhythmic rap music thumps crescendo and then fade as an unseen car passed four stories below. Even with his apartment windows closed, the vibrations easily reached his ears. Amazing. He wondered what those thundering decibels of sound energy must be doing to the delicate nerve endings in the driver's cochlea. *Nothing good,* he decided, and imagined an entire generation of prematurely deaf—but hip—citizens. Any hearing aide stocks to invest in long-term? Assuming, of course, he ever got out of debt from the student loans his tough-love, pull-yourself-up-by-your-bootstraps father forced him to accumulate. Which wasn't completely fair, he admitted. Alimony from divorcing his first, alcoholic wife had been a killer on his financial resources.

He sucked in a deep breath and tried to weigh what to do in the morning about Larry Childs's death. Certainly report it to Risk Management and the clinical trial principal investigator, Nick Barber. But JCAHO was a different matter. Having once been burned,

he couldn't afford to get involved in something having any potential for severe blowback on his job. What if the root cause
analysis pointed a finger at him? Would he be fired? His stomach
turned sour. It reminded him of what happened in California. *Jesus, look how that turned out.*

What would Dad do in this situation? More to the point, what
was the right thing to do?

Another peek at the clock radio: 1:37 A.M. The alarm was set for
5:45. Four hours. Enough time to chew an Ambien into a bitter
paste and rub over his gums with the tip of his tongue to speed
up absorption to a couple minutes rather than the twenty or so
it'd take if swallowed.

No! He had to stop relying on sleepers. For all sorts of reasons,
all of which he could recite as easily as the twelve cranial nerves.
But the most important reason was the possibility of starting over
with Nancy. For a Ph.D. molecular biologist, she had a peculiarly
strong prejudice against taking medication she didn't believe was
absolutely critical and lifesaving. She'd rather suffer through a
cold than pop an antihistamine. On the other hand, she'd readily
ingest any number of unscientifically proven herbs prescribed by a
traditional Chinese naturopath. Got an ache? Chew a weed, but
don't take Ibuprofen. A heritage that obviously migrated from
Hong Kong to UCLA with her. In San Francisco she occasionally
visited Chinese fortune-tellers, although claiming to not take their
forecasts seriously. Tyler didn't believe it for a second, suspecting
she'd rescheduled her entire thesis defense because of one such
prediction. Quirky, yes, but one of the little things he loved about
her. Almost as much as he appreciated how she cheerfully set aside
her studies when his unpredictable schedule allowed for a few unexpected hours together—only to get up an hour or so earlier than
usual to make up the time.

Besides, her caution for Western medicine provided a healthy
contrast to his willingness to pop medication at the first sign of a
cold or an athletic-induced pain, which, now that he thought

about it, had probably contributed to his present reliance on sleepers.

But he needed sleep. Besides, he could break the pill in half. That way . . .

Tyler focused on the clock radio again: 1:39 A.M.

Don't do it.

But I need the sleep.

Sure you do, pal, but when will it stop? You know it has to stop. Especially now. You can't let Nancy know you've developed this little problem.

It isn't a problem.

No?

Tomorrow night. I'll stop tomorrow night. I just need some sleep.

Tyler swung his legs out of bed and headed for the bathroom and the amber bottle of white Ambien tablets in the drawer just to the left of the sink.

CHAPTER 6

Tyler hurried into the crowded cafeteria and checked his watch for the fifth time in two minutes. Four minutes late. Not like him. He beelined for the latte stand, eyes searching for a likely Jim Day, saw a man the color of bittersweet chocolate and about his age and perhaps two inches shorter standing, latte in hand, with an expression of anticipation. Tyler approached and asked, "You Jim Day?"

The man turned and studied Tyler a moment. "Dr. Lawrence?"

Tyler extended his hand. "No. Actually, Dr. Lawrence called you last night for me. I was busy in the ICU." He paused, looking for a place to carry on a conversation. "Sorry I'm late. Got delayed on rounds. How about that booth over there?"

Day gave a sarcastic grunt. "No way we're broaching that subject out here where someone might hear. My office." He started toward the exit.

Tyler waited until they were seated in the small cramped office before broaching the subject. He got straight to the point by explaining the discrepancy between Larry Childs's treatment dosage recorded in his PDA and the one in the EMR. Next, he explained the consequences—a lethal case of radiation necrosis. Not that he had pathological confirmation yet, but there could be no other reasonable explanation.

Day said, "I believe you about your patient . . . that he has a se-rious problem and all. That much is obvious. I just can't believe someone outside the system could change the data field once it had been populated. The only way that field could've been changed is someone holding EMR privileges changed it. Even then, they'd have to have superior privileges and that could only be a doctor with direct responsibility for the patient. Even then it's hard to do, what with all the cross-checks and all. And if they did, there'd be a record of it."

"I can't imagine a doctor changing that dose. It just doesn't make sense. I mean, for what possible reason?" Especially consid-ering Larry Childs was such a low-profile person. "You can check that, can't you?"

"Sure."

"When?"

Day shrugged. "Later today, I guess . . . possibly tomorrow." He studied Tyler a second before asking, "Why"—his eyebrows furrowed—"you want me to check it out this minute?"

"Hell, yes. My patient died this morning. Don't you think that makes it a priority?"

Day shrugged. "Fine. I'll check it." He turned to the computer and started typing.

"Let me ask you something. Instead of a physician, doesn't it seem more likely it'd be someone else fooling around in the sys-tem? Maybe someone who didn't realize how serious a seemingly simple change might become?"

Day hit a key hard, then looked up. "Your hacker theory?"

"Why not?"

Day's look hardened. "Because, my man, that system is one im-penetrable sonofabitch. It's that simple."

The answer surprised Tyler. No computer system connected to the outside world was impenetrable. "You honestly believe that? I sure as hell don't."

Day sighed, gave a resigned let-me-explain-it-to-you look. "Doc, listen up. I know what you're driving at—that old theory that no network's secure? Maybe true for just about everything outside the NSA, 'cept this one? This one insecure? Uh uh, nooooo. I've never seen security like this one. That, my man, is the absolute strong point of the Med-InDx system. That and its database engine."

"Sure, easy for you to say. The company signs your paycheck every two weeks. Your 401K's probably overflowing with stock options."

"Hey, man, lighten up." Frowning, Day held up his hand, his expression one of genuine hurt. "I'm telling you straight up, breaking that system's security is harder than knocking off a Federal Reserve Bank."

"So you say. But I have a patient whose brain rotted out from a radiation overdose and the dosage field says he got two hundred gray. So are you going to check it out or what?"

"Sure, I'm checking it out as we speak. You got me interested now." He held up a wait-a-minute finger and returned to his computer. A moment later, "Nope. No evidence that field was altered."

Tyler thought about that a moment. "Bear with me a moment on this. If a hacker had enough access to change the data field, couldn't he also have enough access to cover his tracks?"

Day's eyes widened. "You mean, like, alter the validation fields? You out of your fucking mind, man? No way."

"I want you to check it out."

Day studied him a moment. "You're serious, aren't you."

"My patient just died. Of course I'm serious."

"I don't know if it's possible to really check that out, but to do it right I'll have to go back over a few of the oldest backup tapes. They're stored off site. A place outside Salt Lake City. I'll have to request they upload them for me to take a look at. That'll take a few hours at best. At best," he emphasized. "Assuming, of course, I can whip up some enthusiasm from the unlucky bastard who gets my request." He slid out of the chair, an obvious sign the meeting was over. "You can wait a day or so, can't you? No way I'm going to get that answer for you sooner."

Tyler stood up also. "Hell no, I can't wait a day or two." He flashed on a potential hot button that might get Day's attention. "Besides, this has to be reported as a sentinel event. Which means a root cause analysis with—at this very moment—you in the spotlight. That means getting JCAHO involved. Understand?" Anger flickered across Day's eyes. Good. Maybe that would get some action out of him. "If I don't have word back from you by tomorrow, I'll report it as a suspected hacker intrusion. Then it's your problem to prove otherwise."

Day's expression grew even harder. "I wouldn't advise that."

"Then get me the information so I can file the report accurately." Tyler turned and stormed out of Day's office.

9:45 A.M., MMC BOARDROOM

"Can you be a little more specific about the exact reasons you and several of your committee members are in Seattle at this particular time, Dr. Vericelli?" The reporter glanced down at the glowing little red RECORD light on her portable Sony cassette recorder.

Sergio Vericelli straightened his posture and elevated his goateed chin an inch—a posture he felt befitting his stature as committee head. He cleared his throat while reaching for the nearby glass of water. Both well-rehearsed ploys to kill extra seconds while mentally reviewing his answer for potential chuckholes. As a full-time employed physician for the Joint Commission on Accreditation of Health-care Organizations—otherwise known as "Jay-Ko" by health professionals in the trenches—he was a press conference combat veteran. However, he knew full well this was not just your usual lightweight collection of hacks from the local rag and television station of some Podunk Hollow community whose one-hundred-bed hospital just passed accreditation. No indeed. This was The Big Time. He recognized the stringer for *The*

Wall Street Journal, the *Forbes* writer, the cute CNBC reporter in a miniskirt with her video cameraman joined to her shoulder, to name just a few of the industrial-strength media at the other end of the highly polished boardroom table.

Sergio flashed his newly whitened teeth in a benign smile. "Maria"—he loved calling her by her first name—"that's a fairly open-ended question. Could you be a bit more specific?" He knew exactly the point the question was intended to ferret out, but wanted to toy with her a moment, see if she was really as bright on her feet as rumors indicated.

"Fair enough. We all know your committee is charged with making a decision about the new JCAHO EMR, eh, electronic medical record system, requirements within the next thirty days. And it's no mystery your committee's been looking very seriously at the Med-InDx solution. Is there any reason to believe this trip signifies any problems for the Med-InDx product?"

Sergio's smile widened. Perfect. "No, Maria. In fact, quite the contrary. To answer your question, we are here to review the last four months of data from Maynard Medical Center. I must admit, *those* data continue to demonstrate an outstanding consolidating decline in medical errors." He loved to emphasize the correct grammatical plural of datum since so many illiterates missed this particular fine point. "In particular, it demonstrates the remarkably low level of common medication errors that can be achieved with a high-quality, comprehensive EMR."

He cleared his throat again and readied himself to launch into his dog-eared speech. "By EMR I am referring to an Electronic Medical Record—not a complete clinical information system such as offered by the Med-InDx company. JCAHO's emphasis on the switch to computerized charts represented a drastic change from the time-honored clinical chart so characteristic of medical-record keeping for the past one hundred years. As I'm sure you are all aware, in November 1999, the Institute of Medicine concluded a study entitled *To Err Is Human: Building a Safer Health*

System. It focused attention on the issue of medical errors and patient safety. The report indicated that as many as forty-four to ninety-eight thousand people die in hospitals each year as the result of preventable medical errors. But the point is, very little progress has been made to correct this problem. Think about it. If the airlines had the same record of crashes, who would fly?" He glanced around the room knowingly and smiled as this thought sunk in.

"Look what happened to American auto manufacturing when they got sloppy. Several automakers went bankrupt. The big three lost a huge market share to the foreign automakers. Well, it's time to reform the error rate in hospitals.

"The Institute's report estimated that medical errors cost the nation approximately $37.6 billion each year; about $17 billion of those costs are associated with preventable errors. About half of the expenditures for preventable medical errors are for direct health-care costs. These preventable errors are exactly what electronic medical records are intended to reduce."

The *Wall Street Journal* stringer piped in: "Hold on a moment, Dr. Vericelli, you're straying from the point of the last question. Some of us would like to drill down on this. Would you share the exact figures with the group?"

He raised his eyebrows in mock surprise. "Figures?"

"Yes. What are the error figures for the Med-InDx system?"

Sergio shook his head with a good-natured grin. "You know I'm not at liberty to disclose data of that nature at this time. Once the committee has reached their final decision and made their finding public, those data will be released as a matter of public record. But until then, the committee cannot disclose proprietary information, especially in a case such as this where the company's public offering is slated only days after the committee's ruling."

Frowning, the journalist shook his head. "That's ridiculous, Doctor. With the timing of Med-InDx public offering so close to the committee decision, it is unreasonable for you to withhold this information. One has to wonder if there's more than mere co-incidence here."

Other reporters murmured agreement.

Sergio hesitated, unsure of the reporter's intent. "I understand your eagerness for some preliminary indication of the committee's findings, but even I, as committee chairman, have no knowledge of what that decision will be since there has yet to be a vote." *There, that should answer the bastard.*

"But," the reporter interrupted, "surely you're aware of the committee's sentiments. If the Med-InDx product truly is as superior as rumors have it, then the decision is all but made."

Too smart to get suckered into that game, Sergio shook his head—"Sorry"—and nodded at the next reporter. "Next."

"Any truth to the rumor that so far results clearly favor the Med-InDx product? That Prophesy's solution isn't even considered in the running anymore?"

"I thought I just answered that question, however differently you might have phrased it." Sergio wagged an admonishing finger before turning to Bernie Levy. The Med-InDx CEO sat staring out at the reporters with vacant Bill Gates eyes and a Bill Gates haircut. "I'm sure Mr. Levy would like that to be the case, but so far all I can tell you is the committee believes both products are excellent. This also means there is no clear leader as far as the committee has determined."

Another reporter asked, "If you can't give us the figures, perhaps you can let us know any areas in which Med-InDx shows particular strengths?"

Sergio's face grew serious. He stroked his salt-and-pepper goatee in a manner he believed demonstrated thoughtful consideration. Which was far from the case. He knew the figures cold, but intended on leaving a very different impression. After an appropriate pause, he said, "Their product shows solid strength across the board in all areas in which a complete EMR might be anticipated to compete. Using their solution"—tossing in a little Silicon Valley buzzword—"we have seen a dramatic lowering in patient ID confusion, particularly for those patients with the same last name. The committee has seen a significant decrease in miscommunication among caregivers and an absolute zeroing of wrong-site surgery in the past twelve months. There are other areas of improved performance too, such as medication delivery, especially with infusion pumps. But most dramatically, the Maynard Medical Center trial has demonstrated a remarkable and statistically significant drop in medication and blood product mix-ups when compared to the same period of time preceding the implementation period."

Pausing with a dramatic flourish, Vericelli turned to his right side where Arthur Benson, Maynard Medical Center CEO, sat at military attention. "And this brings me to my next point. I thank Mr. Benson for allowing his medical center to be used as the clinical trial site for the Med-InDx product evaluation. Most of you have no idea of the cost in time and personnel a study of this magnitude and nature requires. Although in the final analysis the Maynard Medical Center will reap the benefit of acquiring a world-class Clinical Information System, the medical center has spent millions of dollars over the past three years phasing in this entire complex system." He paused, nodding his head slightly. "Yes, millions. Think about the increased IT staff required to install and convert the software to the present computer networks and then to train every one of the three thousand employees—the doctors, nurses, admitting clerks, pharmacists, just to name a few—who use the various components of the CIS in their day-to-day activities."

He sipped water from the glass next to the podium while deciding the appropriate words to best conclude the press conference. Slowly he set down the glass and raised his head for proper emphasis and raised his voice like a Baptist preacher reaching the climax of his Sunday sermon. "The groundbreaking report from the Institute of Medicine opened our eyes to the risks every man, woman, and child takes when being cared for in hospitals, doctors' offices, or emergency care facilities. The know-how to prevent these errors exists in the form of electronic medical record systems. We now need to focus on making sure that health care organizations are actually taking these preventive steps."

He turned first to Bernie Levy, shook his hand, then did the same with Arthur Benson before strutting from the boardroom.

– – – – – – – – – – –

Tyler's beeper started chirping. He didn't recognize the number but the exchange indicated the callback number was within the medical center. Tyler reached for his cell phone.

"Dr. Mathews, Joe Delaney. I'm reading histology of one of yours marked urgent. From last night? A patient by the name of Childs?"

Tyler wasn't sure if he wanted to hear the answer now that Larry was dead, but he had to sooner or later. He sucked in a deep breath. "Let's hear it." His chest tightened.

"Don't have much of anything definitive to tell you since most of the specimen shows nothing more than some nonspecific necrosis, but there are a few sections with blood vessels showing changes consistent with radiation necrosis. As I understand it, the differential diagnosis includes tumor, a viral infection, and radiation necrosis. That correct?"

Not wanting to bias the pathologist's opinion, he gave a noncommittal, "Yes."

"Well then, I'd have to say there's nothing to suggest either tumor or a viral infection. The latter, as you know, can't be totally excluded until the EM studies"—electron microscope—"are completed, but . . . well . . . I'll let the entire pile of chips ride on radiation necrosis."

Tyler's gut tightened as he thought again about the apparent radiation dose mix-up. Jim Day hadn't called back yet. How many hours had it been?

The pathologist asked, "Anything else I can help you with long as you got me on the line?"

Tyler's mind refocused. "No, nothing more. Thanks for getting back to me so soon. I appreciate it."

Tyler replaced the cell phone in his white coat and picked up his latte. Cold. He set it back down just as a premonition burst into his consciousness. At first it was nothing more than amorphous foreboding, a feeling that something awful, something he had no control over, would trample his new life—especially now that there was hope of getting back with Nancy. Then, he realized what the feeling was. *Because I've lived this before,* he thought. *Therefore it isn't really déjà vu, is it?*

He thought about calling Nancy and talking over the situation. But what was there to discuss? A simple case of paranoia? A residual feeling from California?

Tyler stopped rotating the latte cup on his desk. Regardless of who was responsible for the radiation overdose to Larry Childs's brain, the result was the same: a disastrous complication resulting in death. At the very least, he should file a report with the study Principal Investigator, Nick Barber, who in turn should notify the NIH bureaucrat with overall study responsibility. That person would file an immediate written report with the DMSB—the data monitoring and safety board—who would review the problem within twenty-four hours and quite possibly shut down the entire study.

Jesus, what have I done?

Tyler looked up a telephone number and dialed.

"Do me a favor and pull up the data sheet on study patient MMC-LC1."

Nick Barber said, "Hold on a sec."

Tyler heard the click of computer keys in the background.

"Okay, got it."

"What was the treatment dose?"

It took a few seconds before Nick answered, "Ten gray. Why?"

Tyler realized the skin on his arms and neck carried a patina of sweat in spite of the relatively chilly office.

"We have a real bitch of a problem, Nick." A drop of sweat rolled into the corner of his eye, stinging, triggering a series of blinks.

Tyler stared at his hand computer on the desk in front of him, the notes on Childs still visible on the screen.

Nick said nothing, leaving Tyler with the task of continuing. Tyler sucked in another deep breath.

"Our records show he was given two hundred gray."

Tyler heard Nick draw in a very deep breath. "Holy Mother of Christ."

He went on to describe in detail Larry Childs's clinical course.

"I have no idea how this happened," Tyler felt compelled to add. His heartbeats were clearly audible in each ear now as rhythmic swishes.

"Christ," Nick Barber muttered. "How could you have let this happen?"

"Let it happen?" The rototiller started in his gut. "I just found out about it."

"My point exactly." Another pause. "I need to report this to Margaret Heit."

Tyler recognized the name. The NIH section chief unfortunate enough to hold their grant in her portfolio.

"Nick?"

"Yes."

"I think a hacker may have been in our system."

Nick gave a sarcastic grunt. "A hacker? Yeah sure, Tyler. What-ever." He hung up.

— — — — — — — — — —

Dog-tired after a full night up doing cases, Michelle looked for-ward to a lingering soak in a hot Jacuzzi tub filled with bubble bath before taking a two-hour nap. She opened her condo front door with a sigh of relief, then locked it behind her. She dropped her purse on the granite kitchen countertop and headed straight for the bathroom, but stopped.

A man, a stranger, stood just inside the bedroom door.

CHAPTER 7

During his short tenure at Maynard Medical Center Tyler had never walked this hall of thick maroon carpet and surreal serenity. The ordered stillness proved a sharp contrast to the operating rooms or patient floors. No crash carts, stretchers, or half-folded wheelchairs littering the hall. No nurses in Brownian motion. The galvanized HVAC air held no trace of feces, tincture of benzoine, or dirty dressings. No cacophony of beepers cutting through dozens of simultaneous conversations. The wall on his left displayed precisely aligned parallel rows of eight-by-ten photographs of the Board of Directors, past and present, each tastefully framed in brushed silver.

Tyler found the correct office number. An engraved brass plaque to the right of the open door read Jill Richardson, Vice President of Risk Management. Inside, an anorexic-looking mid-thirties male with a moussed brown crew cut and goatee glanced up as Tyler entered. "May I help you?" A tasteful faux mahogany desk sign identified him as Tony Colello, secretary.

"Is Ms. Richardson in?"

The man frowned. "Do we have an appointment?"

"No."

The secretary smirked. "I'm so very sorry, Ms. Richardson's day is absolutely chock-a-block. You will just have to make an appointment."

"Look, this is extremely important. I need to report a patient death."

Jill Richardson glanced once again at the Movado Elliptica adorning her left wrist and hurried down the hall. The weekly Senior Steering Team meeting had exceeded the designated two hours by an additional fifteen minutes—which now limited her ability to sift through the ever-accumulating stack of pink While You Were Out notes, voice mails, and e-mails before her meeting in forty-five minutes with that bitch union representative from Local 188. Goddamned self-serving nurses were crying foul by claiming that staffing pattern changes—using skilled nursing assistants to do some of the menial tasks previously done by RNs—placed inpatients at increased risk. Bullshit of course, but bullshit that once stated had to be negotiated. With contract renewals only three months away, the butt-ugly bull-dyke union representative elected last year by the militant nurses was saber-rattling again. Loudly. The bitch.

Rounding the corner to her outer office, she would have run smack into a man coming from the opposite direction but he gently grasped her upper arms, said, "Whoa," and stopped her.

"Thank you," she muttered, adjusting the sleeves of her black Donna Karan suit. Once back together, she looked more closely at the white coat and scrub suit standing directly in front of her, recognized him without placing the name. A good five inches taller and sixty pounds heavier than her five-foot-six 115-pound frame, the thing that struck her was his eyes. Not their color, but a gentleness and intelligence deep beyond the hazel iris.

"Ms. Richardson, Tyler Mathews. I need to talk with you. It concerns a complication that may put us at risk." He reached out to shake hands.

She glanced again at her watch, judged the ever-accumulating mound of work on her desk and the meeting, and decided she just didn't have time right now. "Can it wait until this afternoon or tomorrow morning?"

"No. A patient died this morning. A totally preventable death that probably qualifies as a sentinel event."

The last two words blew away any time concerns. "Yes, of course, that is important. Please come in." She extended an arm toward her office door while ignoring Tony's admonishing frown.

She followed Mathews into her cramped office, "Have a seat," and noticed him glance at the massive L-shaped desk with matching credenza. Those and the floor-to-ceiling bookcases left little room for her task chair and two visitor chairs. "Atrocious, isn't it. An inheritance from my predecessor. Apparently a man with a sense of design but lacking any sense of proportion. It does allow a lot of surface area, however." She noticed him admiring her lesser glass pieces on small risers. "Original Dale Chihuli . . . during his time as Artist in Residence at Pilchuck." She believed these gave the room a personal feminine touch while leaving the sense of power the furniture created.

She dropped into her desk chair and leaned back against the black leather. "Tell me about this complication." What had she heard through the administration grapevine about Mathews? Something about his past. Drug abuse? A drug rehab program, maybe? Whatever, he didn't look like an impaired physician now. In fact, intense and dour were the words she'd pick to describe him.

Tyler Mathews explained Larry Childs's unfortunate death due to the radiation overdose, the NIH supported clinical trial, the report to the Principal Investigator, and finally, "I believe this qualifies as a sentinel event. What do you think?"

"Most assuredly."

He frowned. "What do I need to do next?"

"First, let me make sure I understand what's been done thus far. I believe you said you've already notified the study PI, who presumably will notify NIH. Correct?" She decided to wait until he left the room before considering the proactive legal damage control needing to be attended to. Which would be considerable in a case like this. Always best to launch an aggressive defense before the family contacted a lawyer, assuming, that is, they hadn't already.

Tyler nodded again. "Correct."

"Then that part is taken care of." Her thoughts returned to the primary and most important issue he'd raised. "As you said just a moment ago, we should probably consider this a sentinel event. As such, we are obliged to file a report with JCAHO. That is, of course, after we've performed a thorough root cause analysis. Have you started that process?"

A wave of relief washed over Tyler. By agreeing with him, Richardson had just removed the burden of decision from his shoulders, as well as assumed some of the responsibility. Who could blame him now for one hundred percent of any blowback?

"No, I haven't." Her questioning smile unnerved him. He found her attractive now that they were interacting one-on-one. The only other times he'd seen her was at the podium during quarterly Medical Staff meetings. Typically dressed in well-tailored business suits with an expensive-looking scarf around her long thin neck, his first impression had been the quintessential ice maiden. A persona mandated by the job, he decided.

"Why not?" This time her tone had an edge to it.

"Well, actually I *have* started one," he said defensively.

Her smile faded. She glanced at her watch. "Dr. Mathews, I'm already way behind schedule, so I'm in no mood to waste time here. Have you or have you not started a root cause analysis?"

He felt his face redden. "Yes I have. This morning I talked with one of the Med-InDx techs about the problem."

She made a note on a yellow legal pad. "I see. Who was that?"

"Jim Day."

"And can you speculate at this time about the cause of the overdose?"

"Only way I can explain what happened is a hacker cracked the system and changed the dosage."

Her head jerked up from the notes she was making. She frowned. "That's a most serious allegation, Dr. Mathews. Does Mr. Day agree with you?"

"No. But I have him checking to see if there's any hint of the chart being tampered with."

She seemed to consider this a moment. "Well, Dr. Mathews, it seems like you're off to the right start in this matter. But I think it only fair to advise you that because of the medical center's investment in the Med-InDx system—both in time and money—we should be extremely certain of any and all the facts before filing any type of report with the Joint Commission. Don't you agree?"

This hadn't really concerned him until she spelled it out just now. "No, I don't agree. A patient is dead, his brain zapped with an overdose of radiation. It's fully documented in the chart. Seems very clear to me it deserves to be reported to JCAHO." A warning bell rang in his mind—he was experiencing the same force of indignation that led him down the path to destruction in California. He amended his last statement. "That is, of course, after I get word back from Jim Day." He stood, prepared to leave.

She stood and smoothed the front of her skirt. "I want to be kept in the loop on any and all developments. Are you clear on this?"

He saw no problem with that. "Crystal."

She extended her hand. "Good. Call me as soon as you find out anything. If what you say is true, and I have no reason to doubt you, we definitely have a problem on our hands. If, however, this is just another example of human error, well then, it's nothing new. Agreed?"

"Agreed." He turned to leave, knowing it wasn't just a simple case of human error.

– – – – – – – – – – – –

Sylvia was both pissed and concerned. Forty-eight hours since hearing from Michelle. And that just wasn't like her. On the other hand, Sylvia was all too aware of Shellie's roving eye. Wouldn't be the first time she claimed to be on call only to be having a one-night stand with some bitch she'd picked up after downing a few Buds at the Wild Rose.

She sat in the front seat of her black Ford pickup tapping aqua-blue fingernails on the steering wheel. Fucking Shellie. Go up and confront her or let it pass and act like nothing was happening? Again she studied the condo building and Shellie's bedroom window. The shades were still drawn. For only one reason, she decided.

No, she couldn't allow this sort of thing to go unnoticed. If Shellie wanted a lasting relationship, then she'd have to respect some degree of propriety and not jump in the sack with every cunt that happened to smile at her.

Her anger grew, drying her throat, tightening the muscles fanning out across her temples.

This was too much.

Sylvia jumped down onto the concrete sidewalk and slammed the truck door, not even bothering to lock it. Now committed to a knock-down drag-out, she stormed toward the building, each clomp of her boots ratcheting up the tightness in her chest. She would almost welcome the release a good shouting match would bring. Maybe even get physical.

Hmmmmm . . .

The thought excited her, bringing fantasies of post-confrontational sex, making her nipples harden under the loose-fitting tank top. Yes, a fight, then some hard sex to make up . . . Shellie being submissive . . .

She used her key to open the front door of the building, now more excited about the possibilities than the actual anger.

Maybe the cunt would still be there . . . perhaps a three-way? They'd done that twice before, three ways. She'd introduced Shellie to the concept.

She reached Shellie's front door, mussed her spiked hair in one final primp, then keyed the lock and threw open the door.

"You fucking cunt!" She strutted into the living room.

Silence.

"Michelle?" Something didn't seem right. What?

A sudden icicle stabbed her gut.

"Michelle!" She ran to the closed bedroom door but stopped on the other side, afraid to see what was inside. "Honey, are you in there?"

With deep foreboding she slowly opened the door and gasped. "Oh, God, Shellie . . . what have you done?"

CHAPTER 8

Sergio asked, "What did she cost, if you don't mind me asking?"

"I believe you have not answered my question. Are you trying to dodge the issue?" Arthur Benson began merging into the right-hand lane. I-5 southbound was in the throes of congealing into the clot of vehicles typical for late afternoon. A graphic symptom of Seattle's traffic problems.

Was he serious? Sergio glanced at the man's face, but as always, his attention riveted on the shock of white hair in Benson's widow's peak. Solitary against the background of black, it served as an eye magnet. Benson briefly made eye contact before returning his attention to the task of defensive freeway driving, leaving Sergio without a clue what he thought, which disturbed him.

Sergio's index finger traced the inlaid burnished walnut dashboard. "How much? Eighty, ninety thousand? More?" *Probably more.* He made a mental note to stop by a Mercedes dealer and check it out.

"You still driving that rusted-out Toyota?"

"Hey, fuck you," Sergio snapped. "I had to pay my sons' college expenses." The bastard had done too good a job researching his background.

"Oh, really? Then what about their scholarships? Those didn't count?"

"There were other expenses too, I'll have you know. Besides, my boys won them on the basis of academics, not Neanderthal machinations on the playing field," he said with pride warming his chest. "They certainly did not inherit that brainpower from that stupid sow of a mother." Her image flashed across his memory. "Pig!"

"You still blame her for losing your practice? It had nothing to do with—"

"Of course," Sergio interrupted before the bastard could rip off the old scab like he'd done before. "I never would have started drinking as much if she had been more attentive to my needs."

Benson laughed sarcastically. "Sensitive issue? Fine, let's go back to my question. Are you going to answer it or not?"

Sergio sighed and forced his attention to the matter at hand. Too many hours of angst had already been wasted analyzing the what-ifs and the role of his wife in his fall from grace. "I'm fifty-four, it's time I planned for my future," he mumbled.

"I should think so, I should think you wouldn't want to spend too many more years choked by that insufferable job of yours."

"It pays the bills," Sergio said without enthusiasm. He knew where this was headed: another hot button.

"Ever wonder, Sergio, what do the doctors and nurses think of you as you step across into their world to pass judgment on their practices? They fear you and JCAHO, of course, but underneath that fear is a loathing. And you know it, don't you? Because you harbored it too when you were one of them."

"I do not see it that way. I am a better interviewer because of my background. I know exactly what it's like to be in the trenches. And they know that."

"You actually believe that crock of horseshit?" Benson laughed. "I bet you try to make them envious, probably make a point of telling them all the benefits of being a nonpracticing, bureaucratic, paper-pushing surgeon. No pager to wear. No 3:00 A.M. telephone calls from some tight-sphinctered nurse requesting a verbal order that'd be self-evident to a sixteen-year-old candy striper. Nurses! The epitome of anal-retentive, blinder-restricted, professional vision."

Sergio felt his anger spike. "You know nothing of what the practice of medicine is like."

"Maybe not, my friend, but I know that most of you salaried, bureaucratic ex-surgeons—the AMA officers and JCAHO lackeys—are either the product, or should be a product, of a substance abuse program." Benson laughed again.

The words stung like a slap in the face, turning embarrassment into more anger at those who piously judged his past rather than accepting the good person, the provider father, he actually was. "You think this is funny? You enjoy mocking me like this? I tell you I am much happier in this role. Let all those *real* doctors and nurses—those who you say think so little of me—struggle with the nursing shortages, falling reimbursement, the unbalanced distribution of doctors to geographic areas, and on and on and on. Let all those small little professionals deal with that morass. You can kiss my ass."

"Not the answer I was looking for, Sergio. And I need an answer before this ride is over."

Sergio blinked at the green highway coming up: SEA-TAC AIRPORT NEXT RIGHT.

Sergio shook his head. "Sorry, I was thinking of something else."

"You still haven't answered my question."

Ah yes, the committee and the all-important endorsement. "First, let me ask you . . . how many billions will I generate for Med-InDx? How many dollars is that endorsement worth now? Millions. Possibly billions. You duped me. Yes, duped me. Embarrassing, but true. One hundred thousand dollars is so-called chump change compared to what that endorsement is worth now."

"Rant and rave all you want, but I'm losing patience, my Italian friend. Your answer?"

"In terms of the IPO, how many points will that endorsement elevate the price on the first day of trading?"

Benson opened his mouth as if starting to say something, then closed it, his jaw muscles rippling.

A surge of power buoyed Sergio's confidence. "I ask only an

innocent question, my *Texas* friend." He sat back in the seat, thought, *Fuck him if he doesn't like it.*

Benson's smile was not friendly. "There is no way I can predict what will happen to the stock. You should know that."

Sergio gave a derisive snort and turned to look out the side window. "Ah yes, but we can imagine, can't we?"

"When it comes to financial matters I don't like to work with imaginary numbers. They make me nervous. I prefer reality."

Up ahead the bare concrete Sea-Tac control tower loomed above a ten-foot-high chain-link fence, an overcast sky dark with swaths ranging from battleship-gray to black as storm clouds rolled in from the Olympic Mountains.

"I was too generous. You and your colleagues knew that and have taken advantage of my good nature. It is time you and your colleagues rethink my, ah, consultative compensation."

The car approached the passenger-loading zone.

Silence.

"How much do you believe your compensation should be, amigo?"

"More along the lines of two million."

"Two million," Benson echoed without emotion, then nodded his head almost appreciatively.

The car came to a stop. Sergio opened the passenger door but did not step out. "I am sure Prophesy would be interested in a similar discussion. Yes?"

Benson turned blank eyes to him. "Don't be so quick to jump ship. I'll need to discuss this with my colleagues. In the meantime, I suggest you not talk with anyone from Prophesy. Is this perfectly clear?"

Benson's eyes spiked fear in Sergio's heart. A moment later he shook this off. He was the one in control, not the Med-InDx investors. They needed him more than he needed them. "I am quite serious. Either pay me two million dollars now or the endorsement goes to Prophesy."

"Do not worry, amigo, you will be taken care of."

Smiling with the satisfaction that power brings, Sergio stepped from the car. The trunk lid popped. He retrieved his bag. But not before checking out the model number on the trunk hood. A 420 CLK.

He would stop by the Mercedes dealership tomorrow.

– – – – – – – – – – – –

Tyler locked the door of his beat-up, used Range Rover, pulled his leather bomber jacket over his head to shield him from the driving rain, and splashed through shallow parking-lot puddles toward the restaurant, a sports bar on Lake Union, not far from the Fred Hutchinson. He'd never been here before, but a colleague of Nancy's had recommended it as being close to work and serving to-die-for fish and chips. He smiled. She remembered his tastes.

He found her at a table for two by a large picture window overlooking slips filled with white powerboats with tinted windows and sleek sailboats with skeleton masts. She smiled as he approached, which he took as a hopeful sign. Her black hair was pulled straight back in a ponytail, her preference when working. Instead of contacts, plain wire-rim glasses. No makeup over her flawless skin, an attribute she took great pains to shield from direct sunlight. The assistant professor look. A conscious effort to keep her Asian beauty disguised. He believed she felt people automatically devalued a beautiful woman's intelligence by about fifty percent.

"Hello, Tyler." Her smile faded. "My God, what's happened to you?"

He stopped short of sitting down and glanced at his soaked Dockers. "I forgot to bring an umbrella."

"No, I mean your weight . . . your face . . . just look at you . . . you look like you just escaped from one of those awful Nazi concentration camps or something."

"Just working hard, I guess," he lied. Unsure whether to kiss her or not, he decided to just sit down and took the other chair.

"Have you had a physical lately? Is something wrong?"

"You mean like terminal cancer?" he joked.

"No, I didn't mean—"

"I'm surprised you chose this place," he said, nodding toward the window at her back.

"You mean the water?" She didn't turn to look at or out the window.

"Yes." With her phobia of water so strong, coming here must have taken a goodly amount of resolve, he realized.

"I know how much you love fish and chips. My roommate said this place has the best in Seattle."

Resisting the urge to touch her arm, he said, "I've missed you," then blushed at his own frankness.

"Well, I've missed you too." She blushed too and dropped her eyes. "You're one of the reasons I jumped at this Hutch opportunity."

His heart warmed at her confession and shyness. "You like it then, the job?"

She beamed at him. "I love it. You should see the lab they gave me."

The waiter asked for their drink orders. She settled for water, explaining how she planned on returning to work after dinner. Tyler ordered a Red Hook beer, seeing how the restaurant didn't serve his favorite from the San Francisco Anchor Brewing Company.

When the waiter left she continued. "The whole thing just came together beautifully, kind of as if . . ."

"As if it were predestined."

She blushed, "Yes," and glanced away in embarrassment.

Probably consulted a fortune-teller before accepting the job, he thought.

"I mean," she continued, "when the offer came I had, like, maybe a week—ten days at the most—to decide. Then Carol, you remember her? She told me about this friend with this apartment on Capital Hill. Said she was looking for a roommate. So I called her. She's the kind of person you'd like just talking with her over the phone. I couldn't believe it."

"So you took the job. That's great."

"No, you haven't heard the best part." She leaned back beaming, as if about to lay down a royal flush. "She works at The Hutch too. I mean, we drive to work together most days."

He shook his head in dismay. Amazing, but typical. Somehow she always fell into things like this. Lucky. "That's terrific. How's John?" Her brother.

Her smile widened. "Sumitomo, the Japanese conglomerate?"

"Uh huh."

"They hired him. He's working in Los Angeles now. Loves it. I mean, talk about good fortune, he didn't even have to look for it. They recruited him just before graduation."

"Your parents?"

"Still in Hong Kong. I tried to get them to move over here, but they wanted to stay put. Said they didn't think it was any safer in the United States, what with all the crime and terrorist threats. They'd rather face an infectious disease."

Tyler asked, "May I ask you something?"

"Sure. What?"

He felt his face redden. "Nah . . . forget it." He decided certain questions were completely off base. He considered mentioning that he had not been dating, but figured this would only look like an oblique way of putting the question back on the table.

"What?"

He shook his head. "It's nice . . . being here with you. Like it hasn't been all that long."

"Yes, I know."

Tyler's heart accelerated. He wanted to reach out and touch her cheek but didn't want to rush anything for fear of putting her off.

"How's your job?" she asked.

"Fine."

"Are you sure?"

"Why?" *Here we go,* he thought.

"I don't know . . . you don't look so good. Your weight . . . how much have you lost?"

"I don't know," although he knew exactly. "Can we drop the subject?"

"You're not . . ." The words seemed to die on her lips.

"What? Not using? You mean, you still believe I was?" He felt the old anger ignite.

"No. That's not what I meant."

Liar.

"Don't give me that look, Tyler. It's important. You know that."

Tyler sucked in a deep breath, blew it slowly out between pursed lips. "Look, let's not get started. I was really looking forward to seeing you. I don't want to get into an argument. Okay?"

Their orders arrived: his fish and chips with a bottle of vinegar, her taco salad with an extra portion of salsa—just the way she always liked it.

They ate for a moment in silence. She finally said, "I checked on you through a friend."

He set down the piece of fish he was ready to take a bite from. "You what?" not certain he'd heard correctly.

"Don't get angry with me, Tyler. I wanted to be certain you were doing okay before I took the chance of moving back up here."

He pushed the plate away. "I don't believe this."

She reached across the table, grasped the back of his hand in hers. "Hear me out before you get that way." She looked directly into his eyes. "I still love you. I didn't want to take the chance of moving up here if you were still . . . still spiraling downhill."

"Spiraling downhill? Jesus, Nancy. After I got fired and no one wanted to hire me . . . what . . . ?" He let the question die. Old ground. All of it. Baggage, the Dr. Phils of the world call it. He thought about her last words, trying desperately to focus only on the best part of them. "You still love me?"

"Yes, I do. I want to see if we can get it back together. But before we do that, I want to know that you're back on your feet completely. That means no drugs."

"Believe me, I am."

"Good. Then there's a chance for us." She glanced at his partially eaten meal. "Why don't you finish it? I know how much you like fish and chips."

He picked up a now cold piece of fish and forced himself to nibble part of it.

Dinner ended. An awkward lull hung over the table like dense San Francisco fog.

Finally she announced, "Time to get back to the lab."

"When can I see you again." *How bizarre,* he thought, *asking your wife for a date.*

She looked away. "Let's not rush this, Tyler. I'm still settling in and . . ."

"And?"

"Just let's not rush it. Okay?"

CHAPTER 9

"You can stand in the shower now and let the water run over your head, just don't shampoo." As always, Tyler was explaining wound care to a post-op patient in for removing the staples holding the wound together after removal of a small benign brain tumor. She was sitting on the exam-room table smelling of rubbing alcohol and cotton dressings as he removed the clips one by one. One exam table, one rolling stool, two chairs, and a small desk on which to write notes. A small counter along the wall contained a small stainless-steel sink with cabinets above and drawers below.

"It has nothing to do with the chemicals in the shampoo—the wound's healing beautifully—it's that I don't want you to stress the wound edges and pull them apart." With a snip of the staple remover, he popped out the last one. A puncture site just behind the hairline began oozing blood. Tyler picked up a two-inch square cotton sponge and pressed it firmly over the spot. "Hold still a minute while I put a little pressure on this."

For a moment he admired his handiwork. When the redness vanished and the hair fully grew back in three months you would really have to search to find this scar. A definite advantage of private practice over academics: closing your own wounds instead of allowing a first-year resident to do it. But he still missed teaching residents, probably always would. Would he ever make it back to an academic appointment? Maybe. If enough time passed. Memories dim. His past problems might be forgotten.

"Ah, Dr. Mathews . . ."

"Yes?" He glanced at her face. The crimson ascending her cheeks triggered a suspicion of what was coming.

"Brad . . . my husband . . . wanted me to ask . . . when I could have sex again."

He smiled at her. "Anytime you want, but only with Brad. I don't want you getting too excited."

For a moment she looked blankly at him, mouth slightly agape. Then she giggled and gave his hand a playful slap. "Oh, Dr. Mathews, bad puppy!"

His beeper started chirping.

He let up on the wound, made sure the bleeding had stopped, then checked the beeper readout. A number he didn't recognize.

"Be right back, Mrs. Gowers." He opened the door and headed for his office down the hall.

"Dr. Mathews. It's Jim Day. Sorry it took so long getting back to you, but I've been up to my ass in alligators and the swamp's still rising. I checked the history on that medical record you asked about."

Tyler's pulse accelerated. "Yeah? What'd you find?"

"I'm afraid it's not what you want to hear. Far as it shows, there's been no alteration to that field, or any field on that medical record ever. What you see is what was put in there from the git-go and that's the end of it."

A paralyzing chill hit Tyler. Did this mean it was *his* mistake? "Are you sure?"

"Hey, Doc, there's no way no how any field can be altered without that alteration being recorded. Don't know how to say this any more clearly than I just did."

Dizzy, he dropped into his desk chair and sucked in a deep breath. "Bear with me a second . . . I need to make certain I have the facts straight." He paused to collect his thoughts. "Any time any entry is made into any field in the medical record, the identity of the person making that entry is recorded. That's correct, isn't it?"

"That's right."

Tyler palm-wiped his mouth. "Okay then . . . who entered the radiation dose in Larry's chart?"

"Thought you might want to know that." Tyler heard Day's keyboard clicking away in the background. "Record shows that it was transmitted electronically from outside the center by Dr. Nick Barber, but that since he's not privileged here, it was validated by you per your research protocol."

Precisely per protocol. But the overdose still could not be accounted for. "Hang in here with me a little longer. Okay?"

"It's your dime."

"Let me walk you through this one more time, then you tell me how come Larry Childs got an overdose. I checked with Barber. Their records show they ordered a ten-gray dose. My independent records confirm a ten-gray dose was ordered. But the chart says he got zapped with a two-hundred-gray dose and his brain rotted out from too much radiation. Explain how the hell that can happen."

Day gave a sigh of exasperation. "You know damn well I can't tell you that. All I can tell you is that field hasn't been changed since it was populated."

"What makes you so goddamned certain? If I hear you, you're saying it wasn't changed by the *standard* means . . . by another person with privileges, like a doctor. But I still don't see why it couldn't have been changed by someone *without* privileges, like a hacker."

"Because that's flat-out impossible. It just can't happen."

"And I say that's bullshit. You just told me that Barber ordered a dose and I confirmed it. Both our records show a ten-gray dose. But he got a two-hundred-gray dose. That means we—by that I mean you, me, and Maynard Medical Center—have a major problem on our hands." Tyler flashed on his conversation with

Michelle. He made a mental note to call her and go back over the story. *Better yet, check with Doctor . . . what was her name?*

Day said, "If you know so much about computer security I suggest you tell me how that could happen and the field not show evidence of being tampered with."

"Thought we went over this before. If a hacker had access to the source code he'd know how the system security was written. If he knew that, it makes sense he could get in and out without leaving a footprint."

"Now that's a huge stretch. Chances of that happening are worse than me hitting Mars with a brick." Day paused, exhaled an audible breath. "Anything else you want to know? If not, I'm gonna sign this ticket out."

"You sign off on this and I'll personally see that you're named on the root cause analysis as obstructing an investigation into a patient death. Is that clear?"

– – – – – – – – – – – –

Arthur Benson said, "Goddamned straight it's a problem. It's a big problem, bucko. In fact, it's more than a problem. It's a potential catastrophe waiting to unfold on us. And don't give me any of your it's-only-hypothetical horseshit. I'm in no mood to hear it." *God, what I'd give to strangle that fucking little Jew geek.*

Benson realized the portable phone was pressing his ear so tightly that a headache was radiating into his right eyeball. He let up on the pressure and stood. Pacing always helped at times like this, and the office was large enough that he could do laps around the eighteen-chair conference table. His eye caught the oil portrait of Chester Maynard staring down at him. The old man's piercing green eyes seemed to follow him through the room.

Bernie said, "Chill way down, dude. What are we talking about, a minor problem, right? Go and get your panties in a knot and you'll elevate your cholesterol, have a stroke maybe. You don't want that and I don't want that."

That's all he needed, more of the little fucker's attitude.

"Minor problem you say? Minor fucking problem? You think some NIH bureaucrat calling to ask about a research patient who died of brain rot is a minor fucking problem?" His heart pounded his ribs. Maybe Bernie had a point about needing to calm down. But not until the fucking geek understood the potential hazard they were facing.

"Let me make this perfectly clear to you, Mr. Bill Gates wannabe. Your entire fucking company will be a one-paragraph postmortem on page fourteen of *The Wall Street Journal* if you don't fix it."

When Bernie didn't respond, he said, "I thought you'd fixed it."

"No shit. I thought so too. But obviously that isn't the case. What do you want me to do, fall on my pencil? Cut my throat?"

"Wrong answer, Bernie." Benson pictured Bernie in his chrome and black leather office, probably wearing suntan Dockers and a pale blue, button-down oxford, open at the neck just like Bill Gates. Every book Gates had ever written lined up on the credenza like a shrine. Even named his daughter Willamina. Jesus!

"Let me ask you something, Bernie."

Bernie said, "Shoot," seemingly unfazed.

"If it's such a minor problem, why hasn't it been fixed yet?"

"Gimme a break, dude. You know I've been wickedly busy. What with the IPO and everything."

"Oh, yeah, busy. Important things like schmoozing reporters at press conferences. Maybe you should be spending more time taking care of business rather than working on that klieg-light tan of yours."

"Oh, a little sensitive, are we? What are you saying? I should not be pushing our product? I should, like, hide it? I'm telling you we have the wickedly superior solution and that is what's going to win in the end. Med-InDx rocks, man, but every piece of software ever written has a few bugs. They all do. And they all get ironed out sooner or later. At least the important ones do."

"You seem to be forgetting something, amigo. This is a hospital. We're in the business of healing people, not killing them. According to you, this type problem would never happen."

"Hey, dude, way I see it, you're *way* overreacting. So one lousy patient gets a wicked case of brain rot. You think that condemns the whole product? Hell no. You trying to tell me everything that's done at your fancy carriage trade medical center is perfect? That you're the Martha Stewart of health care? That your staff doesn't have their fair share of screwups? Helllloo . . . Earth to Arthur . . . screwups are what this little escapade is all about. Reducing them . . . and that's exactly what we're doing. *Reduce* them. Not *eliminate*. That, dude, is the *big* picture."

"Jesus, you really don't get it, do you. The *real* big picture is that any of this leaks, you can stand back and see Prophesy trample you to death. The big picture is the longer that bug stays in there, the more risk we're taking. Get it?"

"How many times I gotta tell you? I'm on it."

Arthur kicked a chair that wasn't aligned perfectly with the table. "Horseshit you are, otherwise we wouldn't be having this conversation." A bolt of pain shot up his leg causing his knee to buckle. He caught himself and hopped on one foot, cursing silently. "I don't see why you can't assign some of your hotshot coders to it."

"Like I said before, the medical record is my baby. No one else codes it. No one."

"And as I said before, your fucking ego isn't the important thing here. That bug is."

"Hey, great thinking, Arthur . . . so I tell a few coders there's a wicked bug in the system . . . and so now we have even more people know about it. That what you really want? Some disgruntled employee shooting off his mouth? Worried about Prophesy finding out? Hey, here's a perfect way to do it. Brilliant, just absolutely brilliant."

Benson picked a decorative crystal paperweight off the desk

and threw it the length of the office. It smashed into the wall leaving a noticeable dent. "Just fix the fucking thing."

"Speaking of which, who found it?"

"No one's found it *yet*. That's the whole fucking point to this little conversation. We don't want to take the chance someone will find it. We want it fixed."

"Understood. But if I knew where the problem popped up it would help me troubleshoot it."

"Bernie, it's the same goddamned problem as before. A data field apparently changed. Spontaneously, so I'm told."

"Yeah yeah yeah. You got to give me more than that. Which data field?"

"A radiation-treatment dose."

"Huh! That's just wonderful," he said with a hugely sarcastic edge in his voice. "Not even in the same general area as last time. See? This is what I'm talking about. It's, like, an intermittent. They're the worst kind to troubleshoot. You never know where or when to look."

"I know. You've said all that. You've also said quite convincingly you can fix it. Just see that you get it done this time, got it? Meanwhile I'll keep a lid on things from this end."

With that, Benson slammed down the receiver.

CHAPTER 10

1:25 P.M.

Lunch finished, Tyler hurried back to his office via the back hallway, having learned the hard way to never enter through the reception area where he'd been sandbagged once too often by a patient asking a question about their problem before having had time to review their chart. He dropped into his chair, hit the intercom for the receptionist, said, "I'm back," in a mimic of the Terminator.

"Have a good lunch?"

"Depends on what you think of cafeteria food."

"Sorry I asked." She paused a beat. "Your one o'clock canceled but as luck would have it we have a work-in for you. Sharnel put him in Room Three."

"Thanks." He used the desk computer to call up the new patient's chart. He scanned meager information but didn't see the Chief Complaint—the problem that brings the patient to the doctor—listed.

He punched the intercom again. "He mention what his problem is?"

"No, he didn't. Said it was confidential."

Tyler shrugged this off, thanked her, and picked up the tablet computer for electronically recording the patient's history and headed for the exam room. He knocked on the door as a warning, then pushed it open. In a chair, reading an outdated copy of *Newsweek,* sat a blond, freckled-faced man about Tyler's age wearing gray slacks and a blue blazer, a white shirt with rep tie, and a military crew cut.

"Mr. Ferguson, Tyler Mathews." Tyler set down the computer on a small table and extended his hand.

After the handshake Ferguson withdrew a wallet from his inside blazer pocket. "Doctor, I'm not here about a medical problem. Here." He flipped open the wallet and proffered identification. "Special Agent Gary Ferguson, Seattle Field Office, FBI."

Caught totally off guard, Tyler inspected the identification. Appeared official enough, but then again, what did he know? An uneasy feeling skewered his gut. Tyler tried to think of something benign the FBI might want from him but couldn't come up with anything. *More repercussions from California? Had to be.* "I don't understand." His heart started pounding. His fingers tingled.

Ferguson waved a palm toward a stainless-steel rolling stool beside the small charting table. "Why don't you sit down so we can talk?"

"Why? How long is this going to take?" He folded himself onto the stool.

The FBI agent jutted his chin at the computer. "You're using Med-InDx on that, aren't you?"

Tyler glanced at the computer. "Yes." A sinking feeling replaced the tightness in his gut. Maybe this wasn't about California.

"Like it?" This was said in an overly conversational tone that implied anything but casual interest.

Tyler wiped both palms on his thighs, then rubbed them together. "I didn't realize the FBI does marketing surveys for software companies."

Ferguson's eyes hardened. "I am. Had any problems with it?"

Tyler's gut tied a square knot. "No."

"Huh! Really!"

Silence.

"Why would you even ask?" He felt the agent's eyes sizing up his awkwardness. *Never have been a convincing liar, pal.*

Silence.

Tyler started to stand. "Look, if there's nothing else, I'm busy."

"Sit down, Doctor." The agent's eyes hardened further. "We're not done yet."

Tyler stood. "Far as I'm concerned we are."

"Doctor, we think there's a problem with Med-InDx and we think you know about it."

"A problem? What kind of problem?" The rototiller in Tyler's gut roared to life.

"You just had a serious complication on one of your patients, didn't you?"

Tyler dropped his voice to almost a whisper and bent forward. "How'd you know about that?"

Ferguson nodded. "A kid's brain rotted away because of Med-InDx, didn't it."

"Why didn't you call me on the telephone? Why did you go through all this charade to talk to me?"

Ferguson stood, handed Tyler a card. "You familiar with Lowell's Café in the Market?"

Tyler accepted the card without looking at it.

The FBI agent gave a sharp nod. "Meet me there at five o'clock. My cell phone's on the card if something comes up, but I think it's in your best interest not to stiff me on this, if you get my drift."

"No, I don't get your drift."

Ferguson smiled, "Be there," and walked out of the exam room.

3:50 P.M., OFFICE OF JILL RICHARDSON

"She's busy."

Tyler craned his neck to the left for a straight shot through the open door into Jill Richardson's office. She sat at her desk facing the computer monitor. Raising his voice he said, "Is that right, Ms. Richardson? You're too busy to see me?"

She turned and smiled. "No, of course not."

To Tony, Tyler said, "See? She's not too busy to see me," as he walked past.

The red-faced secretary shot back an expression that could only be interpreted as angry embarrassment.

Tyler dumped himself into one of the two chairs facing her desk. "As I warned you I was going to do, I reported Larry Childs's death to the project PI."

"So soon?" Her brow furrowed. "Was that wise, considering we have no idea what the cause of death was? Shouldn't you have waited until we found a cause?"

"We know exactly the cause of death. Radiation necrosis."

"You know what I mean. We haven't completed the root cause analysis yet." She studied him a beat. "Don't tell me you've finished it."

"Look, a patient in a federally funded research protocol had a complication and died from radiation necrosis. I'm obliged to notify our own Institutional Review Board as well as the study Principal Investigator who then has the responsibility to notify the chairman of the Data Monitoring and Safety Board. There's no controversy here." He said this with a tone of conviction that did not invite rebuttal.

Before she could say anything he added, "What NIH plans on doing with the information is their business and remains to be seen. They have the choice to stop the study until the committee reaches a decision on whether to shut it down entirely. I have no doubt this is a grave enough complication for them to seriously consider that option."

She cleared her throat and straightened her posture. "I didn't mean to imply you did the wrong thing. I guess I'm still shocked that your patient died, that's all."

"And another thing. The on-site technician, Jim Day, says there's absolutely no evidence that someone messed with the data field. Basically, he says the treatment dose is exactly what was entered into the computer. When I talked to Nick Barber, I had him check his records. They're the same as mine. Ten gray. I could conceive of one of us possibly making a typo, but both of us? Not a chance. On top of that, the computer would have to accept the two-hundred-gray dose. And since it's way out of range that couldn't happen without an override by the treating physician. And that didn't happen either. Bottom line? There's no other explanation—someone had to change the dose after it was inputted."

She cocked her head to the right. "And Jim Day says that's impossible?"

"Correct."

"So what you say must be correct. The dose was changed. The question is how?"

"How much do you know about computers?"

She considered this a moment before answering. "The sum total of my knowledge is how to turn them on and off and use e-mail."

"Well, the only way I can see this happening is a hacker."

"But that's what I don't understand," she continued, "I thought you said Day said that was impossible."

"Look, I'm no computer expert but there are a few things I do know. I know that a good hacker can exploit just about any system that's connected to an outside phone or fiber-optic line. If the system can accept incoming connections, it's vulnerable to intrusion. And everyone who knows about Med-InDx knows it's being touted as having impenetrable security. Man, oh, man, making a claim like that, that your system's uncrackable . . . and making a huge public deal about it, is a direct challenge to any self-respecting hard-core serious cracker. Do that and you're sure to be hit."

"But how could someone change the record and not leave any evidence?"

"That takes work, but obviously it's not impossible because that's the only reasonable explanation for what happened."

"But you said Jim Day said that can't happen."

"You know what source code is?"

"No."

"It's the original program written in whatever language the

software is written in. Once you get a copy of the source code, you can figure out any number of ways to work around the security. You know what a trap door is?" He added, "In reference to software programming, not cellars."

"No. But how do you know all this?"

"My college roommate used to code game software. He was also a hacker, but just not as devoted as the real ones. He told me about how coders leave trap doors in programs for easy access. The idea is, if you're debugging a complicated program, you want access to advanced segments without having to work through all the prior steps that take you up to that particular point. When they finish the product they usually leave them in, for when they need to revise or troubleshoot the software later. Maybe the same thing applies to an application as complex as our medical record."

She frowned. "So you're suggesting if a hacker knew about one of these trap doors and had the source code he might be able to change a data field without leaving any evidence of being there?"

"Absolutely. What other explanation is there?"

She stopped taking notes and started tapping her MontBlanc pen against the paper. "That's all very interesting, Dr. Mathews, but where is this going?"

"I've always figured if one person can't give you the answer you're looking for, go to the next person up the line. Maybe we should go directly to Day's boss at Med-InDx, see if he or she is more receptive to the idea that their system's been breached."

She set the pen down, tapped both thumbnails against her lower teeth, apparently pondering this. "For what it's worth, let me make a suggestion. Before going to someone in Med-InDx, why not talk to our CIO. After all, if we're dealing with a security issue, our IT Department needs to know about it too. I think this approach would be more politically advisable, and if you want, I can arrange an appointment today."

Her suggestion made sense. "Go ahead, phone him."

CHAPTER 11

Arthur Benson leaned forward in the desk chair, combing fingers through the shock of white hair just to the left of his widow's peak. His other hand held the telephone to his ear. He said into the mouthpiece, "We can't take that chance."

The man on the other end of the line responded, "So, what do you propose?"

Behind the desk, above the matching credenza, hung an oil portrait. The piercing eyes of a distinguished, serious-faced man in a three-piece suit stared through round wire-rimmed glasses at anyone who cared to look at him.

This isn't rocket science, Benson thought. *Not even close. Why do I have to spell it out like this?* "Way I see it, we have only two options. Pay the sombitch off or off the sombitch. My vote? The latter."

"Did he say how much he would settle for?"

"That is not the point." He drummed his fingers and reconsidered his answer. "The point is, we can't let him hold us up like this. It's extortion, blackmail. It's going against a fundamental rule. It's not right. It's bad business. It puts us in a position to be hit up again. It's the reason the Israelis don't deal with terrorists. We can't let this pissant hold a gun to our heads. How else can I explain this to you? What is there you don't understand about this?"

"Got your point the first time. Just answer the goddamn question. How much does this pissant terrorist blackmailing sombitch— as you call it—want?"

"What difference does it make? We're not paying it."

"Just give me the figure instead of a headache."

Benson exhaled, exasperated. "He didn't give an exact figure. But the general tone of the conversation came in at around two million. Not exactly what you'd call chump change."

"But only a fraction of what we've sunk into this."

"So what are you saying? It's the cost of doing business?"

"Could be."

He squeezed out a sarcastic laugh. "Fat chance."

"So what are you saying? Off him?"

"Yes."

"And just how is that going to play to the feds? A couple weeks before the committee's report is due the committee chairman has a goddamn automobile accident? That'd be just what Prophesy is looking for."

"I have it from a very good source that our amigo has a heart problem. It could be made to look like a heart attack. Anybody gets suspicious enough to do a post, they'll find a good enough reason for him to croak."

The other man admitted, "It *would* solve a few problems."

– – – – – – – – – – –

Yusef Khan stood outside his open office door, hand extended. "I am glad to meet you, Dr. Mathews."

A slender man Tyler pegged for five feet nine inches and mid to late forties, his black hair and flawless dark complexion accented strikingly chiseled, handsome facial features. He wore a gray herringbone tweed sports coat, blue Brooks Brothers button-down oxford, maroon tie patterned with a blue, green, and gold school crest of dubious authenticity, navy Dockers, cordovan penny loafers. *A Dartmouth assistant professor could not have done it better,* Tyler thought. Then considered that his dad, the professor, dressed pretty much the same.

Khan ushered him and Richardson into his office. "Please forgive my office, it is a mess," and shut the door behind them, confining them in a room cluttered with computer printouts, computer journals, overflowing bookcases, and stacks of CD jewel cases on the floor. The room smelled faintly of paper and printing ink, reminding Tyler of a secondhand bookstore.

From the mix of accents, Tyler guessed Khan had been schooled in Pakistan by the Brits before immigrating to the States.

The Chief Information Officer bent to remove a pile of computer journals and printouts from a chair in front of his desk. "What may I do for you." He stood for a moment looking for a free spot to place the pile.

Richardson reached out to stop him. "Don't go to the bother. I know you're busy, so we won't take up much of your time."

Setting the stack back down with an embarrassed blush, he said, "I do not receive many visitors in my office." He straightened, brushed off his hand, his gaze turning to Tyler. "This is about your unfortunate patient, Larry Childs, yes?"

"How did you know?" He turned to Richardson. "Did you say something I didn't hear?"

Richardson stiffened. "No. You were right there when I called."

Khan gave Tyler a quizzical smile. "You act surprised. You do not know that Dr. Golden from the NIH contacted me and asked me to verify this alleged error?"

Tyler's fists tightened. "Alleged?"

Khan's face became more puzzled. "This is not the correct word?"

"Nothing's alleged. It happened. I can prove it." But since Khan apparently knew the punch line, Tyler decided to skip the preliminaries. "There was a dosage error. I checked Childs's medical record the evening he was admitted. The intended dose was ten gray. He received two hundred gray."

Khan's face wrinkled in apparent confusion. "But I found no evidence of this alleged error."

"What!" Tyler glanced at Richardson. She was studying him

with a strange, almost-bemused expression. Was Khan's English so bad that this represented a massive communication problem?

"Apparently you don't understand. Let me go through it again. The other day the record showed Childs received two hundred gray of radiation to his brain. Two hundred gray is a massive overdose, I guarantee you."

Khan flashed a puzzled smile, "Come," beckoning while moving to his desk. "I will show you."

Khan typed a command. Larry Childs's chart popped up on the monitor.

Khan said, "I will open his chart," and moused the tab for radiation treatments. The radiation dose showed ten gray.

Tyler blinked, looked again. "That can't be." He checked the name on the chart. Correct—Larry Childs. The treatment date was also correct.

Richardson asked, "What?" and craned her neck to see over his shoulder.

Tyler straightened up, bumping her out of the way in the process. "Goddamnit! Day must've changed it."

She shot him a funny look. "Why would he do that?"

"He's on the company payroll, for christsake. He was the last one to open the chart. He's had every opportunity."

"But are you forgetting," Khan piped in before Richardson could respond, "such orders can only be changed *before* a medication or treatment is being given. This one"—tapping the flat panel screen with a pencil eraser—"cannot be changed, not now." He shook his head adamantly.

Tyler looked from Khan to Richardson. "Bullshit. It was two hundred gray the other day. It's ten gray now. It's been changed in the past twenty-four hours!"

Richardson said, "Looks like ten to me, Dr. Mathews."

Tyler's temples tightened, his head feeling ready to explode as he looked at the screen again. Had to be Day who changed it. No other explanation seemed reasonable.

"... a mistake." He realized Khan was speaking to him. "I am thinking it is entirely possible."

Tyler stormed to the door.

"Stop."

Tyler felt Richardson's hand on his arm. He stopped, glanced around. They were in the tunnel connecting the Annex to the main hospital building. He must have walked down the two flights from Khan's office on autopilot, his rage so intense.

"What the hell's going on, Tyler?" She drilled him a hard look.

"You have to ask? You stood right there and saw the record and you have to ask? They changed it."

"*They?*"

"Stop it! You know what I mean."

"*They?* No, I don't know what you mean."

"Fine, then let me be very specific. Jim Day must've changed it."

Her intense blue eyes turned questioning. "For what earthly reason, Tyler? Besides, you heard what Khan said. The only time a treatment field can be changed is before the treatment is logged as given. After that, no one, not even God can change it."

Tyler threw up his arms in exasperation and frustration. He was sounding crazy and knew it. "It's a cover-up."

"A cover-up?" She spoke each syllable slowly and deliberately, each one with a questioning tone.

"Don't start with me. You heard me. *They*"—throwing it right back at her—"don't want anyone to know a hacker's been in the system."

"They? A cover-up? You mean, like the Warren Commission? Are you into some sort of conspiracy theory here?" She coughed a cynical snort.

He glared back at her. "Oh, right, you think I'm crazy! Then how do you explain Larry Childs's brain?"

"C'mon, Tyler . . ." She glanced at an expensive watch on her left wrist. "It's just about Miller Time . . . or at least it is in Topeka.

What say I buy you a drink so we can talk this out without you doing a Ted Bundy on my bones. Is that a deal, or what?"

He studied her a moment. "Don't try to blow this off, Ms. Richardson. It won't work." He turned and headed toward the exit.

CHAPTER 12

Tyler glanced at his watch. Seven minutes late. He broke into a trot just as the traffic light changed to green in his direction, leading to the narrow one-way street bisecting the Pike Place Market with its eclectic meld of funky shops. Ahead, above the green two-story structure, towered Seattle's large trademark PUBLIC MARKET sign Hollywood directors love to showcase.

He crossed First Avenue, passed a sidewalk flower vendor, continued into the dead end of Pike Place with its signature tourist spots smelling of fish, vegetable earth, and musk—the large bronze pig children ride and the seafood stall where salesmen toss fifteen-pound salmon like baseballs to delight gawking tourists. A few feet farther he started threading his way between passage-clogging shoppers and sightseers through an endless block of produce stalls, the air thick with spices, coffee, and sweat.

Another block brought him to the wood-framed glass doors of Lowell's Café.

He preempted the hostess with, "I'm looking for someone." He walked along a lunch counter toward the back of the restaurant where a line of tired wood booths with half-open single-pane windows allowed customers a urban back alley view of the waterfront/harbor scene below. A huge white and green Washington State ferry departing Coleman dock blew its horn.

Ferguson was already seated in one of the booths, a bowl of chili and a bottle of red Tabasco sauce in front of him. Tyler slid onto the opposite hard wooden bench. The warm inside air, thick with the smell of corned beef hash, reminded him of his dinner date later.

Ferguson propped his spoon back in the bowl and reached for the hot sauce. "Thanks for showing up, Mathews." He uncapped it and began shaking drops over his chili.

Tyler glanced about. No one seemed to be watching. "I don't have a lot of time. What's this all about?"

Ferguson raised an index finger before mixing the hot sauce into the chili with the spoon. He brought a small dollop to his mouth and contemplated it like a wine taster. "Needs just a little more." He sprinkled several additional drops on the thick brown mush before capping the bottle. "You like hot?" He pushed the bottle aside and nestled his elbows on the wood table.

"I didn't come all the way down here to discuss our respective tastes in chili seasonings."

Ferguson set down his spoon again. "Fine. Let's talk about Med-InDx. I asked if you've had any problems with it and you became defensive as hell. What was that all about?"

"Hold on a minute. I find it short of astounding that the FBI would even have the slightest interest in a software product. What's the deal?"

Ferguson shoved the bowl of chili toward the center of the table, leaned forward on his arms. "Fair enough. Where do you think the money comes from to start a company like Med-InDx?"

Tyler took a moment to dredge up a reasonable answer. "Since it's a start-up, my wild-ass guess would be venture capital."

"Exactly. So my next question is, who are the investors bankrolling Med-InDx?"

Tyler rolled his eyes. "Jesus, I don't believe this. You get me down here to ask me something like that?" He stood up to leave.

The right corner of the agent's mouth twitched as if suppressing a grin. "Sit down and don't be copping an attitude with me, Mathews. It's what we call a preparatory question."

Tyler leaned over the table. "Don't tell me what to do."

Ferguson held up the Tabasco sauce bottle. "Have any idea how much money the initial investors are going to be worth when their stock goes public in a couple weeks?"

How many more of these inane questions should he endure before just walking out? Tyler looked at the FBI agent in disgust. "I guess that depends upon how well the market treats it."

"Correct. But consider this . . ." He waved the red bottle as if it were the company. "The success of the Med-InDx IPO will be directly impacted by the JCAHO committee report. They give it an enthusiastic two thumbs-up and a pat on the back, say 'That's our baby,' that stock will pierce the ionosphere. Any investor holding shares before it hits the secondary market is going to make a megaton of bucks. But"—he paused—"if the committee's nod goes to Prophesy, Med-InDx stock will be as valuable as two-day-old dogshit."

Tyler shrugged. "So far all this conversation is nothing but Economics 101. What's this have to do with me?"

Ferguson pointed the red bottle cap at him. "Just stick with me on this for a second."

Tyler checked his watch again. "Speed it up. I have another engagement. And an important one."

Ferguson shot him a warning look and shook his head. "Not as important as this one, you don't."

A gut feeling warned Tyler that Ferguson had a trump card he was about to play. Something to do with the incident in California? Couldn't possibly be. That had been closed long ago. Still, he didn't trust the man.

Tyler said, "Go on."

"I had a high school teacher once told me everything can be explained by studying history. That if you understand the past, you'll be able to explain the present. Having said that, you know what the Mafia did after a few of their big guns ended up in the slam for tax evasion?"

Unable to resist the feeling of being watched, Tyler glanced over his shoulder again. "No, but I bet you're going to tell me."

Ferguson set down the bottle. "They started buying up legitimate businesses with cash flows that made it easy to launder beaucoup bucks from illegal operations."

"I still fail to see what this has to do with me, Ferguson. And your attitude is beginning to grate on me. Make your point or this conversation's over."

Ferguson's expression hardened. "My point is this: since the crackdown on terrorists after 9/11, those international factions who are, shall we say, unsympathetic to the United States have been forced to be a wee bit more canny about how and where they generate money to finance activities. They can't just tap some Middle Eastern billionaire on the shoulder and expect a few million bucks to flow into their bank accounts unnoticed. Because of this, they started looking around for innovative ways of getting high returns on legitimate investments. Venture capital is one of them."

"You're saying terrorists funded Med-InDx?"

Ferguson tapped his temple. "Smart thinking. Problem is we don't have enough hard evidence to do anything about it."

"Got it. If you can't prove the company's backed by dirty money, you'll settle for a way to destroy the entire company. That about sum it up?"

Ferguson leaned back in the booth and grinned. "Score one for the doctor."

"But you don't know for sure the money's dirty."

"Stow the soapbox, Mathews. I don't want to hear any righteous crap. I didn't say we didn't know it, I said we couldn't prove it . . . not in a court of law, we can't."

Tyler almost told him how someone was diddling the system. Thing was, he didn't have any proof. Especially now, with Larry Childs's record changed back to normal. And after what happened in San Francisco, he didn't trust the FBI.

Ferguson continued. "There was a technician worked for Med-InDx at your hospital. Helped troubleshoot problems. He surreptitiously contacted a member of the committee and leaked that he suspected a flaw existed in the database engine . . . one that causes data fields to be corrupted at random. Once a value is inputted, it might stay stable or it might change at random for no obvious reason . . . maybe it became corrupted when another patient's data was entered." He shrugged. "He didn't know how exactly. All he knew was, it was happening.

"We found out about it, but before we could fully debrief the man he took an abrupt vacation. Turns out he died in a scuba-diving accident down in Mexico. Very convenient, don'tcha think?" The agent's face was grim.

"Corrupt random fields . . . you mean change information at random?" A sense of relief washed over him. The overdose wasn't his fault.

Ferguson asked, "You gonna answer my question or just sit there stealing looks over your shoulder like a bunny rabbit in a carrot patch."

Anger shot through Tyler.

"Why the hell are you leaning on me, Ferguson?"

"Because you reported a complication involving an overdose of focused radiation. From what I understand, that kind of treatment is directly under medical record control and shouldn't happen. If that's the case, it might be an example that supports his allegation of spontaneous data field corruption. So, Mathews, tell me about this patient of yours."

"How did you find out about it?"

"Your patient's problem? Through NIH. Contrary to popular opinion, we feds *do* talk to each other. Especially since the Homeland Security Act reorganized our job descriptions a wee bit."

"You know anything about my recent past?"

"Tyler, we know more than you could imagine. I know what hand you wipe your ass with."

"I'm talking about what happened to me."

"I know you grew up in Los Angeles. I know your dad was professor of neuropathology—whatever that is—at USC and raised you to have high academic ideals. His first wife turned out to be an alcoholic, so he dumped her and married a younger woman, a grad student who does obscure Gaelic translations. Kind of similar to the way you picked your wife, Nancy. Right?"

Tyler sat in silence.

Ferguson continued. "I know you attended an inner city public school because your father believed this was a better character builder than private school. He supplemented you with lessons on the side to make up for any educational deficiencies public school might've offered. I know you wanted a collegiate basketball scholarship—UCLA, to be exact—but your high school ranking blew it. Seems you always took impossible shots with only one second left on the clock . . . messed up your average, so you were never seriously considered for college-level point guard. Got your MD degree at UCLA medical school. Did a residency at Moffitt in San Francisco with an interest in brain tumors. You even spent some time at NIH. How am I doing so far?"

Ferguson's knowledge angered Tyler. "I asked about my recent past."

"What? That you dropped the dime on your chairman for bilking Medicare out of several million dollars?" The twitch returned to the corner of Ferguson's mouth. "You seem so surprised. Why should you be? Shit, Tyler, we investigated your allegations. Why shouldn't I know all these things. It's all in your file." He paused to lick his lips. "Tell you something else that'll blow your mind. I was assigned to the case."

"Then you know what happened." Long-festering anger boiled deep within Tyler's chest. "I got fired on trumped-up drug charges. No one would hire me. I was lucky to get the job I have."

Ferguson's expression softened. "I know. I'm sorry about your career, but at least you did the right thing."

"The right thing?" Tyler coughed a sarcastic laugh. "Considering what happened, that's debatable. But you know what? I learned from that experience. And here's what I learned. One"—holding up a finger—"don't get involved. Two"—up came a second finger—"don't trust the FBI to stand by you. They're only out to win their own game. They don't give a damn about the people they ask to help them get there."

"What happened to you was unfortunate, but believe me, there was nothing we could do to help the situation."

"Bullshit." His anger flared. "I trusted you guys when you agreed to protect me. Protection? Jesus, what a joke. Nothing happened to Weiss, not even a slap on the hand. But me? Hey, my professional record is stamped 'Impaired Physician' and I get carted off to a drug rehab program and my wife leaves me. Wow, what a hell of a good deal that turned out to be. And now you've got the nerve to ask me to make the same mistake twice? Jesus, where do you guys get off?" Tyler realized a waitress and two customers were staring at him. He dropped his voice to a hiss. "You have any idea what that's done to me?"

Before Tyler could answer his own question, Ferguson leaned forward. "Believe me, there was nothing we could do. Someone got word to Weiss before we had a chance to subpoena the records. That gave him enough time to blow the smoke from the gun barrel before we could nail his sorry ass. We could've protected you from any collateral damage, but once those drugs were found in your locker there was nothing we could do about it."

"So you just watched me go down the toilet on trumped-up drug charges? Like a chump? Jesus!" Tyler slammed his palm on the table. His heart was pounding his sternum like a sledgehammer.

A moment later he added, "This job at Maynard? It's all I could get coming out of rehab. Nobody wants an impaired physician on staff. It's like asking a sex offender to live next to a grade school." He turned to Ferguson. "Know what my dream was going into neurosurgery? To be a department chairman at a good university.

Know how much chance I have to get there now?" He raised his hand, thumb tip to index finger. "Zero. You guys ruined my career and my marriage." He started to slide out of the booth.

Ferguson grabbed his arm. "Sit down and listen up."

Tyler jerked away, but couldn't break the agent's grasp. "Let go. I've listened up enough."

Ferguson's grip released. "Sure, have it your way, hotshot, but before you go, take a look at this." Ferguson handed him a folded piece of paper.

Tyler snatched the paper from his fingers and opened it. A mixture of embarrassment and rage hit.

"Where'd you get this?"

In the next instance he realized it would've been easy to obtain if the FBI had wanted it. They must've targeted him a while ago.

"We have every one you ever wrote, Mathews, so sit down and listen up."

He remained standing, undecided what to do.

"I said, sit down."

"Asshole!"

Ferguson grinned but not one of amusement. "In my job that's a term of endearment."

"You think it's funny what you guys did to me? The way you ruined my life?" He caught himself from saying anything about Nancy. He didn't want to jinx the possibility of getting back together.

"That's in the past." Ferguson held up the paper Tyler had dropped on the table. "This is the present."

He felt compelled to justify the prescription. "You have no idea what it is like, being railroaded into a drug rehab program, then having your wife walk out on you. I couldn't sleep . . . still can't . . . another doctor, a friend of mine . . ." He let the words die. No sense trying to justify it.

"You think I give a damn why you did it? Think again." Ferguson's malicious grin widened. "But I do give a damn it's a federal offense. 'Cause it means I have a hammer on you. So, here's the deal, plain and simple. Bring us solid evidence the software's flawed, and get it to me within the next seven days, or I turn this evidence over to the DEA with the recommendation to prosecute you for forging prescriptions for a controlled substance."

Tyler didn't try hiding his disgust. "You enjoy doing this to people, don't you?"

"Think I give a shit what you think?" Ferguson laughed. "Know a doc name of Michelle Lawrence?"

A heavy premonition hit. He'd forgotten to check back with her. "Yes . . . ?"

"She was found dead yesterday morning. Narcotics overdose. Only problem is she had no other signs of prior use." He wagged his eyebrows again. "Seems kind of strange to the cops to OD the first time out, especially all alone in her bedroom with the door closed. Know what I'm saying?"

Tyler swallowed a wave of nausea. He thought of Michelle's fingernails, her manly swagger, her totally screwed-up self-image. A real character, but a person he really liked.

Although he suspected the answer, he had to ask, "What does that have to do with me?"

"I don't know. You tell me."

"I have no idea."

"No? Not even the fact she was your anesthesiologist on your unfortunate patient? Think about it, Mathews. And while you're at it, think about one other thing. That JCAHO committee report's due to come out in two weeks. They endorse Med-InDx and it will become the de facto standard. Prophesy, its only competition, will be forced out of the business. That happens, and Med-InDx becomes the only game in town. It'll become kind of like Microsoft and operating systems. That software will be in all major hospitals in this country within five years. You think there's a problem at Maynard with the present system? Well, think what it'll be if that problem's magnified a couple thousand times.

"And another thing," Ferguson added before Tyler could respond, "our source believed the problems are much worse than they appear. You know for a fact that for the past two decades medicine has been moving toward more outpatient procedures. Only the sickest patients are the ones in hospitals now. Our informant firmly believed that the mistakes that software's making are at least three times what's being noticed. Probably worse than that. The problem is that many of the deaths are simply being chalked up to the fact the patients have life-threatening problems in the first place." He shot Tyler a serious look. "You getting any of this? It making any sense?"

"Yes."

"Okay then. We have maybe a week before the committee's report is sealed. After that . . . well, it's on your conscience, Mathews."

Ferguson pushed out of the booth. "One other thing . . . a word of advice. We think some of the Maynard upper echelon are fully aware of the bug and are helping to keep a lid on it. What I'm saying is don't trust *anybody*. And I mean nobody. Learn something from your friend's death, Mathews. Be smarter than you're acting now."

Ferguson glanced at his bowl of chili, slapped a five-dollar bill on the table. "Damn! Chili got cold." He glanced at Tyler as if realizing he was still there, straightened up, adjusted the fit of his blazer. "I was nice a minute ago. Let me put it this way . . . if I don't have something with which to bring down Med-InDx within a week I'll have the DEA do a number on you that'll make what happened in California look like foreplay."

CHAPTER 13

Nancy said, "Why don't you cut the small talk, Tyler. I can tell it's forced. Just tell me what's got you so upset."

They occupied a corner table of a small Thai restaurant she claimed to be within walking distance of her apartment. The crammed-to-capacity interior buzzed with dinner conversation white noise and busy kitchen clatter. The air smelled of peanut sauce and spices.

Her frankness triggered a short laugh. Pure Nancy. She could read him so easily no matter how hard he tried to disguise his emotions. *Then again, I usually have my mood de jour displayed in block letters across my forehead.*

"I want to talk about you, and possibly us . . . not me."

"Fine, but as long as you seem so preoccupied with something else, we won't be able to talk about anything at all. So you might as well cough it up."

He set his beer on the table and considered how much of the problem to divulge. He wanted to confide in her but couldn't. Not as long as the Ambien thing threatened. Any chance at getting back together would be out the window if she knew about that.

"Well?" She was eyeing him with that inquisitive Chinese face he loved to kid her about.

"There's this problem at work."

"Oh, Tyler . . ."

He finished the sentence for her, "not again," with the weight of her unspoken condemnation heavy on his shoulders. She had warned him last time not to get involved—a stance he chalked up to growing up in a politically oppressive country.

"Sorry, Tyler, that wasn't called for." She reached across the table and took his right hand in hers. "Go on, tell me about it."

"As long as *that* issue's come up . . . you need to know I was never abusing. The drugs found in my locker? They were planted."

"We've been through that a hundred times, Tyler. What about the urine tests? How could they turn up positive?"

"Simple. Someone switched samples and gave the lab someone else's . . . someone who was using. It's easy enough to pull off if you really want to."

"I want to believe you, Tyler." Her eyes softened and met his directly, underscoring the sincerity in her voice.

"Think back, Nancy. You know the symptoms. Did I ever act like a user? Did I have any of the characteristic signs?"

She looked down at her folded hand in her lap. "I have thought about that. No, you didn't. That's one of the reasons I took this job. To give us another chance."

A rush of vindication swept over him, almost making him cry with joy. Without thinking, he reached out and took her hand. Maybe there was hope of salvaging their marriage.

"Go on, tell me about what's wrong at work," she said.

He told her about Larry Childs and the clinical trial he was involved in, the radiation overdose, the question of how it happened, and finally Larry's death. He said nothing about Special Agent Gary Ferguson or the implication of their earlier conversation.

She listened intently, asking only an occasional question to clarify a point.

When he finished she asked, "How do you explain the mix-up in radiation dose?"

He paused to sip his beer and consider just how much detail to delve into. He thought of Michelle, and Ferguson's implication. "Only thing I can think of is a hacker," he lied.

At this point the waitress brought their orders of Pad-Thai and Swimming Rama. Grateful for the distraction Tyler used it to steer the conversation back to Nancy and her work.

Dinner finished, bill paid, Tyler folded the yellow Visa copy and stuffed it into his wallet. "It's still early. Want to go someplace for a drink?"

Nancy covered a yawn with her hand. "I better get home. I need to get up early tomorrow."

Both stood. "I'll walk you home."

Outside, the summer sky was transitioning through deepening purple hues. To the west a burnt orange glow highlighted the Olympic Mountains. The air still contained enough warmth for Tyler to throw his windbreaker around his neck and be comfortable in short sleeves. As they started along the sidewalk he reached for her hand. She gave him a little squeeze, as if to say, good move, Tyler.

Their conversation dwindled into a soft comfortable silence bred from familiarity. They crossed Pine, then Pike Street, leaving the Capital Hill neighborhood for "Pill Hill"—an area dominated by hospitals and professional office buildings. Her brick apartment building was built in the 1930s and encircled a courtyard. A path entered the yard then teed to entrances on opposing sides.

Climbing the three stairs to the courtyard, Tyler said, "I like some of these older buildings. They have more character." He thought of his parents' home, the one he grew up in. It was older too.

"The rooms are bigger but the downside is the bathroom. There's only one. And that's a problem in the mornings when we're both trying to get out of there. But it suits me for now."

Tyler wondered what "for now" meant.

As they reached the building's front door she rummaged a key from her rucksack and turned to him. "I'd ask you up, but . . ."

"But?"

She nestled against him. "I have a roommate."

Without thinking he wrapped his arms around her and hugged. Gently he leaned down and brushed his lips against hers. It felt as natural and familiar as if they had kissed good-bye at the door this morning.

"Next time, your place," she murmured.

"How about tonight?"

"Poor timing." She broke away from his arms, stood on her tiptoes, and pecked him on the lips. "Thanks, Mathews."

"Thanks, Fan."

She turned, put the key in the lock.

"How about tomorrow night?" he asked.

"I forgot to tell you. I have to fly back down to San Francisco tomorrow. It's just an overnight trip to clean up some things in the lab. I'll call you when I get back." She blew him another kiss, then slipped inside the door.

Tyler walked the six blocks back to his car fantasizing what it would be like to have his wife back. The months away from her had blunted just how much he missed her. Although she had not followed through on the divorce, each passing month had left him with less hope of reconciliation. Now she was stepping back into his life and it appeared she was serious about making a go of it. Or if not, at least considering it. All of a sudden, today's turmoil seemed to pale against the possibility of renewing his marriage.

– – – – – – – – – – –

The man turned toward a car and acted as if he were having difficulty with the door lock as Tyler Mathews stepped down from the apartment courtyard onto the sidewalk. He'd seen Mathews and the woman kiss and had read their body language well enough to back away just before Mathews had turned and started his way.

He let Mathews walk away. The woman was of interest now. Who was she? He stepped up into the courtyard and into the shrubs. He'd wait, watch for a window to light up.

12:07 A.M.

Flat on his back, arms at his sides, Tyler stared at his bedroom ceiling as parallel lines of light from car headlights passing on the street below periodically streaked across gray shadows. He had yet to fall asleep. And it didn't feel like he would anytime soon. Hard as he tried, his muscles seemed incapable of relaxing. Or if they did, it was for only as long as he concentrated on them.

His mind ruminated obsessively on Michelle. Was her death quick or had she suffered? Was it connected to the Med-InDx cover-up? Ferguson implied as much, but without much more than an apparent hunch. *That's the kind of implication that can make you even more paranoid, pal, if you dwell on it.* But, Tyler realized, there was no way he couldn't dwell on it.

Once again he ran a mental list of things to do tomorrow. Contact Robin Beck and Gail Walker. Find out their stories. *Does Ferguson know about them? Should I even tell him?*

Take an Ambien.

No way. Not now that there's a chance of getting Nancy back.

Go ahead. It's been a rough day. You deserve it. Practice abstinence tomorrow night.

But why should tomorrow night be any different?

Face it, pal. You're not going to get to sleep in this fucked-up state. Sooner or later you're gonna have to take that pill if you have any hopes of relaxing. Besides, there're only five more pills in that prescription before the jig's up. Special Agent Gary Ferguson saw to that, now didn't he!

What to do about Ferguson was the big question. Spy for the FBI? What were the chances of getting caught? Especially with Khan in the way. To spy he'd have to use the computer. And if Khan—or anybody else in the organization with hooks into IT—suspected him, it would be a chip shot to track every one of his keystrokes. Which made the sixty-four-thousand-dollar question: did *they*—whoever "they" were—suspect him?

For christsake, pal, what do you mean, does anybody suspect you?

Khan knows damn well you suspect a hacker diddled the field. Not only that, but with Michelle dead . . .

Sure, but that's the only thing Khan knows. What if I simply make it look like I let it drop? Then what? Will Khan believe I dropped it?

He doesn't have to believe anything. All he has to do is insert a routine to monitor for your log-in ID and then record anything you do. Spy and sooner or later he's going to know it.

The apartment's air conditioning flicked on. Tyler listened to the soft hum, welcoming the distraction.

12:21 A.M.

On his left side, Tyler stared at the glowing digits and reconsidered half an Ambien. Maybe just a half. That way he could stretch the remaining few out.

He thought of Nancy. What was he going to do if she spent the night?

Hide one, stupid. Where you can sneak it. If you needed it, that is.

12:37 A.M.

Tyler stood in the bathroom, amber plastic prescription bottle in hand, thinking it over. If he took a half tablet, he would be that much closer to running out of the damned drug. Once that happened there was nothing more he could do. So, considering it from that angle, he owed it to himself to take it.

Tyler opened the bottle, broke a pill in half, and chewed it to a paste he spread along his gums with the tip of his tongue. On the way back to bed he vowed to not take the other half tomorrow.

Tomorrow . . . Among other things, he'd look up Beck.

– – – – – – – – – – –

Confused, the man stood in front of the apartment registry. The woman he'd seen in the restaurant was Asian. None of the names listed seemed Asian. Then again, maybe she was married. He smiled at the thought. Mathews . . . dipping the wick with another man's wife. Perfect.

He turned to leave the building lobby but he wasn't satisfied. He'd be back, he decided, opening the door and stepping into the night, and next time he'd follow her in and find out which apartment she lived in.

CHAPTER 14

"I'm sorry, Doctor, Dr. Beck doesn't work here anymore," the young pimply-faced ward clerk answered in a singsong voice.

Tyler stood in front of the Emergency Department work desk, the expansive main hall to the exam rooms and trauma bays stretching out to either side of him. His peripheral vision caught a flash of blue as a nurse in scrubs hurried by. From behind the desk the squelch broke on a fire department scanner. *Tuned to the paramedics' frequency,* he figured. Even at this hour the department churned with activity, some nonemergency patients being treated after signing in during early morning hours.

Tyler asked, "Really?" trying out his best friendly smile. "When did she leave?" *Funny, I'm not surprised.*

"I'm sorry, Doctor, we're not allowed to give out any personal information about our staff."

"Then I suppose her home phone number is out of the question," unable to hide a note of frustration.

"I'm sorry, Doctor, yes it is."

Tyler nodded, "Thanks," and walked away wondering if he'd just carried on a conversation with a robot.

One flight of stairs up and a block-long hallway brought him to the physicians lounge. He punched in the access code, opened the door, and hung a right. Two of the three small computer cubicles were occupied. This time of morning the internists were printing out patient lists, most surgeons having already passed through the lounge an hour or so ago before starting rounds or heading to the operating rooms.

After settling into the unoccupied cubical, he picked up the telephone, punched 0. When the operator responded, he said, "This is Dr. Mathews. I need to reach Dr. Robin Beck. Can you put me through to her home number?" No way would she give him the number, he knew.

After a brief pause, "Sorry, Doctor, she's no longer listed as being on staff."

Tyler thanked her and hung up. Seeing no telephone book, he pulled over the computer keyboard and opened Internet Browser and requested QwestDex. A moment later he dialed Robin Beck's telephone number.

The phone was answered on the third ring. "Hello?"

"Dr. Beck?"

"Yes?"

"I don't know if you remember me," he lied, having never met her—that he could remember. "I'm Tyler Mathews, a neurosurgeon at Maynard. I was wondering if I might be able to meet with you later today?"

A pause. "About?" sounding mildly suspicious.

"About the complication you had a while back. I had a serious one the other day and I think it may have some similarities to yours."

"This some sort of sick joke?"

"No, no, please . . ." He scrambled to find the words to subdue her anger. "I'm serious. A patient of mine died because of an overdose of radiation to his brain. I think the computer may be responsible."

After several seconds, "Dr. Beck, you still there?"

"Your name again?"

"Tyler Mathews. I'm a neurosurgeon—"

"Yeah yeah, you already said all that." A pause. "Where do you want to meet?"

"Wherever would be best for you."

"You can come here." She gave him her address. "What time?"

He calculated how long it'd take to drive to that part of town, figured in the few other things he needed to do, and checked his watch. "How 'bout around ten-thirty."

"See you then."

Tyler entered the ICU nurses station and glanced around. At one of the charting computers sat a male nurse he recognized. When he approached, the young man glanced up. "Something I can do for you, Dr. Mathews?"

He decided to use the plausible story concocted during the eight-floor elevator ride. "Here's the deal"—he glanced at the nurse's ID tag dangling from a neck lanyard—"Paul. I'm writing up a case report to submit to *Neurosurgery.* In going over the chart I discovered a nurse, name of Gail Walker, took care of the patient. She works on this floor, doesn't she? She working today?"

Paul scratched his cheek, seemed to think about it. "Walker? Yeah, I seem to remember her. She left Maynard several months ago, I believe."

"Think you could find out where she went?"

"No problem."

Paul used the telephone to call the nursing office. After a brief conversation he hung up, turned to Tyler. "Story is she didn't show up for work a couple months ago. No one's heard of her since."

Back in the physicians lounge Tyler logged into QwestDex again. It listed two G. Walkers but neither phone answered after twenty rings. The G. Walker he was searching for could be married and listed under her husband's name. Or, she might live in one of the numerous suburbs of Seattle, leaving too many possibilities to search.

From his wallet he pulled a business card of a King County detective in his basketball league at the Seattle Athletic Club. He dialed Jim Laing's number with little hope of actually catching him, figuring he'd leave a voice mail. To his surprise, Jim answered.

"Jim, Tyler Mathews . . . yeah, I know, I missed the last game . . . look, this isn't about hoops. I need a favor . . ." He asked the detective to run Gail Walker's name through the DMV computer. A moment later he had an address.

8:10 A.M., SEATTLE FIELD OFFICE, FBI, FEDERAL OFFICE BUILDING

Special Agent in Charge Nina Stanford made no attempt to hide a yawn as she picked up a black Braun coffee carafe on the credenza behind her oak desk.

"My flight out of National had a cockpit light that wouldn't shut off when they tried to button down the plane, so we sat there for an extra goddamned hour while some engineers worked on it. I assumed it was either fixed or irrelevant since, in the end, we landed intact. In any event, I didn't get into Sea-Tac until eleven-thirty. Which meant I didn't even get to bed until after one this morning. Want yours black?"

Ferguson answered, "Black is fine." They were in her sixteenth-floor office of the Federal Building. The west side, with an expansive view of the harbor and huge orange dock cranes lining the Harbor Island piers. Framed pictures of the Director and the President hung on the drab federal green-gray walls as the only attempt at decorating.

Stanford wore one of her smartly tailored business suits. This one was light chocolate, which contrasted well with her flawless ebony skin. Ferguson wore his uniform—classic navy blazer, white shirt with a rep tie, and slacks. Slacks was the one change he made in recognition of the only two seasons he figured occurred in Seattle: suntan for summer, charcoal gray for winter. The routine had simplified his morning wardrobe selection ever since Susan, his fashion police, filed for divorce.

"Enough of my trip to Hooverville," Stanford said, handing him a white ceramic mug—the no-handle navy style she preferred. "Tell me what happened with the good Dr. Mathews?"

He accepted the warm mug. "That's one nervous-as-hell doc. Couldn't wait for the interview to be over once I broached the subject. Bottom line, he went out of his way to dodge answering anything. He was definitely holding back."

She swept a palm toward a chair in front of her desk. "Please." Then settled into the executive black leather chair behind the oak monster.

"What exactly was his reaction when you told him about it?"

"That's what made my impression. Guy didn't even bat an eyelash. It was like he expected to hear it. In fact, I got the impression he was kind of relieved to find out about it."

She blew across the surface of her coffee. "Then my next question is, is he likely to cooperate?"

"Didn't commit one way or the other. Guy's still gun-shy from the raw deal he ended up with in California . . . and I can't say that I blame him."

She sat, swiveling the chair side to side. "Couldn't be helped. You know that."

"True, in all likelihood . . . but still, you have to admit Mathews got handed the brown end of that particular stick."

Stanford hitched a shrug. "You present him with his *options*?" Her perfectly groomed eyebrows arched.

"Yep. And he's not a tail-wagging puppy over it."

She barked a sarcastic laugh. "Wouldn't expect him to be."

"Way we left it, he'll get back to me."

"When?"

"I plan on giving him two days before I start applying pressure."

"I wouldn't wait any longer than that." She paused a beat. "And if that doesn't work what's Plan B?"

8:10 A.M., Office of Jill Richardson,
VP of Risk Management

Tyler closed the door behind him. "Good morning."

Richardson looked up from her keyboard. "What's wrong? You look annoyed."

He dropped into the chair directly in front of her. "When are we going to file the sentinel-event report?"

"Never."

He sat in stunned silence for a beat. "You're joking."

She broke off a chunk of bagel sitting on a white paper plate next to a latte, both next to the keyboard. "Not at all. Right now there's not a shred of evidence Childs received an overdose. Sure, he suffered an unfortunate outcome from treatment—which, by the way, I know for certain, since I checked on this, is a known complication. And a complication in and of itself is not a sentinel event." She popped the bagel into her mouth.

She stopped chewing, put a hand to her mouth, asked, "What?"

"You're part of it, aren't you."

"Part of what?"

"The cover-up."

"Oh, for Pete's sake. That's ridiculous." She held up a finger until she could swallow. "Where's your evidence that the record was manipulated? The way I see it, your patient died. Understandably you feel some empathy toward him and the family. That's natural. I would hope any good doctor would react that way. But complications happen, Tyler. You need to move on."

"Bullshit. There's a problem with the computer and I'm not moving on 'til I find out what it is and get it fixed. And if you won't help me, I'll file the sentinel event myself."

She studied him a moment. "You're serious."

He let out an audible breath of exasperation. "Jesus, what does it take to get through to you? Damn right I'm serious."

"Do that with what you have now and you'll make a fool out of yourself. I don't want to see you do that."

"Then help me so I won't make a fool of myself."

"Fine. What do you want me to do?" She crossed her arms.

"I don't trust the information I've been getting from Day. I need to have someone outside this medical center and Med-InDx have a look at the backup records. I know for a fact that backups are made daily in a thirty-day cycle. There should be several days of records still out there with the original value still present. I want you to ask Khan to freeze the backup records for the day Childs was admitted. Then I want an independent evaluation of them."

Richardson swallowed again, dabbed her lips with a paper napkin. "I'm not going to do that."

He felt his jaw muscles tighten. "Why not?" They were giving him a headache.

With a resigned sigh she glanced away. When her eyes returned a moment later, she asked, "Did anyone else see the overdose value?"

An alarm went off in his mind. "Why do you ask?" He thought of Michelle.

"I simply want to know if you have any witnesses. Is there something wrong with that?"

"I don't like your tone. It implies I made the whole thing up."

"Why don't you answer my question instead of dodging it with righteous indignation? Is there a problem, Tyler?"

His gut said she knew something he didn't. "Dr. Lawrence, the anesthesiologist, saw it," and watched her response.

Another dismissive wave. "Lawrence of A Labia? The Dickless Dyke? Hah! Nobody in their right mind is going to believe her."

"Why not?"

"Because, Tyler, she's on probation for sexual harassment and she's really pissed about it. She'd just love to find a reason to slam us." She shook her head in apparent disgust. "Got anybody else who can back your story?"

Obviously she didn't know Michelle was dead. Or if she did, she covered it well. No, he decided, she didn't know.

"Jim Day. But under the circumstances . . ."

"Then let me tell you something I shouldn't. But I think you need to know this. And I'm telling this to you as a friend." She paused. "The other day, after we met with Khan, I went back to see him. I asked him to check the data field to see if there was any record of it being changed. There were two attempts to change the record but they were both unsuccessful."

Tyler's gut did a double somersault. "Did it show who?"

Her eyes hardened. "You know the answer, Tyler. Why do you even ask?"

"No, I don't know. What did it show?"

"You tried to change it the day after Larry Childs was admitted."

CHAPTER 15

Paranoia, fear, and anger began boiling in his chest. "Whoa, hold on a moment. What possible reason would I have to do something like that?"

"Ohhh, c'mon, you're a smart man. I can think of all sorts of motivations, most of them financial. I did some checking on you, Tyler. When you were ten your birth parents divorced. Although your mother wanted custody of you, you chose to live with your father. Although he could have afforded to send you to school, he believed his son should have to pull his own weight. As a result, you financed your own education with student loans. You were just climbing out from under a mountain of debt when you fell into"—with fingers of both hands she carved quotation marks in the air—"other problems. So, after my talk with Mr. Khan I asked myself, what possible motivation could Dr. Mathews have for diddling a data field? Know what the two primary motivators are for criminal actions?"

Before he could answer, she continued. "Money and sex. And since I could see no sex angle on this, I thought, 'Aha, money!' So I asked Mr. Khan to do some checking on you. Guess what he found? A Charles Schwab account in your name. Guess what else? It has only one stock in it. And lordy, lordy, guess which stock that might be? You guessed it, Prophesy. But instead of common stock, it's ten thousand calls. Now that's what I'd call leverage. How do you explain that, Tyler?"

Tyler jumped up and leaned over the desk to within a foot of her face. "This is bullshit. I'm being setup."

"Bullshit?" She pulled a sheet of paper from a stack and set it down in front of him. "This is bullshit?"

He picked it up. A Charles Schwab statement, his name and address listed correctly as the owner. Just as she claimed, December calls on Prophesy Inc., the only holding.

"Right now those calls are out of the money," Richardson said. "But should something happen to discredit Med-InDx, something that might sway the committee's recommendation, well then, those calls will be worth a small fortune."

"Where did you say you got this?" He held up the paper.

"Like I said, Yusef Khan."

He folded it. "Then you can get another copy." Could Ferguson find out who opened the account? Probably.

Tyler's beeper began chirping. He checked and found a STAT page to the Emergency Department.

John Brown, the ED physician who paged Tyler, lowered his voice and said, "I was hoping to catch you before you went in there." They stood inside the physicians work area—three walls of desk space with four computer terminals, three phones, and four rolling task chairs, two of which were occupied by scrub-clad ER docs typing and mousing instead of writing. The area always seemed too hot and carried a trace of body odor, as if this large alcove off the main hall had no ventilation.

"Is there a problem?"

"Frankly, yes. He's Roland Rowley's patient and although neurology isn't my specialty, I think Roland's missed the boat completely on this one. He didn't want me calling you, but I insisted."

Terrific, another turf war. "What's the issue? You said something about the patient blowing a pupil. If that's true, there shouldn't be any problem with you calling me." He'd consulted on a couple of Rowley's patients. A modestly competent neurologist although a bit pompous and opinionated.

"He's down here." Brown led Tyler down the hall to Trauma

Three. Ironically, the same room Larry Childs had been admitted to. "You'll see."

Brown opened the door and entered. Tyler followed. Hunched over the stretcher, Rowley peered through an ophthalmoscope into the patient's right eye. On the other side of the gurney a nurse busied herself tidying up the cardiac monitor leads. Brown cleared his throat, said, "Roland, Dr. Mathews is here."

Without looking up, the neurologist grumbled, "Everything is under control, Dr. Mathews, you can return to whatever you were doing. John made a huge mistake bothering you. I apologize for him." The nurse glanced nervously from Brown to Rowley and back again.

The emergency physician said, "Sorry, Roland, I know Mr. Torres *was* your patient, but the moment he was admitted to the ED he became my responsibility. And I'm telling you I want Tyler's opinion on this one." He turned to Tyler. "Mr. Torres is a forty-two-year-old Hispanic male who last week began to develop symptoms of aphasia—"

Straightening up, Rowley glowered at Brown and said, "It's a straightforward, garden-variety TIA for which I put him on some persantin and aspirin. But, unfortunately, it seems to have progressed on into an infarct. Textbook classic. No need to consult neurosurgery."

Ignoring him, Brown continued. "Thing is, before this all started he presented to the ED with complaints of ear pain. A diagnosis of otitis media was made and he was placed on Ampicillin. Today his wife brought him in saying she couldn't wake him up. He's been running a low-grade fever all week."

"Yes," Rowley interrupted again, "and the cultures proved Ampicillin to be the drug of choice. The ear infection was treated correctly. It's effectively a red herring. It has no bearing on the present diagnosis." He replaced the ophthalmoscope in the wall holder.

Tyler knew Brown was hinting at a brain abscess, a rare but potentially deadly complication of ear infections, treated or otherwise.

Moving closer to the stretcher he realized the patient's arms were rigidly flexed. Even from where he stood he could see the left pupil was dilated compared to the right. *Déjà vu all over again.* He thought of Larry Childs.

Tyler asked Brown, "Ordered a scan yet? A CT will do."

Brown shook his head. "Both MRIs are tied up with other emergencies and our CT is down."

Just then Torres's arms locked into rigid extension—a grave sign of brain deterioration due to increased pressure inside the skull. Tyler said to Rowley, "Even if this is a stroke, he's slipping down the tube as we speak. And there *is* a chance we're dealing with an abscess. If we don't do something now, sure as hell he's going to crash and burn." To the nurse he said, "Get me ten of Decadron and twenty-five grams of Mannitol STAT."

Brown said, "Oh, shit, here we go. Look at his respirations, he's gone into central neurogenic hyperventilation."

Tyler looked. Sure enough, Torres's breaths were rapid and deep, his neck muscles straining at each inhale. Another dire sign.

"Now just a minute here—" Rowley interposed himself between the stretcher and Tyler as if protecting the patient.

"Out of the way, Roland. I don't have time to debate this." Moving around the internist, Tyler asked Brown, "You have a twist drill set here?"

"Can't say that I've ever heard of it."

"I take that as a no."

Brown nodded.

Tyler picked up the wall telephone and punched zero. When the operator connected he said, "Give me surgery central supply." Then to Brown, "Call for a respirator and technician, pronto."

Rowley threw up both arms. "Mathews, this is too much. You're overstepping your boundary, here."

"Stow it, Roland." Then back into the phone, "This is Dr. Mathews. I'm in the ER. I need a twist drill tray and I need it now. Have someone run it over. *Now.*" He hung up.

Tyler grabbed the otoscope from the wall holder and peered into Torres's right ear. Clean. The tympanic membrane glistened back at him. Next, the left. Here the membrane was inflamed and bulging from yellow pus trapped behind it.

The nurse charged into the room holding two syringes. "Here they are. Which one you want first."

Tyler grabbed the one closest. "I'll give this one. Push the other." He glanced at the label: 10 mg Decadron.

Another nurse hurried in. "What can I do to help?"

"I need hair clippers, razor, and a prep kit. Then get a Foley into this guy."

Tyler put a palm against Rowley's chest and pushed him away. "Look, either help or get out of the way." He grabbed the IV line, found the rubber injection port, and plunged in the needle.

The nurse returned with the shaving equipment. A second later a surgery tech carrying a sterile pack came through the same door-way. "Someone call for a twist drill set?"

Tyler pulled over a stainless-steel Mayo stand. "Just dump it here." He turned Torres's chin toward his right shoulder and with the hair clippers cleared a patch of black hair just above his left ear. After shaving this with a safety razor, he painted the area with Betadine.

As Tyler pulled the Mayo stand next to the gurney, Rowley said, "I am personally going to see that this is brought up to the Medical Executive committee. You're doing this without an operative consent."

Brown called over, "Hey, good point. His wife's out in the waiting room. I'll go get one from her."

"Thanks." Tyler slipped on a mask and sterile gloves, opened the sterile layer of the pack, and draped off the prepped area with four blue sterile towels, which he clipped together at the corners of the opening.

He waved a syringe at a nurse. "Need some Xylocaine with epinephrine."

The nurse held out a vial. Tyler punctured the protective membrane with a needle and withdrew five ccs which he injected in the skin where he intended to drill. He stabbed a small scalpel blade through the wheal and for the next thirty seconds pressed a small cotton sponge over the wound to stop the bleeding. Next he selected a small drill bit from a choice of three and tightened it into the chuck of a stainless-steel hand drill. Carefully, he slipped the drill through the stab wound and hit skull.

He jutted his chin toward Torres's head, told the nurse, "Need some help here. Give me some counterpressure.

Gently at first he drilled, feeling the tip bite into bone. Ninety percent of this technique was feel, he knew. Now that he could appreciate the force against the bit he turned it a little faster. A few turns and the bit advanced, dropped through the outer bone layer into the thin marrow space. It "caught" again as it started cutting into the inner bone layer. He drilled slowly now, waiting to feel the final slight catch as the tip penetrated the skull and pushed up against the dura. There! He felt it.

Not wanting to drive bone flecks into the underlying brain he withdrew the drill and wiped the bloody tip clean with a fresh sponge. In the background he could hear another Rowley rant. *Fuck him,* he thought and concentrated on sliding the drill bit back through the scalp wound on into the skull hole. He gently tapped the drill point against the dura, feeling the tough membrane give way ever so slightly. With a quick twist, the drill point shredded the dura, giving him a path to pass a needle.

Brown entered the room waving a piece of paper. "Got it. You can shut up now, Roland."

Tyler replaced the drill on the tray and sorted through the long biopsy needles. He picked a long round-tipped one with a single side port and a core filled with a removable stylet, which he tested to make sure it removed easily.

For a moment Tyler studied Torres's head, imagining the underlying anatomy in three dimensions, a process he excelled at. His drilled hole was directly above the left ear, placing him above the mastoid sinus, which, he believed, would be the nidus the infection had spread up from, probably spreading along the veins that drained the brain. If so, if he passed the needle slightly downward toward the base of the skull, chances were he'd hit the abscess.

Big if, he realized, as Rowley's threats echoed in his mind.

He glanced up. Rowley glared back at him. "You've done it now, Mathews. You better pray you're right, otherwise I'll have the executive committee strip your privileges from you."

Suddenly his confidence vanished. Other diagnostic possibilities began to flood his brain, none of them very likely, but neither was a brain abscess—statistically speaking. *C'mon, pal, what else can it be?*

Holding the needle between thumb and forefinger, bracing the side of his hand against Torres's scalp, Tyler gently slid the needle into the hole. Probing, layer by layer, he worked the needle tip down to the dura. Next the tip entered soft mushy brain with a feel obviously much different than normal tissue.

"Feels too mushy," he muttered to no one in particular, trying to buoy his confidence.

Means nothing except it's abnormal, he decided. *Could still represent a stroke, just like Rowley claims it is.*

Slowly, gently, he pushed the needle deeper, the tip of an index finger transmitting subtle, tactile messages to his brain.

"There! It hit resistance."

He probed again. Clearly resistance. An abscess capsule maybe? Or even tumor. His fingertip tapped the needle a little deeper, breaking through the resistance into another mushy area.

Left hand holding the needle perfectly still, his right hand pulled out the stylus. Green, foul-smelling pus poured out. Relief surged through his body. He glanced at Rowley who turned away muttering.

"We need some culture tubes," he called to Brown. "Anaerobic and aerobic. And I want a STAT gram stain, culture and sensitivities, and . . ." so relieved, his mind went blank. "Shit, just give me the whole enchilada."

He selected a glass syringe from the sterile tray, attached it to the needle, and slowly aspirated a full ten ccs of pus. He handed the gunk-filled syringe to Brown and picked up another. Again he filled it. A total of twenty ccs withdrawn. *That should make a huge difference,* he thought.

Torres began to groan and tried to move his head. "Hold on, José." Tyler pulled the needle from his brain, having withdrawn enough pus to decompress the life-threatening pressure.

With a butterfly Band-Aid Tyler closed the small stab wound, then stripped off his gloves. Off in one corner Rowley chewed his lower lip. Tyler caught his eye for a moment and held it before turning to Brown and saying, "I'll go put a note in the chart."

Just then his beeper went off.

"This is Dr. Mathews. Did someone page me?" Tyler sat in front of a computer terminal in the Emergency Department work area, his left shoulder wedging the phone against his ear while he held up his beeper and rechecked the displayed number. It wasn't familiar but the prefix could very well be within the medical center exchange.

"Dr. Mathews, thanks for calling back so promptly. This is Lieutenant Campbell, Maynard Security. Could we meet outside your locker in the dressing room." It was not a question.

CHAPTER 16

A fist gripped Tyler's intestines and twisted. A cold feeling of déjà vu swept through him like an arctic gust. "My locker?" He flashed on California.

"Yes sir."

He glanced around the area in panic, instinct urging him to get out of the hospital. "Why would you want to meet me at my locker?"

"I don't want to go into it over the phone." This said with a sharp edge of impatience. "If you please, just meet me at your locker in, say, two or three minutes."

"Sorry, I'm busy in the Emergency Department at the moment."

"You know what, I'm a very busy person too, so I don't exactly have a world of time to dick around with you about this. Let me put it to you this way. That locker of yours *will* be opened in three minutes with or without you standing there to witness it. After that, closing it will be *your* problem. Understand?"

The line went dead.

Tyler quickly terminated the connection to Torres's chart and told the nurse he'd be back in a few minutes. He chose a side stairwell to climb from A Level to the second floor, taking stairs two at a time. As he walked the block-long hall from the south to the north end of the building, a nauseating premonition churned his gut. Another setup. He was certain of it. Someone knew exactly what happened in California and was copying it.

The question was, who?

He would need a lawyer, of course. A criminal defense lawyer. And a good one. But how to find one?

He rounded the corner to the short hall that ended at automatic double doors serving the operating rooms. On his right, the women's locker room. To his left, the men's locker room. An officer in a black MMC security uniform stood outside the door, waiting. Presumably Lieutenant Campbell. Dr. Jean Anderson, Director of Medical Affairs, stood next to him wearing a dour expression and a pale violet Armani suit with a blue silk scarf around her neck. Both went well with her short-cropped silver hair.

She said, "Sorry to have to do this, Tyler, but . . ."

"Your lack of sincerity is deeply touching, Jean."

Campbell said to her, "I'll go in first, make sure everybody's ready to receive a female visitor."

With Campbell gone, Tyler asked her, "What's this all about, Jean?"

She hesitated a second. "Someone swiped some narcotics from the anesthesia pharmacy."

"And an anonymous tip just happened to finger me, huh? How convenient."

She adjusted the gold Lady Rolex on her wrist. "Sarcasm isn't going to win you any Brownie points on this one, Tyler, so stow it. Besides, you're in more trouble than just this. The Quality Assurance committee has been asked to review a recent surgical mortality. Larry Childs?"

He started to defend himself when Campbell's head popped out from behind the door. "Coast is clear."

Heart pounding, fingers tingling, Tyler led them to his locker. He picked up the combination lock, missed the first number, and started over again. This time the lock clicked. He opened the narrow metal door and stepped aside without even looking, knowing exactly what they'd find.

Campbell stepped up to the locker. "My, oh, my, what do we have here?"

Tyler heard the clink of glass vials being collected but said nothing. A bonfire erupted in his chest but instinct warned not to say a word at this moment.

Anderson said, "Dr. Mathews, as of now your admitting privileges are suspended pending a hearing with the Medical Executive Board. You have the right to care for any patients still in hospital, but you will not be allowed to admit any new patients. Is this clear?"

Fuming, Tyler sat in his office and tried to think through his next move. Call Ferguson, tell him what happened, and ask for help? Only way Ferguson would help is if Tyler spied for the FBI and that too was an almost certain route to self-destruction—a lesson he learned too well the last time he tried to help the feds. And even if Ferguson agreed to intervene, what could he possibly do or say? Support Tyler's claim that the drugs were planted in his locker? Hardly. Ferguson would never believe him. Not when he held a fistful of Tyler's forged Ambien prescriptions.

Shit! He reached in his desk drawer for a Tums.

And what would happen to him now? Sure, he could deny stealing the drugs, but who would believe him? Especially with him recently graduating a drug rehab program.

He flashed on Nancy. She'd never take him back if she found out. The gut rototiller revved its engine.

You're really screwed this time, pal.

He noticed the time and realized he'd completely forgotten his interview with Dr. Beck. He picked up the phone and dialed her number. No answer.

For a distraction Tyler turned to the computer and moused the Med-InDx icon. Might as well finish the note on Torres. The chart popped up along with a message notifying him of some preliminary lab results. He clicked the dialog box and found the gram stain findings were back from microbiology. Interested now, he clicked that tab.

And saw:

Gram stain shows numerous white cells, a large degree of necrotic debris, and four-plus gram negative rods. Cultures and sensitivities pending.

Gram negative rods? Tyler vaguely remembered Brown saying something about gram positive cocci, not rods. A completely different type of bacteria. He checked the lab report from Torres's earlier visit, the one prompting treatment with Ampicillin. Correct. Gram positive cocci were cultured from the original bacterial cultures.

Tyler leaned back and stared at the ceiling, mulling this over. "Huh!" He leaned forward, grabbed the telephone, and dialed the Emergency Department and was put on hold. A few moments later Brown picked up.

"John, Tyler. Look, I was calling about our patient Torres."

"Nice job, by the way. You ran out on me before I had a chance to thank you."

"What I'm calling about is, do you remember the results of the original gram stain?"

"I'd have to look to be sure, but I'm almost certain it was gram positive cocci. Why?"

Tyler's suspicions increased. "It's now gram negative rods."

Brown gave a long slow whistle. "Holy mackerel! No wonder the bug juice didn't touch him. Jesus. How could I have given him the wrong drug?"

"Not necessarily. Maybe the abscess came from a different source. Blood borne, maybe."

"Nice try, Tyler, but I wasn't born yesterday. I screwed up if it's gram negative."

"Don't be so sure," he said. "Let's see what the sensitivities come back as. Even treated otitis can become an abscess if it wants to." In the background phone noise, Tyler heard Brown's name paged over the intercom.

"Uh-oh, gotta run."

"Bye."

Tyler sat back and thought it over again. Brown was a superb ER doc. Not one to make a mistake of that magnitude. He checked the chart again. The original culture clearly documented gram positive cocci, not gram negative rods.

Tyler burnt a copy of Torres's prior lab results to CD. He knew full well that Khan, or anybody else with system administrator privileges, would be able to document the download if they were monitoring him, but so what? He was on record as having treated the patient in the ED. He had a perfect right to access this chart.

A plan began crystallizing in his mind.

Five minutes later Tyler knocked on Yusef Khan's open office door. Khan glanced up from a printout on his desk and smiled. "Yes, Doctor, what is it I can be doing for you?"

Tyler entered the office. "I believe I've found another chart error."

The man slid off his reading glasses and placed one stem in the corner of his mouth. "Another chart problem? Another one of your so-called hacker problems?" He grinned at Tyler.

"Yes," he admitted, studying Khan's reaction. "Only now I've changed my thinking. I don't think a hacker's the problem at all. I think the problem's in the system. A bug in the software."

The grin vanished from Khan's face. "A bug in the system? What kind of bug?"

"One that corrupts database fields."

"This is so?" Khan stiffened and removed the stem from the corner of his mouth. "You have proof of this?"

"Suddenly you're interested, are you? Sorry to disappoint, but no, I don't have proof. I just have an example." He gave him Torres's name and chart number, then had him pull the chart up on the monitor. Tyler pointed out the problem with the initial gram stain and the one taken earlier and explained the resultant disastrous abscess from an erroneously treated infection.

"But cannot they be different, these two infections?" Khan asked.

"Theoretically, yes. Probabilistically, no."

"And why are you showing me this?"

Tyler's turn to grin. *Gotcha!* "Because, my friend, if anything in that record changes now, you'll have to believe me. Yes?"

From Khan's office Tyler headed straight for Jill Richardson's office. When he got there her inner office door was closed. He said to her secretary, "I need to speak with Ms. Richardson, it's important."

Tony glanced at the wall clock. "She should be finished in another ten minutes if you'd like to wait outside. I'll fetch you when she's available."

After making himself comfortable on a contemporary couch in the administration general waiting area, he pulled out his cellular phone and again dialed Robin Beck's phone number. After ten rings he hung up. Still no answer.

After about fifteen minutes of cooling his heels, Tony floated forth to announce, "Ms. Richardson will see you now."

She was leaning toward the computer monitor, apparently catching up on e-mail when he entered the office and closed the door.

Jill double-clicked the mouse, then turned to him. "So, Dr. Mathews, what can I do for you?"

"I found another patient whose treatment was compromised because of a problem with the EMR."

Her face turned serious. "Really! Tell me about it."

Tyler told her how Torres's bacteria had been erroneously reported as gram positive cocci when they probably really were gram negative rods and how this more than likely resulted in an inadequately treated infection becoming a life-threatening brain abscess.

"Couldn't it be possible that both organisms were present initially and the antibiotics treated one, allowing the other to become the abscess?"

He shook his head. "Nope."

She sat back, fingers steepled, tapping her lips, and seemed to consider his story. After a moment she said, "What do you plan to do?"

"Do? I'm doing it. I'm reporting this to you as head of Risk Management. And as such I expect *you* to do something about it. There's a serious security flaw in the Med-InDx software." He folded his arms and met her stare. "So, Ms. Richardson, what are *you* going to do about it?"

She studied her manicure. "I'm not a doctor but I doubt seriously you can prove those results were reported inaccurately."

"The cultures will prove it."

She shook her hair, then combed it back in place with her fingertips. "One case doesn't prove anything."

"Perhaps. But you and I both know there are other cases, don't we."

She didn't answer.

He decided to push the gambit. "We both know there's a problem with the medical record. The only way I can prove it is to find some other cases like mine. I want you to give me the names of any other patients who've had any complication you believe might have resulted from a record error."

She cast a puzzled expression. "I'm not sure I understand where you're coming from. I thought you didn't have enough data to show there's a problem. Now you do? On what basis?"

"Why is this sounding like you're stonewalling? The more you and Khan insist there's no problem, the more I think there is. All I'm asking is for you to help me do a root cause analysis. Are you telling me you—VP of Risk Management—refuse to investigate a problem that's a potential risk to patient safety?"

"Are we back to the conspiracy theory now? Hackers and cover-ups? Because if you are, I have to tell you I think that's ridiculous. Yes, of course I know about any major complication that occurs in this medical center. I have to. That's my job. Be proactive; make sure there's nothing that's going to result in adverse medical center exposure. And if there is, enact the appropriate damage control. If there had been a serious concern about any computer security problems affecting patient safety, I'd know about it. There isn't."

"You're blowing smoke at me, Ms. Richardson. Surely there are cases where physicians or nurses have blamed the system. Are you telling me there's been nothing even close to that?" He locked eyes with her.

"I don't understand why you're so adamant about this hacker theory. Do you have any idea how much testing was done before we allowed that software to be installed and tested here? The HIPAA requirements alone required an entire extra layer of security. Do you really believe Med-InDx and Maynard would allow a security-flawed system to be used on patients?"

Tyler laughed. "C'mon, you're joking, right? No software system—especially one that's still in development—is secure. Certainly not one that hasn't been in widespread use. Hell, look at Microsoft. They send out Windows patches every week and still don't have it right. And that's only an operating system, not a complete information system. Tell me you're not trying to sell me on the possibility our EMR's the one and only exception in the universe." He shook his head slowly. "I won't buy it."

She seemed to consider this.

He added, "Look at it this way. Let's say you're right and nobody's ever mentioned a problem before. Does that mean there isn't one? One that no one knows about? Of course not. And if there is, it's killing patients. Would you, as the head of Risk Management like to stand by and know that possibility was never investigated?"

When she still didn't answer he added, "I already know about Dr. Robin Beck. She claims there was a problem with the computer. So there must be others."

She gave a resigned sigh and threw up both hands. "Alright already. I'll give you the chart identifiers of three cases that struck me as suspicious, *but* only on one condition."

"And that is?"

"If anything turns up, you'll discuss it with me before doing anything foolish."

Tyler punched his chest with a thumb. "Me do something foolish?"

She grimaced. "Especially you." She paused, seemed to be thinking of something. "But for what it's worth, you should also know a few things about Dr. Beck. The incident was investigated. She clearly made a mistake. Also, she's an impaired physician. Alcohol and drugs. We have a long record of complaints about her. The incident you're speaking of was the final straw. We had no choice but to let her go. She's now got a ten-million-dollar malpractice suit against her on the case in question and that's probably going to settle before the insurance company spends any more money on expert witnesses. And she's now in rehab."

"I still want to look at the record."

6:15 P.M., QUEEN ANNE HILL

With an uneasy gut feeling, Tyler approached the front door to the small, gray with white trim Dutch Colonial. Beck hadn't answered any of his phone calls all day. That alone didn't bother him as much as the fact that no voice mail had picked up either. He didn't know many doctors who made themselves totally unreachable. None that were successful, that is.

He rang the front doorbell.

No answer.

He rang again.

Still no answer.

He took a cracked concrete path around the house to a postage-sized, dandelion-infested patch of grass surrounded by a weathered cedar fence. An unattached garage held a red Mazda Miata. Top down.

He walked up onto the back porch and peered through the

glass window in the center of the door, saw a commercial-grade stainless-steel gas stove, a Sub-Zero refrigerator matching white European-style cabinets. Obviously remodeled within the past few years. A coffee mug sat on the Corian counter next to the sink. The well-equipped kitchen of someone who likes to cook. Not the kitchen of a substance abuser.

He rang the back bell and pounded on the door.

Two minutes later he sat in his car trying to curb a bad feeling brewing in his gut. He'd start calling again in the morning.

CHAPTER 17

Back in his car, cell phone in hand, Tyler unfolded the scrap of paper with Gail Walker's phone number scribbled across the top. He dialed. It rang twice before connecting to a computerized female voice informing him the number had been disconnected. Just as it had earlier that day. He punched off and for a moment stared at the paper—her address scrawled below the phone number—weighing his next move. Walker's address appeared to be in Ballard, a neighborhood not that far from Beck's Queen Anne residence. Why not?

He fired up the ignition, took a route off the northwest side of Queen Anne Hill down onto Fifteenth NE, then north across the Ballard Bridge. He found her building more easily than a parking space. After dumping the Range Rover next to the curb on a side street, he walked two blocks back to the five-story stucco building. Either condos or apartments, he reckoned, while jogging up three concrete steps to a glass front door. Recessed into the wall to the right of the door was an intercom system. He scrolled through the directory without finding Walker. A small sign at the bottom of the intercom read Manager, Unit 102. He punched in the number, hit the # key. A moment later a woman's voice answered.

Tyler asked, "Are you the manager?"

"Hold on a second. I'll get my husband." The intercom clicked off.

Just as Tyler was about to punch in the number again, a tall thin man in Levi's and a denim shirt appeared in the lobby and approached the door. He cracked it enough to look out and ask, "May I help you?"

"I'm trying to find Gail Walker."

The man's eyes narrowed. "And you are?"

Tyler pulled out his wallet. "I'm a doctor from Maynard Hospital. She used to work there." He displayed his Washington State professional license. "I need to speak with her about a case she was involved with several months ago."

The man opened the door farther but didn't offer Tyler entrance. "Doesn't live here no more."

"When did she move?" The uneasiness in Tyler's gut intensified.

"Don't know, exactly. Matter of fact, we're not sure what happened to her. One month she didn't pay her rent, which wasn't like her at all. I started going to her apartment, knocking on the door, but she never answered. Got to the point her mail completely filled up the mailbox, so I finally felt forced to open her unit. All her things were there, but she wasn't. Haven't seen hide nor hair of her since."

"And you've never heard from her since? No change of address notice? Nothing like that?"

The man shook his head. "Nope."

"And her furniture and things? They still in the apartment?"

"Nope. In storage. We ended up renting the unit a month ago." He gave a guilt-absolving shrug. "Had no choice, what with her not paying rent."

8:55 P.M.

Flat on his back, head propped against a pillow, Tyler clutched a longneck Red Hook and studied his beige living-room ceiling while a cloud of anxiety churned his stomach. On the stereo Esther Phillips was singing "Sweet Touch of Love." How long had it been since he'd last listened to this CD? He loved Esther's distinctive voice. Even more, he loved these particular lyrics. They reminded him of Nancy.

The irony of his fondness for Phillips's singing hit him. Throughout her career she battled narcotics addiction. Now he was battling a narcotics rap even though not addicted. *Shit!*

Unable to lay still, he got up and paced.

What to do? The only way out of this mess seemed to be finding proof of the software bug. But both Beck and Walker were gone. There had to be another way.

He set the beer on the faux rattan coffee table and picked up the portable phone and thumbed redial. He let Nancy's phone ring ten times before hanging up. He needed to talk with her, get her take on the situation. That's what they'd always done in the past when either one had a problem. God, he missed her now that she was back in his life.

The song ended and the next cut began. Tyler checked the time. He'd already made up his mind: tonight no sleeping pill. No excuses. No matter what.

He shut off the CD player and headed for the bedroom. If need be, he'd lie in bed all night staring at the ceiling rather than pop even half an Ambien.

11:13 P.M.

Tyler listened to an overhead jet head for Sea-Tac and tried to force his muscles to relax. But Michelle's death served a premonition warning about Robin Beck. The fact that neither she nor an answering machine had answered the phone ate away at his mind, leaving unsettling anxiety. He changed positions, tried to think of Nancy.

12:32 A.M.

Tyler sat on the edge of the bed and palm-wiped his mouth. What would be worse eight hours from now, being too tired to think carefully or having taken a half Ambien to get to sleep? Once he put the question in this light, the answer seemed obvious.

Weighed down with regret—but, hey, what was he supposed to do?—Tyler walked into the bathroom and chewed a half tablet of Ambien.

7:45 A.M.

With the all-too-familiar fuzziness of sleep deprivation accentuated by residual Ambien molecules coating his neurons, Tyler set a Starbucks latte grande on his desk and flipped on the computer.

Morning rounds, or the lack of them, had ignited another surge of anger at whoever planted the drugs in his locker. He had discharged his last post-op patient and then rounded on Torres, the bright spot of the morning. By now Torres was sitting up in bed talking fluently. Rowley hadn't yet seen him today, but from the looks of things, Torres could be transferred out of the Neuro ICU.

The nauseating Windows introductory melody played, bringing Tyler back to the task at hand. He spread the paper listing the patients' names and chart numbers on the desk and moused the medical record icon. A moment later he was ready to begin. He entered the first patient's chart number and hit ENTER.

REQUESTOR NOT AUTHORIZED appeared on the screen.

He typed the second patient's name. Same response.

Tyler crumpled the piece of paper into a ball and threw it against the wall. "Shit!"

Fuming, he typed in Torres's number. The chart immediately appeared, no problem. He requested the chart of the patient he had discharged a half hour ago. It popped up too.

He picked up the wadded paper and smoothed it on the desk, then tried accessing the third patient. Again, access denied.

Still fuming, he picked up the telephone and dialed the IT help desk. A young-sounding female answered with a chirpy, "Help desk, may I have your name and department?"

"Tyler Mathews, Neurosurgery."

He heard keyboard clicking followed by, "And what can I do for you, Dr. Mathews?"

"I can't seem to access several medical records. Is there something wrong with the server this morning?"

"Not that I know of. Hold on, let me check." A moment later she returned with, "All servers are functioning, Doctor. Tell you what, let me check on your account. I'll be right back." *Click.*

Vivaldi's "Four Seasons" filled the cyber void. Tyler waited.

About thirty seconds later she was back on the line with, "I'm sorry, Dr. Mathews, it appears that your account is restricted to only patients you're presently seeing either as an inpatient or outpatient." So mechanical was her delivery, Tyler almost mistook her for a recording.

His anger spiked again. "Does it say who placed that restriction on my account?"

"No, sir. I guess you'd have to ask one of the system administrators for that kind of information."

"Thank you."

"Have a nice day."

You've got to be kidding. He slammed down the receiver.

Khan's office door was closed when Tyler arrived, so he banged on the frosted glass window, almost breaking the pane. From inside came a muted, "Come in, please."

Khan sat behind his cluttered desk, his white shirtsleeves rolled to the elbows, computer printouts spread across the surface before him. His expression remained masked when Tyler locked eyes with him.

"Good morning, Dr. Mathews. May I interest you in some tea? I am just fixing myself a cup." He nodded at a chipped royal blue mug on the credenza behind him. A heating element plugged into a nearby wall outlet submerged in the water.

"I want to know why my medical-records privileges have been restricted."

"Ah yes." Khan interlaced his fingers on the desktop and straightened his posture, striking the pose of a high school teacher about to address the class. "You see, Dr. Mathews, I am only following protocol."

"And what protocol is that?"

Khan now seemed uncomfortable, "Ah, well, yes . . ." and broke off eye contact. "For some reason—and I am not told these reasons, Doctor—you are being classified as impaired. The rules regarding access to medical records forbid impaired physicians from accessing all but their own patients." His eyes dropped to his folded hands. "I am sorry but I am only following orders."

"Bullshit. Orders from whom?"

This time Khan met his stare. "This I cannot tell you."

"You can't tell me or you won't tell me?"

Khan shrugged. "What difference does this make if in the end you do not find out?"

Only better judgment restrained Tyler's reply. Instead, he turned and stormed out of the office, slamming the door behind him.

"Got a second?" Back in the Neurosurgery Department, Tyler stood at the door to Bill Leung's office. His partner sat at his desk sorting through a pile of phone messages. Tyler wondered if Bill—or any of his partners for that matter—knew about the drugs in his locker yet.

"What's up?"

Tyler entered Bill's office. More spacious than his own, more personal touches too—like the green shade banker's lamp and the silver-framed picture of his wife, Anita. It made Tyler want a picture of Nancy on his desk too. The joke, Tyler realized, was that with Bill married to a Caucasian, if the four of them ever went out to dinner, people would automatically assume Nancy was Bill's wife.

"Want your opinion on a case." He moved to Bill's desk. "The patient's name is Torres." He watched Bill turn to the computer and pull up Med-InDx and log in. Once the chart was on the screen, he went through the case with him.

Leung drummed his fingers on the desk. "I'm not sure I understand the problem. Looks to me like you handled this situation perfectly. Oh, sure, Rowley can be a real butthook when he's on the defensive, but hey, who isn't at times?"

"Thanks. Just wanted to know if you would've handled it the same way."

His partner scrutinized him a moment. "Sure there isn't something else to all this?"

"Nah. Thanks." Tyler saluted, turned, and left.

Back in his own office Tyler glanced back up and down the hall he'd just traveled. Satisfied no one was watching, he closed and locked the door—a practice completely foreign to him. Before now, his office door always stood open and unlocked. He sat down at his desk, flipped on the computer. As he waited for the machine to boot his eyes wandered out the window. Across a small alleyway another professional office building loomed. He pushed out of the chair and pulled the cord to close the Venetian blinds. Satisfied no one could observe from the other building, he dropped back down, sucked in a deep breath, and wiped both palms on his thighs.

Using Bill's password, he signed into Med-InDx. Once there, he pulled up the record of Tyrell Washington, the first of three patient names Jill had given him. His fingers froze over the mouse. The admitting physician was Robin Beck. Michelle's image flashed through his mind along with their conversation in the cafeteria the night of Larry Childs's admit. This had to be the incident Michelle had mentioned.

He punched the left mouse button, moving the screen deeper into the record. Washington had been admitted to the Emergency Department last November in coma. Robin Beck made the diagnosis of diabetic coma based on the history in the record. She had treated him with a large dose of insulin and charted the reason as being the suspected diagnosis of ketoacidoses due to lack of insulin. Problem was, the chart now showed that Washington wasn't diabetic and certainly wasn't taking insulin. Washington died in cardiac arrest only minutes after being treated.

The telephone rang. Tyler jumped, his heart rate racing. He picked it up.

Click. Then dial tone.

The caller ID was already blank by the time he thought to look. A chill snaked down his back. Coincidence or simply a wrong number? Another chill nudged a sense of urgency into his work. He picked up the paper and typed in the second medical record number.

The next case was just as interesting. Later that same month a second case had been reported to Risk Management. A GI bleeder in the Intensive Care Unit had been transfused with mismatched blood resulting in a massive transfusion reaction and then in fatal cardiac arrest. It took a few mouse clicks to find the nurse of record, Gail Walker.

How could this possibly happen, he wondered. *This is exactly the type of screwup electronic medical records eliminate.* He knew before even checking what the record would show. Sure enough, it appeared that Walker had never scanned the bar-coded label on the bag of red cells before hanging it. Clearly Walker's error. Or at least, that's how it looked to anyone investigating the complication.

Tyler paced nervously around the cramped office, his need to move fueled by restlessness and a gnawing anxiety in the pit of his stomach.

He dropped back into the chair and entered the last of the three names, hit ENTER.

This case occurred just last January. A nurse injected a patient in the Cardiac Care Unit with a potent antiarrhythmia medication less than an hour after a prior dose of the same drug had been given. The second nurse, the one responsible for the mishap, swore that the prior injection had not been recorded on the medical record. In fact, upon review of the record, the pharmacy portion clearly showed the drug being prepared and delivered to the CCU twice in less than an hour, a finding directly supporting the nurse's assertion. The nurse responsible for the first injection also swore she had given and charted the injection—a claim the chart clearly supported.

"This isn't right," Tyler muttered. He stood and paced, trying to figure exactly what didn't set well with this case.

Then it hit him. If, as the first nurse claimed, the first dose had been ordered, filled by the pharmacy, and injected—as the chart claimed—a second could *not* have been given unless specifically ordered by the physician. This is because safeguards embedded in the software would have alerted the pharmacist that a second dose was being ordered during the period when a second dose would have been lethal. So, if all were working properly the managing physician would have had to overwrite the system with a detailed explanation to justify a second dose within this short time frame. Clearly, that step hadn't happened.

Whoever was behind the cover-up had done an elegant job hiding the first two cases. Not so for this third case. This was exactly the type of information Ferguson was looking for and exactly the type of proof Tyler needed to exonerate himself.

Tyler burned a copy of all three cases to a CD.

Finished, he removed the silver disk. For a moment he sat still, rocking it back and forth slightly, staring at the rainbow dancing across the disk's shiny surface. Another idea hit, he slid the disk back into the still open bay and pressed it home.

In the search field he typed Torres's name, hit ENTER. A moment later his brain abscess patient's chart appeared on the screen. He moused the Laboratory tab, then the microbiology section.

This time, instead of gram positive cocci, the gram stain reported gram negative rods. Next, he checked Torres's pharmacy records. Changed also.

Tyler fought off a faint smile of satisfaction. *Just like surgery,* he thought, *when you get too sure of yourself, that's when a complication jumps up and bites you in the ass. Be careful now, pal. Don't let your guard down.*

He burned Torres's information to the CD also.

Task finished, he removed the silver disk from the computer and glanced around the office for a place to hide it.

CHAPTER 18

Yusef Khan's computer emitted a series of beeps like a robin chirping. They drew his attention away from the work at hand. A glance at the nineteen-inch LCD screen immediately focused his eyes to a red flashing dialog box. This general alarm was programmed to trigger for events of a security nature as well as any number of other contingencies a person holding his administrator-level privileges chose to set. During any given day he might monitor for any number of incidents, such as if any of his technicians were sneaking time on porn sites. As Chief Information Officer he also spent some time each day spot-checking the work of his system administrators—those people who made sure the hundreds of Maynard Medical Center PCs continued to function seamlessly across a network of numerous servers and storage units.

He moused the cursor onto the box and clicked.

The computer responded with: 191.90.26.05 ACTIVATED.

His interest in the message perked up. This was the medical center internal network address for Tyler Mathews's computer. But all the number told Khan was that the computer in Mathews's office was logged into the network. It did not reveal its user. Keeping the present window active, Khan queried another program for the password used to log onto the system.

It did not match Mathews's password.

Next, he ran the password through the database and found

it belonged to a William Leung. A quick scan of the user directory showed Leung was a neurosurgeon, one of Mathews's partners.

This left two possibilities. Leung could be using Mathews's machine. Or Mathews had borrowed Leung's password. There was a good way to settle the question.

Khan dialed Mathews's telephone. It rang once before Mathews answered with, "Mathews here."

Smiling, Khan hung up. Persistent fellow, that Mathews. Sly too.

He checked another program he'd set to monitor all keystrokes from Mathews's computer. It was functioning well.

Out of curiosity, Khan downloaded what had been recorded so far this morning. One by one he issued the same commands and was pleased with what he found. Tyler had called up the medical record system and then a patient's chart. A bit more searching perked up Khan's interest further. The record of interest was of a patient who had died last November. Not only that, Mathews had never been involved with the patient case. Interesting.

He cross-checked the patient's record number with a list he kept hidden in the top drawer of his desk. It matched a number on the list.

Khan picked up the phone again and dialed a number from memory. A moment later a man answered. Khan said, "It's me, Khan. Just as we suspected, our friend is snooping again."

– – – – – – – – – – –

Tyler decided to hide the CD in a plain manila business envelope and leave it in clear sight on his desk, figuring something out in the open wouldn't draw any attention if someone came looking for it. He couldn't shake the feeling of being watched— either directly or electronically.

You're losing it, pal. That was totally paranoid.

The telephone rang.

"Mathews here."

"Tyler, Steve Rolfson."

Tyler exhaled a deep breath and relaxed. "Hey, Steve, did you just try to call me a few minutes ago?"

"No. Why?"

"Nothing." The chill returned. "Wrong number, I guess."

"What I'm calling about, I just finished the brain cutting on your patient Childs. Thought you might want to hear what I found."

Tyler picked up a pen and pulled over a piece of scratch paper. "Shoot."

"You already had it nailed. Clear-cut case of radiation necrosis. Not a doubt about it. Want to come down and view the specimen before I sign off on the case?"

Tyler started drumming the pen against the desk. "No, Steve, but thanks for asking."

"Anything else you want to know?"

Yeah, but you can't help me with those questions. "No. That was all. Thanks again." Tyler hung up with a sense of anticlimax.

For a long time he sat staring at the manila envelope, wondering what to do with the information inside. Without a doubt it verified Ferguson's claim of a problem with the Med-InDx system. He considered calling him but immediately rejected the idea. Before turning anything over to the FBI he wanted a tangible assurance of immunity from repercussion. Not only that, he wanted it in his lawyer's hands. Once bitten . . .

Talk to Jill about it? Ferguson's warning to trust no one in the MMC administration popped into his consciousness again.

Nancy. If there was one person he needed to talk to, it was Nancy. He glanced at his watch. She should be back sometime this evening. He dialed Alaska Airlines to check arrivals from San Francisco.

3:30 P.M.

"What do you mean it's finally over?"

Still dripping sweat from a five-mile jog, Tyler stood in his apartment kitchenette toweling his face with one hand while pressing the phone to his left ear with the other.

Nancy said, "Just what I said, Tyler. It's over between us. I'll call my attorney and have her file the papers."

CHAPTER 19

"Don't I at least deserve to know why you're having this sudden change of heart? The other night when we went out, I got the impression things were going well between us. What changed all that while you were in California?" A thought suddenly hit: did she have some guy in San Francisco? Maybe she'd come up to Seattle to test their relationship. And maybe she'd gone back to San Francisco to cut things off with him but it hadn't worked out that way. A huge empty hole suddenly opened up below his diaphragm.

"Oh, Tyler, don't play innocent with me. You know how that pisses me off."

He threw the towel against the wall. "I'm not *playing* innocent, I *am* innocent. I don't know what the hell you're talking about." Maybe the-other-man fantasy wasn't the operative problem here. If not, what? He kicked the towel away from where it had landed.

"Well then, let me spell it out for you. You swore to me you were clean and sober. Today I learn that isn't quite true, that you were hiding narcotics in your locker, just like last time."

A jarring numbness engulfed him. "Who told you that? Believe me, that isn't true." He ran a mental list of possible candidates and immediately stopped at Ferguson. He was the only one who knew about Nancy. And he was the only one to have a motive. Then again, how in hell would Ferguson know about the drugs? Didn't make sense.

"Oh, Tyler, how can you say that? This is exactly like the last time." She sighed in exasperation. "Why in the world would someone lie about something like that?"

He slammed his hand on the countertop. "Listen to me, I'm being framed because of what I know about the medical record system!"

"And who's behind this?" She sounded blatantly skeptical.

"I don't know, but I have some suspicions." He considered mentioning the FBI, but quickly decided with her probing it would only lead to more problems.

Another doubtful sigh. "This is sounding way too familiar. Just like last time."

He knew better than to argue any further. Nancy would just dig in deeper. Best to let her vent, decompress, and try to reason with her later. "Who called and told you? At least tell me that."

"What difference does it make?"

"It could help me a lot."

"To get off of drugs?" This said with barbed sarcasm.

"Please."

"Tyler, I don't know. I received a phone call. That's all I know."

"Male or female. What exactly did they say."

"This conversation is going nowhere. I'm going to hang up now."

"Just one last thing. Please."

A pause, then, "What?"

"Don't file those papers just yet. Give me one last chance to prove myself. Give me a week. Please?"

She hung up.

1:15 A.M., NAPERVILLE, ILLINOIS

Even at this time of morning the outside temperature hung at a muggy seventy-eight degrees Fahrenheit, the air cloyed with Lake Michigan humidity. Tangible air, the kind you could sweep off your arm one minute after stepping out of air conditioning. The back side of a 175-unit condo complex faced a park bordering a river. A path for strollers and joggers meandered through the greenbelt kissing the riverbank every now and then. Two stocky men in black long-sleeved mock-tees and black jeans left the path and crossed the lawn toward the building. Both men wore black nylon fanny packs.

Approaching the basement door they slid on thin latex gloves before the taller of the two pulled from his pocket a cheap metal ring holding two keys. In the dim moonlight he selected one key and slipped it into the lock. The door clicked open, automatically triggering a hall light. They quickly stepped inside and quietly shut the door and stood still, listening for sounds of someone in the basement storage area. Quiet. Satisfied, they moved forward.

To their left, a fire door opened into a stairwell. They entered and climbed steadily to the fifth floor. Although both men pumped iron and jogged at least two hours a day, they stopped on the landing to slow their breathing and make one final check. The same key that opened the outside door opened this one. Door cracked, they listened for hallway sounds. The target's unit was one door down the hall to the right. Having gone through the same drill yesterday while the owner was at work they slipped adroitly inside the unit within seconds of leaving the stairwell.

With the target's front door now closed behind them the short entranceway into the living room was completely dark. They deftly removed penlights from their packs and waited for their eyes to accommodate. The penlight bulbs had been changed to red, reducing the risk of light reflecting off windows or, worse, being seen by the target. They remained in place for two minutes, their eyes adapting to the darkness before flicking on the lights. The soft hum of air conditioning became the only sound. The apartment carried the smell of fried cube steak, probably from earlier this evening.

They crept forward.

The telephone rang.

From the direction of the bedroom came a sleep-laden, "Hello," followed by a gruff, "Wrong number."

The lead man hand signaled retreat. Both men sank back into the dark entrance alcove.

Next came the padding of bare feet. A moment later the sound of water hitting water, then a toilet flush. Another few seconds and the condo interior again became silent.

They settled down to wait.

2:10 A.M.

With soft snoring now coming from the bedroom, both men moved forward. A right-hand turn followed immediately by a left turn took them inside Sergio Vericelli's bedroom. Enough moonlight filtered between the curtain edges to work deftly without penlights.

Their next moves had been well choreographed. The heavier of the two intruders, at 210 pounds, quickly stepped to the right side of the bed while his partner moved to the left. In one fluid move, the heavier one dropped down on Sergio, cupping a pillow over his face to mask any shouts yet allowing him air to breathe, since signs of suffocation could easily be discovered by a good medical examiner. The other intruder held Sergio's left arm extended, palm up.

Vericelli's violent struggle was no match against stronger, heavier men. Even in the faint light, the man holding Sergio's arm saw one vessel stand out like a sewer pipe. His free hand withdrew a syringe from the fanny pack. With his teeth he removed the plastic guard. Carefully, making sure not to bruise the skin—for this would surely draw a medical examiner's eye to the puncture wound—he slid the needle into the distended vein.

Seconds later Sergio's movements stopped.

The heavier intruder pushed off Sergio and felt for a carotid pulse. Feeling none, he put his ear to Sergio's chest. A moment later he nodded to his partner.

In a well-practiced routine, each man removed any sign of a struggle. They smoothed the sheets, fluffed the pillow, and arranged the victim to appear to have died peacefully during sleep.

Five minutes later they retraced their path to the front door, opened it, and checked the hallway. Moments later they were strolling across the freshly cut lawn away from the basement door, latex gloves stuffed deep in their front pockets to be burned later.

The outside temperature remained a muggy seventy-eight degrees.

CHAPTER 20

Tyler entered the large cafeteria at one of those "down" times when the breakfast crowd vanishes and coffee breakers have yet to start trickling in, leaving only a few odd-hour employees—mostly midlevel administrators—planted sparsely at tables. At the far end of the room, the diagonal corner from the entrance, the latte stand was doing a steady business. He recognized Jim Day as the second person in a two-person line. He passed a shadowy wall alcove with a continually moving conveyor belt to buss dirty dishes and brown plastic trays into a cloistered area wafting the smell of dirty dishwater over to the nearby booths, making it a mystery to Tyler why anybody would eat near there.

Jim Day said, "Make it a grande latte with two shots of vanilla."

Tyler waited for the moon-tanned, anorexic barista to acknowledge Day's order before tapping him on the shoulder. "Been looking for you. One of your colleagues said I could probably find you down here."

Day turned. He seemed surprised, then disappointed. "Oh, man, you again."

"What can I get for you?" Already tamping espresso into the stainless-steel steam filter, the barista craned his neck and shot Tyler an expectantly bored expression. Tyler wondered if the guy was experiencing carpal tunnel symptoms yet from palm-banging the steam filters into the espresso machines. So far, he'd treated two Starbucks employees for the problem.

"I'm here to see him," with a nod toward Day. Then to Day, "Need to ask you a favor."

"It figures. I didn't think you were here to ask me out for dinner. Can it wait until I get my drink?"

Tyler decided to push. "I want in to see Bernie Levy and I want you to set it up."

Day laughed, shaking his head as if to say: don't be ridiculous. "No one gets in to see Levy unless they're Bill Gates." Then he seemed to think about what he just said. "That is, not without a very—and I mean very good—reason."

"Someone's screwing with his system. That's good enough."

Another laugh. "What? You still on a tear about your mysterious hacker? The one who comes and goes without a trace?" He leaned over toward Tyler's ear, whispered, "With all due respect, Dr. Mathews, take my advice: get a life. There's no hacker fucking with you or the network." Day straightened up and glanced expectantly at the latte stand.

Something in Day's eyes told Tyler he knew about the drugs in the locker incident.

"Is that right? Is that what you're going to tell some nosy reporter two days from now when another Maynard patient dies and word's been leaked you were warned there was a bug in the system and you did zip about it?" He let the point simmer a beat before continuing. "Since Med-InDx is a start-up, I assume a goodly amount of your compensation—at least your retirement compensation—is in stock options. What if somehow, through some nasty little twist of fate, The New York Times or Wall Street Journal gets wind of this bug between now and the stock's IPO? What do you think those options would be worth if that happens?"

"Here you go." The barista held out Day's latte.

Frowning, Day tossed four dollars on the counter, then snatched the drink from the man's hand. Without waiting for change, Day marched toward an empty booth. Tyler followed.

Seated, Day lowered his voice. "Is that what you plan to do? Go to the press with some funky ginned-up story that could potentially ruin a good company? Just because *you* may have screwed up and overdosed a patient? You think that's fair?"

Tyler met Day's eyes. "You think it was fair for Larry Childs?"

Day set the coffee on the table and pushed it aside. He leaned toward Tyler. In a harsh whisper, "We've been over this. What does it take for me to make the point? Listen to me one more time: there's not a lick of evidence that medical record's been tampered with. That's a fact."

"So *you* say."

Day's face tightened into a scowl. He glanced around the area, turned back to Tyler. "You suggesting I'm covering up something?"

"Did I say that?" Tyler mimicked Day surveying the room, then looked back at him. "Consider it from my viewpoint. If I were you and I were sitting on a pile of options, I'd do everything possible to protect them. Last thing you'd want is to have a security breach become public knowledge. Especially right now with the IPO looming."

For ten long seconds Day glared at Tyler as if ready to pounce. Then he gave a bitter, dismissive laugh and slumped against the molded plastic seat back. He shook his head in resignation. "And a personal chat with Bernie Levy is going to resolve it for you? Then you'll lighten up on this?"

Tyler nodded. "At least I'll know I've done everything possible to fix the problem."

"You know, don't you, that Levy personally coded the system's database engine?"

"Why should I know something like that?"

"He did, and he's still working on it. And considers it his baby too. A good deal of the other system components—like the accounting package—were bought from software coders who got buried when the dot-com bubble burst a few years back . . . we cobbled it together kinda as a plug-and-play system."

"I'm not interested in Med-InDx company folklore. What I want to know is if you'll set something up?"

Day pulled a cell phone from his breast pocket. "Yeah, sure, I'm his personal fucking secretary." He pushed in some numbers. "I can't promise anything."

Tyler decided to push the issue. "Tell him if he doesn't see me today, I'm going to the *Seattle Times* tomorrow."

2:05 P.M.

So far Med-InDx fell short of Tyler's expectations. For some crazy reason, he'd fantasized glossy, high-tech furniture and minimalist German interior design. Then again, he reminded himself, this was a venture capital–funded start-up, not some fat cat NASDQ corporation like Microsoft or Prophesy. He found the primary corporate office located on the third floor of a tired, twenty-story, black glass office building off Fourth Avenue in the low-rise transitional neighborhood sandwiched between the central business district and residential Queen Anne Hill. There was no way of telling how much additional space the company occupied because the elevator opened directly across the hall from the Med-InDx front door and Tyler didn't take the time to snoop around. The waiting-area decor was heavily into a secondhand office furniture motif. Instead of a svelte, smartly tailored female receptionist, a middle-aged, potbellied male Tommy Hilfiger enthusiast was positioned at a desk guarding the reception area. He glanced up at Tyler. "May I help you?"

"I'm Dr. Mathews. I have an appointment to see Mr. Levy."

The man typed something into the computer, shook his head, typed again, seemed to find something agreeable, and said, "Have a seat. I'll tell him you're here."

Tyler dropped into an uncomfortable chair and wondered yet again what might be accomplished in this interview. Surely Levy knew about the flaw. The question was, what was he doing about it? Did he realize it had caused at least one patient death? Probably not, or they would've fixed the problem by now. *No company would knowingly push a defective product. Would they? Nah.*

"Bernie will see you now."

Tyler followed the receptionist along a hallway flanked by glassed-in offices to the right and a sea of cubicles to the left. The small offices appeared chaotic, most desks layered with computer printouts and one or two oversized plasma-screen monitors. One wall in each office displayed a large white board filled with multicolored hieroglyphics and/or hasty sketches. Work areas teemed with casually clad men and women looking to be in their mid-twenties, radiating enough high-intensity intellectual energy to power a nuclear submarine. Just walking past them invigorated Tyler.

"Just go on in. Bernie will be with you soon as he finishes."

Tyler stepped into the office. The door closed behind him. A man in his early thirties slouched behind the desk, lips pursed, brow furrowed, fingers furiously clicking a keyboard. Tyler stood waiting.

Levy's office appeared no different from the other employees', except for being a bit more spacious and containing a larger desk and a small round conference table with five matching chairs. Two cables from two twenty-one-inch LCD monitors ran to the computer through the desk kick-panel via a splintered hole that looked like it'd been enlarged by a methamphetamine junkie with a wood file. On the wall to the left hung a poster-sized framed picture of Bill Gates, below which an engraved plaque stated, HE DID. SO CAN YOU.

The cut of Levy's brown hair, the sleeves-rolled-up-open-at-the-neck blue button-down oxford, the weak double chin and style of eyeglasses, gave Tyler the impression of a Bill Gates clone.

Levy finally glanced up, muttered, "Be with you in a minute."

A minute turned into two, making Tyler wonder if this was some sort of ploy.

Another minute passed. Levy tapped a key, said, "There!" and turned to Tyler. "Dr. Mathews, I presume." He smiled a set of obviously whitened teeth.

"Yes."

"What can I do for you?" Levy tilted back his chair, swiveling side to side.

"I assume you talked with Jim Day earlier today?"

"Yes." Eyes fixed on Tyler, Levy continued swiveling.

"Then you should know I'm here because there's a problem with your EMR."

Levy sucked a tooth for a beat before saying, "Dude, from what Jim tells me you *believe* there's a security problem . . . maybe some unknown hole a cracker found and exploited. But Jim also says there is no evidence to support any such hypothesis. Unless, of course, you're holding back information Jim isn't privy to."

Tyler glanced at the two chairs in front of Levy's desk, then back at his host, then folded himself into the one directly in front of the desk. "Did Jim tell you what happened to my patient Larry Childs? How he died from a radiation overdose?"

"Yes." Levy's tone questioned its relevance to the meeting.

"You don't seem too upset about it."

Levy seemed genuinely puzzled. "Why should I be? Our company can't be held responsible for your mistakes."

Tyler shook his head. "Therein lies the rub. It wasn't my mistake."

"You wouldn't be the first person to think they're right when, in fact, they're wrong. From what I've been told, the record speaks for itself. There isn't a shred of evidence it was altered. And as I'm sure you understand, an electronic medical record unequivocally documents any change to any record field. It just didn't happen."

Tyler selected his next words carefully. "Are you saying that it's absolutely impossible that my patient's radiation dose didn't change between the time it was entered and given?" He wished he'd thought to bring a tape recorder.

A momentary flicker that looked like fear traced through Levy's eyes.

"It's Tyler, isn't it?" He nodded agreement to his own question.

Without waiting for an answer, "Tyler, I've been programming computers since I was seven years old. The one thing I've learned is that once the software's been validated any data field error is always human error. Machines simply don't make those types of errors, humans do. Rest assured that I personally coded that particular database routine, so I know those lines backward, forward, upside down, and down side up. I've sweated over each line command by command. You can be absolutely dead certain there's not a god-damn thing wrong with that program."

"It's Bernie, isn't it?" Without waiting for an answer, "Bernie, I never said anything was wrong with the program." There! It was out. He watched Levy's reaction.

Bernie Levy studied the man sitting across the desk from him. Intense seemed the best descriptor, if forced to pick only one. Intent would be the second. Question was, intent on what? Ruining the company he'd spent ten years building from nothing? For what reason? Some ill-defined sense of self-centered righteous indignation? As if critically ill patients didn't die every day in hospitals all over the freaking world. A flash of hatred speared his heart. How dare that sanctimonious sonofabitch walk in here and act so freaking smug.

Carefully masking any emotion, Bernie slowly nodded agreement. "Perhaps not, Tyler, but somehow you gave me the distinct impression that was exactly what you implied."

"Then again, it may well be what I believe. What would you say if I told you I have a couple examples of errors that resulted in serious—hell, fatal—complications that can only be explained by an intrinsic problem with your database?"

Bernie tapped a mechanical pencil on the desktop—*tap tap tap*—and considered his options. For sure, talk to Arthur soon as this little shithead left. Arthur would know how best to handle this. "I want to know more details. Do you have any direct proof to back up your insanely preposterous allegation or is this all purely hypothetical."

Mathews looked smug. "Nothing's hypothetical at all. I have several other cases documented in addition to Larry Childs."

Levy flashed his winning smile at Mathews. "Tell me about them."

Mathews leaned back in the chair, arms folded across his chest. "Why so interested if there's no problem?"

He considered his next answer carefully. Was the sonofabitch joking? "I don't get it. What's with you? You get off on being a royal pain in the ass?"

"Pain in the ass?" Face red, Mathews pushed out of the chair. "My only reason for coming to talk with you was to warn you that you have a problem with your database. I hoped to come away with some assurance you're going to fix it before there are any more catastrophes. But apparently you don't give a rat's ass. All I've seen from you and your company is stonewalling. You apparently don't give a damn you've got a serious problem. Perhaps I should tell my story to someone who gives a shit."

Without thinking, Levy picked up the violet nerve ball next to the mouse, started squeezing it. He watched Mathews turn and take a step toward the door. "Is that a threat? I think not. You're in no position to threaten me."

Mathews stopped and without looking back, said, "Really! And why is that?"

"Good day, Dr. Mathews."

"If that's supposed to be a threat, I suggest you need to rethink your position."

"I said good day, Mathews."

Bernie watched the sanctimonious putz leave the room. Soon as the door closed his finger punched speed dial. Benson's voice answered.

"Mathews just left the office. He knows everything. Worse than that, I think he's stupid enough to try to do something about it."

CHAPTER 21

"And just what in the world am I supposed to tell the Finance Committee next time they ask? I'm running out of excuses."

Arthur Benson looked Neddy Longmire up and down while wondering whatever possessed him to hire the fucking little wimp in the first place. *Because you could control him, that's why,* he thought.

Neddy. Even that prissy Ivy League name was beginning to piss him off. What kind of parents named their son Neddy, for christsake?

The kind of people who can get their kids into Dartmouth or Yale, that's who, his inner voice answered again.

And that's exactly where Neddy had matriculated. Fucking Dartmouth. Then an MBA from Columbia. In contrast, Benson thought bitterly, he'd attended the University of Texas at Austin before entering the University of Minnesota School of Hospital Administration.

They were in Benson's office, Neddy pacing, making Arthur nervous with his jerky little squirrellike movements. As a kid growing up in Plano, Texas, Arthur used to shoot the pesky little tree rodents with his .22 rifle. Too bad he couldn't shoot Longmire now. That would chill him out. Arthur smiled, visualizing it.

"For christsakes, Neddy, I know damn well you can come up with something. That's why I gave you the title of Chief Financial Officer. So you can dazzle those sombitches with enough financial spin to keep them off our backs for one more month. One stinking month. That's all we need."

Neddy pulled on his collar, hooking his index finger over the edge and running it back and forth like the heat was set too high even though it was a crisp seventy degrees in the room. Arthur couldn't remember if he'd ever seen the little fag with his collar unbuttoned.

"But McCarthy keeps asking questions."

"Fine. Let him ask. Just keep stalling with your answers. The thing is, just be careful, don't trip up and say something you'll regret." *What a whiner.*

"But he's the chairman of the Board. I can't hold him off forever."

Neddy clasped both hands in front of his heart. Just like that fucking two-faced Baptist preacher Arthur's parents forced him to listen to for hours on end every Sunday morning growing up.

"Oh, dear," Neddy moaned, "I wish I hadn't let you talk me into this. I don't know if I can hold up."

He certainly couldn't argue with that last part. Neddy looked about ready to decompensate any second now. But maybe he was right. Maybe he'd made a mistake using Longmire to help float the deal. Maybe he should've picked someone else. Too late now. "I'm telling you, Neddy, there's nothing to worry about."

"Easy for you to say. You're not the one has to account to the Finance Committee. Lord, if they ever get wind of what we've done . . ."

"Horseshit!" Longmire's words punched a hot button in Arthur's soul. "You know damn well every cent I own's tied up in this deal too, so don't be preaching to me that this is easy." That much was dead-on true. Fact was, he was leveraged up to his fucking eyebrows on this one. Eyebrows and then some.

Neddy started hyperventilating.

Christ, just what he needed right now, Longmire passing out in his office. Then he'd have to either leave him on the floor until he finally came around or call a Code 199 and have the whole damn resuscitation team pile into his office like a fucking Chinese fire drill. There'd be questions and that'd upset Neddy even more and maybe that would be all it took to push the nervous little faggot over the edge.

"Now slow your breathing down or you're going to have one of your spells," Arthur said, finally pushing out of his high-back executive leather chair and coming around the desk to lay a calming hand on his CFO's slumped shoulder. "We don't need that right now." He was behind Longmire now, massaging the man's deltoids like a trainer might do to a prizefighter between rounds. "There's not a damned thing to worry about. This is going to play out just fine. It's orchestrated to a tee. Once we get JCAHO's thumbs-up, we can cover the loan with stock options. Nice and easy, Japanesy. Then you can throw the bank statements in Aldridge's fat boozer face and tell him to piss up a rope."

The CFO inhaled a slow, deep, calming breath and dropped his chin toward his chest. "I just wish this was over. The pressure's getting to me."

Never would've guessed it, Neddy, you little queen. "It's all going to be over in a few weeks. You'll be fine. We'll be rich. You can even quit this job after a respectable amount of time passes, if'n you wanta." He was slipping into his down-home, folksy tone now. People liked that. Made them feel he was sincere.

Times like this triggered second thoughts in Arthur about the scheme. But, he reminded himself, it was a sure thing. Or at least the closest thing to a sure thing there was. His mind drifted back to how it all started, how Bernie Levy had come to him asking if prestigious Maynard Medical Center could be used as a showcase beta site for his company's state-of-the-art solution to an electronic medical record. Coincidentally, Arthur, having read both the federal regulatory tea leaves and the hospital's slipping bottom line, had decided an integral strategy to the center's survival was to completely retool their antiquated IT Department.

Levy's proposition couldn't have come at a more opportune time. Med-InDx needed a high-profile medical center to test their product and Maynard Medical Center didn't have the ten million dollars it would take to buy a complete Clinical Information System, install it over the next two years, and train three thousand employees and fifteen hundred physicians in its use. It was a marriage made in heaven.

Or so it seemed.

What he hadn't done well and regretted, Arthur knew, was good due diligence. He never really looked into the venture capital behind the first and second rounds of funding. And then, during one dinner meeting Bernie mentioned a need for an additional ten million dollars to satisfy the current capital burn rate until the product was ready for prime time and the company could slake its remaining capital thirst on an IPO.

Ten million.

Arthur realized he could get his own hands on the sum. Nine million sat in the MMC reserves collecting paltry returns from T-bills and high-grade corporate bonds after the dot-com bomb market crash. Benson could leverage the final million from his personal assets. The problem, of course, was how to borrow from the reserves without the Finance Committee discovering the "investment."

A week after assuring Levy of being able to fund the rest of the project he orchestrated an accidental meeting between Neddy and a gay prostitute at the medical center's annual black tie fundraiser. Two weeks later he and MMC were partial owners of Med-InDx.

Shortly after that he met the other investors.

The telephone rang. A moment later Bernie Levy was saying, "Mathews just left the office. He knows everything."

— — — — — — — — — — —

With no particular place to go—since he no longer had any responsibilities at the hospital—Tyler sat in the front seat of his Range Rover. There were a couple of times during the interview that Tyler swore he hit a nerve. A look in Levy's eyes, the quick masking of a spontaneous expression.

His cell phone rang. He fumbled it out of his pocket and pressed the send button. "Mathews here."

"Hello, dear, it's your spurned lover, Special Agent Ferguson, calling to check on you. Guess since you answered the phone you're alive and well. What a relief."

"What the hell you talking about?"

"Before I get around to that, let's just say I've been getting worried about you since I didn't hear back, like we'd agreed upon."

How in hell did he get my unlisted number? Stupid question. He's the FBI, pal. "I'm working on it."

"Working on what?"

Good question. "Just working on it. That's all."

"Well, Mathews, while you're working on it, the chairman of the JCAHO EMR committee turned up seriously dead this morning."

A chill burrowed between his shoulder blades.

"His cleaning lady found him in bed when she entered the condo."

"You didn't say murdered. But that's what you're implying, right?"

"That's not affirmative yet." A pause echoed over the airwaves. "Someone tried to make it look like death by natural causes, but there's a highly suspicious puncture mark directly over a vein on his left arm. Certainly caught the attention of the medical examiner. From his read, it's fresh. Probably minutes before death. Vericelli's being posted as we speak."

"What are you trying to tell me?"

"Wise up, Mathews. You don't want to play games with Levy's buddies. If you know anything about that flaw, tell me. Don't be a fool."

Tyler flashed on being stood up by Robin Beck, the visit to her house, the feeling he got looking into her kitchen. For a moment Tyler wanted to tell him everything—the drugs in his locker, Nancy leaving, the Levy discussion, everything. But if he did, he ran a high risk of losing Nancy forever. He had to hang in there a little while longer and see what he could do to salvage the situation.

"Tell you what. There is something you might want to look into." He told him about Robin Beck, how she'd seemingly disappeared after agreeing to meet with him.

"I don't get it. What do you want me to do about it?"

Tell Ferguson about the drugs found in his locker and the stock options in the Schwab account? With him holding the forged prescriptions, what were the chances he'd believe they were planted? Probably zero.

"Check on her. Go into her house, see if she's alright."

"And why would I want to do that if there's nothing wrong with the software. C'mon, Mathews, we both know you're holding out on me. What's going on?"

"Here's the deal. You check out Robin Beck. Then we'll talk."

CHAPTER 22

"What the hell's his hang-up?"

"Have no idea," Ferguson said to Nina Stanford's back. They were in Nina's office, Stanford was standing at the window, peering out at the magnificent view of the harbor and an anchored container ship waiting its turn to be unloaded. Ferguson's cubicle had a view of the water cooler.

"You'd think with us holding evidence against him he'd play ball."

"You'd think so. But I have another idea."

Stanford grunted for him to continue.

"His wife moved to town. I think there's a chance she might be testing the waters for a reconciliation. I think maybe there's an angle we can play here, you know, leverage that."

Stanford turned a quizzical expression on him. "How's that supposed to work? I thought they were divorced."

"Not exactly. Seems she had the papers all drawn up, but never filed. From what I can determine she was never quite sure of what to do. I think there's a good chance they're trying to get it back together."

A trace of a smile crossed her lips. "So what do you propose? Squeezing him? Thought we were already doing that with the prescription thing. Look where it's got us. Nowhere."

"Yes, but—"

"Gary, you can't make a career out of this case. You know that. The kid's either going to play ball or we'll turn him over to the DEA. There's no other way to deal with it. Besides, I've got other things for you to focus on."

"What if I convince her to work on him, get him to cooperate with us?"

Nina hiked a noncommittal shrug. "Thought we just went over that. Why should that work?"

Ferguson frowned. "Just a hunch I have." Just then Ferguson's cell phone rang. He held up an index finger to his boss as his other hand plucked the Motorola from his blazer breast pocket. He punched the SEND button, said, "Ferguson."

"Gary, Tom Washington. I'm over at Beck's house. I think you wanta get your ass over here and see this."

5:30 P.M.

Tyler leaned his trail bike against the wall while he unlocked the door to his apartment. From inside came the annoying beep of the answering machine. Had Nancy called while he was out riding? Maybe she reconsidered? A flame of hope ignited in his chest.

Right foot propping the door open, he rolled the bike into the apartment, then let it shut on its own while he wheeled the bike to the sliding-glass door and then out to the small balcony. He propped it against the wall, next to a rusted charcoal-fueled hibachi. He'd driven up to Whistle Lake on Fidalgo Island to ride his favorite five-mile trail over rocks and gnarled tree roots. The exercise and round-trip three-hour drive allowed him to put things in a little better perspective. And he'd come up with an idea. Maybe he could strike a deal with Ferguson: turn over what he knew about the patient complications in return for the FBI convincing Nancy the drug cases—both in San Francisco and here—were trumped up. Hell, Ferguson knew the truth, what difference would it make for him to set the record straight with her?

The plan's potential downside was the risk of losing his job and more. If MMC filed charges of narcotics theft, he could kiss his medical career good-bye. The way it was now looking, Ferguson was his only way out.

He pressed the answering machine PLAY button.

"Tyler, it's Jill Richardson. I just found out something that really, really spooked me. The JCAHO committee chairman, Sergio Vericelli, died last night. Someone found him dead in bed this morning. They're saying natural causes . . . his heart maybe . . . but I don't know . . . seems kind of fishy, the timing thing . . . give me a call. It's got me spooked, what with everything that's been going on."

Why would Vericelli's death spook her? And why call him about it? To scare him or warn him?

Ferguson's warning echoed in his mind. Should he trust her? She'd given him the names of the other patients who'd had complications. Didn't that count for something?

In the meantime, maybe it *was* time to start playing ball with the FBI.

He decided to put off talking with her until morning, and removed Ferguson's card from his wallet and dialed the cell phone number. One ring and a simulated male voice announced the subscriber's phone was not in service. Next, he dialed Ferguson's office number.

"FBI," a male voice answered. No "May I help you," simply "FBI."

"Agent Gary Ferguson, please."

"Office's closed. You want his voice mail?"

"No, this is important. Can you beep him or something, have him call me back?"

"Who's calling?"

Tyler gave him his name and home phone number and hung up.

From the refrigerator he pulled a piece of lasagna bought earlier that day from an Italian deli on the next block. For a moment he studied it, then replaced it. Instead, he grabbed a Red Hook long-neck from the fridge. He knew in his gut that Michelle's and Vericelli's deaths were linked. He just had to figure out how.

9:55 P.M.

Tyler hung up the bath towel after drying off and caught a glimpse of himself in the mirror. Nancy was right. He looked like hell. All skin and bones. None of the muscle he'd had when playing ball. Well, his life had turned to shit. No wonder his body had followed. He shrugged, slipped into a pair of well-worn scrubs he used as pajamas, then opened the below-sink drawer and picked up the amber plastic Ambien bottle. For a moment he almost opened the white plastic lid. Nancy's image floated by his mind's eye. He dropped the bottle back into the drawer and slammed it. He'd rather spend the entire night wide awake studying the ceiling and listening to passing traffic than take the damned thing.

He slid between the sheets and clicked off the bedside lamp.

Flat on his back, interlaced fingers under his head, staring into the gray shadowy ceiling it dawned on him: Ferguson hadn't returned his call.

CHAPTER 23

6:53 A.M.

Tyler awoke almost an hour later than usual. The last thing he'd done after crawling into bed the night before was turn off the alarm. No need to get up at the usual time since he had no surgery or inpatients to do rounds on, nothing to do at the medical center anymore.

Sitting on the edge of the bed, he raked his fingers through his hair and realized he'd actually fallen asleep sometime during the night. The more he thought about it, the more he realized he *had* slept through much of the night. In contrast to the heavy chemical slumber so familiar to him, natural sleep had been so light it seemed like no sleep at all. His dreams—realizing now he *had* dreamed—were filled with more vibrant colors and clearer sounds, a state responsible for initially believing he'd lain awake all night.

Still, he didn't feel refreshed. More like he'd repaid only the first installment to a huge sleep debt. But the fact he'd gone his first full night in God knew how long without Ambien left him hopeful— probably, he decided, padding toward the toilet, like the alcoholic who completes his first twenty-four hours without a drink.

9:30 A.M.

"Do you know about the drug thing?"

Sitting on the opposite side of the desk from her, Tyler watched

Jill Richardson's eyes as the question hit. She held his gaze, said, "Yes, of course I know," as if considering the question ridiculous.

"Don't you find that a bit coincidental, the timing I mean?"

She frowned. "What? Coming on the heels of your assertions?"

Her tone wasn't at all assuring, certainly not what he expected.

"It's a setup. To impeach my credibility. That's what that was."

She said, as if totally disregarding his statement, "I can only imagine how embarrassing it was, Khan showing you Childs's dose was recorded as normal."

A surge of anger ignited in the center of his chest. "What the hell are you saying? I planted those drugs to make it look like I'm being persecuted?" Had it been a mistake to trust her? At least he hadn't mentioned Ferguson.

He immediately reconsidered this last thought. Would telling her that the FBI suspected a software flaw redeem some of his credibility? Did it even matter at this point? He pushed up out of the chair, started pacing a tight circle in the cramped office, tightening and loosening his fists, trying to calm down.

"I haven't said *what* I believe. Fact of the matter is, I'm not sure what *to* believe. But I have to admit the possibility did cross my mind." She said this in the same voice he'd heard psychiatric nurses use on distraught, possibly violent patients.

He glared at her. "You don't have to say anything. It's clear that you think I planted the drugs. Well, let me tell you about me and drugs . . . how I've been through this before. Maybe then you'll understand."

She watched him now with both hands on the edge of the desk as if ready to jump up. "Want to take a break? I could have Tony bring us a couple cups of coffee?"

He stopped pacing and leaned over, hands on the top of the chair he'd been sitting in. "Nice try. No. You're going to hear this."

She shot a nervous glance at the phone.

He continued. "The story goes like this. The place where I got fired? My chairman, the head of Neurosurgery, was heavily into

Medicare fraud . . . not that he didn't always spout off all the requisite rationalizations to justify it: the lousy reimbursement, the overwhelming federal bureaucracy forced on the practice of medicine, the huge cost of malpractice insurance. I could go on and on but you get the point. He was just greedy and it got outrageously egregious. Doing things like billing for cases residents did when he wasn't even near the operating room. I mean, not even close. It wasn't like he was down the hall and available if a problem came up. Hell no. One time he was in Hawaii slamming down mai tais while the billing office was submitting a week's worth of cases the residents were doing under other faculty members' guidance. They were billed under his name.

"I didn't like it, but I couldn't say much since I was low man on the totem pole. I tried to steer clear but then one day I couldn't dodge it any longer. He asked me to cover a few cases . . . you know, make myself available if there was a problem. I told him no. His response was classic him. He threatened to fire me if I didn't play ball.

"See, the thing you don't know about me is I always wanted to end up chairman. He knew that. He also knew that his department was the big time, the job that'd launch me in the fast track. If he fired me I'd be screwed. I'd never get another chance." Tyler snorted a bitter laugh. "Turned out I got fired anyway. Which means in the academic circles I'm now a pariah. He made sure of that. What chairman wants to hire a faculty member who blew the whistle on his last boss?

"It became a classic double bind. I wanted to keep my job, but the more he had me cover cases the more I could end up in a federal penitentiary with no chance of ever practicing medicine again.

"The feds assured me they'd protect me." He barked another sarcastic laugh and shook his head in disgust. "Didn't happen. My boss found out about their investigation in time to kick a lot of dirt over his tracks. Once that happened the Federales backed off.

The moment that happened, drugs were discovered in my locker. I mean it was exactly like happened here. I find that a little too co-incidental. Somebody knew what happened to me back then and is now using it to set me up again."

"So you were never abusing?"

"There's no way I could practice neurosurgery and be a junkie. Maybe an anesthesiologist could—hey, all the gas passers do is sit next to their computerized machines and read *Road and Track* or *PC Magazine* during cases anyway—but neurosurgery? No way."

She seemed to consider his story a moment. "Why would someone plant drugs in your locker?"

The question surprised him. Then again, not if she missed the ramifications. "I just told you why. To silence me. Why? Because they know this job is my last chance to salvage my career. I get busted for narcotics one more time, I lose my license forever. They're telling me to keep quiet and in the process making certain they have a way of impeaching my credibility just in case I don't."

"And who are *they?*" She used her fingers to signal quotes around the word "they."

He studied her. *Trust her? Better not.*

"Look at the facts. The medical record *is* flawed somehow. A se-curity hole. Something. It's killing or severely hurting patients. You know that's fact. You've seen examples. And I don't need to spell out the potential trouble I pose by being aware of it. I'm not trying to threaten or hurt anybody with this knowledge, I'm just trying to get the problem fixed. And because of this, someone's trying to de-stroy me."

"And you expect me to help you?"

"Yes."

"Why?"

"Because as head of Risk Management you should damn well know there's a problem. You can back me up." Again he consid-ered telling her about his visit to Bernie Levy and Ferguson but de-cided against it.

"Last time you asked my advice I suggested we talk with Khan. That didn't seem to work too well. Now you're asking me again. Is there any reason to think things will turn out better this time?" She smiled as if questioning his judgment.

He resented her tone. "Yes."

"Then before you consider doing anything else, I suggest we talk with Art Benson. If there's something wrong with our medical records system, he needs to know about it." She gave him a scrutinizing look. "Are you absolutely certain of your proof this time? I don't want to go through a repeat of our conversation with Khan."

"I'm sure."

"Fine, but you'd better be damned sure because Art's up to his hips in preliminary budget planning meetings this morning. If I pull him out of that, your story better be bulletproof." She shot him a sideways warning look and reached for the telephone.

"He'll be with you momentarily," said the frumpy secretary before shutting the door, leaving them alone in Benson's spacious office.

Richardson and Tyler stood next to a rectangular conference table capable of seating eighteen. A few feet beyond the table's far end a ceiling-recessed screen hung down in front of the wall. Beyond the other table end sat a large desk behind which, over the credenza, hung an oil portrait of a distinguished-looking man with piercing eyes.

Tyler kept his hands clasped together to keep them from fidgeting. To distract Richardson from noticing he asked, "Who's that?" with a nod toward the oil portrait.

"Chester Maynard, founder and first surgeon at Maynard Hospital."

Tyler had seen pictures of the medical center's humble roots. A three-story house atop a forested hill, which at the time was beyond the Seattle city limits.

Richardson said, "Tell you what . . . I have a meeting with the main honcho in the nurses union in a few minutes. It's going to take all day. If this runs on too long I'm going to have to leave."

"No problem."

"No, that's not what I was getting to." She reached out, touched his arm. "You know where Isabella's restaurant is?"

She gave him the address and said, "I want to hear the outcome of this. Why not meet me there for dinner, say six-thirty?"

Her proposition caught him off guard. He had no plans, not now with Nancy refusing to see him. "Sounds fine."

Arthur Benson entered the large office with the loping stride of an ex-athlete. At six feet one inch and two hundred pounds he struck Tyler as being in extremely good shape for his age and demanding job. He wore dark gray suit pants but no suit coat, his white shirtsleeves rolled up to the elbows with the collar button undone behind the loosened knot of a black and white checkered tie. He nodded to Jill. "Morning Ms. Richardson." He extended his hand to Tyler. "Dr. Mathews, I'm embarrassed to say I don't believe we've formally met yet. Arthur Benson."

The thing that caught Tyler's eye was the shock of white hair just to the left of Benson's widow's peak. After shaking hands Benson offered them seats at the south end of the conference table.

Richardson led off with, "I know you're busy with the budget, Art, but I consider this extremely important." She turned to Tyler. "Dr. Mathews came to me with what he believes is a problem with our EMR. I recommended he tell you about it before doing anything else." She nodded for him to begin.

Tyler explained Larry Childs's complication and how the field had been changed to a normal value after filing the NIH report. He went on to explain the near-disastrous result from a mix-up with the gram stains. For a brief moment he caught Jill's eye. Then he mentioned there were other "examples" but didn't elaborate. She seemed to understand.

When he finished, Benson turned to Richardson. "Would you please excuse us, Ms. Richardson."

Rising out of the chair, she checked her watch. "Not a problem. I'm due for a meeting with your favorite Teamsters bull dyke." She shot Benson a wide-eyed innocent look. "Should be loads of fun."

Once Richardson was out of the office and the door closed Benson locked eyes with Tyler. "Obviously you aren't as smart as brain surgeons are cracked up to be or you would've taken the hint. Guess that means I have to spell things out for you. Mention another word to one more person about any alleged computer problems and I'll personally see to it you're brought up to the state Quality Assurance Board for narcotics theft. I'm quite certain you're smart enough to understand the repercussions of that. Do you not?"

CHAPTER 24

"Hey, sailor, looking for a date?"

Tyler snapped out of ruminating over his encounter with Arthur Benson, The Asshole, and glanced up to see Jill Richardson removing an ankle-length black raincoat. She handed it to the Ristorante Isabella maître d', then slipped into the chair across the table from him. She wore a simple white silk blouse beneath a tailored black linen blazer and slacks, a single string of pearls her only jewelry. She looked stunning in the tastefully simple outfit.

The maître d' asked, "And would you like to start with a cocktail?"

Without consulting the menu Richardson said, "A glass of the house pinot grigio, Gregory."

"Very well, Miss Richardson." He turned to Tyler. "Sir?"

"I'll have the same."

"Very good." Their tuxedoed host turned heel.

"So"—Richardson smoothed the tablecloth immediately in front of her—"how did the rest of your meeting with Art go?"

"It sucked." He described Benson's threat.

When he finished, she said, "I can see why that upset you but you need to appreciate what the medical center has at stake."

"Are you serious? He threatened me, goddamnit. Don't even try to defend that. Jesus, you'd think he'd want to correct the problem. What's going to happen to Maynard's precious image if word gets out he covered up a flaw in their medical record system? Think that's going to play well with the media?"

She reached across the table, squeezed his hand, said, "Simmer down," but held on a second longer than needed to make the point. "Yes, their reputation is at stake, but that's only part of it, Tyler."

"Oh, I see . . . and that makes it okay for him to threaten me." He felt pressure build in his head.

"Oh, Tyler, you're so intense." She shook her head, making an admonishing *tsk-tsk* sound. "No, not at all. I'm just saying I can see why he might have reacted the way he did."

Fists clenched, Tyler started to push out of the booth. "I can't take this. I'm outta here."

She grabbed his arm. "Please don't leave. At least not until you hear my side of this." She released his arm.

"There is no other side of it. The fact is a patient died from a radiation overdose. Now Benson's trying to cover it up. That in itself should be enough to cause a serious investigation. Give me a break here."

"From your perspective they might. But where's your proof? Look at the other facts. You claim a hacker's diddled Childs's medical records but the head of IT claims it never happened." She shrugged. "Who's Benson supposed to believe? You or his own lieutenant?"

Tyler felt his face go red with anger. "Don't you get it? He didn't even listen to me. I bet he never bothered to check the pathology report on Childs's brain."

She put her hands to her ears. "Okay, okay, keep your voice down." She paused a beat. "Let's go with that last thought of yours. Let's assume for a moment he bought your hacker story. Why would he want *you*"—pointing a finger at his chest—"mouthing off to the press?" She cocked her head questioningly. "You have any media training?"

He waved dismissively. "No, but why would I need media training if I was simply telling the truth?"

"Why? Well, let me tell you, a press conference can be a real bitch if you don't know how to control it to give your own message. You get a couple of aggressive reporters on your tail and you'll lose control in a millisecond. So, if there's any media coverage of this, Art's going to want Cynthia Wright from communications to handle it. *Not* you. Understand what I'm saying?"

"In other words, whitewash it."

"Oh, Tyler . . ." She sighed. "What are you planning to do about this mess?"

"Larry's funeral is tomorrow. I thought I'd stop by."

"I don't do funerals unless I have to." She cocked an eyebrow. "I've never heard of a doctor going to his patient's funeral. Isn't that kind of against union rules, kind of like admitting you did something wrong?"

"Don't know. Never thought of it that way."

Their drinks arrived. Richardson picked up her glass in a toasting gesture. "Here's to better days."

He thought of Nancy, of repairing the damage and getting back together. "To better times."

"May I ask you something?" Richardson looked at him now with an impossible-to-read expression. "You wear a wedding ring."

He glanced at his left hand, nodded, sat back in the booth, and became aware of the clatter and chatter of diners, the interlaced fragrances of garlic and pesto and melting butter.

"We're separated," was all he said. Then, on impulse, "How about you, you ever been married?"

She chuckled. "No. The only men I've hooked up with have been one colossal series of Mr. Wrongs. I seem to have perfected the knack of zeroing in on good-looking, self-assured, financially well off, narcissistic bastards, any one of whom would've resulted in an unmitigated disaster as a husband. A couple months ago I consulted a therapist about it, to see if I could snap out of the rut. But I never really had faith she'd do me any good so I dropped out."

Her unguarded frankness seemed completely out of character with her at-work persona. "You're kidding."

————

When the waiter brought the bill Tyler reached toward it. "I'll take care of it."

She snatched it away. "Why? This was my idea. You can pick it up next time."

Next time?

As they headed for the coat check she slipped her arm through his and asked in a soft voice, "Would you like to stop over for a nightcap?"

"Sorry. I have some things to do tonight."

She seemed to take this in stride. "Then how about this. If you're not busy tomorrow, why not come over for dinner?"

"Look, I'm not trying to be high maintenance or anything, but I don't know what kind of mood I'm going to be in after the funeral. Understand what I'm saying?"

She nodded agreeably. "It's Saturday. I don't have anything planned. I can walk down to the market and find a few odds and ends to throw together at the last moment. Just give me a call and let me know, but don't make it later than four-thirty if you expect me to cook."

He reconsidered. "Tell you what . . . a home-cooked dinner sounds great. I accept."

1:13 A.M.

For a moment Tyler stood in the shadows cast by the solitary low-wattage bulb atop the corner of the long, one-story storage building directly across from his own ten-by-ten-foot rental locker. The complex of storage buildings was closed this time of night forcing him to scale a high Cyclone fence to sneak into the grounds, making him wonder if the owners kept a watchdog on duty. Before climbing the fence he'd scouted the area but saw few security measures—no CCTV or movement sensors—an oversight when renting the stall. Next time—if there was a next time—he'd know better. Then again, why? No one would want to steal his junk. He listened again for sounds of a dog. Nothing.

Tyler moved to the side of the roll-up metal door to keep from casting his shadow on the heavy brass padlock and spun the dial. After leaving Jill, he'd returned home to burn another copy of the CD that he then placed in an envelope with a note to Nancy saying if anything should happen to him to turn it over to Gary Ferguson. He'd mail it in the morning when the post office opened. The original was in an envelope wedged in his left armpit as he worked the padlock free.

Paranoid, maybe. Cautious, yes. Considering Michelle's and Vericelli's deaths, Walker's apparent disappearance, Benson's threat, and Ferguson's warning, he felt this precaution seemed definitely warranted.

Kneeling, he grabbed the bottom of the storage-locker door and raised it with a grinding metallic clatter. From his back pocket came a flashlight. For a moment he used it to survey his stuff. That's exactly what it was: stuff. Meaningless items to others, precious to him. The game-winning basketball from the state championship he'd played as point guard. Already out-of-date medical school textbooks, a photo album chock-full of worthless snapshots taken with his childhood Kodak.

He slipped the envelope into the photo album and replaced it lovingly in the cardboard U-Haul moving box.

A moment later he rolled down the metal door and secured the lock.

CHAPTER 25

The last somber face hurried across the parking lot through thick unseasonable drizzle to disappear past the plate-glass door into the Bonney Watson Funeral Home. Tyler Mathews waited for the clustered mourners to clear the lobby before climbing out of his Range Rover and following. Just inside the door a marble-top desk held an open guest book. He didn't sign it. To his left, organ music played a hymn vaguely familiar from long inattentive hours perched on a hard oak pew beside his parents during obligatory Unitarian services. That was thirty years ago when he still believed in God and the goodness of people.

A left-hand turn and twenty-five feet of oriental runner brought him to closed double doors. Inside, heavy organ chords accompanied a female's soprano lilt. Careful to not attract attention, Tyler pushed open one side and slipped into the back of a room crammed with parallel rows of blond oak pews. The air smelled of the tiger lilies arranged around the podium in front. The room was packed; which surprised him. Friends of the family, he decided. Larry Childs had not been the kind of young man to garner sympathy, to be popular.

He stood along the back wall, drifting into thoughts about the series of bizarre events this past week, when a sudden vibration against his left hip jerked him back to the funeral. He plucked the beeper from his belt and checked the display. A number he didn't recognize, but the exchange was for the hospital.

He slipped out the door into the deserted hallway. Twenty feet away a single glass door exited to a wheelchair ramp and the parking lot.

Outside now, pulling his cell phone from his suit pocket, a voice demanded, "Dr. Mathews, what are you doing here?"

He spun around. Leslie Childs held something out to him. "Want a hit?"

He recognized a roach proffered between chewed, unpainted nails. Her choice of the "layered look"—a hand-embroidered amateur crafts vest, untucked dress shirt over a tee shirt—couldn't hide her unhealthy thinness. Bulimia or a bad macrobiotic diet? An eating disorder either way, he decided.

"No thanks."

"Whatever." She shrugged, prepared to take another toke, but paused. "You didn't answer my first question. Why are you here?"

He wanted to ask why she was out here getting lodded while her brother was inside being laid to rest, but instead replied, "Came to pay my respects to Larry."

Lips in a tight O, she held the marijuana smoke deep in her lungs, a raised index finger delaying her response. Finally, she exhaled with a phlegmy cough. "Sure it's not out of guilt?"

He met her incriminating stare. "Perhaps a bit. Larry was my patient. I always feel guilty when a patient dies. I wish I could've done more to save him."

Her eyes softened. "Even if there is nothing you could do to save him?"

"Especially then."

When she didn't respond he felt compelled to justify his answer. "Makes me feel useless as a doctor."

"You knew Larry didn't have a chance when you took him to surgery, didn't you?"

Once more he saw no good answer, one that would end the conversation. He remembered the reason he'd come out here. "Excuse me"—holding up his cell phone—"I have to call the hospital."

Without waiting for an answer he turned and moved a few feet away, staying under the eves of the roof to keep off the heavy drizzle, his back toward her.

"Dr. Mathews, Christine Dikman. Sorry to bother you on a Saturday, but this is important. You have a moment?"

He glanced at the building, thought about the service in progress, and decided to stay outside. "Yeah, sure."

"You don't know me. I'm a nurse up on peds." She paused as if searching for the right words. "There's this kiddy up here, his name's Toby Warner. He's been diagnosed with agranulocytosis."

Tyler tried to remember what he'd learned about that in med school. No granulocytes, or white cells. Could be caused by medications. That was about it. "You sure I'm the person you want to talk to about this? I'm a neurosurgeon."

"I guess I'm not making much sense. Okay, here's the story. This kid's studies show his bone marrow is completely wiped out. I mean fried. His hematologist, Norton Sprague, you know him?"

"No."

"Well, he's placed Toby in protective isolation and is socking it to him with some big-time bug killers. But that's not all. Sprague wants the kid to have a bone marrow transplant and the parents aren't buying into it."

Marrow transplant? "Why not? Admittedly, it's a major procedure with a lot of risks, but if it's indicated it's indicated. What, they have some religious issue with that?"

"No, it's not that. It's they just don't believe the diagnosis."

"And the reason you're telling me all this is?"

"Hold on a second, let me close the door to this office."

Tyler watched two-way traffic zip by on Broadway, the cars' windshield wipers slapping clear arcs across windshields. A moment later, "There's a rumor going around the hospital that you think there might be something wrong with the medical record system. Is that right?"

"Where did you hear that?"

"Is it true?"

"I don't know."

"Will you come up here and take a look at Toby?"

Tyler decided he couldn't just walk away from Leslie Childs without saying good-bye, so he turned.

She was gone. So was the smell of marijuana.

1:45 P.M., SATURDAY

"Nancy Fan?"

Gary Ferguson stood in the open doorway to a laboratory of black countertops and scientific instruments he couldn't even begin to name, looking in at an attractive Asian woman hunched over a microscope. She wore a knee-length white lab coat with her lustrous black hair rubber-banded into a ponytail. Her large glasses did nothing to hide or detract from her intrinsic beauty.

Her head jerked up. "Yes?" She glanced nervously around the room, perhaps looking for the familiar face of a colleague, her right hand delicately touching the base of her throat.

"No need to be frightened." He pulled his ID wallet from his blazer inside pocket. "Here," offering it to her for inspection. "Special Agent Gary Ferguson, FBI."

She tentatively accepted the ID but handed it back immediately, as if it were contaminated. "Is something wrong?"

"Sorry to startle you. I tried your apartment but your roommate said you were here working."

"Is this about Tyler?"

"What makes you ask that?"

She blushed, glanced around the room again, tense. "Nothing . . . I mean . . . nothing."

He returned the ID to his blazer pocket. "You're Tyler Mathews's wife, correct?"

She seemed to consider her answer. "Yes?"

"May I?" Ferguson pointed to another counter-high lab stool and accepted his own offer. He leaned an elbow on the counter. "Yes, Dr. Fan, this is about Tyler. I need your help with something."

"What?"

"What has he told you about the problems he's having at work?"

She hesitated. "That's a leading question, Mr. Ferguson. What did you have in mind specifically?"

"He tell you we—the FBI—suspect there's a problem with their computerized records system? That it may be responsible for a recent death of one of his patients?"

She frowned. "He mentioned something about a problem, but we've not seen that much of each other. We're separated."

Ferguson nodded. "Yes. That's part of the problem. You see, we were notified of the complication through the NIH. For reasons I won't bore you with, we're investigating any leads that suggest a software bug in the system. Because it involved your husband's patient I contacted him, but because of his past encounter with the Bureau, he has been unwilling to assist us."

"What does this have to do with me?"

"I'm hoping you'll help me convince him to help us."

"I don't know if I can. We're not seeing each other right now."

Ferguson studied her a moment, wondering if she too blamed the FBI for the disastrous outcome of Tyler's last encounter with federal law enforcement. "I understand the feeling you and Tyler have about how the California debacle ended up, but if it's any consolation, I know Tyler didn't steal those drugs."

She stared back at him. "What did you just say? He didn't make up that story . . . the drug thing, it wasn't true?"

He wasn't sure if she just referred to the forged prescriptions or not. "I'm not sure I follow. What drug thing?"

She flashed a look of confused relief. "He didn't tell you about the drugs in his locker?"

"No. Tell me about them."

Soon as Ferguson was out the door, Nancy went straight to the wall phone, a mixture of guilt and anger tugging at her heart. Anger at herself for not believing Tyler. She dialed his number and listened to it ring. By the tenth ring she thought it strange his answering machine hadn't picked up.

Too upset to work now, she decided to go home and continue unpacking. She'd try again later.

– – – – – – – – – – – –

Christine Dikman closed the door to the Charge Nurse's office and said to Tyler, "Thanks for coming, Dr. Mathews. I know you didn't have to." She wore purple scrubs, a stethoscope draped around her neck, and chestnut hair ponytailed with a rubber band. She was tall and skinny with a thin, attractive face he estimated had at least fifteen years of nursing stress etched into it. She folded herself into a black task chair behind a utilitarian desk with a glowing LCD monitor. He took the only other chair, a simple maple one.

She looked at him. "Here's the rest of the story I didn't tell you over the phone. As I mentioned before, the parents don't buy into the diagnosis. And after I finish telling you the whole story I want you to take a look at Toby."

"But I'm not a hematologist."

"You don't have to be. Just take a look at him. You'll see what I'm concerned about. I've taken care of a ton of leukemia kids and I know what the ones with their marrow shot to hell look like. He's not one of them." She glanced at the fingers of her right hand with a hint of regret he'd seen in nurses who scrub too often. "The parents rejected Sprague's push for a bone marrow transplant and asked for a second opinion. Sprague felt the risk to Toby of leaving protective isolation was too great to have him obtain that from outside the hospital so another hematologist was brought in. Of course, all she did was look at the lab studies and agree with Sprague." She opened a desk drawer, removed a plastic tube, and squirted a dollop of white lotion on her palm.

"When it turned into a standoff Sprague contacted our in-house attorney who's gotten a judge to issue an order for the transplant."

"Oh, Jesus. When is it going to take place?"

"Soon as Toby's strep throat clears up. At least that's the plan as it now stands."

CHAPTER 26

Tyler stood in the entrance to his apartment building and swiped the key fob over the security sensor. The front door lock responded with a metallic snap. He pulled open the door and entered the deserted lobby. The rain had picked up since leaving the hospital and the run from the parking lot across Third Avenue to his apartment building had drenched him, washing clumped strands of brown hair over his forehead. With a brisk swipe he pushed them straight back, then headed to the wall of mailboxes.

"You should invest in a piece of property. A small house or condominium. Otherwise you are throwing away good money. Build up some equity," his father had advised when hearing he'd rented an apartment in Seattle. The senior Mathews fancied himself Tyler's personal financial advisor based on his status as department chairman.

"But I don't plan on staying there more than two years, Dad. You know that." They'd discussed that particular strategy too. Numerous times. The MMC job would be Tyler's ticket back into academic medicine. Or so he hoped. Now that hung in the balance.

Ignoring the elevators, he headed for the paneled exit door to the stairwell. Only four flights up to his floor and he needed the exercise. Starting up the bare concrete stairs he thought of Nancy again. Could Ferguson somehow help salvage the situation? He still hadn't been able to reach him to negotiate a deal.

As usual, the hallway to his unit was deserted. Rarely did he see other tenants. He pushed open his apartment door, stepped inside, and stopped, his hand frozen on the key still in the lock. Something felt wrong, out of place.

After folding the key back into the wallet, he slowly closed the door and stood very still, searching his senses for what seemed odd. A deep sense of foreboding mushroomed beneath his diaphragm making it difficult to suck in a full breath. His heart accelerated.

"Trust no one." "Sergio Vericelli was found dead in bed. We're looking into a needle mark on his arm."

A chill tickled the spine between his shoulders.

Only paranoia? he asked himself.

No. Something *was* wrong and in the next instant he knew exactly what. A trace of stale nicotine floated in the air. The kind that clings to smokers' clothes.

Did the manager come in for some reason?

Heart racing, nerves tingling, he stepped cautiously into the living room and surveyed his meager furnishings. Nothing looked disturbed. Then again, he wasn't a Martha Stewart–grade housekeeper.

A floorboard creaked. His head snapped around toward the bedroom. Two men shot forward, each grabbing one of Tyler's wrists. They jerked his arms behind him and before he could react, kicked the back of his knee, buckling his leg, and dropping him to the floor. He screamed in pain and fear as a clear plastic bag—the kind used to sheathe laundered shirts—slipped over his head. Lungs now empty, Tyler gasped for air but the thin plastic barrier snapped taut over his open mouth and flared nostrils. Another bolt of adrenaline shot into him. He would suffocate if they kept it on.

He struggled with the strength fear of impending death provokes, but both men outweighed him by at least twenty pounds and each one had an arm pinned to the floor. He bucked, swinging up his feet to kick at their heads and missed. One man moved over him, straddling his hips and twisting his wrist into a painful position.

Tyler tried to buck the man off, but his vision began dissolving into a pinhole as his consciousness ebbed away.

Tyler surfaced from darkness, both lungs filled with precious air. A bad dream? Was that what it'd been? His eyes cracked, saw the familiar ceiling above his bed. He tried to move, to turn over, but was stuck spread-eagled, arms and legs held rigid. Another wave of panic surged through his arteries.

"What the hell . . ." Tyler turned his head, looked over his right shoulder. One of the men was filling a syringe from a glass vial.

A hoarse voice whispered in his ear, "Shut up or I'll stuff this pillow down your throat."

Tyler tugged at the restraints, then noticed the padded leather. Exactly the same tethers used by hospitals. *The kind that leave no marks.* He still wore suit pants, but the coat was off, his right shirtsleeve rolled up past his elbow exposing a bulging vein.

A wave of cold tingling raced through him. "Jesus Christ, what the hell you doing?" He flashed on Michelle. Was this exactly what happened to her?

Syringe Man said, "He warned you. Shut up."

"Fuck that noise. Help!" he yelled as loud as possible, hoping a neighbor would hear.

A pillow slammed over on his face, then pressure over his mouth. Tyler tried to rock back and forth, but couldn't free his mouth. Something sharp pierced at the skin over the vein. He tried to wiggle and dislodge the needle, but a cool sensation rushed upward under the skin into his shoulder and then vanished.

CHAPTER 27

He tried to scream, "No, don't!" but it came out as a muffled grunt.

The pillow vanished. The panic and fear began evaporating into a warm, delightful cocoon of well-being.

"Who are you guys?" If he could get them talking he might negotiate something. Maybe they just wanted information.

The big one looked at the smaller one, asked, "How long?"

The other one said, "Couple minutes, more or less."

Tyler asked, "This have to do with the medical records?" Strange, he thought, he no longer feared them even though he knew they meant him grave harm.

The first one bent over Tyler and studied his eyes. "Maybe a bit quicker, way he looks."

Tyler watched the restraints vanish from around his wrists, then tried to hold up his arm and study the area they'd wrapped around but found he couldn't even focus on the hairs on his arm no matter how hard he tried. Strange.

Through his muddled mind it dawned on him. They'd injected him with a narcotics overdose, just as someone had done to Michelle and then Vericelli. The drug effects were quickly hammering his brain into submission. First he'd slip into unconsciousness. Then, unable to support his respirations, his breathing would become more and more shallow until it would cease altogether. He'd be dead in a few minutes. He fought the funny tingling starting in his lips and tried to refocus on his hand but was amazed to see his fingers holding the syringe. He let go, letting it roll off the bed. Too bad. Pick it up later. Instead, he struggled to prop himself on one elbow. "Please, don do this to me . . . I'll tell you whatever you wanna know."

"Know?" The big one continued collecting the leather restraints. He snickered. "We don't want to know shit."

Tyler let his heavy head flop back onto the soft pillow. That felt good. "But then . . . why?" Strange, they wore latex gloves.

"Are you religious?"

"What?"

"Because you got maybe twenty seconds before you're out. After that? Hey, you're dead." With another laugh, he turned and followed his partner from the room.

Unable to sit, no longer caring that he couldn't, Tyler nestled back onto the mattress and took comfort in knowing that in a few moments he'd discover the answer to a question that had subliminally bugged him almost thirty-eight years now.

Familiar sounds began seeping into warm weightlessness . . . then vanished . . . then appeared: the steady bleep of a cardiac monitor, distant murmurs . . . Was this surgery? *Should I be scrubbing?* He wrestled with the sounds, trying to make sense of them. He could perform the surgery if he knew what the case was. Or was this just another variation on the recurring dream of being on campus and realizing in one hour he was due to take the final exam for a course he signed up for but somehow never attended?

"Tyler."

Slowly rotating his head toward the familiar female voice he realized he was flat on his back, eyes closed, drifting somewhere north of semiconsciousness.

"Tyler."

He willed his eyelids open a crack. They reflexively scrunched tightly shut from blinding light. He tried again, this time more slowly. Jill's blurry face floated inches away, her eyes searching his.

"Jill?" he croaked. His dry tongue flicked over equally dry, cracked lips. "Water."

A smile curled the corners of her mouth. "Welcome back, Tyler. You had me worried there for a while."

He realized she was sitting by him in what looked like a familiar room, then realized why it seemed familiar. It appeared to be the Maynard Intensive Care Unit. *What happened? Was I in an accident?* He felt no discomfort other than a desire to shift positions and wet his mouth.

"Water."

"Here." She guided a white plastic straw between his lips. The tepid water came with a hint of plastic, but was wet and that's what mattered. He let it fill his mouth before swallowing and tonguing the residual moisture over parched gums.

"More."

She replaced the straw. "Easy. Don't drink too much until you know your stomach can handle it."

The details of the apartment struggle trickled back to him. "They tried to kill me," he croaked.

"What?"

He glanced around again, then looked at the back of his hand. An IV obscured the injection site.

"What time is it?"

"A little after midnight."

"Midnight! What day?" His voice cracked again. He tried to clear his desert-dry throat.

"Sunday morning."

He thought about that a moment.

"How did I get here?"

"When I didn't hear from you by six o'clock I started to worry. By the time six-thirty rolled around I was getting really worried. I tried calling but no one answered. Not even your answering machine came on. That's when I really started to worry. So I came over to your apartment and had the manager let me in. Good thing I did because otherwise you might have checked out for good." She paused, seemingly searching for difficult words. "Maybe this will be a lesson to you, Tyler. Maybe you should consider a drug rehab program."

He palm-wiped his face, removing unseen cobwebs. "What?"

"You OD'ed. The ER doc says you must've miscalculated your dose."

"Bullshit. I was attacked. Two men. They tried to make it look like an OD. Probably the same thing happened with Michelle."

She seemed to study him a moment. "And you fought these two men?"

When he didn't answer, she said, "There wasn't any sign of a fight," in the objective tone of a therapist. "They didn't find any cuts or bruises on you and the room looked normal."

"Goddamnit, they straightened up the room."

"Oh, Tyler . . ."

"I'm telling you . . ." Her expression said it all. "Shit, you think I'm making this up!"

She sighed. "All I know is that if I hadn't found you, you'd probably be dead by now. I'd hate to see that happen." She took hold of his hand.

He tried to push up on his elbow but the room spun and his brain felt coated with more cobwebs. They probably gave him narcan to reverse any narcotic, but who knew what other medications had been in the syringe. "They tox screen me?"

"Yes."

"Know what they found?"

She nodded. "Fentanyl and a benzodiazepine."

He considered that a moment. Good news and bad. He probably had a fair amount of tolerance for the benzodiazepine considering all the Ambien he'd downed over the months. Fentanyl—that was another matter.

"If you think I'm lying, check with the police. I bet it's the same drug combination they found in Michelle's blood. They killed her too."

He sensed something in her body language. "What is it you're not telling me?"

She straightened up, her face taking back the ice maiden expression. "When they admitted you through the ER? The staff recognized you." She wrung her hands nervously. "Being an overdose, they had no recourse, Tyler."

"What exactly are you telling me?"

"The fact that you were admitted with a narcotics overdose had to be reported to the Chief of Staff."

There it was. His third strike. He'd lose this job, his license, his career. He was totally screwed.

Or was there something he could do? What if Ferguson verified his story? Wouldn't that exonerate him? "Can you get me a telephone?" He scanned the room for his wallet with Ferguson's card in it.

She placed her hand against his chest, gently pushing him back down onto the bed. "Hey, take it easy. I'll see if I can get you a phone. In the meantime, just lay back and take it easy. Be back in a few minutes."

He settled in against the pillow thinking he could call the main FBI number and tell whoever answered he needed to reach Ferguson for an emergency. Wasn't sure if last try he'd mentioned an emergency . . . He closed his eyes praying the room would stop spinning.

Tyler snapped wide awake with the sudden realization time had passed. How much? No way of knowing, but instinctively it felt like more than just minutes. He squinted into the darkened room. The recessed overheads were dimmed and it was complete darkness outside the tinted windows. *Still early morning,* he figured. Jill was gone, the chair empty. He sensed movement and looked right. In a shadowy corner stood a male in pale blue scrubs.

"What time is it?" Tyler asked the nurse.

"Oh, you're awake." The nurse approached the bed.

He sensed something familiar. *What?* "What time is it?" It hit him—the odor of stale nicotine. He felt his heart accelerate in his chest, heard it on the monitor. The fear fed on itself, making him push up on one elbow for a closer look.

"A little after three." The nurse picked up the clear plastic IV line connecting a half-full saline bag to a vein in the back of Tyler's right hand.

He noticed a large syringe in the nurse's other hand. "What is that?" The fear gripping his heart intensified.

"A little medicine to help you relax."

Something familiar in the man's voice jolted Tyler further toward panic. He yanked his arm away and sat up. "I don't need anything to relax. I want up and out of here." He started to reach for the lock to lower the bed rails.

"Sorry, no can do." The nurse grabbed at the IV injection port.

It all clicked—the same voice from his apartment.

Tyler's hand clamped onto the man's wrist, twisting it violently, causing the syringe to tumble onto the bedsheet. Tyler's free hand snatched it away before the man could react. Rolling onto his right side, Tyler held the syringe as a weapon. "Back off, asshole."

The killer retreated a step but didn't seem particularly threatened. He rolled his neck, loosening up his shoulders, and crouched.

Tyler noticed a lanyard hospital ID dangling from his neck. The picture looked nothing like the man. With his free hand, Tyler released the bed-rail lock, letting it drop with a bang. He slid off the side of the bed. His free hand tore off the EKG leads. The man stepped closer, both muscular arms outstretched like a sumo wrestler. Tyler edged around the bed, keeping a good space between them.

Tyler yelled, "Don't! I'll inject you," hoping someone would hear.

The man shot one quick nervous glance toward the glass door. Closed. The curtain pulled, effectively sealing off the outside from sound transmission. He smiled with apparent satisfaction. "Make my fucking day."

Tyler ripped out the IV but couldn't remove the indwelling IV line without setting down the syringe. Blood began dripping from the open port. The killer lunged for Tyler's arm but he sidestepped, causing him to miss hitting full force, but his shoulder crashed into Tyler's chest, slamming him back against the wall, causing his grip to give. The syringe tumbled to the floor.

Tyler grabbed for it, but the other man was quicker and already bent over, hand outstretched. Instinctively, Tyler kicked, driving his knee directly into the man's face, connecting hard, producing a sickening crunch of shattering bone and cartilage. Warm fluid spurted over his bare leg. Blood. But the killer dropped onto all fours, both hands groping frantically for the syringe. Tyler kicked it just before the man's right hand reached it, sending it spinning across the floor. He broke free and lunged, his fingers reaching. He scooped it up, spun around, rammed the needle through the thin scrub shirt cloth into the man's back until it bent against the shoulder blade. He rammed the plunger home just as the man rolled right to get away, but the needle was now hooked into his back and moved with him. Empty now, Tyler released the syringe, letting it hang from the man's back.

Still crouching, the man swung. The roundhouse blow clipped Tyler on the chin, spilling him backward and into the wall. He scrambled back onto his feet, sprang for the door as the man also pushed up onto his feet. Tyler slid open the door only enough to slip into the hall, then slammed it closed and held it. He glanced around for help. Fifty feet away, outside the waiting room, stood the second killer. The man's eyes widened in surprise but he said nothing, just started walking hurriedly toward him.

CHAPTER 28

Tyler yelled at two nurses in the nursing station, "Help! Call security," and started running.

The door crashed open behind him. Tyler turned his head. The killer was hanging on to the edge of the door, struggling to remain upright, his eyes no longer focusing.

Tyler sprinted bare-footed to a side stairwell, slammed his left hip into the horizontal door release at full speed, flinging the door open, crashing it against the concrete wall. Using both hands to help slide down the tubular metal railing, he jumped down stairs three at a time, his feet stinging against the cold bare concrete. He never turned to see who was following him.

Tyler paused on the second-floor landing for a quick listen. Rapid footsteps hammered the concrete stairs above, heading his way, echoing off the cinder-block walls. He threw open the door and turned right at a dead run. The dimmed, deserted hallway stretched out in both directions. If he could round a corner before the other guy burst through the door, he might be able to gain time. His feet stung from slapping the bare concrete stairs and his lungs hurt from lack of oxygen and the lingering effect of the narcotics. At least now his soles were hitting vinyl.

Up ahead a man in gray housekeeping work clothes waltzed a large electric circular buffer side to side across the floor. The man didn't seem to notice him at first, probably because of earphones connected to a silver Discman hanging from his belt. Just then the man's head jerked up, eyes wide. His mouth dropped open as Tyler shot past. At that moment the door banged open behind him. Tyler rounded the corner.

Twenty more feet and he reached the men's surgery locker room. Frantically he punched in the four-digit security code. The lock snapped open. A moment later he was inside, gasping for air, leaning against the closed, locked door. His pursuer probably wouldn't know the security code. And if he asked the housekeeper? Odds were fifty-fifty he didn't know it either. But he couldn't bank on those odds.

Tyler grabbed a set of scrubs off the metal rack and hurried to his locker. A moment later he threw open the narrow metal door and tore off the patient gown. On came the scrubs followed by his dedicated surgical shoes—a pair of Nike runners on the locker floor. Now dressed, he closed the door, then tore off the tape and removed the Intracath still dripping blood from his vein. He pressed two fingers firmly over the puncture site and shook his head in an attempt to rid it of the last brain cobwebs.

He leaned his back against the cold locker door to steady himself and sucked in a deep lungful of air while trying to collect his thoughts.

Call security? Probably not a good idea. They'd most likely see him as nothing more than an escaped substance abuser gone berserk. Besides, what if the medical center security was cooperating with the killers? Call Ferguson? Okay, but only after finding a secure hiding place. Nancy? No. She didn't believe the drugs-in-the-locker story anyway, so why would she ever believe this one? Especially after being hospitalized for an overdose. That left Jill.

He looked at the door through which he'd entered just minutes ago. So far no one had tried to come in here. Maybe the housekeeper said nothing. Maybe his pursuer gave up. Maybe the asshole was outside waiting. And maybe he was surrounded like Butch Cassidy in the final scene of the movie. No way to tell without opening the door and that was simply an option he wasn't about to exercise.

Over in the hall that led to surgery was a row of dictation booths. They contained phones. He dialed. When the operator answered, he said, "This is Dr. Leung. I need to be connected to Jill Richardson's home phone, STAT."

A moment later Jill's sleep-laden voice answered.

"It's me, Tyler. I need help," he blurted between breaths, his heart still hammering his sternum.

"What? What's happened?"

In rapid-fire sentences he explained the ordeal in ICU.

She asked, "Where are you now?"

Something stopped him from telling her exactly. Instead he said, "I'm still in the hospital. Can you help me?"

"You have to ask? Yes, what?"

His plan crystallized. "Drive up here as soon as you can. Park in the Emergency lot. Go to the cashier and claim my valuables—tell them the police want my wallet."

"They'll never give those to me."

"Sure they will. You're the head of Risk Management, you can pass off a credible enough story."

She didn't answer immediately. "You may be right . . . okay, where will I find you?"

"After you get my things, just go back to your car. I'll meet you there." He hung up.

The locker room had two exits: the way he'd entered and a second door to the main hall serving surgery. No reason the killer would know about the second exit unless, of course, the housekeeper or security told him. *Then again,* he thought, *what were the odds he's still in the building? By now his disguise should be blown. Unless, of course, security was helping him.* Now that he thought about it, more than likely it probably *wasn't* the killer who'd pursued him . . . it was probably one of the nurses or someone from security. The killer would have had to help his buddy since he'd been injected with whatever the syringe contained.

This time of night the operating rooms would be dark and silent unless there was an emergency case under way. But with forty ORs available, chances were, even if one was being used, he could make it to a back hall exit without being noticed. And if they did, he'd look completely in place. Just another surgeon wandering through the area.

He cracked the door displaying a large red sign, AUTHORIZED PERSONNEL ONLY BEYOND THIS POINT, and peered out into a graveyard-still hallway. He heard no sounds.

He slipped out into the hall, quietly closing the door behind him. The main hall formed a large rectangle circumventing a huge core of back-to-back operating rooms sharing a common dirty area and central supply. Over on the other side of the rectangle, a stairway led down to the first-floor surgical waiting area. From there it would be a relatively easy matter to slip out through a side door and walk around the block to the parking lot. Piece of cake.

"Hey you. Hold it right there."

Tyler glanced over his right shoulder. A large black man in a Maynard Medical Security uniform started jogging his way, each step accentuated by metallic jangles.

Tyler darted across the hall, shouldered through a heavy swinging door into an OR illuminated only by light angling through a small window in the single door to the central area. Unable to see well, he ran into the heavy stainless-steel operating table, banging his left knee, shooting pain up his thigh and buckling his leg, making it impossible to run. Cursing silently, he dropped behind the anesthesia machine, frantically rubbing the kneecap.

The double doors cracked open as the security officer whispered, "I repeat, in pursuit of subject. Second floor, main surgery." A pause. "Roger that."

Shit!

A moment later a flashlight beam cut through the enlarging crack between the swinging doors. In a normal voice, the man asked, "That you in there, Doc Mathews?"

Tyler ran his fingertips down the back corners of the anesthesia machine until he could feel the small back wheels and their locks, then slowly rotated the flanges forward into the unlocked position.

One side of the door was completely open now, the flashlight beam exploring the room's white tiled walls and interior. "Don't worry, Doc, we're your friends. We don't mean you no harm. Come on outta there. We know you in there." The beam cut across the top of the cart, passing overhead.

Tyler heard the metallic jingle of keys and peeked around the cart. The guard, silhouetted from the weak light filtering in from the hall, was moving slowly toward him now, flashlight still sweeping the room, but seemingly concerned now with the possibility of Tyler hiding behind the operating-room table. "You can run, but you can't hide, Doc. Believe me on that one."

It dawned on Tyler. The guard was flanking the OR table. If he just stayed perfectly still, the guy might assume he'd gone out the other door and follow. He peeked around the cart edge to see where he was. The flashlight beam caught him directly in his eyes.

"Gotcha," the guard yelled with obvious glee.

Tyler heard the jangle move his way, estimated the closing distance, and forced himself to wait one more beat before throwing all his weight against the anesthesia machine, rolling it forward as fast as he could until it came into thudding contact with something solid enough to stop it abruptly. He heard a groan and rushed past as the guard slumped to the floor, flew through the doorway and into the hall where he turned left, heading for an exit. Just as he approached the junction with the hall to the recovery room another security guard jogged around the corner in his direction. Without breaking stride, Tyler dropped his shoulder like a determined fullback and caught the surprised man in the chest, spinning him around and crashing him against the wall.

Tyler rounded the corner at the end of the hall and slammed his hip into the emergency exit crossbar, throwing the door open and triggering a deafening, clanging fire alarm. But rather than fleeing down the stairs, he turned and sped across the hall into another blackened operating room. Gasping for breath, hand over his mouth to muffle the sound, he peeked through the small window in the swinging door at the limited view of the hall.

A moment later the guard he'd smashed against the wall flew through the open emergency door and began clambering down the stairs in pursuit. A few seconds later, the first guard limped after him.

Cautiously, being careful to make no sounds, Tyler slipped into the utility room, cut across central supply, through another dark OR, and back into the hall on the opposite side from where he'd entered the area. Here was the door surgeons used to drop down to the first-floor waiting area. Moving as quickly as possible but without making any noise, he made it to the first floor, cut out into the lobby waiting room, ran across the main lobby to the front doors, then out into the driveway.

"Were you able to get my wallet?" Tyler asked, sliding into Jill's Lexus coupe, scanning the area yet again for another security guard.

"Here." She handed it to him, then fired the ignition. "But you'll have to be the one to claim the rest of your clothes. I didn't want to have to explain that too." She gave him a strange look. "Was that you who set off the alarms?"

Tyler scrunched down in the seat so that just his eyes peered over the edge of the window. "I had no choice."

"I'm getting out of here before you get yourself in another calamity." She turned, looked over her shoulder to back up, and hit the door lock button. "How about we go to my place so we can both catch our breath and figure out what to do next."

Anything sounded better than hanging around the Emergency Department parking lot while hospital security kept searching for him. "Sounds good." He opened the wallet. Good, Ferguson's card was where he'd left it.

She nosed the car into the street. "From the top . . . tell me exactly what happened."

He went through the entire story again. When he finished she said, "Lucky you woke up when you did. Otherwise . . ." She reached over and stroked his cheek. "I don't even want to think about it."

The eastern sky glowed with the first orange-red streaks of dawn. Traffic remained sparse. The start of another Seattle Sunday morning. To Tyler it looked as bleak as his future. Did hospital security have enough juice to request Seattle police look for him also? He sucked in a deep breath, tried to calm his nerves, the pain in his gut and knee.

"You don't have any Tums or Maalox with you, do you?"

"No, but I have something at my condo."

"Thanks." He straightened up in the seat.

Neither one spoke as she drove down Madison to Fourth, then north to Stewart. A few minutes later they waited as a large steel parking garage door of a high-rise building rolled up, allowing them access. Car parked, he followed her to a carpeted elevator atrium. From there they rode up to the twenty-first floor.

Once inside her condo she pealed off her lightweight black raincoat and hung it in a closet close to the door. "Give me a second. I'll get you some Tums."

He watched her disappear down a short hall to the master bedroom. A moment later she reappeared, handed him an open roll of antacids. "Here. Want a stiff drink, something to calm you down?"

A drink was the last thing he wanted or needed. "What I need is to figure out a way of getting some real clothes." He pulled at the sides of the scrub pants to emphasize his garb.

"Maybe I can sneak into your apartment, if you tell me what you want." She waved him into the living room and offered him a seat, but he was too edgy to sit. Instead, he moved to the wall of windows providing a breathtaking view over the roof of the Pike Place Market to the harbor and West Seattle. A white-and-green ferryboat was pulling away from its slip.

"Maybe you should call the police and tell them what's happened," she offered.

He waved that idea away. "Ridiculous. It'd be too easy for Benson to convince them I'm just another druggie after medications . . . the asshole."

"Maybe so, but one way or the other you need help with this. Let's face it, any help I can give only goes so far. I draw the line at hand-to-hand combat." She smiled, said, "Here," and offered him a chair again. "If not a drink, then how about some coffee?"

Although caffeine was the last thing his jangled nerves needed at this point, it might just paradoxically calm his mind. "That'll work." He started toward the kitchen area. "I'll supervise."

Two barstools were parked in front of a granite counter. He tried to perch on one but couldn't sit still and opted to stand. He watched her pull a bag of beans from the Sub-Zero, ran his hand over his head, and tried to think of his next move but all that came to mind was contacting Ferguson.

She stopped working, eyed him questioningly. "You're planning something . . . What?"

"There's this guy . . . Ferguson. I think he might be able to help get me out of this mess."

She poured coffee beans into a black and chrome Braun grinder. "Oh? And what does this Ferguson fellow do that he can help?"

He hesitated, trying to decide if he could trust her. She capped the grinder and turned toward him. "Well?"

She'd saved his life. Why not trust her?

"He's an FBI agent."

"Really!" Her finger stopped just short of pressing the grinder switch. "Is this a personal friend or did you contact him about our little problem with the medical record?"

He tensed at her reply. Something about it left him even uneasier than a moment ago. "Neither. He contacted me."

She glanced down at her frozen finger and pressed the button.

The rattle of beans quickly segued into a smooth whir. A moment later she released the button, looked him in the eye again. "About?"

"About two or three days ago," he said. "I don't know . . . I've sort of lost track of the days."

She rolled her eyes, sighed exasperation. "C'mon, Tyler, don't try to be funny. This is important . . . what the hell did he want from you?"

"He wanted to know if there was a problem with the medical record. Why?"

She set down the grinder and leaned against the counter. "And why would he come to you with that particular question?"

"This is beginning to feel more like an interrogation than idle conversation."

She shot him a hard look. "It's important, Tyler. Now answer my question."

"Because I reported Larry Childs's death to NIH. He was following up on it. Now get off my back."

She frowned. "Odd. Why would he be interested?"

"I have no idea," he lied.

She seemed to consider this a moment. "And what did you tell him?"

"I told him what I knew . . . that Larry Childs had a bad case of radiation necrosis and despite the record saying he received a normal dose, he didn't."

"And that's *all* you told him?"

"Right."

Seemingly relieved at his answer, she poured the grinder contents into an espresso machine, put two cups beneath the outflow scuppers, and pressed a button. "And when you talk to Ferguson this time, what do you plan on telling him?" Brown liquid began flowing out of the scuppers into the cups.

He studied her body language a moment, looking for . . . what? "Why so curious?"

Her eyes held his a moment. "You have to ask? You just had

two attempts on your life. Should I not be concerned about that?"

He believed her. "I'm going to tell him everything I know about this mess."

"Fine, but do you have anything to back up your story? Last I knew you had nothing to prove the Childs thing."

"True, but I have the other patients you turned me on to." He almost forgot Torres. "And my brain-abscess patient."

"Yes, but do you have direct proof? That's the real question. Without it, who's going to believe you?"

"Yeah, I have proof," he said reluctantly. "I burnt all of it to a CD. If anyone changes those records now, it'll be even better evidence."

She seemed to think about this a moment too. "You stored that someplace safe, I presume."

"Yes." He waited to see if she'd ask the obvious.

Instead, she said, "And when you get to the part of your story about last night . . . the killers . . . who are you going to point the finger at?"

CHAPTER 29

"Arthur Benson."

"Arthur Benson! You're joking. Why? Because he threatened you?" She barked a little you've-got-to-be-kidding laugh, like clearing her throat.

"Seems like a good enough reason for me. Besides, he's got a hell of a lot to lose if word gets out of a flaw in the system."

"Tyler, we *all* lose if that word gets out. Every one of us . . . from Benson on down to the dishwashers in dietary. Think about it . . . sure, the CEO always takes the fall for a bad decision, especially one of that magnitude, but it was the board that signed off on the commitment to Med-InDx. My God, if it got smeared all over the press a security flaw was causing problems, no one would ever want to be admitted to Maynard again. If that happened, the whole hospital would go under. Every nurse, clerk, pharmacist, and doctor—including you—would lose their job. Is that what you want? To lose your job?"

He slammed the countertop with his palm and stepped off the barstool intending to leave. "Jesus fucking Christ, I don't believe what I just heard. What are you suggesting? That I not talk to Ferguson? That I turn my back on the fact patients are dying because of a software bug? That I simply forget that twice in the past twenty-four hours two thugs have tried to kill me?"

Her right eyebrow arched. "Software bug? What's this about a software bug?"

Mistake. He'd forgotten. Far as she knew, he still believed in the hacker theory. He tossed a dismissive wave. "It makes more sense to suspect a software problem than a security breach by some serial killer hacker." He couldn't leave now, not until he deflected her attention from the software. "You didn't answer my question. What are you suggesting, stay away from Ferguson because I can't prove who's trying to kill me?"

"No, that's not what I'm saying at all." Anger filled her voice. A second later she held up a hand. "Time out."

She came around the counter, took him in her arms, and hugged him. For a moment he did nothing, too caught off guard to know how to respond. His arms encircled her and for a moment he relived the fantasy from the other night.

Nancy's image floated into his consciousness. He pushed Jill away. "This is bullshit. I have to go."

She straightened up, a hurt look on her face, and brushed her hair back into place. "Hear me out on this, okay?"

He glanced at his wrist, realized he didn't have his watch. "One minute and I'm out of here."

She raised her finger. "All I'm saying is you'll be more convincing if you can go to Ferguson with facts, not suspicions. If I understand you correctly you have some evidence from four patients' charts that suggests complications. Isn't that true?"

"Yes, but it's more than just suggestion. They died because of errors in the records."

"But you have no idea what really caused those complications, do you? What I mean is, couldn't some of them—if you really look closely—have been human error?"

"You and I both know it wasn't human error. Even you must've thought there was more to it than just human error. Why else would you give them to me?"

"I never said I was convinced. They looked suspicious, that's all. And as far as accusing Benson of hiring killers . . . man, oh, man, that's one serious accusation to make without something other than an undocumented conversation between the two of you." She shot him a questioning look. "Does any of this make any sense?"

In fact, it did. He nodded. Any move against Benson without absolute proof would result in exactly the same type of reprisal his ex-chairman had leveled on him. Only this time it'd be worse, he'd lose his license to practice medicine. Maybe his life.

Jill rotated her cup, seemed to consider asking something. "Is there any way to get more supporting information before you call your FBI contact?"

"There might be."

CHAPTER 30

Jill asked, "What?"

Trust her? He wanted to. For what reason, he wasn't certain. If nothing more, he wanted someone to bounce the idea off of. Who else was there?

"My only hope of finding the kind of evidence you're talking about is to convince someone inside of Med-InDx to help me. I only know three people even remotely associated with the company. Jim Day, Yusef Khan, and Bernie Levy. Levy sure as hell isn't going to do anything. Ditto with Khan. That leaves Day."

"You're not planning on going near the hospital are you?"

"Not if I can help it," he lied.

She seemed genuinely concerned. "After all that's happened, what makes you think you can trust him?"

"He may not have a choice."

Tyler could feel the doorman's eyes size him up as soon as he exited the elevator and headed through the lobby of Jill's condominium to the front door. Too discreet to ask a point-blank question—like, Who the hell was he?—the doorman pulled open the huge hinged hunk of plate glass protecting the high-end building from outside urban uncertainties and uttered a simple, "Good morning, sir," without completely masking a distinct note of curiosity in his voice.

Tyler figured probably not many homeowners come strolling through the lobby in scrubs. And the pair of heavy, black Zeiss binoculars in his left hand did little to clarify the picture. Or maybe it was something very simple—a security thing—like the guy had never laid eyes on him before now. He decided whatever the issue, it was the doorman's problem, not his. Avoiding eye contact, he muttered, "Thanks," and stepped out onto the sidewalk.

He stood to the side of the door mentally running through his plan. Although the street was still in the building's shadow, the air temperature was now on the chilly side of mid-sixties. The scent of salt water from a gentle harbor breeze had washed away all evidence of Saturday night car fumes but did nothing to calm the brewing anxiety in his gut. A moment later he turned away from the harbor and started toward the next corner.

9:40 A.M.

Tyler crouched, binoculars steadied on a rusted, metal-capped parapet, studying his apartment windows across the street. The downward angle didn't allow an entire view of the living room and kitchen, but gave him enough coverage to believe no one was waiting inside. He'd been crouched up here on this stinking tar roof for what felt like a half hour but was probably more like fifteen minutes, making his knees ache, making him edgy to move on. Besides that, the black roof was radiating enough heat to make breathing the putrid exhaust from a nearby vent a real pain in the ass.

Leaning forward, the heavy German glasses angled downward, he studied the cars and pedestrians once again, coming back to an anthracite BMW 7-series still curbed just down from the entrance to his building. It had been parked there doing nothing since he'd first looked. The driver's side window was down, an elbow perched on the edge, a wisp of what could be cigarette smoke curling up over the top edge every once in a while. Short of walking up and asking what the hell the driver was waiting for, there was no way to prove they were watching for him or not and it seemed highly doubtful it would be Ferguson's car.

Might as well get on with it, he decided.

He duck-walked back from the edge before standing and heading for the bare concrete stairwell. A few minutes later, on the basement level of the apartment building, he hit a button switch. A roll-up, metal-slat garage door groaned upward, allowing him to walk up the steeply angled driveway into the alley. From here he traveled two blocks north, turned east for two blocks before heading south for another two blocks, bringing him to a 24/7 convenience store. He entered and nodded to the familiar counter clerk, the air thick with the smell of spicy hot dogs rotating under a set of heat lamps.

He passed a wire stand stocked with various potato chip choices and followed an aisle to a large cooler filled with beer, soft drinks, and half-gallon milk cartons. A narrow hall led past a unisex lavatory radiating ammonia fumes to a metal fire door.

Tyler cracked the door and peered out. The alley, atherosclerotic from green Dumpsters, was impassable to any vehicle wider than a Volkswagen Jetta. Twenty feet away a man in soiled clothes was urinating against a brick wall.

Tyler crossed the alley to his apartment building back door and punched a six-digit security code onto an aluminum keypad. The door lock responded with a hard, metallic snap. He stepped inside and for the next thirty seconds stood on the stairwell landing breathing deeply, trying to slow his heart and lightheadedness. He listened for someone in the stairwell. Nothing. Slowly he cracked the door and peeked into the first-floor lobby. Seeing no one, he slipped into the hall and punched the manager's doorbell and waited down the hall so that he couldn't be seen from the street. A moment later the door opened, framing an unshaven face with bloodshot basset-hound eyes.

"Doc Mathews." The manager combed nicotine-stained fingers through greasy salt-and-pepper hair.

"Sorry to bother you, Carlos, but I—"

"Y'don't have no keys." The man yawned, scratched both love

handles, and nodded. "You okay, man? Sure as shit din look worth a damn last night when they drug you outta here. Juz a minute." For a beat he vanished from view only to reappear, keys in hand. He wore a faded Grateful Dead tee shirt and black jeans, no socks. He started toward the elevator without bothering to close his own door, probably figuring no one would have the nerve to enter, much less steal anything.

"I gotta tell ya, Doc, the owners don't want no druggies livin' here. I'm gonna cut ya some slack this time, but anything like last night happens again . . . Well . . ." He let it float.

Fed up with trying to defend himself, Tyler answered, "Understood."

Carlos pulled a ring of keys from a retractable belt holder and opened his door. "Here ya go, Doc."

"Hold on a second, I want to give you something."

Carlos shot him a suspicious look. "Gimme something?"

Tyler swept his hand toward the entrance. "A thank you for your trouble here."

The manager grinned, showing a missing canine. "No need."

"You can wait here or come on in." Tyler entered his apartment, figuring if someone were waiting for him Carlos could run and call the police. Carlos followed him in.

"Hold on." Tyler made a quick tour through the one-bedroom apartment before stopping in the kitchen and grabbing the only bottle of wine in the place, a Merlot he'd bought in hopes of cooking dinner for Nancy. "Here you go."

Carlos smiled. "Hey thanks, man, but ya know, you don't need to do this." He held up the bottle. "Ya sure?"

Tyler gave him a shoulder pat, ushering him toward the door. "For all your troubles. Thanks again."

A moment later he locked the door and surveyed the place more closely. His keys were on the counter where he'd left them. There were no signs of a struggle in either living room or bedroom. Even the syringe was gone. He checked the answering machine. Unplugged. At first he considered plugging it back in, then decided to let it go. If the killers knew it was unplugged, called, and found it plugged in again, they'd know he'd returned.

A floorboard creaked. Tyler froze.

Could he have overlooked something?

Both eyes on the bedroom, Tyler backed up toward the coat closet where he kept a baseball bat for the occasional pickup games between MMC surgeons and anesthesiologists. It was a well-used Louisville slugger from high school. Bat raised, ready to swing, he moved toward the bedroom and stepped inside. His breath caught. The bathroom door was closed—something he never did living by himself. Tyler turned the doorknob until he heard it click. He waited a beat before throwing it open and stepping back into a batting crouch. He waited.

No one.

Tyler dumped the Range Rover two blocks from the hospital, fed the parking meter with enough quarters to stave off the meter maids for an hour, and took off on foot. He was wearing black Levi's, a black cotton mock tee, and his Nike jogging shoes. A few minutes later he approached the main loading area for the medical center. As expected for this time of morning, a truck was backed up to the dock. With his ID badge clipped to his belt, in clear sight but difficult to read, he moved briskly along the sloping driveway, up a set of chipped concrete stairs onto the loading dock. With a cordial nod to a worker, he slipped inside, jogged down a set of stairs to the subbasement, then a tunnel to the annex. Moving quickly and purposefully, he climbed the stairs to the correct floor, darted through the hall to the office.

Jim Day looked up from his desk with a startled expression. "What the hell are you doing here?"

"Keep your hand away from the phone and your keyboard." Tyler surprised himself with the force of his command. He shut the door, isolating the two of them from the hall and anyone passing by. He leaned over the desk, both hands on the surface, and locked eyes with Day. "How long have you known about the bug?"

Day's face went expressionless. "Excuse me?"

"The bug. How long have you known about it."

Day glanced nervously around as if someone else might hear. "The fuck you talking about?"

"Don't start with that shuck-and-jive routine. I know you know exactly what I'm talking about. The medical record system. It's got a bug and it's killing patients. And if word gets out, you and everybody who hid the fact is going to be running for cover. And you know what? Those of us on the low end of the totem pole are the ones going to take the fall for the other guys. Know what I'm saying?"

Day coughed into his fist. "Man, I don't need this shit. You been shooting again? That what this is all about? 'Cause sure sounds like you high."

"Think so? Think that's why the FBI came sniffing around two days after I filed the NIH report on Childs?"

Day stopped fidgeting and stared back.

"Yeah, that's right. Wasn't even forty-eight hours before a federal agent was in my office asking about it. Seems that one of your predecessors got worried about what was happening and . . . well, you know . . . went to Mexico scuba diving and never came back."

Day picked up a ballpoint pen, started drumming it on the edge of the desk. After a moment he said, "So, what are you trying to say?"

"I think you know about the bug. Least that's what I told the FBI."

"You what!" Day slammed down the pen, started drumming his fingers on the desk instead. "You fucking crazy?"

"That's right." Tyler smiled insanely. "I told them you not only know about the bug, but that you're part of the cover-up. They've had you under surveillance for the past week."

Day studied Tyler's eyes a moment, perhaps looking for a bluff. "And what's this bug supposed to do?"

"Hell, you know more about this than I do. You tell me. What can go wrong? A value gets corrupted because of a magnetic flaw in the storage media? Maybe two values are inputted at exactly the same time so the CPU confuses them? What? I don't know *how* it happens. I only know it *does* happen. So"—meeting Day's eyes full on now—"you tell me."

Day continued drumming the table and studying Tyler's face. "It's possible, I suppose . . . just not likely."

"Why not?"

"Because we'd know about it already. That's what this past few years of beta testing's been all about."

"Now there's an interesting answer. It can't be happening because we don't know it's happening. I think there's a name for that kind of logic but I can't exactly remember it at the moment."

Day just sat glowering at him.

"Know what I think?"

Day shook his head. "No, enlighten me."

"I think everybody in your company knows about it but prays to hell word doesn't hit the media before the IPO hits Wall Street. Either that or you believe by some sort of miracle it's going to be fixed in time to hold a press conference in which your PR guru or Bernie Levy will announce to the world that you discovered it just in the nick of time, before it could cause trouble. That's what I think."

Day looked away, the overhead neon light glistening off two beads of sweat over his upper lip. "You can say what you want to whoever you want. But you can't prove shit."

"Before you just blow this off and stonewall again, think about what'll happen if Med-InDx gets the JCAHO nod and becomes the gold standard. You really want to know you had a chance to stop this but didn't because you wanted to boost the value of your stock options? Is that what you *really* want?"

"Hey, don't cop an attitude with me." Day sat upright. "This FBI dude . . . you really tell him about me? Like what?"

Tyler saw fear in Day's eyes. "Like I already told you . . . said you knew about it and that I'd asked you to help me."

"And?"

"That discussion's not over yet. So, I guess that depends on how much help you give me."

An idea flashed in Tyler's mind. He raised his hand, cutting off Day's next remark. "Hold on, let me ask you something first. Every time I asked about changing the radiation dose field you told me *you* couldn't. But what about someone like Bernie Levy, could he do it?"

Day wagged his head. "Oh, man, Bernie? Nerdy Bernie?" He seemed to mull this over. "Yeah, guess maybe . . . He's the man who penned the code. Don't see why he couldn't. But then again, there'd be a record of it."

"Yeah? Well maybe not." He remembered his college roommate, a computer programmer who wrote games as a means of supporting his tuition and board. "I assume since Bernie wrote the code, he'd know the program's trapdoors."

"He'd have to. He wrote them."

From the intensity of Day's eyes he could tell the technician had already anticipated the next logical point. "Then couldn't it be possible for Levy to change the value of, say, Childs's radiation dose and not leave a record of it?"

Day let out a long slow whistle. "Lord have mercy, this is getting a bit heavy."

"You didn't answer the question."

"Shit yeah, it's possible. But I don't know, man . . . geeky old Bernie doing something like that . . . ?" He wagged his head. "Man, that's cold."

"So let me ask you once more . . . have you heard anything about a system flaw? A bug that can corrupt or change parts of records?"

Day exhaled a long slow breath and stroked his upper lip. After a moment he leaned forward. "Okay, so maybe there's been some rumblings and shit for maybe six months now, maybe longer. No one's sure what the problem is but, hell yeah, there's a problem."

Tyler's heart accelerated. If a record existed of troubleshooting the bug and he could get hold of a copy, it could go a long way toward settling the score with Ferguson even if his career as a neurosurgeon was finished. "You know if there's any formal record of it?"

Day gave a resigned nod. "Not something formal, but more than likely there'd be notes or a list of traps to troubleshoot it. Word has it someone's been working on it. Probably Levy since he's so proud of that part."

"Where would those notes be?"

"Only one place they'd keep something like that. Levy's office."

The other day he might have been sitting within ten feet of that information and didn't know it. But more than that, Day had just confirmed what he'd suspected all along. Levy had been lying.

"I want you to help me get in that office."

Day laughed. "You what? Man, that's fucking insane."

"I'm serious."

Day settled back in his chair, shooting Tyler a funny look.

Tyler asked, "You going to just sit there admiring my overbite?"

"Whoa, guess you *are* serious."

"How do you get in the building at night?"

The right corner of Day's mouth curled up. He rolled his eyes. "Can't fucking believe you. The building has security. Not Fort Knox security, but security. For starters, you need a swipe card."

Tyler decided to press his luck. "Let me borrow yours."

Day barked a sarcastic grunt. "No fucking way, man. They'd be on my sorry ass like Dragnet."

"Okay, then I'll find my own way into the building. How about the main office? How do you get in there?"

"Oh, man . . ." He hung his head. "You use a key."

"Yours will do fine."

Day shook his head adamantly. "Uh-uh, noooo noooo. You ain't getting it."

"Yes I will. You're going to get me a copy of yours. And you know why you're going to do that?"

Day didn't answer.

"Because if you do, I'll tell the FBI you helped me blow this thing apart. If you don't, I'll stick to my story that you aided and abetted a cover-up."

Day's head dropped back, his eyes looking straight up at the ceiling. "Fuck." A moment later he said, "I need some time. Give me a couple hours, then meet me in Pioneer Square," and gave Tyler an exact location.

3:34 P.M.

From an alley across the street Tyler watched Jim Day saunter into a combination coffee shop and bookstore in historic Pioneer Square. Tyler watched for an additional three minutes before starting across the street. The day was perfect Seattle August—bright, low seventies, low humidity—the type of weather that packs the area with tourists and locals alike. Waterfront salt water, drying kelp, and creosote tinged the air.

On the other side of the street now, he peered in the shop's front window. Day sat at an ice cream table for two inspecting a self-standing table menu sandwiched in plastic. A moment later Tyler folded himself into the opposite chair and said, "You got it?"

Day set down the menu. "You're a real asshole, you know that."

Tyler looked nervously over his shoulder at the front door. "I don't have time for pleasantries, my friend."

Day removed a key wallet from his pocket, unhooked one from a loop, handed it over, muttered, "Oh, man, sure hope you know what the fuck you doin'."

CHAPTER 31

Tyler watched Jim Day walk out of the café. He decided to sit for a moment and try to come up with a plan of how to break into Bernie Levy's office. He reconsidered Day's advice to stay away from the place. Who knew what kind of security they had or if Day was setting him up. What about just calling Ferguson and handing over what little information he had? He wasn't convinced it wouldn't turn out to be a repeat of the California disaster. "History repeats itself," was one of his father's favorite clichés. Tyler believed it. No matter what, his medical career was over. Arthur Benson would see to that.

Tyler decided on a reasonable plan. One he would carry out tonight. The more he thought about it, the more tonight, Sunday, seemed like the best time. Fewer people in the building. More than likely the janitorial services would have already been through the place Friday evening, leaving him only security to deal with. Just how much additional security Med-InDx might have in addition to routine building guards was the real unknown. Being a start-up company they probably didn't have the cash to support much extra, if any at all.

"May I help you?"

He looked up at a waitress. "Sorry. I'm just leaving." He stood. Time to get going anyway. He decided to empty his bladder before leaving and walked to the hall in the back of the store.

A few minutes later Tyler reentered the store, froze, and did a double take. One of the killers—the stockier one—stood just inside the entrance, cell phone against his ear. He hadn't seen Tyler yet.

Tyler backed up a step, frantically searching his memory—had he noticed a back exit? Had to be one.

The man's eyes locked on to Tyler. He gave a sharp nod, slammed the cell phone shut, and stuffed it into his pocket. Grinning, he started toward Tyler.

Tyler turned and ran, searching for an exit sign. The hall turned right past the toilet, then left into a dead end with doors to either side. He pulled open the one to the right. A set of open stairs with a flimsy metal pipe railing led down into darkness. His forehead brushed something. He reached up and touched a pull string. He pulled. Lights flicked on below. Looked like an abandoned cellar. He slammed the door and threw the deadbolt, then scrambled down the rickety stairs to hard-packed dirt.

A quick scan of the large area revealed an old boiler room, maybe the original for heating the building. In a distant corner, an old abandoned coal furnace stood on a cement pad.

A loud crash of splintering wood came from the top of the stairs. He spun around to look. The door held, but it looked as if another good kick would open it.

He ran around the room inspecting the bare cement walls for any way to escape. No windows, no doors. He was trapped.

The boiler—any way to hide in there? He jerked open the heavy cast-iron door. Not enough room. Besides, it'd be the first place to look. Anything to use as a weapon? He scanned the floor again.

Another splintering crash from the door. He glanced up at it again. The hinges were barely hanging on now.

Instinctively he moved behind the boiler as if to delay the inevitable.

On the bare cement wall a four-foot-high iron door hung on rusted hinges. Discarded on the dirt below lay a small length of rusted iron pipe. Not a good weapon, but . . .

He wedged the pipe under the door edge and pulled, trying to pry it open. It wouldn't budge. Tyler mustered all his strength and gave one more pull. Metal screeched against metal as the door cracked open two inches, enough to curl his fingers around the edge. Leaning against the cement wall, he yanked with every ounce of strength. Slowly, screaming in protest, the door opened.

What he saw totally confused him. The door shielded an opening but it was entirely bricked in. He reached out and fingered the mortar. It crumbled to his touch. It dawned on him—he was looking at a remnant of the Seattle underground. He remembered the story he'd heard shortly after moving here and taking a city tour. How after the original city burned, a new city had been built on top of the old one. Which meant there was probably a passage or even an old abandoned street just on the other side of the bricks.

"Shit."

He swung the pipe against the bricks and was amazed to see large chunks of mortar and brick fall away. He swung again, this time punching a brick back into a black void. With his back firmly against the cold iron boiler, he kicked the flat of his foot into the bricks. More fell away, landing on the other side of the wall with distant thumps. Another kick gave him an aperture barely large enough to crawl through.

One more crash from above and the door came bouncing down the stairs.

Tyler stuck his head through the opening into black dank air, fouled with urine and feces. Had to be underground Seattle. Long since abandoned except for tours through limited areas. He'd heard stories of the homeless and psychotics living down here in the sub-sidewalks.

He wiggled headfirst through the opening hoping the tight constriction would slow down the bruiser coming down the stairs. His fingers sank into a layer of foul-smelling muck. He hand-walked forward, wiggling his torso through until he managed to free his legs. Standing on slippery ground now, he flicked both hands. Globs of mess splattered against the wall.

Which way to go?

He reached out, touched the wall he'd just climbed through. Keeping his right hand against the wall, he stumbled along the side of the building without any idea where it would lead.

The unstable footing slowed him in spite of the intense urgency to run. He forced his pace to quicken. With his next step his right foot came down on something that rolled away with a clink, driving his full weight onto his twisted right ankle. A bolt of pain shot up his leg. He groaned and steadied himself against the wall while working his ankle back and forth, trying to determine how badly it was injured. A moment later he gingerly placed weight on it. Sore and sprained, but functional.

Up ahead dim light filtered down from overhead.

Behind him came a crash. Bricks splashed into the same muck he'd just left. Frantically, he limped forward toward the dim light.

Footsteps started splashing in his direction now, faster than his own. He tried to speed up but his ankle wouldn't tolerate it. He tried pushing through the pain as he'd done so many times on the basketball court, but his ankle only throbbed more and threatened to buckle. He accidentally kicked an object. Glass shattered, giving away his position. "Shit," he muttered and glanced over his shoulder. A circle of pale light angling in from the wall opening silhouetted the killer as he lurched forward.

A raspy voice whispered, "Come to mama, Mathews," then chuckled.

Ahead about fifteen feet, up where the ceiling should be, anemic rays of light filtered down. He remembered examples of surviving old sidewalk-windows that looked like really thick soda pop bottle bottoms arranged in six-by-eight-foot concrete panes embedded in the sidewalks. With his retinas more adjusted to the darkness, the old skylight allowed enough luminescence to pick up his pace in spite of his protesting ankle. Moving more quickly now, his eyes searched the dim light for any sort of weapon.

Echoing, sloshing footsteps were closing in. *How can such a monster move so fast, especially through this darkness?* The fetid overpowering air made it impossible to take in a deep full breath.

He stumbled, fell to his knees, jamming both hands into rubble, scraping his palms. His hand brushed something and his fingers explored it a second before his mind connected an image. Pipe. A piece of discarded water pipe. Old lead pipe. He picked it up, examining its length with his other hand, felt its heft.

The approaching footsteps slowed. He could hear the man's breathing now.

The hoarse voice said, "Nothing personal, you understand. Just doing my job."

Tyler gingerly planted his right foot, then turned to look. The behemoth stood just inside the rays from the overhead skylight. "Tell me something," Tyler said.

"What?"

Tyler threw his entire body into the swing, bringing the pipe around at full force into the man's left tibia. There was a sickening crunch of bone. The man gasped but didn't go down. Tyler scrambled to his feet, bringing the pipe back for another swing.

He didn't get the chance. A fist the size of Alaska slammed into his stomach, doubling him over, stealing his breath. Another fist crashed into the back of his neck, sending him down onto dirt and chunks of concrete and brick. Sparkling lights danced where his vision should be.

Miraculously his right hand still clutched the pipe. Gasping for breath, he rolled onto his side just as a foot stomped the dirt next to his ear. A sharp edge poked into his back. He rolled once more, moving a little farther away from the hulk. Obviously hurt, the man limped forward clutching something in his right hand. Tyler tried to scramble to his feet, but a round object under his foot rolled, dropping him to his knees again. Kneeling, using a two-handed swing, he swung the pipe for the man's groin and connected solidly.

The huge shape groaned and dropped the object as both hands groped toward his groin. He bent forward, trying to deal with the pain yet still do the job he came for. Tyler scrambled to stand, but rammed his head into something hard. For a second he could only kneel, stunned. The killer started to straighten up.

Tyler raised the pipe and brought it down squarely on the back of the man's head with a satisfying *thunk*.

The man went down and remained still.

For a few seconds Tyler crouched, still trying to breathe normally, his weapon ready to hit again. The killer stayed motionless but breathing. Slowly, step by step, Tyler backed away, putting space between them. Finally convinced the battle was over, he turned and hobbled into protective darkness in search of a way out.

CHAPTER 32

Ten, maybe fifteen minutes later, Tyler stepped around a wood slat barrier into a well-lighted cavern of old storefronts and a wood sidewalk. Early Seattle, a replica of Seattle's business district before the fire that destroyed the young city.

Fifty feet away a guide told a group of tourists, "In 1889 an overturned glue pot in Jim McGough's paint shop started the Great Seattle Fire. What happened was the city burned down, leaving only tough brick shells of the main part of the old city. Since the area had been repeatedly inundated as a saltwater flat, it was decided to lay down iron beams and build a new, higher city on top of the old. Parts of that underground still survive and you can see the doors, windows . . ." He stopped to peer, open-mouthed, at Tyler.

Tyler limped forward, his ankle aching like hell, his clothes smelling of gunk. He asked, "Which way's out?"

The guide looked him up and down with obvious distaste and pointed to his right. "Just follow that sidewalk. It's about a half block." He nodded at Tyler's hand.

Tyler glanced down at the two-foot length of pipe still clutched tightly. "Oh, that? Been hunting rats."

9:15 P.M., TYLER'S APARTMENT

Jill asked Tyler, "Can you think of anything you might've forgotten?"

Stupid question, Tyler thought. *How would I know if I'd forgotten it? She's just trying to be helpful,* he decided. He told her, "No. I think I have everything," and tried to ignore a hollow anxious weightlessness filling his stomach.

They were in his apartment, Tyler wearing a fresh pair of black Levi's, a black mock tee and a black windbreaker, and his dark navy trail-biking rucksack. Perfect for blending into shadows.

After climbing out of the underground, he'd caught a bus uptown and spent fifteen minutes limping around the perimeter of the building housing Med-InDx before heading back to his apartment to dump his soiled clothes into the washer and stand under a hot driving shower for ten minutes before tending to the various scratches on his face and hands. He'd taken six hundred milligrams of ibuprofen, iced his ankle, and elevated it.

Then he'd tried to nap but couldn't sleep, worrying instead about how the killers knew where to find him in the café. Obviously, someone told them. Who? Only three possibilities existed: Jim Day, Jill Richardson, and, unwittingly, himself. Day was the obvious choice since he had the best motivation: to save Med-InDx's reputation. But if that was the case, why give Tyler the key? To set him up to get caught breaking into Levy's office? If so, why tip the killers to come for him in the café? Didn't make sense.

What about Jill? She knew he was going to meet Day. But if she wanted him killed, why rescue him from the overdose and then the hospital? *Why not just have the killers pull her car over after picking him up?*

Which left himself. Had he inadvertently tipped off the killers? *Was someone listening in to his cell phone? A bug in his apartment?*

The telephone rang. Tyler debated answering it. The killers checking to see if he was home? He picked up. "Hello."

"Dr. Mathews, Christine Dikman. Sorry to bother you at home, especially this late on a Sunday evening."

"No problem."

"I just heard from the charge nurse that Toby's been scheduled for the marrow transplant tomorrow morning. She just received a consent signed by a judge. Have you been able to find out anything yet?"

Tyler glanced at Jill, who seemed to be watching him closely. "Not yet."

"Is something wrong?"

"No."

"Is there anything you can think of that I can do? The thought of that poor kid undergoing . . ."

"Tell you what. I might have something tomorrow. I'll call you then. Can I reach you on the ward?"

"Yes," she said hopefully. "I'll be there from seven o'clock on. If anyone says I'm busy, just have them pull me out of whatever it is."

"Talk to you then."

"Who was that?" Jill asked when he'd hung up.

"One of my partners. Wants some information I'd promised him before he does a case in the morning."

Jill paced a tight circle, nervously rubbing both hands together. "Tyler, I don't like this . . . it's too dangerous."

"Stop it. You're making me nervous. Besides, we've been through this. I don't see any other way out of this. I'm totally screwed without proof there's a software flaw." He thought of Ferguson's threat. *Why were you so stupid to forge your own prescription, pal?*

He slipped the rucksack over one shoulder. "Your cell phone turned on?" He popped a Tums in his mouth and pocketed the rest of the roll.

She flashed exasperation. "Yes."

"Good." He patted his pockets for one final check. He had everything. "I'll call soon as I'm out and away from the building."

"Why don't you just come over to my place?"

He opened the front door. "I don't know how long this is gonna take."

"Oh, right! Like I'm going to be able to sleep tonight!" She followed him out.

He locked the door, wondering when or if he'd see his apartment again.

They walked the stairs to the first floor, neither one saying a word, Tyler already worrying about getting into the building undetected.

Once through the lobby and out the front door, they stood for a moment of awkward silence on the sidewalk. She came to him, stretched up on tiptoes, and kissed him. "Be careful."

He kissed her back. "I will."

She turned and walked away. Tyler headed in the opposite direction.

Jill turned the corner and moved along the street to her car. She thumbed the electronic key, snapping the locks open, and slid into the front seat.

From the shadows of the backseat Arthur Benson asked, "He on his way?"

She nodded. "The fool."

Benson glanced at his watch. "What say we give him ten minutes before going back in." She thought about this a moment. "Sounds about right."

9:15 P.M.

Nancy Fan listened once again to the telephone ring and combed anxious fingers through her hair. *Damn him, why won't he answer?* She checked the clock. Quarter after nine. Six hours she'd been trying. She'd even checked the hospital. He wasn't on call and wasn't in surgery. Just to be sure, she'd had the operator page him overhead. Nothing. And another thing, his answering machine wasn't on and his cell phone responded with, "The Verizon customer you are trying to reach is not available." Both alarming. For as long as she'd known him he'd been compulsive about being reachable 24/7—even when not on call.

She'd not been to Tyler's apartment, but had the address. Perhaps the manager would let her in. After all, she *was* Tyler's wife.

She grabbed her coat off the davenport arm but stopped. *What if he's with another woman?* Barging in on him would be embarrassing. *Goddamnit Tyler!* But if that was the case, she needed to know it now. Didn't she? *I mean, if we're serious about getting back together?*

With her roommate out on a date, there was no one to tell where she was going or when she'd be back. She slipped on the lightweight coat, tossed her keys in her purse, and slammed the apartment door behind her. Maybe he wouldn't be there. But doing something was better than just waiting around an empty apartment doing nothing.

CHAPTER 33

10:30 P.M.

The sky hung low and black, stars masked by clouds swollen with potential rain, leaving the sidewalk aglow with the sickly hue from mercury-vapor streetlamps. Hidden in the doorway to an auto repair shop, Tyler studied the front entrance across the street as occasional cars sped past. Tall plate-glass doors and matching windows provided an almost unobstructed view into the lobby where a security guard perched on a swivel chair behind a desk. Tyler remembered the layout from his appointment with Bernie Levy. He'd noticed the back side of the guard's desk, remembered seeing it filled with two parallel rows of CCTV monitors where some views probably switched between several cameras while others were probably dedicated to security-sensitive areas like the garage entrance. Every now and then the guard picked up what looked like a handheld radio and appeared to say a few words—most likely checking with other guards roaming the building.

Tyler noticed a young man hurrying down the opposite side of the street carrying two large pizza boxes stacked one atop the other. He waited until he started up the three concrete steps to the entrance before running across the street after him. Balancing the boxes in one hand, the kid pulled a swipe card from a retractable cord on his belt and ran it through a reader.

Tyler reached the door just as the lock snapped open. "Here, let me get the door for you."

"Thanks." The man passed through the doorway.

Just as Tyler was about to follow, another guard stepped from an alcove into the lobby, giving him a scrutinizing once-over. Tyler got a strong gut premonition to not challenge the man and let go of the door, turned and walked away. So much for going in the front.

Back onto the sidewalk he headed south to the end of the block, turned the corner, and approached the downward-angling driveway into the basement garage. The entire concrete slope was ablaze from two high-intensity spotlights mounted on the header just above the rolled-down security door. Casually he sauntered down to the door and peered through the slats. Sure enough, on the ceiling twenty feet away, a TV camera angled directly toward him. So much for the strategy of following a car in before the metal door could roll back down. Sure, there was a small chance of getting away with it, but the odds were against him. He needed something better.

He returned to the sidewalk and continued on to the alley that he'd walked earlier in the day. He'd noticed the loading dock, figuring it had possibilities. He stopped to peer into the darkened narrow passage. The only light in the alley came from the loading dock. With a slow casual stride he entered, eyes searching for a back door or alcove from which to watch. He found it a quarter of the length in; a recessed back door. Perfect. Close enough so that the viewing angle included ninety percent of the dock, yet sufficiently out of range of the high ceiling lights to remain hidden. On his right a large green Dumpster blocked any view into his hiding place from the street. Even so, with his dark clothes he'd probably remain invisible if someone walking past looked directly at him.

Two workmen in denim overalls were sitting on the dock, legs dangling over the edge, smoking and talking. He was close enough to hear most words. One cracked a joke. The other laughed, then, after a deep drag, flicked his cigarette into the center of the alley where it hit with a shower of sparks.

Tyler dropped down on his haunches, back against the door, and waited.

Five minutes later, the other man mashed his cigarette ember against the metal edge of the dock sending another shower of sparks to the ground. Both workers stood, brushed their hands on their gray overalls, and reentered the building through a steel fire door.

Tyler waited two minutes before sliding from his hiding place. To the left of the dock, stairs led up from the alley to the deep loading platform backed by a set of roll-up steel doors. Near the top of the stairs was the single pedestrian door the workmen had used. Heart pounding, he climbed the stairs. And tried the door-knob. Locked. He looked down at a small hunk of wood lying just to the side of the jamb. *Must've used it to prop the door open.*

What now, pal?

Tyler returned to the shadowy doorway, hunkered down, and waited.

Twenty minutes later a man wearing a security uniform came through the same doorway. This time Tyler saw him kick the block of wood into place with the tip of his shoe, letting the edge of the door come to rest without quite closing. The rent-a-cop pulled a pack of cigarettes from his breast pocket, tapped out a smoke, and lit up with a clanky Zippo. About two drags into it his radio squawked. After several staccato words into the mike, he pinched off the ember, replaced the cigarette in the pack, opened the door, but either forgot or did not bother to remove the block from the jamb.

Tyler stepped tentatively into the alley and was about to take his first step toward the loading dock when a familiar voice behind him ordered, "Stop."

He turned. Yusef Khan stood next to the Dumpster aiming a gun at Tyler's heart.

————

"Fuck! Where is it!" Benson threw a CD case on the floor.

Jill Richardson shot him a hard look. "If I knew where he hid it, we'd have it by now, Art." She continued surveying Mathews's small living room/dining room combination looking for another spot to check. They'd been through the small desk and the PC— the most likely places to start.

"You sure he said it was here? I went through these with a fine-tooth comb," he said, picking up another music CD.

"Damnit, Art, must you always use such tired old clichés? Come up with something more original once in a while, for christsake." Her eyes continued searching the room. "How about the DVDs . . . we haven't checked those yet." She crossed the room to a small TV and DVD player, a small stack of DVDs immediately to the right. She picked off the top box, opened it, threw it on the floor. Then the next.

A knock came from the door.

Jill's arm stopped in the middle of tossing another container. She locked eyes with Benson. He mouthed the words "Who is it?"

Jill shrugged.

Another knock. This one harder, more insistent. From the other side of the door came, "Tyler? I know you're in there. I can hear you."

Jill kicked off her shoes, moved to the door to peer through the security hole. An Asian woman with determined eyes raised her knuckles to knock again. It clicked. Jill had noticed the silver-framed portrait on Tyler's desk. The same woman. Presumably his estranged wife.

She turned to Benson, mouthed the word "wife" before opening the door. With a beaming smile, she swung the door open, said warmly, "Come on in. It's Nancy, isn't it?"

The woman hesitated, her face displaying obvious confusion. "And you are?"

Jill extended her hand, "Jill Richardson. We work with Tyler." She tossed a quick nod toward the living room. "This is Arthur

Benson, Maynard's CEO. We were just having a talk with Tyler."

The woman's face brightened in relief as she stepped over the threshold.

Jill shut the door and nodded for Benson to take over.

CHAPTER 34

Khan waved the gun left, whispered, "Step back, in the doorway, please."

Tyler couldn't take his eyes off the barrel aimed dead center at his heart. And when he did, it was to fix on the finger pressed against the trigger.

The gun flicked sideways. Khan whispered harshly, "Move, Mathews. Before someone sees us."

"What the hell . . . ?" Tyler stepped back into the shadows. "I haven't . . . I don't understand . . ."

"What I'm doing here?"

"Yeah, that's a good place to start." He looked at the gun again but couldn't see it, it was so dark in here. His heart hammered his sternum. His throat constricted into a straw. "Jesus, I mean . . ."

Khan waved, whispered, "Keep it down," and glanced toward the loading dock.

"Why?" Tyler asked, voice normal, hoping someone on the street might hear. "I mean, what's the problem?" He stepped toward the street.

Khan grabbed his arm and whispered, "Don't be foolish. Those men you saw? They're security guards and they're waiting for you. That whole act on the dock? A setup. You think it was an accident the last one left the door open? No, don't be foolish."

Something nagged Tyler. He studied Khan's face a moment before it hit him. "Your accent . . . it's—"

"Gone?" Khan gave a humorless laugh. "Disarming, is it? First time you met me, I bet you thought I was just another incompetent rag head right off the boat."

"No, I—"

Khan waved again. "Some other time. Right now we need to talk."

"Can you put that gun away. It scares the shit out of me."

Khan raised a finger to his lips, whispered, *"Shhhhhh,"* and pointed over Tyler's left shoulder.

He turned. Back out on the loading dock stood another man dressed in denim bib overalls. For a moment the man scanned the area before turning and exiting through the same door.

Tyler felt a tap on the shoulder. Khan whispered, "Come on, this way."

Staying in the darkest part of the shadows, Khan moved along the brick wall toward the street.

Tyler followed Khan out the alley in the same direction he'd entered, across the deserted street, and into a similar garbage-scented alley on the next block. While crossing the street, it occurred to Tyler that he could simply turn and run up the block and escape. What was Khan going to do? Shoot at him? Run after him and tackle him? But at this point what Khan had to say definitely held his interest. They stopped just a few feet in from the street at a point no longer bathed in streetlight yet not completely dark.

"How do you know about the guards?" Tyler asked.

"Easy. As head of information services I have the ability to access every computer, telephone, pager, and cell phone supplied to any medical center employee. Including Arthur Benson. And I have this." He held up a handheld radio. "Here"—he offered it over—"you want to listen to their conversation?"

Tyler waved it away. "But—"

"Either of you gents spare any change?"

Startled, Tyler spun around. An emaciated pale woman, early thirties perhaps, stringy ends of dishwater-blond hair brushing bony shoulders, in a faded tank top, shorts, and flip-flops, stood at the entrance to the alley, eyes darting from Tyler to Khan and back again.

Tyler slapped his pockets and remembered purposely not bringing any change for fear it might make noise. "You're out of luck." He turned back to Khan.

"How 'bout a blow job? Twenty bucks for the two of you," she offered hopefully.

Tyler shook his head and turned to her again. "Not interested. We're busy."

Khan told her, "Wait, don't go," then to Tyler, "I have an idea."

Shocked, Tyler started to protest but Khan waved him silent, and moved a few steps toward the depths of the alley, pulling Tyler along. "Hear me out on this."

Fidgeting, left hand rubbing her right arm, the woman eagerly watched, apparently waiting for whatever deal Khan was going to offer. Khan turned back to her, "Give us a minute here, okay?"

She shrugged. "Whatever," but did not take the hint and move away.

Khan sidled up next to Tyler, lowered his voice. "Look, six months ago I started to notice some"—he made finger quotation marks with both hands—"problems with our new EMR. I—"

"What kinds of problems?" Tyler broke in.

Khan shook his head, frustrated. "Same kinds of problems you noticed. But the point is I became concerned after there was a report of a patient who died. The doctor who submitted the report was convinced the computer made an error but when the root cause analysis came back it showed human error. I wasn't convinced the report was correct. What really happened, although I can't prove it, was someone—someone with super-user privileges—changed the record to make it look like human error. I kept my mouth shut and acted dumb, but I also started tracking all bug and error reports turned in. Every one of them got channeled through Jim Day. So, I started keeping an eye on him."

"Keeping an eye on him?"

Khan shrugged. "Electronically. I started reading his e-mail and voice mail. Eventually I started recording his phone calls. That's how I knew about tonight."

Khan's lips drew up into a faint smile. "Come, I'll prove it to you." He held out his hand. "Your key to Med-InDx, please."

Tyler considered this a moment. Other than the key, what did he really have to lose? If he lost the key in the deal, he could still go to Ferguson with the evidence accumulated so far. The FBI was the one thing neither Khan nor Benson knew about. His trump card. He pulled the key from his pocket and handed it to Khan.

Khan moved to the fidgeting blonde. "I forgot my attaché case this evening when I left the office earlier. I'll give you twenty dollars to fetch it for me."

Her tongue flicked across her lips. She scratched the back of her neck. "What? You think I'm stupid? No fucking way, man."

"No, I know you're not stupid, but I think you need the money for whatever you're on. This is all quite simple. I need my case. I want you to get it for me. You need the money. You do the task, you get paid. That's all there is to it." Khan started across the street toward the alley they'd left moments ago. She followed, Tyler just behind her. They stepped into the street.

"Man, what a crock of shit. You want some frigging attaché case, go get it yourself. I don't need to be starting no trouble." She rubbed both biceps and shivered in the warm air.

Khan stopped at the entrance to the alley, pulled out his wallet, held a twenty-dollar bill up in front of her face. "You want this, you earn it by going in that building down there." He pointed toward the loading dock. "And get that case." His other hand dangled the key. "Here's the key to my office."

The woman's eyes riveted on the bill fixed between Khan's fingers, then shot to the key and back again. "Ahhh, man, if this ain't a huge crock of shit . . ." She glanced up the street as if wrestling with a decision, then back to Khan. "Why don't you dudes just settle for a blow? I'm good, man . . . I can suck the paint off a Ford pickup truck."

Khan had another twenty in his other hand now. "Twenty now. Twenty when you return with my case."

"Fuck!" Her hand shot out, snapped the bill from between his fingers. "Let's get this show on the road." She muttered, "Know damn well I shouldn't friggin' be doing this."

Khan walked her down the alley, Tyler dropping back to tail them. They stopped a few feet from the edge of the loading dock where Khan handed her the copy of Jim Day's key and pointed out the door off the loading dock. He explained the location of Bernie Levy's office and told her the maroon leather attaché case was inside on the corner of the desk. Khan did such a good job spinning the tale that Tyler found himself almost believing it. A moment later Tyler watched her trudge up the stairs and vanish through the door.

Soon as the door closed, Khan said, "I suggest we move to another location," and started back to Tyler's original hiding place.

They hadn't waited two minutes before the door banged open. Two men stepped out onto the loading dock, the thin woman between them. She said something and pointed to the spot where she had left Khan. The men squinted, jumped down onto the pavement, and glanced around.

Staying in the shadows, Khan and Tyler moved quickly toward the street. Once they rounded the corner, their pace picked up.

Khan glanced over to Tyler. "See, I kept you from walking into a trap. Do you trust me now?"

— - — - — - — - — - —

Nancy listened to the huge man tromp downstairs and say a few words to the tall thin one introduced as Benson. A moment later she heard what may have been the front door close, then the sound of a television being turned on. Before the man left, he'd removed her blindfold. She scanned the combination bedroom/

office again, saw a bed, a desk with a computer, an elliptical cross-trainer, and a sliding-glass door out to what would logically be a deck. Two solid doors. One obviously a closet. The other probably into a bathroom. With the overhead room light on and it being dark outside, the reflection off the glass made it impossible to see more than the first few inches of deck beyond the door track.

The man had told her to sit in a black leather chair, then he'd tied her wrists together with what looked like quarter-inch rope and bound her across the abdomen to the chair. Probably because of her hysterical crying he hadn't bound her ankles or gagged her. More importantly, he hadn't tied her wrists all that tightly. She sniffed the last of her tears and decided there was no one to help her but herself. What to do? She glanced around the room once more. Seeing nothing that might help her, she raised her wrists up and examined the binding. A double square knot. Splaying her hands apart, she worked her mouth down between her wrists until her front teeth could bite a grip on the cord and pull.

The first loop came easily. The second one did not. As hard as she tried, it would not loosen. Just then she heard the heavy tromp of the man's feet on the stairs.

A moment later his huge shape obliterated most of the doorway. She looked up, saw his eyes studying her, felt them focus on her breasts. She looked down and tried to quell the urge to scream at him, for if she did, he might gag her.

"Want a beer?"

She shook her lowered head.

"You sure? 'Cause I'm a going to have one. Way I figure, you and me can have us a pretty good party a little later. And there's no sense you being all tight-assed when we do. Might as well get yourself drunk so's you'd enjoy it. Know what I mean?"

She shook her head again.

"Hey, suit yourself. But me? I'm going to pop me a beer, enjoy me a little one-eyed monster, and then, like the Terminator says, I'll be back."

CHAPTER 35

Tyler said to Khan, "Let me get this straight—you never changed the lab results on Torres?" They were sitting in a booth over in one corner of an all-night donut shop that smelled of fried dough, cigarettes, coffee, and sweat. Tyler believed the majority of customers were either crackheads or dealers. Either way, he and Khan were the oldest people in this place and looked pathetically out of context. Out the window, curbed at the other side of the street, a baby-blue SPD cruiser idled with the front windows rolled down, two uniformed cops to either side of a vertical, dashboard-mounted shotgun, drinking coffee.

Khan picked up a paper cup filled with steaming, overcooked coffee, blew across the top. "I monitored that case." He paused to sip. "After you filed the report, I went through the proper protocol and passed it on to Jim Day. You see, the way it is supposed to work—and this is lovely, the way Med-InDx set it up—is if you"—nodding to Tyler—"find a bug or problem with anything in the entire Clinical Information System, you're supposed to report it directly to an on-site technician. Problems of that nature are really not intended to be handled by my department. And it makes sense, in a way . . . since what we have is a beta version, one they're still actively working on. The problem is we have such a turnover of employees, there is always a group who aren't familiar with that policy. As a result, a number of so-called problems come across my desk every week. Most are simple user mistakes, nothing of any importance. And so, I hand them off to the Med-InDx tech like a good little minion." His angry eyes looked up at Tyler. "They all think because I'm Pakistani I'm too stupid to notice what's going on in that medical center and I do nothing to assuage that impression.

"But this does not answer your question. Yes, I followed the Torres chart. I passed on the information to Med-InDx and within hours Torres's medical record had been altered. Believe me, it wasn't me who did it."

Tyler looked into his own cup of coffee. Was Khan telling the truth? He was never a good judge of character when it came to situations like this. Never had been. He took people at their word because that's how he'd been trained as a physician. You'd never make a diagnosis if you doubted everything a patient told you. Sure, you developed the ability to filter and arrange stories into the proper order, but you always accepted the patient's word.

"Who do you think made the changes? Day?"

Khan held up both palms. "Your guess is as good as mine. But keep this in mind: unless Day holds an extremely high security level or is aware of ways to navigate the system without leaving footprints, I would think not."

"If not Day, then who?"

"Without footprints, how can you tell? Could be either someone high up in the information stream or someone who cracked the system's security."

"But it has to be someone with sufficient motivation to want to make the changes. Who would that be?"

Khan shot him a wide-eyed, are-you-crazy look. "Anyone with Med-InDx options is a candidate to make those changes."

"Not everybody's willing to kill for stock options, Yusef." He held up a hand. "Okay, that's beside the point. Point is, we both know the system's flawed. What *is* the flaw? I mean, how can that happen?"

Khan seemed to choose his words carefully before answering. "That's a tough one. The easiest answer is that someone is purposely changing the information. And I must say, the thought did cross my mind. But, to what end? That does not make much sense, does it? Especially since it seems to occur at random."

"I agree."

Khan said, "The other possibility is something's inherently wrong in the code . . . something that corrupts the information either as it's entered or immediately after it's entered. I suspect the later. Otherwise it would be too easily noticed. The other bit of data supporting this theory is, like I just said, the occurrences seem completely random and, for what it's worth, the errors don't seem to be exclusive to only the medical record. I've seen similar problems with the accounting and scheduling software. To be even more specific, the problem seems limited to only proprietary Med-InDx sections . . . and not the ones they picked up from dot-com software casualties."

Tyler nodded. Khan's explanation paralleled Ferguson's story. "I still don't understand how data might spontaneously change, or if Levy knows about it, why he hasn't fixed it."

Khan broke off a piece of plain donut. "A bug like that can be extremely problematic. Especially one that's intermittent and random, like this appears to be. If you can't reproduce the symptoms it's almost impossible to trap and troubleshoot it. The best you can do is develop a patch to work around it." Khan gave a little laugh, "And then, of course, there's the great Bernie Levy." He popped the piece of donut into his mouth.

"Meaning?"

Khan flashed a bemused smile, held a finger to his mouth until swallowing. "You met him the other day. What was your impression?"

"Other than the fact he blew me off, I didn't have time to form one."

Khan's eyebrows shot up. "You took no notice of the shrine to Bill Gates? The shrine that doubles as his office?"

Before Tyler could answer, Khan added, "It goes beyond that.

His obsession has engulfed his personal life too. His daughter's name is Willamina, in honor of Gates. Rumor has it his wife wouldn't let him get away with just plane old William. Oh, no, she insisted it be more feminine." Khan laughed, obviously enjoying the tale. "The point is, he considers the medical record portion of the system his. He refused to delegate any part of the programming. But we're straying from the point, aren't we?" Khan's eyes lost their mirth. "I know you were digging around medical records after I restricted your privileges. Looking for what, other examples?"

"Yes."

"And did you find anything worthwhile?"

Tyler hesitated a few beats. "Guess that depends on what you'd consider valuable. Besides, from what you've told me, you probably recorded every keystroke I punched in that keyboard, so you tell me what I found."

Khan studied him a moment. "Dr. Mathews, let us, as you Americans like to say, cut to the chase. I believe we hold the same goal dear to our heart . . . to stop a flawed system from obtaining the JCAHO endorsement. Unless, of course, they—meaning Med-InDx—can demonstrate convincingly that the bug has been dealt with appropriately. In that case, I have no problem with the software. In fact, if it was not for that little"—he cleared his throat to emphasize the next word—"problem, I'd say it is an excellent solution. Is this not a fair statement?" Khan leaned back against the booth like a poker player laying down a straight flush.

With Ferguson's warning lurking in the back of his mind, Tyler crafted his response so as to get more information without giving away his own. "Sounds like you're on a crusade. I'm not. I just want to practice neurosurgery and get on with my life."

Khan nodded enthusiastically. "Yes, my point exactly. Benson has you very well compromised." He paused, studying Tyler before flipping a dismissive wave. "Yes, yes, I know all about the drugs planted in your locker. Benson's work. All of it. And for one reason only . . . to force your silence. Benson and Levy know you have the power to expose their secret and in the process destroy what they've worked so hard for these past four years. They're deathly afraid of what you might do with that information. That's what this is all about."

Tyler felt a wave of relief and hope come over him. "You have proof Benson did it?"

Khan smiled. "Yes, of course. I have it all on tape." Before Tyler could speak, Khan continued. "You are relieved at this? Does this mean you are ready to cooperate with me?"

"What exactly is it you want from me?" Tyler asked suspiciously.

"Come now, Dr. Mathews . . . I know you are a smart man. But perhaps I should make my position perfectly clear. I have the evidence of a software bug. You, I believe, have evidence to show its consequences. In fact, it has, to put it bluntly, killed several patients. Am I not correct?"

"Yes."

"And you have been able to document this? Unambiguously?"

"There's still something about your story that bothers me . . . if you've been on my side all along, why didn't you say something earlier? Why didn't you help me? I mean, why now?"

Khan leaned forward, both forearms planted firmly on the table. "Ahhh, a good question. Simple enough answer. When you first came to me I had no idea if you were one of Benson's spies. He's a canny one, Benson. He's had concerns about me for several months now but hasn't been able to know for sure."

Khan's explanation sounded too easy, too rehearsed. "Why not fire you? That'd take care of things."

"Because I am upper-level management. He would have to go through the board to fire me."

"So what? Why not frame you like he's done with me?"

"You *are* a suspicious one, aren't you. Fair enough. The answer again is simple. You were easy. You have a past . . . one that made the drug angle very believable. Me? It is not so easy. And unlike you, I would have an exit interview with the board and that's something Benson fears since he doesn't know exactly what I know."

He had to admit, Khan's proposition made some sense. By working together, Tyler would have enough information to get Ferguson off his back and refute the bogus drug charges.

Khan asked, "Are you willing to join forces?"

"Okay—yes, I made copies of the records. In fact, in Torres's case, I made the copy before I let you know about it, so yeah, I have date-stamped evidence the reports were changed after the report was filed."

Khan beamed. "Excellent."

Tyler remembered something else he wanted cleared up. "But let me ask you one more thing."

"Certainly."

"If you knew the drug thing wasn't true, why did you restrict my network access?"

Tyler's cell phone rang. He pulled it from the rucksack and glanced at the face. The number was unfamiliar. A premonitory bolt of panic gripped his heart.

– – – – – – – – – – –

Nancy tugged, felt the cord give a little. Another tug and it started to pull free. A moment later it fell away from her wrists into her lap. Now, with both hands free, she reached down and slid the cord around her waist so the knots at the back of the chair came around to the front. Another few seconds and these knots were untied too. Quickly, she stood up, rubbing the rawness from her wrists where the cord friction abraded them. She moved to the sliding-glass door, flipped the latch, and slid it open only enough to step outside onto the deck.

For a moment she stood in the heavy night air allowing her eyes to adjust to the dark. Off across a void she recognized the three television towers atop Queen Anne Hill. Then it struck her. This must be a Lake Union houseboat.

She was surrounded by water.

A wave of nausea hit followed by vertigo. Arms blindly searching for something to grab onto, she stumbled back to the safety of the room, tripped over the door track, and fell to the floor.

CHAPTER 36

A vaguely familiar voice asked, "You want your wife again alive?"

The words didn't make sense. Tyler glanced at the phone in his hand, returned it to his ear. "What?"

"Do you want your wife back alive?"

A bolt of anxiety slammed Tyler's gut. His mind started racing, running through possibilities, praying for a wrong number or someone playing a sick joke.

The voice continued. "Because, unless you do exactly as I tell you, you'll never see her again."

The voice . . . he'd heard it before. Where? Who?

"You still there, Mathews?"

"Who is this?" Tyler's heart was hammering his temples, his hands tingled. Khan watched with a questioning expression, as if suspecting something.

"Do I have to tell you? You haven't figured it out yet? And here I've been deluded into believing you were such a smart little fucker. Well, guess what! I was wrong about that, wasn't I?" A pause. "You know who I am and I believe by now I have your complete and undivided attention, so it's time to play let's make a deal. Only, in this game there is only one door and only one deal. To put it bluntly, you have no choice or negotiating power. Are you following any of this, or are you still trying to figure a way to sneak into Bernie Levy's office?"

Khan mouthed, "What is it?"

Tyler waved off the question, his total attention on Benson. "I'm listening. What do you want?"

"What I want, my young stupid friend, are three things. One, I want you to sign a statement retracting your egregious allegation that our medical record system has a problem and admitting that your outrageous accusations against me and my administration represent nothing more than an unfortunate side effect of your ongoing battle against substance abuse."

Benson paused. The constriction in Tyler's throat tightened. "And?"

"Yes, well, the next item on the agenda—to be included in the aforementioned statement—is for you to agree to enter a drug rehab program . . . which I might add, will be paid for by your benevolent employer, Maynard Medical Center. Let it not be said that we are unwilling to work with an impaired staff physician, no matter how serious the problem may be."

Another pause.

"Get on with it. What else do you want?!"

"My my, a tad bit testy, are we?" Benson laughed. "Well, dear boy, it's quite simple . . . I want that CD you burned."

"What CD?" Tyler's eyes drilled Khan, who was hanging on every word.

"Don't irritate me any more than you already have or you'll really piss me off. And that you can't afford to do."

It hit Tyler: the only reason Benson could know about the CD was if Jill told him. He hadn't told anyone else, not even Nancy. Or had he? Suddenly he wasn't certain anymore. Did that mean Benson was bluffing about Nancy? Did he have Nancy with him? Unable to think clearly, Tyler tried to come up with a bluff of his own. If only he could get hold of Ferguson. Could Khan help?

"You know, I don't really give a rat's ass if you get pissed off or not."

"Tyler, Tyler, Tyler . . . that is not the right attitude. Let me see if I can help provoke an appropriate adjustment. Hold on, will you?"

Tyler heard movement, then a bell in the background, the kind of bell you might hear from a boat. A moment later came the clatter of the phone being picked up. He recognized Nancy's sobbing, but she couldn't seem to get a word out. Finally she was able to gasp, "Tyler, there's water all around me. I'm terrified."

"Nancy?" Tyler's legs weakened, almost sending him to the floor. The room started to spin. He reached out to keep from falling.

Far off, in the background roar of his brain he heard Benson's voice say, "Take her back to the room," then directly into the phone, "Still so cocky, you little prick?" Another laugh. "Oh, dear, maybe you don't really care about her and I've made a huge mistake. Oh, my, now wouldn't that be something!"

A white-hot ember engulfed Tyler's brain. "You hurt her, Benson, so help me I'll kill you."

"Oh, my, so you *do* care. How auspicious for me. Does this mean you're ready to deal?"

"Where do you want me to bring the CD?"

"That's the spirit! Now, where is it?"

"It's in my storage locker."

"At your apartment?"

"No. It's a rental down in Georgetown."

"Very good. Meet me in my office, in, say, ten minutes. Once we have completed the appropriate paperwork we can drive over and pick it up."

"Nancy better be there or no deal."

"At my office? Don't be ridiculous. You'll see her *after* I have the CD and signed papers. No sooner."

"No deal. I want to be certain she's not harmed."

"Oh, alright. She'll be in my office waiting for you."

"So help me, Benson—" But Benson had already hung up.

Tyler tapped off the phone, his mind still a blur, images of what might be happening to Nancy distracting him. *If Benson so much as lays a finger—*

Khan gave him a funny look. "Benson?"

For the first time tonight, Tyler saw an ally, and it filled him with a subtle sense of relief. He wasn't alone after all. He explained Benson's demands.

Khan asked, "You agreed to hand it over?"

"Yes, of course. What other option do I have?" he asked, interested now. Perhaps Khan saw an angle he'd missed?

"Well, we'd better get going then. Don't want anything to happen to . . . Nancy? Is that her name?"

Tyler slid out of the booth, Khan right behind him.

"Let me come with you."

Tyler started toward the door, now considering Khan's request. Having a friend along seemed comforting, but . . . "You want Benson to know you're in on this?" He stepped out the front door onto the sidewalk, the police car still idling across the street. He flashed on asking the cops for help but immediately rejected the idea as stupid. Any story he told them would sound crazy.

"At this point it makes very little difference what the pompous ass thinks. If we succeed in exposing his cover-up, it will be immaterial."

Tyler turned in the direction of where he had ditched his Range Rover earlier, Khan on his right in lockstep. He thought again of what Nancy must be going through. His pace quickened. They turned onto a deserted side street. He felt a tug on his arm and turned.

Khan said, "Hold on."

"Look, I don't have—"

Khan's gun was pointed at his chest again.

"The CD, Mathews, I want it."

CHAPTER 37

"Christ, Yusef, stick to our plan." He started to move again when Khan cocked the gun, said, "We have no plan."

Tyler stopped. "What the hell's going on?"

"Simple enough. Prophesy will pay handsomely for that information. One lesson I learned well as a young lad is to be loyal to my employer. I have no intention of turning that CD over to anyone else."

Tyler studied Khan's eyes. "You're shitting me . . . you're working for Prophesy?"

"Surprise."

"Jesus, Yusef . . . Nancy . . . I can't let them harm her."

"And I can't let you give Benson that information."

"One way or another, word's going to get out about the flaw. What the hell difference should it make to you or Prophesy if the end result is knocking Levy's company out of the running? They win, Med-InDx loses. Right?"

"Not necessarily."

"How so?"

Khan shook his head as if to say, stupid question. "It's a basic tenet we professionals adhere to. The only way to know for sure that the job's done right is to do it yourself. Prophesy can't afford to trust you or even me, for that matter. Too much money's at stake."

"But Nancy. They have her."

Khan shrugged. "Easily enough handled, I suspect. Tell Benson

I double-crossed you. By the time he can do anything about it, it will be too late. He'd be a fool to do anything to her . . . especially if you go to the police. Where is this storage locker of yours?"

Tyler turned and started to walk away. "You won't kill me. You do, you don't get the CD."

The bang was deafening. For a second Tyler waited for the pain to hit. None came. He realized Khan had shot a pile of black garbage bags filling a doorway. Khan said, "I'll shoot to maim, not kill."

Tyler thought of Nancy. "Maim me and you still lose your sweet deal."

"I disagree." Khan stepped closer, aiming the gun at Tyler's kneecap. "You see, there's a good chance the information I have will be enough. On the other hand, if I combine it with what you have, well . . . let us just say it is icing on the cake. I take out your kneecap and I beat Benson. Now tell me the instructions. We do not have much time here, now that I have attracted much attention with that gunshot, the police should be here soon. If so you lose. I will give you five more seconds to decide. One . . . two . . ."

Seeing no other option Tyler told Khan the locker number and combination. When Tyler finished, Khan said, "One final detail. Which computer burned the CD? Your office?"

It took a moment for Tyler to realize what he was getting at. With the evidence still on the hard drive, another CD could easily be created. "I did it from home," he lied.

"Want some advice, Mathews? Don't play poker unless you learn to bluff much more effectively." Khan backed up a step and began to raise the gun.

In a flash Tyler understood Khan's intention before being able to even verbalize it. He feigned a move, then reversed, shifting his weight onto the painful ankle. Caught off guard by the quick fake, Khan swung the gun in the wrong direction and fired milliseconds before Tyler's shoulder rammed directly into his chest, pushing him backward into a brick wall.

Tyler heard the rush of air as the impact collapsed Khan's lungs, then, pinning the smaller man against the wall, brought his knee squarely into Khan's groin. Khan's body seemed to sag and Tyler released, letting him slump, gasping for air, to the asphalt. He kicked the hand still holding the gun and saw it drop away.

For a moment Tyler stood still, mentally sorting through various options. *Pick up the gun? I wouldn't know how to use it.*

Ferguson.

Tyler kicked the gun away from Khan. "Anything happens to Nancy and I'm coming back for you, asshole."

He ran for his car while his thumb punched through his cell phone list.

The Land Rover's tires screeched in lateral protest as Tyler raced the vehicle down the spiraling ramp into the underground parking garage for his office building. Deserted this time of night, the industrial neon lights cast a deathly reflection off bare concrete. Having his pick of any spot, he chose the stall closest to the main entrance and killed the engine. The cold cloud of anxiety floating in his stomach lining intensified.

For a moment he sat very still, struggling to rein in his anger and anxiety, watching to see if anyone was waiting for him here. A moment later he leaned over, opened the glove box, removed a blue plastic Mylanta bottle, took a deep swig, then tried capping it but couldn't quite thread it. Disgusted, he slammed the bottle in the cup holder and threw the cap on the floor.

He surveyed the area one more time before stepping down onto the desolate concrete, his footsteps echoing off bare walls.

He used his ID swipe card to unlock the door, then headed for the main floor and Benson's executive suite, berating himself with each step for allowing Nancy to become involved in this mess. He would never forgive himself if anything bad happened to her. Correction: if anything *worse* than what was already happening.

This part of the deserted, dimly lit first floor was populated only with administrative and support offices. The closer he got to Benson's office, the more intense the anxiety grew. He dried both hands on his pants thighs and, just like in basketball, forced himself to push through the distraction and focus.

The side corridor to Benson's suite appeared darker than the main hall and ended in a dimly lit outer secretarial office, a parallelogram of yellow light slicing out from Benson's inner office. He entered the office. A deep gravelly voice from the shadows said, "Hold it." A strong grip clamped his arm.

He stopped.

"Spread your legs."

"Where's Nancy?"

"Fuck you, Ace. Spread 'em."

Tyler shrugged and did as told. *Confidence,* he coached himself. A set of hands slid expertly over his clothes. "You can go in now."

Tyler found Benson standing, butt propped against the top of his desk, arms folded casually across his chest, talking to another man he didn't recognize. Benson glanced at Tyler with a smug smile. "Well, well, the return of the prodigal son." That's when Tyler noticed Jim Day sitting at the far end of the conference table nervously playing with a laptop computer. The moment they made eye contact, Day glanced away.

Tyler's fists balled involuntarily as his eyes continued searching the room for Nancy. They passed over, then snapped back to a picture on the massive credenza. A framed color shot of Benson, his arm wrapped around the shoulders of a woman about his age, both backed up against a railing overlooking water. Although out of focus, Tyler recognized the background: Lake Union with Queen Anne Hill in the distance. Tyler sensed Benson staring at him so he continued to glance around the room.

Benson became rigid. "You think I'm stupid, Mathews? You think I don't know about your FBI contact . . . what's the name? Ferguson?" Benson's face turned red with anger. "Is that it? You think I got to where I am by being an ignorant paper-pushing *administrator*? That's what you physicians think about us, isn't it? We're nothing more than trivial bean pushers who can't succeed in business—isn't that the party line?"

The other man said, "Art. Keep your voice down and stay focused."

Benson wiped spittle from the corner of his mouth with the back of his hand as he walked a tight circle. "Here's the deal, Mathews. Unless you sign these papers"—he grabbed a manila folder off the conference table and shook it at him—"right now"— he slammed it on the table along with a fountain pen—"and get me your CD within the next few minutes, your precious little slant eye is going to die. Here." He pushed the folder and pen toward Tyler.

Tyler's gut cramped, almost doubling him over. "You agreed to have her here."

Benson beamed, eyebrows raised in mock surprise. "Really? Oh, well, in that case, I guess I lied." He pushed off the desk and stood.

"We had a deal."

Benson's face reddened. "Fuck *the deal. The deal* is, your wife's not coming back until this is signed, sealed, and delivered within the hour. That's *the deal,* Mathews. Now let's get on with this." Benson's hand slammed down on the manila folder. "I'm losing patience with you. Sign these."

"Where is she?"

"Ahhhh, well . . . that little bit of information is not forthcoming until we've settled our agreement. Just in case you've tried to engineer something heroic . . . like calling your FBI buddy . . . Ferguson, isn't it?"

That clinched it. Jill was Benson's information source. No one else knew about Ferguson. He thought of Nancy, how terrified she must be.

"So help me, Benson . . ."

Benson flashed a smug smile. "What?"

Looking at the folder, Tyler shook his head in disgust at

himself for being unable to find the words to express his anger.

Legs trembling, unable to take his mind off Nancy, Tyler moved numbly to the large conference table and opened the folder. Without reading the two typed pages, he scribbled his name on the last page, not caring what the words said. Had Khan already gone to the storage locker? Tell Benson about him? And Ferguson . . . did he get the message and would he be there? He had to get Benson to the storage locker before either Khan or Ferguson.

"Afraid I have some bad news for you, Art."

"Oh?" For the first time a hint of doubt crept into Benson's voice.

"Yes, you see, it seems Yusef Khan's been working for Prophesy." Tyler capped the fountain pen, picked up the heavy bond paper, and blew across the drying ink. "He's had our phones and computers tapped . . . and knows everything, and I mean *everything*. He was waiting for me tonight . . . he was with me when I got your phone call. If you want that CD, we'd better hurry."

Benson's face grew crimson, his jaw muscles rippled. "You little shit . . ." He came at Tyler, his right arm back ready to swing, but stopped abruptly and drew a breath. "How long ago?"

"We started at the same time. I came straight here." Tyler's mind was racing, trying to calculate how much time it'd take Khan to destroy the hard disk.

"Where is it?"

"At a storage locker I rent."

Benson shoved Tyler toward the door. "Get going. You're going to take us there. And goddamnit, Mathews, if that CD's already gone, Nancy's dead."

Tyler rode in the front passenger seat of Benson's gray Mercedes CLK 420 coupe with Jim Day silently in the backseat clutching the laptop while Benson's two thugs followed in another car. Tyler remained rigid, unable to release the aching muscular tension, nervously brushing his thumb against each fingertip—back and forth endlessly—while he mentally stormed through various scenarios, all bad. Had Ferguson picked up the page and voice mail? He hoped not. When making the phone call he'd naïvely believed Nancy would be in Benson's office. Stupid. The anxiety ice cloud froze in his stomach.

After a fifteen-minute drive that seemed to take an hour, Benson turned into the parking lot fronting the storage area. Behind a ten-foot cyclone fence topped with razor wire, parallel rows of increasingly large buildings occupied an entire city block, reminding Tyler of a prison camp. Benson's thugs pulled up alongside and killed their engine.

"The fuck you waiting for?" Benson had his door open.

Tyler stepped onto cratered asphalt and pointed to a section of fence down the block in relative shadows. "There's an area down there where we can climb over without being seen."

The bigger of the two thugs said, "Fuck that noise," and stepped around to his car's trunk. A moment later he held up a bolt cutter. With one whack the lock protecting the swinging gate clanked to the ground. "Any dogs in there?" the cutter asked.

"Not that I know of."

"Better not be, I hate those sonsabitches." From underneath his coat he pulled a flat black gun with a cylindrical suppressor attached.

Benson told the other man, "Stay here and keep the keys in the ignition." To Jim Day, "You come on and bring the laptop." Then to Tyler, "Lead on, but don't make any noise."

Tyler pushed through the gate and led them single file along an asphalt drive flanked on both sides by a monotonous series of similar-sized roll-up metal doors. Other than an occasional soft footstep he heard only a dog bark in the far-off distance. His gut knotted tighter with each storage unit passed. At the end of the row Tyler held up his hand, stopping the procession. He turned to Benson, whispered, "It's just around the corner." Only Benson and Day were with him now, he realized. How long ago had the other man dropped away from them?

They turned left. Tyler's rental was the third one in from the road. The vertical rolling steel door was half open, light spilling out onto the asphalt. Quietly, Benson moved forward, Tyler and Day following. Benson pulled a gun from under his suit coat, glanced around the door, and said, "Find anything interesting, Yusef?"

CHAPTER 38

Tyler stepped away from Benson so that he could see into the storage bin. Khan sat cross-legged, on the concrete looking up at Benson. He shot a glance at Tyler.

Benson asked, "Yusef, you have the CD yet?"

Khan smiled as if nothing were wrong. "Yes, I just found it." He held up the platter, the overhead incandescent bulb reflecting dancing rainbows off the smooth silver surface.

"Give it to him." Benson nodded toward Jim Day who had the laptop open now.

Day leaned toward Khan just enough to quickly grab the CD, then back up, as if wanting as much room between himself and Khan as possible. He slid the CD into the laptop tray.

Benson asked, "How much is Prophesy paying you?"

Khan shook his head slowly. "It is irrelevant."

Tyler scanned the area looking for Benson's thug and Ferguson but saw only blackness and an oasis of light below the low-wattage bulb at the corner of the building. The wind was picking up, chilling the area and probably bringing a thundershower.

"Hardly. I'm after damage control at this point, Yusef. Tell me, how much information have you given them?"

Khan pushed up off the cement floor and brushed off his pants. "That also is irrelevant."

"Not if you want to live it's not."

Khan pointed at the gun in Benson's hand. "You're probably going to kill me anyway, so why should I give you any information?

If I die without you finding out it will be my little victory, you see."

Tyler rubbed his hands together for warmth and said to Benson, "Look, you have the disk. Let's get going."

Benson's head snapped around toward him. "Shut up, Mathews. I'll deal with you when I'm done here."

Day said, "It's all here, Mr. Benson. The CD's full of patient information." He snapped shut the laptop.

Benson smiled. "Good. Now hand it over to Mathews."

Clearly puzzled, Day did as instructed.

"Now," Benson told Day, "move over next to Khan." He waved the gun barrel in that direction.

"What?" Day glanced nervously at Tyler, then back to Benson.

Benson pointed the gun at Day's chest. "You're a Judas. You sold me and Med-InDx out. But instead of thirty pieces of silver, you'll get what you really deserve."

Day licked his lips and blinked at Benson. "The hell you talking about, sold you out? I told you about him from the beginning," with a nod toward Tyler. "I told you everything."

"Ahhh, yes, but you also gave Tyler access to Bernie's office. You were playing both sides of this equation, to see which side won. You didn't have any allegiance to me or to Med-InDx. I despise traitors like you."

Day shook his head. "No, swear to God I didn't."

"Oh?" Benson's voice carried a hard edge. "So you're a liar and a cheat?" He glanced to his left, said, "Timothy?"

Tyler realized what was about to happen and started to yell a warning to Day but heard a *thump*, like a fist hitting a pillow.

Day jerked backward as a hole suddenly appeared in his chest directly over his heart. Khan moved like a rabbit to his left, his right hand appearing with his gun. Tyler saw the muzzle flash before hearing the shot. When he looked again Benson was no longer standing.

Several lights suddenly flashed on. All at once three men

approached, all wearing windbreakers with FBI in large yellow block letters on the front, their mouths moving but without words, an intense ringing deep inside both ears the only sound Tyler could hear. A moment later bits of their individual words began filtering through the noise. That's when he recognized Ferguson as one of the men.

For several seconds Tyler just stood and watched as Benson's thug kneeled, then lay spread-eagle on the black asphalt, an FBI agent training a Glock on him with one hand and a huge flashlight with the other. Then he realized Khan was down on the asphalt in a position too awkward to be intentional. Benson lay on his back gasping for air, rocking his head from side to side. Ferguson kneeled next to him, looked him over, then waved Tyler over.

"Get over here, Tyler, this man's got a bad chest wound."

Tyler moved over to them. "Not much I can do here. He needs a Medic One unit." Then he looked more closely at the hole in Benson's right upper chest. "Awww, Jesus, it's a sucking wound."

"What's that mean?"

Tyler reached down, grabbed a fistful of Benson's hair, and pulled his head up so they were looking eye to eye. "Where is she, asshole?"

Benson coughed, gasped for air, and barely managed to say, "Fuck you, Mathews."

Tyler let Benson's head drop back onto the asphalt. "He kidnapped Nancy."

Ferguson waved a palm downward. "No need to shout. I can hear you."

"What?" The ringing, he realized, was still there, just not as intense.

"You okay?"

"No I'm not okay. Benson has Nancy. He's hiding her somewhere . . . a houseboat maybe . . . on Lake Union. They'll kill her."

Ferguson shook his head. "Benson's in no shape to kill anybody."

"Not him. Guys like the one over there. They have orders to kill her if anything happens to him," pointing at Benson who was now losing color. "There was another one of his men back at the car. Did you get him too?"

"What car? We came from over there." Ferguson pointed in the opposite direction from which he'd led Benson into the area.

"We need to find Nancy."

Ferguson jutted his chin toward Benson. "Right now I got my hands full here. Just hang in there. SPD has a response team on the way. They'll be able to help you."

Tyler glanced over his shoulder at the dense shadows where the police would be likely to come from and saw no one. A bolt of urgency stabbed his chest. He was losing time. "I don't have that much time. Besides, you know my situation. They don't. It'll take too long to explain. *You* have to help me." The sense of urgency invaded the pain in his gut. "Now!"

Ferguson placed a hand on his shoulder. "Heard you the first time. Fact is I can't leave right now. Actually, neither can you. You're a material witness, which means we're going to have to get a statement from you, and this situation needs to be stabilized." Ferguson looked at the agent wrapping a plastic tie around the prone thug's crossed wrists. "Besides, where are they holding her?"

"I don't know for sure, but I think it may be a houseboat on Lake Union."

"You know that for a fact?"

"No!" Frustrated anxiety exploded in Tyler's chest. "But it's my only shot. They've got her hostage and they're going to kill her."

"Fact is, unless you know for certain she's been kidnapped and where she's being held, I can't do anything. And I sure as shit can't go busting into someone's house looking for her without an order from a federal judge. So your best shot is to cool your heels until the metro boys get here."

Unable to ignore Benson any longer, Tyler reached down and tore a large piece of Benson's shirt off. He wadded it into a ball, muttered, "Shit," and stuffed it over the hole in Benson's chest. "Only thing to do for this kind of chest wound is plug it. Here, hold pressure on this until the medics get here." He pushed Ferguson's hand over the wad.

"Where the hell you think you're going?"

"Don't let up on the pressure or you'll kill him."

"Mathews, get the hell back here."

Tyler knew he couldn't wait for the Seattle Police. And if he did, what would they do? Probably nothing. At least not in enough time. . . . He stepped back into darkness, then began to run, picking up momentum as the distance increased from the small oasis of light.

Seconds later he crouched and peered through the chain-link fence at Benson's Mercedes. It remained exactly where they'd parked it but the other car was gone. Tyler sucked in a deep breath and started running for the Benz. He threw open the door, slipped in pulling it shut behind him, and locked it as soon as it slammed. He reached down. Luckily the key was still in the ignition. He revved the powerful engine and backed out of the lot, his right hand fumbling for his cell phone to call Information.

CHAPTER 39

Benson's Mercedes crunched gravel as Tyler drove slowly onto the shoulder of Fairview Avenue. He braked to a stop in the small parking lot of a neighborhood grocery store, the glow from the red brake lights reflecting off a window advertising a special on Washington Hill wines. Tyler cut the engine and set the parking brake. He scanned the otherwise empty lot for cars or people, then did the same for the curving asphalt road. He took in a funky waterfront community bathed in cold, violet-tinged, mercury-vapor streetlamps. Across the road, nestled within trees and shrubs, a mini-park hugged thirty feet of shore.

Tyler slipped out and darted into shadows beside the market wall. If Benson was hiding Nancy here, where would guards be posted? At the house or up here near the street? He watched the park for movement. Satisfied, he crossed the street and crouched between cars.

This side of the street was pocketed with shadowy clusters of right-angled parked cars. On the other side vehicles were sandwiched between driveways and NO PARKING signs, or in any available patch of dead dirt. The street remained devoid of traffic, the warm air thick with the humidity of the coming summer thunderstorm. Staying on the shoulder, Tyler headed toward the moorage, past a large blue recycling bin reeking of beer and wine, then a dented green Dumpster wafting rotting garbage. Next, a two-car garage. Up ahead, on a patch of shoulder, a darkened BMW 7-series hugged an alder tree. He moved closer and looked.

Couldn't be positive, but it looked suspiciously like the one he'd spotted outside his apartment. No one inside. He checked the driver's door. Locked. He palmed the hood. Still warm. He tried to remember the car the thugs drove to the storage area but realized he'd never really gotten a look at it. Overhead came the rumble of distant thunder.

Twenty feet farther, a clump of unruly laurel bushes marked the crest of the blacktop drive curving down into the moorage parking lot. He peered over a Dumpster into the shadowy cluster of parked cars, but overgrown shrubs obscured much of the view. From an eight-foot trellis, a sixty-watt bulb swarming with gnats cast anemic light on a rusted metal ramp to the narrow pier, the rest of the area in shadows. He'd have to pass through the light to reach the dock. "Shit!" he muttered.

The waxing and waning hum of I-5 traffic gave a background to the occasional lazy waves slapping pilings. Stagnant lake water, creosote, and dust from bone-dry August asphalt hung in the air. A distant siren dopplered and faded. His heart thumped both ears.

A guard would position himself to watch the dock entrance without being seen, he decided. On the other hand, maybe no one was posted at all. Had to chance it.

A final glance toward the street, then Tyler slipped between a cypress hedge and a weathered wood fence and duck-walked down the drive, each step exposing more of the small shadowy parking lot. The hedge gave out at the edge of the lot. He slipped behind a faded blue Volvo station wagon and waited, eyes adjusting to the lack of streetlights. Ahead, inside the wisteria-entwined trellis was a set of mailboxes. Cautiously he approached. Eight mailboxes; hence eight houseboats, maybe four on each side of the dock. Benson's, it appeared, was number eight. That put it on the right-hand side at the end.

Silently, he stepped across the metal ramp onto a poorly illuminated narrow concrete dock. That's when he noticed a glowing ember at the end of the dock.

The fine hairs between his shoulder blades stood on end. His senses suddenly became more acute, just like in surgery during those awful moments when a complication unravels in your face and every second becomes brutally eternal.

Frightened, yet strangely fascinated, Tyler watched, focusing on the glowing red spot. Now he could make out the shape of a crouching man.

Heart pounding harder, he backed up several steps, never taking his eyes off the ember. It brightened again as the person took a drag. Silently, he retraced his path between the shrubs and fence until he was back up the driveway, then headed back toward the park.

In the park, Tyler crouched beside a cluster of mugo pines to catch his breath and calm his nerves. After a moment, he started down a short path to the water. His face broke a spider's web. He brushed at it only to ball the sticky strand on his fingertip. It wouldn't shake loose. He wiped it on his leg. He listened for footsteps behind him, but heard only waves slapping the shore and followed this sound to a wooden platform above the water.

Three railroad ties served as steps down to a small wood deck a couple feet above the lake. He stepped onto it, the air thickly scented with algae and duck droppings. Across a hundred feet of black water floated Benson's houseboat. He studied it, wondering if Nancy was inside. Was she already dead?

He quickly returned to the car, locked his wallet and cell phone in the glove box, then used the electronic key to lock up.

Back on the wooden platform he slipped off his shirt, shoes, and socks. Another glance at the houseboat floating out in the black water. In the distance came a clap of thunder. Just a quick look, he decided, to see if he could find tangible evidence to back up his suspicions before going to the police.

Sitting on rough-hewn timbers, he carefully dangled both legs into darkness blindly searching for water. His right toes touched cold slime. He recognized the feel. A log. Probably a small breakwater to keep waves from eroding the shore. Stretching out, barely on the edge of the dock now, his toes coaxed it closer, until he could plant both soles squarely across the slippery surface. He pushed off, sending himself upright into a crouch on the log while allowing momentum to rotate him forward, throwing him into a shallow dive. A second later, he slipped noiselessly into the warm upper surface of water.

Careful not to splash, he breaststroked toward the houseboat while his eyes searched for any activity in the lighted windows.

A small speedboat and Jet Ski were moored to a small side deck. He grabbed the boat's coarse bowline and hung there, listening, but heard only small waves slap the white fiberglass hull and the occasional clink as halyards tapped an aluminum mast somewhere off to his left.

Satisfied he hadn't been seen, he worked, hand over hand, along the rope to a cold metal cleat. He released the rope, grasped the porch, and hoisted his body up to where the deck scraped his belly. He leaned forward, chest resting on dry wood, and listened some more. Pilings creaked.

He swung a leg over the edge and rolled prone onto the deck and remained on his stomach perfectly still, his heartbeat competing with the rhythmic creaks and grinds of pilings against the dock.

He crept to the nearest window and saw only an empty kitchen and a slice of an adjacent room. There was no way to see farther into the house so he tried the kitchen door. Locked. From somewhere inside came muffled sounds of a television.

And just what in hell would you have done if it had opened, pal? He didn't have an answer for himself.

An outside stairway led to the second floor. Why not see what was upstairs before swimming back to the car? He climbed silently, reaching a small landing surrounded by a white tubular rail. Across the small deck was a sliding-glass door into what appeared to be a combination bedroom/office. Someone sat in a desk chair, but it was turned so that the back faced him. He crept forward, then froze. *Nancy.*

Heart pounding, head about to explode. He tapped a knuckle on the plate glass.

She didn't respond. *She alive?*

He tried again, harder.

The chair swiveled. Arms duck-taped to the armrest, ankles duck-taped together, a gag across her mouth, Nancy's eyes searched for the source of the noise. Her gaze seemed to sweep over him, then snap back, eyes growing wide.

Tyler almost cried out in joy. Instead, he drew in a deep, calming breath and cautioned himself. *Just like surgery, be careful, methodical, make no mistakes.*

He pointed toward the sliding-door handle and mimed pulling it open.

She shrugged.

He mouthed, "Where's the guard?"

She either didn't seem to catch his meaning or didn't know. She wrinkled her brow and tilted her head.

Gently he tugged the handle. The door shrieked a metallic screech. He froze, but heard only a television from another room. He crept in.

He rushed to her, whispered, "Stay quiet," and tore off her gag. Next he ripped away the tape binding her arms and legs.

"Come on, let's get out of here."

She gave an adamant headshake. "Tyler, I can't, there's water down there."

He gave her arm a gentle tug. "Sure you can. You've got to. Now."

"No, I can't. I've already tried."

"Just close your eyes and let me lead you. There's a set of stairs out there."

"I know. I can't go there, Tyler."

"You *have to*, Nancy." He held out his hand to her. "C'mon, we don't have much time."

Reluctantly, she held her hand out to him, eyes closed. He grasped it and pulled her gently toward the door. Without a sound they crossed the carpeted floor and through the opened door and started slowly, step by step, down the stairs until they reached the landing.

With both hands on her shoulders, he whispered, "Stand here a moment, just keep your eyes closed." He gave her what he hoped was a reassuring pat before moving to the wall next to the kitchen door. Two keys hung there, each dangling from a small red and white plastic float. Had to be for the Jet Ski and speedboat, but which was which? More to the point, which vessel to take? He looked at the speedboat, at the foreign controls, and knew he didn't know how to drive it well enough. The Jet Ski was another matter. He'd driven one before. He pulled it parallel to the dock, climbed on, and tried to slip the first key into the ignition. It didn't fit. The second one did. Leaving the second key in the ignition, he threw the first one out into the lake, then climbed back onto the dock. The wind was picking up, waves now bouncing the small craft against the dock.

He wrapped an arm around Nancy's shoulders. "Open your eyes," he whispered, "but don't say a word."

"You're going to have to climb on that Jet Ski." He felt her body go rigid. "Just take it slow and easy. I'll get on first, then you climb onto that little seat right behind me."

"I can't, Tyler. I just can't do it," she pleaded.

"They'll kill you if you don't. That's what they're planning to do. That's why we have to get out of here."

"I'll die if I have to ride on that thing. I can't, Tyler."

He took her hand, started gently pulling her toward the Jet Ski. She resisted. "No. Tyler, please, I can't . . ." He gently pulled again. She didn't move.

"*C'mon*, Nancy. You can do it. Just keep hold of me." He felt her move forward tentatively, a soft whine coming from her throat as if she were going to cry.

He managed one-handed to wrestle the Jet Ski parallel to the dock again, the other firmly holding her hand. He put a foot onto the Jet Ski, threw the other over the seat, sending the craft rocking side to side with the sudden weight.

"Oh, God," she gasped. "I'll drown, Tyler. I'll drown!"

He tugged her hand. "C'mon. We're running out of time and luck."

She resisted. He tugged again, felt her lurch forward and realized, to his horror, he'd pulled her off balance. For what seemed like eternity she teetered on the dock edge, her free hand windmilling, struggling for balance. He released her hand hoping to give her more balance. Too late. She screamed, and fell forward toward the water right behind the Jet Ski. He watched in frozen horror as she hit the surface with a resounding belly-flop slap, her arms thrashing wildly. He watched, paralyzed, as she sank.

"Jesus!"

Her head broke the surface, her mouth gasping for air, both arms thrashing water. "Tyler," she screamed as she sank beneath the surface again.

She vanished. He leaned over, prepared to dive in but she was gone now.

"Nancy!"

He grabbed the line holding the Jet Ski, the last place he'd seen her, and leaned farther over.

Her hand broke the surface.

Holding a dock cleat with one hand, he reached down, grabbed her hand, pulled her toward him. Her head broke the surface. She gasped for air.

"Here, grab hold of me. Let me pull you out."

From above, "Fuck!"

He glanced up, saw the monster from the underground gawking over the second-floor railing at him.

He tugged Nancy's arm but could only pull her shoulder out of the water. "Here, grab hold of the boat."

She screamed, "I can't. I'm stuck. My jacket's caught on something."

Tyler glanced over his shoulder. Monster was hobbling down the stairs, anger and retribution glowing in his eyes. Tyler forced Nancy's hand to the smaller Jet Ski cleat. "Here, hang a moment."

"No, don't leave me."

With her hand now firmly gripping the cleat, Tyler rolled onto the deck and jumped up to his feet. Across the deck, in the corner, a short canoe paddle leaned against the wall. Just then he heard the heavy thump as Monster's feet slammed the deck and his huge body appeared between him and the paddle. For a moment they half crouched across from each other like sumo wrestlers, waiting for the other to commit a move. An old basketball juke instinctively took over Tyler's limbs, causing him to feign right, then break left, with Monster buying into it, allowing him a fluid drive to the side of Monster's lunge, driving for the oar instead of a two-point slam dunk.

Monster caught himself in time, corrected, and spun around, his left leg obviously in pain. Tyler had the oar now, pulled back like a baseball bat. "Out of our way."

Nancy was still gasping for air, her mouth barely above water, he realized. He'd filtered the sound from consciousness just as he'd done on the court with spectators' roars.

"Fuck you." Monster's arm was reaching behind his back.

A gun, Tyler realized.

Without thinking, Tyler swung the oar toward Monster's leg, the same spot as last time. It connected with a solid, satisfying whack. Monster yelped, fell to his knees, but with his arm still behind his back reaching for the gun. Tyler swung from the other direction, connecting to the man's right temple, felt the wood connect with a solid impact, then watched as he crumpled to the ground.

He rushed to the deck edge, reached down. "Here. Grab on with both hands."

Nancy clamped her hand on to his wrist, fingernails digging into skin, then wrapped her left hand around his other wrist. Using his legs to lift, his injured ankle screaming with pain, he willed every ounce of strength into a pull, felt resistance, then release. Without letting her go, he struggled onto the rocking Jet Ski and jockeyed her up onto the passenger seat.

"Hang on." He settled into the driver's seat, fired the ignition.

Gasping, she pressed fully against his back, both arms locked so tightly around his neck it was almost impossible to breathe. He leaned forward and to the left, pulling her with him, stretching out until his left fingers could barely fumble with the rope. He slipped the loop over the cleat, freeing the small craft just as he caught a movement with the corner of his eye. He forced his head left against Nancy's arms. Monster was up on one knee now, shaking his head groggily, trying to clear it.

He triggered the ignition, heard it catch. The engine coughed to life. He cranked the accelerator, shooting the Jet Ski forward, crashing into the side of the speedboat. The impact threw him into the small windscreen, cutting his lower lip. He straightened up, turned the craft right, and cranked the accelerator again.

"Hang on," he croaked, then realized Nancy was sobbing hysterically. Her grip around his neck tightened. He tried to loosen it but her death grip did not yield.

"You're choking me," he tried to yell, but just then a thunderclap drowned out his voice. He yelled it again but she continued to sob, both arms locked around his neck.

The craft shot out into open lake as a sheet of rain started pouring out of the dark sky. A moment later, he backed off the gas, intent on calming the situation. First order of business was to set a direction, but where to go? Did it matter, just as long as they were free? Directly across the lake loomed Kenwood Air Service. Most likely there'd be people there to help. Maybe he could make a phone call, get hold of Ferguson, and settle things so Nancy would be safe. His shoulders sagged with relief. He'd rescued her and that was the most important thing. Later he could focus on getting the rest of this mess straightened out.

Nancy finally let go of one arm and punched his rib, yelled, "Tyler!"

Realizing her voice had taken a different tone, he turned to hear over the engine roar.

"He's coming after us! And closing fast."

Tyler glanced over his shoulder and in the process unwittingly turned the craft right. The speedboat was bearing straight toward them now, the gap surprisingly short. His heart seemed to flatline, then kick in again at a gallop. He gunned the accelerator and turned parallel to shore. No way he could reach the safety of Kenmore Air before being overtaken.

He yelled to Nancy, "Now you tell me."

"That's what I've been trying to tell you." Then she yelled, "Tyler, watch out!"

He looked up. Directly ahead came the spinning prop of a seaplane touching down. Tyler cut left, missing the plane by no more than twenty feet but the Jet Ski hit the pontoon wake, shooting them airborne. Tyler gripped the controls and braced for impact. "Hang on."

The Jet Ski slammed down, throwing Nancy to the right, pulling him with her. He fought to maintain balance but at that angle he couldn't steer the small craft straight, causing it to turn in a short arc, giving the speedboat an advantage. Straining against the weight he pulled them both upright.

"Tyler, he's gaining."

He glanced directly ahead. No more airplanes. Another quick glance over the shoulder. The speedboat bore down on them.

He scanned the lake ahead of them, searching frantically for a boat or someone to flee to for help but saw nothing out there that looked useful.

He yelled, "Lean forward," and scrunched down below the windscreen hoping to lessen wind resistance. He cranked another millimeter out of the gas and the craft seemed to accelerate slightly, but he knew it wasn't enough. How long could they go before the boat came alongside? Then what?

By now the finger of land protruding into the lake, Gasworks Park, lay dead ahead. Soon he'd be forced to turn right or left. Since they were closer to the west shore, he chose left rather than cut across the larger expanse of open water and make a run for Portage Bay, figuring the closer to the boat moorages, the better chance of ditching the Jet Ski at the last minute—maybe just aim for a populated moorage, run the Jet Ski aground, jump off, and yell bloody murder and hope like hell help would materialize. He saw nothing but marine supply shops, dry docks, and boat moorages along the shore.

They shot under the Aurora Bridge. That's when it dawned on him; they were heading into Salmon Bay, which would very quickly dead end at the locks—the equivalent of a dead-end street. Just then the engine began to cough and sputter. He glanced at the gas gauge. Empty.

"Tyler!"

"What?"

"Behind us!"

Tyler swiveled his head around. A police boat bore down on them, blue lights flashing, Benson's boat no longer in sight. Tyler cut the throttle but the engine had already died.

A moment later the shore patrol boat pulled alongside. A frowning cop yelled down, "You Tyler Mathews?"

Something in the cop's voice alarmed Tyler. "Yes."

"Put your hands in clear sight. You're under arrest."

CHAPTER 40

The cop tied the Jet Ski bowline to the starboard stern cleat, then helped Nancy climb aboard. With her safely on deck, Tyler followed and sat down next to her on a hard bench lining one side of the small cabin. After eagerly accepting thermal blankets from a second policeman and wrapping themselves snuggly, they huddled together, Tyler hugging her but saying nothing. A moment later the idling engines clunked into gear and the bow started cutting a wide circle back to Lake Union.

Nancy wrapped her arms around Tyler's chest and placed her head against him.

"You want to talk about it?" he asked.

"No. I'm just so thankful it's over."

He squeezed her a little more. "You're safe."

She squeezed back.

The trip segued into a haze of engine noise, disbelief. *Under arrest? For what?*

And somewhere during the trip Toby Warner crept back into his consciousness. He'd completely forgotten about him.

The engine rumble cut back and the boat bumped to a stop, jarring Tyler back to the present. As the second cop lashed the vessel to dock cleats the other cop tapped Tyler's shoulder. "Out."

Tyler glanced up. On shore stood two uniformed officers and one gray-haired, stern-faced man in jeans and a navy Gore-Tex raincoat with yellow block SPD on the left breast.

Tyler followed Nancy onto the dock. The gray-haired man

approached, said, "Mathews, I'm Detective Jim Lange, Seattle Police." He held up a badge. "This your wife?" with a nod toward Nancy. The two uniformed officers approached.

"Yes. Why?"

Lange said to Nancy, "Go with these two officers, ma'am. My partner needs to interview you."

She shook her head. "I'm staying with Tyler."

Lange's face grew stern. "No you're not."

One of the officers moved forward, touched Nancy's arm. "This way, ma'am."

"Just a goddamned second," Tyler said, stepping forward. A cop held out an arm to block him. Tyler said, "This is a joke, right? Being under arrest?"

Nancy said, "I'll be alright, Tyler. We just need to resolve this . . . this misunderstanding," and headed to the patrol car with the two officers.

Lange nodded toward an idling unmarked blue Caprice sprouting two VHF antennae from the roof. "Do I look like I'm joking? In the car." The two harbor cops edged closer, as if expecting trouble.

Tyler didn't move. "What are you charging me with?"

Lange shoved him toward the car. "Accessory to murder and fleeing the scene of a crime. Now get moving."

Tyler stepped to the waiting car. "Where are we going?"

"If I say downtown it'll sound like a cliché, but that's your answer."

"Can I at least stop and get my clothes?"

Lange pulled open the thermal blanket. "That's the first smart thing you've said so far."

Dressed in the clothes he'd stashed by the lake, Tyler returned to the backseat of Lange's car. Lange shut the door behind him and climbed into the driver's seat. They were parked alongside of Benson's Mercedes.

"Look, since you seem to know everything about me, you know

I'm a doctor, right? I need to call the hospital. It's important. Can I use your cell phone?"

"No."

"Hey, this is ridiculous. I'm serious. This is an emergency. A kid's life is at stake here."

"Stow it, Mathews. I'm not listening."

"This is bullshit. If you know anything about the shooting you know an FBI agent, Gary Ferguson, was there. He knows what happened. He'll vouch for me."

"Wrong, Mathews. He's the one put out the warrant for your arrest."

Shocked, Tyler slumped back against the seat.

Lange drove around the south end of Lake Union, down Broad to Second Avenue, then south toward the downtown core.

Minutes later Tyler sat up to attention when, instead of heading to the Public Safety Building, Lange nosed into the Federal Building basement garage. The car stopped, Lange popped the door locks. "Out."

Two surly men with close-cropped hair and shoulders the width of a billiards table stood waiting. They ushered him, via elevator, up several floors to an obvious interrogation room: a mirrored window in one wall, a battleship-gray steel table with two mismatched chairs. "Inside," ordered the agent who seemed to be in charge.

"Hold on, I'm a doctor. I need to call the hospital. It's urgent," Tyler pleaded again.

The door slammed with a solid *thunk*.

Within seconds it opened again and Gary Ferguson entered followed by a tall slender African-American woman in a tan pantsuit. He was scowling. She didn't look all that happy either.

Tyler threw both hands up in surrender. "Hey look, Ferguson, if I wasn't supposed to leave I apologize but what the hell was I supposed to do? I mean, Jesus, they had Nancy, you refused to help me, and I sure didn't have time to wait for the police. And like you said, what were they gonna do?"

"I'm glad she's safe, Tyler, but this isn't about her or you. It's about this." Ferguson waved a shiny CD platter in front of Tyler's face. Tyler recognized it immediately. The one from the storage bin.

"So? What about it? That's the goddamned evidence you wanted from me. That was the deal. Our agreement should be finished now."

Ferguson's jaw muscles rippled. "No, no, we're not done yet. This fucking disk is worthless. It's as blank as that wall behind you." He threw the disk onto the table. It hit on its edge, bounced into the air, and fell.

Tyler watched the CD spin around twice before settling on the floor. "But it can't be. I—" He flashed on Jim Day verifying the disk's contents. "Wait a second! Jim Day . . . he must've erased it. If so, it's still there. All you have to do—"

"No, Mathews, it's not there. Who do you think we are"—Ferguson's face grew more crimson—"a bunch of old ladies? Think we don't know shit about data recovery? Think again. And when you do, wipe that condescending tone out of your voice. The fucking disk was formatted. It's been leveled."

Tyler glanced at the large mirrored window and wondered if whoever was watching was recording his words. Did it make any difference? "I burnt it off my office computer. I have a copy there," he said hopefully, thinking maybe this would mollify Ferguson enough to allow him a phone call.

"No, it's not. Someone wiped the hard disk too."

Khan. Tyler finally seemed to notice the other person in the room. "Who's she?"

Ferguson turned to her. "Ms. Hamilton, meet Tyler Mathews." Then to Tyler, "She's with the King County District Attorney's Office."

Tyler looked from Ferguson to Hamilton. "Oh, for christsake, c'mon, I need to call the hospital. You know how important this is."

Ferguson shook his head. "You're not calling anyone until we get this settled."

Tyler looked directly at the mirrored glass. "I demand to call my lawyer."

"It's not going to happen, Mathews. Not until you agree to a couple things."

The pressure in Tyler's head increased. "Hey, what about my constitutional right to a lawyer?" He wasn't certain if this was true, but it sounded good.

Ferguson spread his stance a little, interlocked both arms across his chest. "Not under the Patriot Act you don't. You don't cooperate with me, you're aiding a terrorist organization. In that case I can keep you here as long as I want and there's nothing you can do about it."

Tyler blew an exasperated breath between pursed lips, threw his arms in the air, and turned a tight circle. "Everything I had was on the computer and that disk. What do you want from me?" He thought of the disk he'd mailed to Nancy. He decided not to mention it yet.

"A couple things," Ferguson replied. "I want everything you have against Med-InDx and I want you to go public with it in a press conference." He turned to the ADA. "Owita?"

The woman cleared her throat. "Your buddy Benson survived and was taken to Harborview a few hours ago. Just before they rolled him into surgery he asked for his lawyer. You ever heard of Mel Tomkins?"

"No."

"Well, he's the local equivalent to Johnny Cochran. Now, with what we got so far my boss is thinking murder. Whether we're talking murder one or two we haven't decided. Not until we get more information." She shrugged and rocked her hand back and forth suggesting ambiguity. "But whatever we decide on, your testimony's going to be crucial. You following this, Mathews?"

Tyler sighed and shook his head at Ferguson. "Why can't *you* be the one to blow Med-InDx out of the water? I do it and my professional career will be toast."

"That should be obvious, Mathews. Because you're a doctor and the software killed one of your patients. You'll have much more credibility. Besides, my boss and I will see to it that you're protected from any reprisals from Maynard. You have my word on that."

"Your word, huh," Tyler repeated the phrase with sarcasm and thought about California, about the assurances then, about how it had all blown up in his face. "What time is it?"

"Stay on point," Ferguson answered.

Tyler locked eyes with him. "And what about Nancy? She still thinks those drugs were mine."

CHAPTER 41

Tyler gripped the podium edges, squinted, and listened attentively to the disembodied voice asking the question out there in the blinding supernova of klieg lights. All he could see were the shoes and ankles of the participants seated in the front row. Nancy was one of them, he knew, because he'd planted her there early, before the room filled up. Toby Warner's parents were too, and he smiled knowing Toby was safe at home with his baby-sitting grandmother.

Question finished, he stalled and wiped a bead of sweat from his forehead while choosing his words. "I am a neurosurgeon, not a computer programmer. I guess you'll have to ask Mr. Levy that question. Assuming, of course, that you can find him."

"Any truth to the allegation he's been murdered?"

"I have no knowledge of what's happened to Mr. Levy. You'll have to address those questions to the appropriate law enforcement officials. Next question?"

Another voice, this one female, came from the right side of the room. "Is it true that one of your patients died as a result of the computer flaw?"

Tyler wiped another bead of sweat away with the back of his hand and considered his agreement—a debriefing was what they had called the meeting—with the chairman of the MMC Board of Governors. His hospital privileges would be returned and the bogus drug charges removed if he would agree to not press charges against the Board or MMC for Arthur Benson's transgressions.

"One of my patients suffered an unfortunate complication during the course of treatment. Because of the severity of this complication we instigated a root cause analysis. As a routine part of the root cause analysis we looked closely at the electronic medical record." There! Close enough to fact to not be considered a lie. Far enough from the truth to keep Maynard's halo untarnished.

How much longer, he wondered, *do I have to endure this?*

Another voice asked, "Doctor, what steps is the medical center taking to assure a similar problem will not and cannot happen again?"

Tyler smiled and cleared his throat. "Nothing. We sort of like the idea of random treatment errors. It adds a degree of excitement in our otherwise drab, retched lives. In fact, we have built an employee lottery around these events. The person who guesses the exact number of days from one complication to the next one wins a one-week paid vacation. And I must say, it's done wonders for morale."

He heard a gasp. The continuous murmuring from the audience hushed. His smile widened. "Next question."

"Okay, okay, okay, Dr. Mathews . . . I think I get the message. We've rehearsed enough. It's time now anyway." Suhee Lee, head of Communications for Maynard Medical Center, stepped up on the riser. She turned and said to someone off the podium. "Cut the lights. It's like a damn oven up here."

The large klieg lights died, taking with them the 110 degrees Fahrenheit of radiated heat.

She turned back to Tyler. "You think you're ready?" She leaned a bit closer, inspecting the fine makeup patina powdered over his cheeks.

"Let's get this over with."

"Just remember, Tyler . . . a press conference is *your* opportunity to control the flow of information. Whatever question they ask, give them *your* message. Don't let them take you down a path you don't want to go. You understand?" She handed him a Kleenex.

"Yes."

"Hold still a second." She retrieved the tissue and dabbed it on his forehead. "That last question . . . what should the answer be?"

"Maynard Medical Center stands committed to providing the best quality of care regardless of ability to pay."

She nodded, swept a palm in the direction of the door. "Good. Now let's go meet the real press."

Holding Nancy's hand, Tyler negotiated his way past gawkers and lookie-loos clogging the hall to Gunther Auditorium. Real reporters now lined the route in ambush, throwing out questions, eager for a jump-start on their colleagues stupid enough to wait inside the crowded auditorium, thirsty for a slip of the tongue that would provide the sound bite with which to scoop the others. He nervously reached inside his navy blazer. His finger touched the folded paper holding his formal statement to be read before the Q&A session would start. Yes, it was still there, exactly as it had been the last fifty times he checked this afternoon.

Suhee Lee whispered in his ear, "I just got word that the new head of the JCAHO committee will be attending. The one appointed after what's-his-name died."

A familiar voice called, "Tyler." Something grabbed his arm.

He turned to look for the voice. Jill stood next to him, a serious-looking three-piece suit with round tortoiseshell glasses immediately at her side. She wore one of her severe suits, a silk scarf inside the collar and pinned at the base of her neck. Her signature ice maiden look. She smiled. A forced smile, but a smile nonetheless.

"Tyler, I'd like you to meet my attorney, Barney Ruleman. I assume you've heard of him." Barney Ruleman nodded at him with lawyerly solemnity that probably cost six hundred dollars an hour.

Jill continued. "I think it only fair to warn you that nobody is going to believe that I had anything to do with what happened with those unfortunate patients. Also, if you imply anything to the contrary, I am fully prepared to have Mr. Ruleman take corrective measures. Do you fully understand what I've just told you?"

Tyler smiled and nodded back at her. "I believe you will be hearing from the Board of Governors. Any problems you might have with any fallout from this can be handled by them. Now, if you'll excuse me."

She shook her head. "I don't think you heard me clearly, Doctor—"

He cut her off. "To the contrary."

He turned to Nancy, wrapped his arm around her shoulder, said, "Come on, this is cutting into our vacation," and walked away.